Surrender My Heart (Book #3)

IndieReader Discovery Award Winner for Romance (2018)

"LG O'Connor delivers an intense and well written saga of young lovers connected by a multitude of heartbreaking secrets, misunderstandings, and the possibility of second chances in SURRENDER MY HEART. A must read for lovers of romance, with a bit of mystery." **~IndieReader**

"If you're looking for a contemporary romance/women's fiction hybrid featuring...a compelling story, a poignant second chance, and affirmation that a man and woman in their fifties can still create sizzle, look no farther. Like Jillian and Raine, Kitty and John are characters who are going to stay with me for a long time." **~The Romance Dish (4.5 stars)**

I0586797

Surrender My Heart

Praise for the Caught Up in Love Series

Caught Up in RAINE (Book #1)

2017 IPPY AWARD WINNER (Bronze) in Romance

"O'Connor's contemporary romance is very realistic and will tug on the heartstrings of probably more readers than she expected...Jillian and Raine have faced a lifetime's worth of secrets and heartbreaks...you'll want to cheer them on until the very end." ~**RT Book Reviews**

"The plot is driven by a May-December premise that is blown away in the sexy love scenes." ~**Library Journal**

"For all the contemporary romance fans out there, this book is for you." ~**Night Owl Reviews**

"Urban fantasy author O'Connor (Trinity Stones) branches out into romantic women's fiction with a sexy tale of angst, guilt, love, and hate." ~**Publishers Weekly**

"LG O'Connor had me at "hello" with this plot. Phenomenal writing skills at work is what has made Caught Up in Raine a hard to beat Romance for 2016..." ~**HEA Romances with a Little Kick Blog**

"This story is both beautiful and haunting...I loved every second of this sexy, sweet and romantic book!!!" ~**The Romance Reviews, Top Pick, 5 stars**

"O'Connor delivers a unique women's fiction story packed with emotion, humor and sexiness. I could not turn the pages quickly enough..." ~**Caridad Pineiro, NY Times & USA Today Bestselling Romance Author**

"WOW! What an absolutely fantastic story! I absolutely fell in love with Raine, and wanted Jillian for a girlfriend! Well written and very relevant as a contemporary romance with two amazing, memorable characters." ~**Carla Susan Smith, Author of A Vampire's Promise**

Rediscovering Raine (Book #1.1)

"The writing is gorgeous; it's a beautifully touching story that warms the heart and gives you hope. I am truly in awe of Ms. O'Connor who could make me feel so much in just a few pages."~ **Book Obsessed Chicks Book Club**

"Proving herself a force to be reckoned with in the world of contemporary romance, L.G. O'Connor does not disappoint with this addition to her series." ~**Amazon Review**

Caught Up in Rachel (Book #1.2)

"If *Caught Up In Raine* is the cake, and *Rediscovering Raine* the frosting, then *Caught Up In Rachel* is the decoration on top. L.G. O'Connor has once again proved herself an exceptional story-teller, able to capture all the fear and wonderment of becoming a new parent with this welcome addition to her series. A remarkable gift for inviting her readers to experience all the joys and heartache of her characters, I can hardly wait to see what she has in store for future novels." ~ **Amazon Review**

Shelter My Heart (Book #2)

"A well polished, wonderfully written love story driven by believable characters whose strengths and flaws add complexity to a fairy-tale romance." ~**IndieReader, 4.5 stars**

Caught Up in Love

Three Women. One Story.

A unique blend of contemporary romance and romantic women's fiction, the multi-award-winning *Caught Up in Love* series centers around three New Jersey women: romance writer Jillian Grant, her sister, Kitty, and Kitty's daughter, Jenny. All part of a family that is plagued by loss, each woman harbors her own guilty secret and must confront her past to find redemption and surrender her heart for a second chance to get caught up in love.

Jillian & Raine's Story
Caught Up in RAINE (Book #1)
Rediscovering Raine (Book #1.1)
Caught Up in Rachel (Book #1.2)
Caught Up in Raine Collection (All of the above)

Jenny & Devon's Story
Shelter My Heart (Book #2)
One Summer Day (Prequel Novelette)

Kitty & John's Story
Surrender My Heart (Book #3)

COMING SOON
Caught Up in Christmas (A novella)
Join Jillian, Kitty, Jenny, and their families for one last tale, and the bittersweet conclusion to the Caught Up in Love series.

Sign up for the CAUGHT UP IN LOVE NEWSLETTER at www.lgoconnor.com for release updates and extras!

Surrender My Heart

Surrender My
HEART

Caught Up in Love
Book 3

LG O'CONNOR

COLLINS-YOUNG PUBLISHING

Copyright © 2018 by L.G. O'Connor

Published 2018
Printed in the United States of America
ISBN: 978-0-9970623-5-9 (Trade Paperback)
ISBN: 978-0-9970623-8-0 (eBook)
Library of Congress Control Number: 2017962371

For permission requests, please address:
Collins-Young Publishing, LLC
23 Quimby Lane #893
Bernardsville, NJ 07924

Cover Design: By Hang Le

Sign up for the CAUGHT UP IN LOVE NEWSLETTER at www.lgoconnor.com for release news and special updates.

Dedication

To all my readers and fans ~ you are the ones who make this all worthwhile. Thank you for sharing my stories and for letting them into your lives!

Surrender My Heart

Playlist

Thanks to some of the great musical artists who supplied an amazing soundtrack to Kitty and John's high school years and later as they embarked on a thirty-five-year journey to find forever.

Songs in order of mention (Song, Album, Year, Artist):

Surrender (Cheap Trick at Budokan, 1978), Cheap Trick

Hopelessly Devoted to You (Grease Soundtrack, 1978), Olivia Newton-John

Any Way You Want It (Single, 1980; Captured, 1981), Journey

Show Me the Way (Frampton Comes Alive, 1976), Peter Frampton

Simple Man (Pronounced Leh-Nerd Skin-Nerd, 1973), Lynyrd Skynyrd

Freebird (Pronounced Leh-Nerd Skin-Nerd, 1973), Lynyrd Skynyrd

Don't Fear the Reaper (Agents of Fortune, 1976), Blue Öyster Cult

Find Your Way Back (Modern Times, 1981), Jefferson Starship

Second Chance (Rock & Roll Strategy, 1988), 38 Special

MacArthur Park (Live and More, 1978), Donna Summer

Roar (Prism, 2013), Katy Perry

Cake by the Ocean (Cake by the Ocean, 2015), DNCE

I Was Made for Lovin' You (Dynasty, 1979), Kiss

I Want You to Want Me (Cheap Trick at Budokan, 1978), Cheap Trick

More Than a Feeling (Boston, 1976), Boston

Comfortably Numb (The Wall, 1979), Pink Floyd

The Flame (Lap of Luxury, 1988), Cheap Trick

You Make Me Smile, (Lucky Man, 1993), Dave Koz

Listen to Kitty & John's Playlist on Spotify:
http://spoti.fi/Kitty_John_Playlist

Surrender My Heart

Memorial Hospital

Kitty

October 2016

BLIP. BLIP. BLIP.

In the dead of night, fighting a cocktail of controlled panic and exhaustion pulsing through my veins, I hunch in a padded chair next to John's bed, holding his hand. I take comfort from the steady beat of the heart monitor that he's alive and in there somewhere.

I say the first and most important thing that comes to mind. "I love you, Shaw. . . . I've never stopped. Come back to me. . . ." The words travel over a raw ache in my throat. Words I never thought I'd get a chance to say again. Lowering my lips to his knuckles, I kiss the nearest part of him not bandaged or hooked up to a hanging bag or monitor. "I'll be waiting."

Sitting quietly for a few minutes, I breathe in the mild scent of disinfectant that lingers in the air. My hand covers his as I listen to the opera of whirring, whooshing, and beeping that accompanies the costume of tubes snaking in and out of him.

A fluorescent light behind the bed provides the darkened room's only illumination, casting shadows over him and giving his skin a stark, translucent pallor in contrast to his short salt-and-pepper hair. With the breathing apparatus, his face carries only a glimmer of the strong, craggy-but-handsome middle-aged man he's become — the man I've loved, at times secretly, since I was seventeen.

1

I study him, searching for my first love, the high school football player with a bright future, and then the ex-Marine with ten more years of life behind him, and now the police detective, on the cusp of one last chance for us after thirty-five years of me choosing the best of the worst choices.

He just has to live first . . . and if he survives, I need to tell him the truth.

Before

Surrender My Heart

Chapter 1

Kitty

August 2015 (15 months earlier) – Night of Aunt Vera's Memorial Service

"JILLIAN, ARE YOU sure about this?" I ask my younger sister and warily eye the O'Connor's Irish Crème de Menthe in my hand. A supersweet, minty version of Baileys, it's guaranteed to leave a hangover in its wake if consumed in quantity.

At least that's what I remember from a covert raid on my parents' liquor cabinet when I was eighteen. A flicker of remorse bubbles up as I think, even for a sliver of a second, of the significance of that night with John.

John Henshaw. He's been on my mind more than usual lately. Not a surprise, considering Vera's death and the past we both shared with her. I ignore the unwanted flush of warmth that arises with the long-ago memory.

I sigh and set the bottle on the kitchen counter. Vera's instructions were clear: have two drinks in her honor. A nod to our Irish roots. Jillian and I decided to share the wealth, each having a glass. *But of this?*

Jillian shrugs and snorts a chuckle. "I'd prefer something else, but it was Vera's favorite."

She pulls two cordial glasses from the bar cabinet in her Spring Lake beach house, the place our family has gathered for a weekend of togetherness and mutual support after Vera's passing. A place chosen because of its proximity to the ocean.

"If you say so." I frown at the offending bottle. Leave it to my irreverent eighty-two-year-old aunt to love something this vile. Then again, if I hadn't overdone it at eighteen when Jillian was too young to remember our parents grounding me for stealing it, maybe I wouldn't dread drinking it at fifty-three. The memory wasn't all bad. No, not at all. I may have regretted stealing the alcohol, but I never regretted stealing the time to spend lying with John on that blanket under the stars.

I glance at Jillian and, for a second, glimpse a shadow of our mother's likeness. At forty-two, Jillian has the same chestnut-brown hair, striking amber-colored eyes, and easy elegance. Something I could never hope to replicate with my wider girth. I shudder and refrain from projecting the feelings I have toward our mother onto Jillian.

Twenty-eight years after Mom's death, I still carry her secrets and resent the hell out of her for it. Vera's identical twin, Vivian McNally wasn't remotely the same as her sister. A darker soul lit my mother's amber eyes. God help me, but I loved my aunt more.

Patting my hair — the grays covered for the first time in years — I hope the ponytail I'm wearing provides a moderate defense against the sea breeze at the water's edge. Togged out in black from head to toe, Jillian and I look more like a pair of cat burglars preparing to break into a neighbor's house than two women in mourning, preparing to illegally cast the remains of our beloved aunt into the ocean under the cover of darkness.

"I guess it could be worse," I bemoan. "It could be tequila." I have even worse memories of tequila, which involve a lot of puking. But that was in college.

"What's wrong with tequila?" Raine asks, walking in behind Jillian and slipping his strong arms around her waist. Tall, blond and blue-eyed, he's built like a Viking warrior who could grace the cover of a romance novel. Exactly where Jillian plans to feature him — on the cover of her next book.

She melts against him. "Hey, sweetheart. We're just grabbing the rest of the stuff we need for Vera's send-off." Her eyes close for a moment as she languishes in his embrace.

I paste on a smile, secretly fearing the day he wakes up and realizes my sister is old enough to be his mother, though I hope that's not the case. She deserves the happiness they seem to have found together. I pray it sticks and has nothing to do with Raine's resemblance to Drew, Jillian's first love who died the summer before she left for college. A resemblance eerie enough to have stolen my breath the day I met Raine at Vera's wake.

Still, Jillian's face hasn't glowed like this in years. She looks ten years younger. If Raine gives her a second chance at the love she lost, who am I to judge?

Raine points at the O'Connor's. "You're not seriously going to drink that, are you?"

"We sure are." Jillian sighs.

" 'Fraid so," I chime in, unable to fake a shred of enthusiasm.

"Better you than me." He chuckles and kisses Jillian's hair. "Add a little whiskey, it'll taste better."

Jillian's eyes light up. "Good idea." She reaches for the bottle of Jameson.

I fix a disapproving stare on the whiskey. "Jillian, really?" To say I'm not a whiskey lover is an understatement, though I'm inclined to trust Raine's judgment. He should know — he bartends part-time at an Irish pub.

"Live a little, Kitty. Vera would approve. It'll cut the sweetness and keep us warm." She tucks the Jameson into our backpack along with the Irish Crème de Menthe and cordial glasses. I can't argue her point. We'll need some warmth with this evening's lower-than-average August temperature. But . . .

Live a little? Did I mention my run-in with whiskey? Though justifiable, I'm amazed I made it into adulthood without becoming an alcoholic. Jillian would be shocked, I'm sure, to see the part of me that hasn't existed in decades. Far from the teetotaler I am now. A passionate girl named Kat who had dreams with a boy from the wrong side of town.

My thoughts slip back to John, and I wrestle down a flush of shame over not inviting him to Vera's memorial service. He loved her, too. Probably as much as I did. At least Jillian had caught my neglectful misstep and invited him. Still . . . it should've been me. A point John would agree on. Damn life for being so complicated.

Raine gives Jillian one last squeeze and drops his arms. "We're going to start the movie. You taking your cell?" he asks Jillian, who turns and presses up against his muscled chest. She nods and says in a voice all honey and silk, "We shouldn't be too long."

"Call me if you need anything." He kisses her nose and then grabs a few bottles of beer from the refrigerator before heading to the door. "Later, Kitty."

"Enjoy the movie," I reply with practiced cheer. My acceptance of Raine means a lot to Jillian. Lucky he doesn't make it difficult.

He smiles back and nods, then disappears through the doorway to join my husband, Bob, my daughter, Jenny, and Aunt Sue, who flew up from Florida.

Jillian looks bereft for only a second before she grabs another backpack and a flashlight. I help her pack Vera's silver urn inside, and then we head for the door. She snatches a dark-colored beach blanket on the way out.

The sea-scented air brushes over my face as we steal quietly across the street.

We pull off our shoes before stepping onto the beach. My toes dig into the cool sand, chilling the soles of my feet as I walk. The full moon lights our path and sparkles over the ocean like a shimmering carpet. Waves lap against the sand with an occasional crash at the water's edge while the breeze carries a briny ocean mist that covers us. I lick my lips, tasting salt on my tongue.

"How about here?" Jillian asks, placing her stuff on the ground. She shakes out the blanket, which catches an air current that keeps it aloft and flapping in the night breeze.

I lower the other backpack to the ground and grab the opposite edge of the blanket. Together, we drift it onto the sand and anchor two corners with the packs. Jillian slips out the Jameson and the O'Connor's and secures the remaining corners with the bottles.

She plops onto the rough wool, draws her knees close to her body, and wraps herself in an embrace. Not nearly as flexible or lithe as Jillian is, I ease down next to her.

A cool, gentle breeze rolls past, and I inhale the scent of the ocean. "I like him," I say.

"Huh?"

Out of the corner of my eye, I catch her glancing my way. Avoiding her gaze, I trace a finger over the wool blanket alongside my outstretched legs. "Raine. I like him. He's good for you. I'm sorry I misjudged him."

"Thanks . . ." A soft, moonlit smile touches her lips for a second and fades. "How are you holding up?"

I trade doodling on the blanket for twisting the rings on my right hand. The "I'll be fine" I intend to say gets lodged in my throat, and a tear slides down my cheek. I'm proud of myself for holding it together this long.

Jillian scoots over, wraps her arm around my shoulders, and tucks her head next to mine. "I miss her, too. I know you were even closer to Vera than I was."

Vera. The only person left who knew the whole truth. The loneliness I feel without her guts me. If she were here, she'd know what to do next. She'd know what to do about the impending implosion of my marriage, and the letter that arrived the day she died. Things I'm not prepared or inclined to talk about with my sweet baby sister.

I nod imperceptibly, and my shoulders pull tight under her touch as I wipe my eyes. It feels odd having Jillian comfort me. I'm the one who does the comforting. That's my job. I'm her protector; she's not mine. Still, I hate that I can't be honest about why I'm crying, but my choices robbed me of honesty years ago.

"This might be a good time to break out the O'Connor's." She stretches toward the bottle.

I grab her arm. "Not yet. I'm not ready for that yet." Instead, I drag the urn out of my pack and cradle it in my lap. "Vera was so proud of you, you know."

Jillian frowns. "She was just as proud of you."

Doubtful. "I wish I was brave like you," I whisper, sharing a different kind of truth. "I admire you for seizing the chance to be with Raine . . . even though we didn't make it easy."

She stares at me in the silvery light and whispers, "Kitty, why didn't you invite John to the funeral?"

I swallow and say nothing. Rather, I tighten my grip on Vera's urn and hug it closer, letting shame wash over my grief.

How can I tell her that every time I see John it's an excruciating reminder of what I did to him and what I should've done differently? How I abandoned him, not once but twice? How, when I look in his stormy blue-gray eyes, I see a reflection of the girl I used to be? How I hunger with every shred of my soul for something that I can't have and don't deserve?

"Vera knew what happened back then, didn't she? Between you

and John," Jillian says, her tone taking on a breathy quality as if a puzzle piece has just snapped into place.

Rather than answer, I press my lips firmly together.

"I saw the way he looked at you today outside the church. . . . Please, Kitty. Tell me something, anything, about you and John. I want to know," she pleads and tugs at my arm.

My breath catches. She has no idea what she's asking of me. I shake my head. "I can't."

"Why not? I don't understand what could be so bad," she huffs, changing tack and displaying her usual impatience at my refusal to answer questions about my past with John.

Everything, Kat — the girl locked inside me — wants to scream, but tepid, mild-mannered Kitty only offers, "You'll think less of me." With that, something else inside me crumbles.

She sighs and gives my arm a soothing stroke. "No. I won't. I promise."

I use the urn as a shield. Apropos. Vera was my shield in life, why not in death? "You will." My voice carries the hollow ring of certainty.

Jillian stills and her golden stare locks on mine. "Kitty . . . ," she whispers, "what did you do?"

I swallow hard. My gaze drifts to the ocean shimmering in the darkness. Rather than offering an escape, it pulls the breath out of me and my tears along with it. They flow in hot, tiny rivers down my cheeks.

When I don't answer, Jillian takes me in her arms and rocks me. "It's all right." She rubs my back in slow circles. "Just tell me something simple, like how you met." Her hand drops away, and she lowers her voice. "It's obvious you both still care for each other . . . even after all these years."

A denial sits on my tongue, but it would be a lie and we both know it.

I stay silent, afraid to speak for fear that something simple will lead to something complex. It's just easier to avoid talking about my past with John. Our history is twisted with deeper secrets, and I'm not ready to shatter my sister's vision of the family she thinks she knows.

As for me and John? Not all love stories have a happy ending. Ours didn't. That's life. But most people want to examine, reexamine, and look for that pearl of wisdom or the justification why a romance did or didn't work out. In this love story, there's a single point of failure, and that's me.

"Kitty . . . *Please?*"

Something about Jillian's plea cracks me open. I take stock of my vulnerable state and realize if I don't release the pressure that's building inside me I'll lose my mind. With a heavy sigh, I relent.

What harm can come of a story or two? But I'll need a drink first. A real one, and I want the good stuff. "How about a little Jameson?" I ask, letting Kat slip her bonds, careful not to resurrect too much of the long-dead girl buried inside me, but unable to keep my armor fully in place for the telling.

Jillian's eyes widen. "Sure." She unrolls the whiskey from the corner of the blanket while I retrieve the cordial glasses.

I hold them up and feel my expression slide into something less reserved. Like riding a bicycle for the first time in years, releasing Kat feels both foreign and instinctual, and unexpectedly better than hiding behind kind, nondescript Kitty. "Drink with me?"

Jillian eyes me suspiciously. "I thought you didn't drink." She'd been surprised when I'd agreed to share Vera's send-off toast.

I shrug. "I don't." *Anymore.*

She *humphs*, letting it go, and we trade. I take the bottle and crack it open while she holds the cordial glasses. I pour us each a shot.

We clink the rims, and I throw mine back in one swallow. The alcohol burns a path down my throat and into my stomach. I hate the taste but love the warming sensation.

A wave crashes at the water's edge, and a sudden spray of mist rolls through the air and gently covers us.

"Another?" I ask.

Jillian's eyebrows lift. "Really? You sure? Wow. Here I thought I'd coerced you into sharing Vera's shots."

"You were the one who said to live a little," I say matter-of-factly, and try to remember what that's like.

"That I did." She shrugs and refills our glasses.

I throw back the second shot and put my empty glass on the blanket. The alcohol hits my bloodstream immediately and does its job of easing my anxiety. My gaze settles on the ocean again, and this time the inescapable expanse doesn't suffocate me. "I can't tell you everything, Jillian, so please don't press. But I'll answer your question about how I met John." I glance her way. "Deal?"

Her lips part, and she tries to hide her enthusiasm. "I'll take what I can get."

We'll see how long that lasts.

After years of her asking and me refusing to answer, I almost smile at her look of stunned victory.

"So how did you meet?" she asks, then grimaces at her second shot of whiskey before dumping it onto the sand. Pity. Waste of good alcohol.

Drawing in a deep breath, I prepare to dance in the flames of my past. On a slow exhale, I begin. "We met during our junior year of high school. . . ."

Chapter 2

Kitty

October 1979 – Summit High School

"OH, NO WAY!" I say, looking at the name I was assigned on the roster for tutoring geometry. All these poor souls are on their way to Flunksville after the first marking period.

Sue squints at the clipboard on the door of the math office then casts a glance at me with a glint of jealousy in her eye. "What are you complaining about? At least John Henshaw is good-looking."

"Yeah, in a big, meatheaded sort of way, like the rest of his jock friends." I snort. "He's probably just doing it so they won't throw him off the football team." As cool as I'm trying to play it, the thought of tutoring a guy who would never look at me twice makes my palms sweat.

"You want to trade him for Shelly 'dumb-as-a-box-of-rocks' Madison?" Sue asks, wearing a hopeful smile that highlights her braces, her eyes magnified behind a pair of superthick lenses.

Sue and I are the resident chess champions at Summit High School, and also part of a small minority of students who actually work for their spending money. Hence our little tutoring gigs.

"You win, she's worse. I'll stick with him." I pivot and head for my locker. Sue trails behind me but quickly catches up.

My heart drops as Karen Stark and her blond, bubble-headed cheerleading clan of popular girls come strutting toward us in their

13

Jordache jeans and Candie's platform slides. Her mouth twists into a sneer when she sees me. "Hey, Checker Butt. Suck any dick lately?"

Not even close.

I surreptitiously study the hall as if it's a chessboard, looking for my knight. Finding him, I suppress a smirk. I usually cower, but this time I have an unexpected move.

My mom and Karen's mother are friends, so I don't like to make waves, but sometimes it's worth it even if it ends up in a cat fight and I'm grounded. Chances are good that won't happen. Knowledge is power, and Karen is one detention away from getting kicked off the cheerleading squad.

A small grin spreads across my face. "Nah. David Ross isn't my flavor, but I've seen he's yours." I do my best to project so people can hear me halfway down the hall.

She grinds to a halt and blanches. Not just her, but her whole crowd. Besides the obvious, what makes this particular piece of gossip juicy is that David Ross doesn't happen to be her boyfriend. That unfortunate privilege goes to Mike Ryan, our quarterback.

"What are you talking about, you pervert?" she snaps.

I shove past them, ignoring the nerves gripping my middle. "You should find a better place to give head than the school parking lot."

"Bitch!" she screams and lunges at me. I prepare for impact, but her flock grabs her by the arms and hauls her backward.

"Not now. Walk away," one of them hisses by her ear. Karen screeches, turns on her heel, and shoves her way through the flow of traffic as she and her horde stomp off with the click-clacking of molded high heels.

I wink at the hall monitor as I pass.

Checkmate.

God, that felt good. But I'm positive I'll pay for it later. Somehow.

Sue beams at me in awe. "Did you really see her blow him?"

I sniff. "Unfortunately. I forgot my lunch in Marsh's car.... Speaking of . . ."

Marshall's gangly frame is propped against my locker as he awkwardly tries to balance a piece of paper on top of a stack of books and write a note. Probably for me. He's a senior and my ride home most days when I'm not attending Chess Club or a tournament.

"Hey, Marsh," I say.

He fumbles with his pen as he pushes his glasses back up the bridge of his nose with his index finger. His lenses are almost as thick as Sue's, but his smile is free of braces and kind of nice. His dark hair is thick, springy, and higher on one side than the other due to an untamable cowlick. Too bad — with the exception of not being green, he looks like Gumby. He steps away, and I spin the lock. My hand trembles from the encounter with Karen.

"Hey, Kitty. I was writing you a note." He waves the paper as his books teeter precariously against his chest. He glances at Sue and flashes his geeky but endearing smile. "Hi, Sue."

She shifts on her feet, blushes, and gives him a nod.

" 'Bout what?" I ask, popping open my locker and exchanging one set of books and notebooks for another.

"I've got to leave early for a dentist appointment. Can you find another way home?"

I roll my eyes. "I have legs, Marsh. I can walk. Besides, I have to meet my tutoree, or whatever the heck you call him, at 2:45 when classes end. Today is his first session."

Marsh's eyebrows lift and his mouth flattens into a line. "He?"

"That's what I said. He. Boy. Male genitalia. Need I get more specific?" I twirl the tumbler on my locker and give him a mischievous smile. "Jealous?"

He turns beet red, and before he can answer I walk away and shout over my shoulder, "See you tomorrow morning."

I'm not being mean; it's just that Marsh and I have known each other since we were in diapers. Our history makes him a little overprotective. Almost like a brother. I've even seen his pee-pee. When we were five. He may be a grade ahead, but we're still the same age. A loophole created by my mother who started me in kindergarten a year late. If my parents had the money they pretended to have, I wouldn't be bumming rides. Sometimes I think Marsh feels responsible for me in a way that's just ridiculous.

Besides, I know it's Sue he really likes; plus he's not my type. Not that I have a type. But if I do have one, I can guarantee he doesn't look anything like Gumby. And he definitely doesn't look anything like a meatheaded football player. Probably more like Shaun Cassidy from *The Hardy Boys*, or maybe even his older brother, David, during *The Partridge Family* years.

Then again, who am I trying to kid? I've yet to have my first kiss or my first real date. As for blowing anyone? Yeah, no. Other than reading a few articles in *Cosmopolitan*, I wouldn't have a clue what do if a guy stuck his dick in my mouth. Other than gag and fight back the urge to vomit.

By the end of last period, my heart is beating faster than normal, and I have barely enough time to swing by the math office to pick up this week's lesson plan and squeeze in a quick application of lip gloss before I get to my appointed spot at the shiny mahogany table in the library. There's a plaque affixed to the corner from the wealthy Summit donor who provided it for the school. The economic divide in my high school is as maddening as it is depressing for those of us less fortunate. Especially when people assume we're rich.

Luckily, they provided name tents for the first day, since I doubt this guy even knows who I am. He hasn't so much as looked at me in the last two-plus years we've been here.

On the upside, he's not one of the mean boys on the football team. The bullies who treat people like crap and have a steady stream of the hottest popular girls—like Karen Stark and her crowd—hanging on them in and out of school. If anything, John keeps a low profile most of the time, even when he's sitting with the team during lunch. At least on the occasions I've noticed him.

Like me, he doesn't come from money. Plus, he didn't grow up here. That much I know.

I sit at my table and tap my fingers on the fine wood surface as other students find their tutors. It's 2:55 p.m. and still no John. I huff and wonder where the heck he is. Either way, I expect to be paid. That's the policy.

At almost three p.m., he strolls in with his books under his arm, wearing his varsity jacket and looking pissed off.

He scans the tables and I give him a wave. Lughead. Where the hell has he been? He nods and walks over. Dumping his books on the table, he mumbles an apology and sits. "Sorry, I'm late. . . ." He squints at a slip of paper in his hand and then my name tag. He holds up the white scrap. "This says Katherine, but your name tag says—"

"Kitty, I know. It's a nickname for Katherine."

A slow smile grows on his lips, easing his pissed off expression.

16

"Kitty, huh?"

I nod and keep a straight face, anticipating a snide comment of some sort to follow.

"What about Kat? Anyone ever call you Kat?" he asks, an unexpected shine glowing in his — what I now notice are — blue-gray eyes. Kind of like a stormy sky that's about to clear.

He's better-looking up close than from a distance. His face is on the rugged side, which fits his broad shoulders and hulking frame. A real guys' guy. Nothing remotely like Shaun Cassidy with his leaner physique and softer good looks. Still, John has a nice mouth and, if the upward pull of his lips is any indication, probably has a decent smile if he'd let his mouth get that far. That said, unless "intimidating" suddenly makes my list of attractive features, he's not even close to my type. But that doesn't mean he's not appealing.

"No, why?"

"It's a more grown-up version of the same feline." His eyes rake over me with a smoldering glance, then shutter just as quickly when he sees my brow pop up.

Perv. I flush anyway, wondering if he sees anything pleasing. My scoop-neck top hints at cleavage, but true cleavage requires more than my smallish B-cups offer.

Two people at the end of our table shush us.

"Is that your attempt at flattery?" I ask in a heated whisper.

He leans closer. "Maybe."

I scowl. "It won't get you a better grade." Damn, this guy's a jerk.

"Ooo . . . the kitten has claws." He winks and opens his book. "Can't blame a guy for trying. Sorry. Maybe we should start." A smile tugs at his lips again. "Kat."

Something about the cavalier way he's dubbed me with a nickname in his thick and unrefined Jersey accent gets under my skin. I want to shriek to relieve my frustration. But that will only get us tossed out of the library.

I skip further banter and cut straight to the lesson plan.

We get halfway through, and I'm happily surprised that he's approaching the work with a diligence I didn't expect. I'm impressed. He's definitely smarter than I thought he'd be. Makes me wonder why he's failing.

I drop my pen and lean forward. "I have question."

His gaze catches mine and I get a full dose of stormy blue. "Ask."

"You're not having any issues with the concepts I'm throwing at you. Why do you need a tutor?"

He blows out a breath and runs a hand nearly twice the size of mine down his face. "I had some . . . personal crap at the beginning of the year. Failed the first exam. The coach threatened to bench me if I didn't get a tutor. Not a good idea with Rutgers courting me for a football scholarship. I need a full ride through college . . . so here I am."

His gaze hardens on mine and he folds his white-jacketed arms over his broad chest. "Contrary to popular belief, not all football players are meatheads." He pauses, his stare unwavering. My stomach goes into free fall, but I refuse to drop my gaze. I have an inkling of what he's going to say, so I hold my breath and wait.

He caves and rolls his eyes. "I heard you mention my name outside the math office."

Crap. Heat spreads like wildfire up my neck, burning my cheeks. I squeeze my eyes shut. "Oh God, I'm sorry."

He surprises me with a chuckle, so I open my eyes. He's shaking his head and there's an amused sparkle in his eyes. "At least you didn't trade me for Shelly 'dumb-as-a-box-of-rocks' Madison."

I smile back, ignoring the warmth still flaming in my cheeks, and say softly, "Really . . . I'm sorry. You're not a meathead."

"That's a relief." He drops his chewed pencil and leans forward. "You'll be happy to know that I don't think all chess players are geeks, Checker Butt." There's no malice in his tone. The opposite— he makes the vile nickname Karen gave me freshman year slide off his tongue like an affectionate caress. He looks at his watch and pushes back his chair. "Gotta go."

"Huh?" I glance at the wall clock, flustered. "You still have ten minutes."

He shakes his head and gathers his things. "Got practice. I need to gear up. See you Thursday?"

I roll my eyes. "I guess so."

He gives me a smooth smile and whispers, "Bye, Kat. See ya around."

My eyes gravitate to his denim-clad butt as he turns to go. Hot damn.

"John?" I whisper.

He turns.

"What position do you play?" I ask.

"Tight end, why?"

I try to suppress a grin. "No reason."

He chuckles and walks away as I stare at what I think is one of the finest tight ends I've ever seen.

Chapter 3

Kitty

Oceanfront in Spring Lake

THE SOFT LAPPING of waves pulls me back. I rub my arms and glance at Jillian. She's grinning at me.

"What?" I ask, feeling my lips pull up in a smile. Telling the story felt good. Cathartic.

"I've never seen this side of you before. I like it."

My smile falters. It's been so long since I've allowed myself to revisit the early days when I still had a solid compass on who I was and where I was headed. Meeting John complemented that piece of me. But Jillian's wrong. She has seen that side of me and the pristine part of my past, unsullied by what came afterward. Only she was too young to remember.

Jillian hugs her knees. "I'm enjoying this. Tell me more. How long did it take you guys to figure things out?"

I lean back on my hands and sigh. "We had a few fits and starts. Things started to change a couple of weeks later. . . ."

November 1979 – Summit High School

WE'RE ON OUR third week of tutoring, and I'm due to meet John in the library for our Tuesday session after my next class. He's got a test on Thursday, so I've prepared a practice exam to put him through his paces. If he passes, he should do fine.

I'm racing toward my locker when I get shoved from behind and my books go flying in every direction. I'm down on my knees with a *thump* and the air is knocked out of my lungs before I fully realize what's happened.

"Oops . . ." Karen Stark says in a silky whisper behind me, and then kicks the nearest book out of my reach. Denim-covered legs and Candie's-clad feet fill my field of vision. I try to get up but a swift kick in the ribs expels the remaining breath from my diaphragm. At least I don't hear a crack.

"Cat fight!" someone yells.

Dread grips me and I curl into a fetal position to protect my body as another foot lands a blow on my thigh. I'm surrounded in a sea of legs and the din of a jeering crowd.

Opportunistic bitch. Dave's out sick today. By the time another hall monitor hears this, I might already have the crap kicked out of me. Literally.

Someone grabs a tuft of my hair from behind and yanks hard enough to pull me to my feet. I scream as loud as I can as nails rake down my cheek, leaving a stinging trail.

I refuse to cry and do my best to pry the bitch's fingers out of my hair, but someone grabs my arms and pins them behind me. The crowd smells blood and eggs the girls on.

When the hell was five on one ever a fair fight? Assholes, all of them.

Karen steps into view and lands a punch to my stomach. Pain ripples through me and whoever has me pinned from behind shoves me to the floor. My knees hit the hard surface and I double over, again unable to breathe.

"What the *fuck* are you doing?"

My head jerks up at the sound of John's low, menacing growl. Glaring, he shoves the girls out of the way until he's shielding my body with his bulk while I stumble to my feet. His fists are clenched at his sides. The crowd goes quiet. He's the biggest guy within a twenty-foot radius. Anger rolls off him in steady waves, giving him a sexy, hero-saving-the-day sort of aura that I can't fully appreciate and still continue breathing. A function I'm already having trouble with.

Gratitude fills my heaving chest at the same time embarrassment heats a trail up my neck. I give him a sideways glance. That's enough to see he's staring at Karen and her friends with murder in his eyes.

"I don't care that you have tits. You fucking touch her again, and you'll deal with me. Understand?" He jabs his finger at Karen's friend Pam, then turns to Karen and says through gritted teeth. "Same goes for you. Now pick up her books."

Karen's nostrils flare and she presses her lips together as she glares back at him.

"Now," he bites.

Her jaw works behind her cheek. She and her friends snatch up my books.

"Give 'em to me," he snaps, his hand out.

I don't know whether to laugh or cry. And I'd be lying if I said John didn't scare me a little. Okay, make that a lot. I'm not sure I can be friends with a guy who might hit a girl. Not that we're friends, unless the increasingly friendly banter during our tutoring sessions is enough to constitute a friendship.

I stand frozen as the crowd dissipates and John stands in front of me holding my books. His eyes lock on mine and soften. He edges closer. "You okay?" he asks quietly.

The shock of what happened washes over me, and my eyes water. I clench my jaw and nod.

He flips his chin and reaches his arm out. "Come here."

I take a step toward him, and he drapes a muscled arm over my shoulder. "Let's go."

He stops for a second to scoop up a second pile of books that must be his and places them on top of mine, then he drapes his arm back around me. The weight of his body near mine makes me feel protected. My pulse has trouble regulating with each brush of his thigh next to mine as we walk, lighting up my nerve endings in a new and unfamiliar way.

"Slummin' it, Shaw?" Matt Ferguson, one of his teammates, chuckles as we pass by.

"Fuck off, Mad Dog," John says in a weary voice, and instead of leading me to my locker, he leads me to the nearest exit and out into the parking lot.

The brisk November afternoon has me shivering the moment I step outside. He sets the pile of books on the ground, slips off his varsity jacket to reveal a long-sleeved thermal V-neck shirt stretched across his chest, and drapes the jacket over my shoulders. I'm hit by the scent of leather, spice, and pine that clings to it along with warmth from his body.

"Where are we going?" I mumble. My side hurts and I ache everywhere.

He snatches up the books and pulls me back under his arm. "My car . . . I thought you might like a minute to get yourself together," he says. His voice is nice, kind. Something I haven't heard in any of our lessons. Bored. Sarcastic. Teasing. Annoyed. Those things I've heard, but never . . . kind.

Until now.

My knees shake and I swallow hard, consumed again in total and utter mortification at what just happened inside. I don't know what comes over me, but the moment my butt hits the leather seat on the passenger side of his black Camaro, tears slide down my cheeks. I cover my face with my hands and cry.

"Hey," he whispers and wraps his arm around me again. He gently pulls me over to rest my head on his shoulder. "*Shh*. It's okay." His fingers stroke my hair as the tears continue in a steady stream. Too embarrassed to speak, I lose myself in his spicy, piney scent. It's the most amazing smell ever. The pressure behind my eyes gives me a headache, but his scent makes it bearable.

"We're missing class," I say in a shaky voice, afraid we'll get detention for ditching.

He lets out a breath. "Missing one class won't kill you . . . or me."

I stay quiet. I realize I'd rather take the punishment if it means I can sit here with his arm around me for the next forty minutes.

"Talk to me, Kat. What happened in there?" he asks, again, concern heavy in his voice. Like he really cares.

"I thought you were friends with her . . . ," I say, not really knowing if he was, only that he knows her boyfriend, Mike Ryan, the quarterback on his team.

He snorts. "Her? You kidding me?" His sarcastic tone is back.

I shrug and wipe my eyes with the back of my wrist. My shoulders slump with my next exhale and I stare at my hands.

He takes my chin in his hand—it's rough but warm—and slowly turns my head to face him. His lips quirk up in a ghost of smile and his eyes take on new warmth. "Hey. I don't waste my time on assholes. God knows there are plenty of them in this school. And I don't let people beat up on . . ." His throat bobs as he swallows. "My friends."

I avert my gaze and try to ignore the butterflies riding motocross through my stomach. The corner of my mouth lifts, and I stare back at him. "So, I'm your friend?"

He smiles for the first time and nods. A real smile, not just the hint of one. I was right. He does have a nice smile. It softens the hard edges on his face that make him look intimidating, and he looks even more appealing. To the point that I want to know what I did to make him smile so that I can do it again.

"I'd like to think so." He rubs a calloused thumb over my cheek before letting me go, and then leans across me to open the glove compartment. He pulls out a fast-food napkin and hands it to me.

I make good use of it.

"You never answered my question," he says.

Yeah, that. I sigh and sniff a half laugh. "Payback. Something from a few weeks ago."

He raises his brow, waiting.

I cringe and rest my hand on my mouth as I guess at the shade of crimson creeping up my neck, based on the heat level above my collarbone. "I saw her giving David Ross a blow job in the parking lot, and I kind of shouted it in the hallway. . . ."

John's silent for a few seconds and then breaks into deep peals of laughter. "You're shitting me?"

I shake my head and try to suppress a smile. "It was well deserved, in my opinion. Plus, it felt pretty good to put her in her place." I rub my middle and frown. "I was wondering what took her so long to retaliate."

Concern fills his eyes and his shoulders stiffen. "Are you hurt?"

"Not unless you count my pride. I'm sure I'll have some bruises, but that's not such a big deal." I clench my teeth. "What a bitch."

He presses his back against the bucket seat, crosses his arms, and beams his appreciation. "You're a feisty little *kitten*, aren't you?"

I narrow my eyes and snap. "Don't call me that or our friendship will be extremely short-lived."

He gives me a look filled with wide-eyed innocence. "What's wrong with Kitten? It's no worse than Kitty. Personally, I like Kat the best."

"Kitten, cat, what's your preoccupation with small furry animals?" I'm not one hundred percent opposed to either nickname, but that's not the point. The intimacy of accepting a name that's solely for his use makes me feel weirdly vulnerable.

He looks at me deadpan. "Would you prefer Pussy?"

My jaw hinges open for a moment and then I laugh until I'm out of breath. I'm not sure if it's to release the tension of the last twenty minutes or if it's his delivery, but I can't stop laughing, and every time I look at him it sets me off all over again. He joins me until tears are streaming down our faces and we're gasping for air.

I shove him. "Oh my God, I can't believe you said that to me!"

He laughs once more and wipes his eyes. "I'll stick with Kat."

Then it hits me and I glance around the interior of the Camaro. It's not brand-new, but it's in excellent condition. "I thought only seniors were allowed parking privileges."

He cocks a brow and gives me that crooked grin of his. "Called in a favor and got an exception."

"Lucky you. When did you get your license?"

"Beginning of the summer," he says, resting a palm on the steering wheel.

"Wow, you turned seventeen even earlier than me."

He shrugs. "I had to redo the eighth grade when we moved here from Bayonne. What's your excuse?" His Jersey accent thickens with the way he says Bayonne. It's not much different than a Staten Island accent. Then again, you can spit and practically hit New York from Bayonne.

"Quirky August birthday. My mother didn't enroll me in kindergarten until I turned six." I hold my pinky out to him and he gives it a questioning look.

I smile. "It's the secret handshake."

There it is again, that smile of his. He lifts his hand and wraps his large pinky around mine. "Handshake for what?"

I shake it and enjoy the warm feel of his finger against mine. "Juniors Who Should Be Seniors Club."

He chuckles and leaves his pinky to linger where it is. "How many members?"

I shift my gaze upward and scrunch my brow in contemplation before I answer. "Two."

He laughs and releases my finger to start the car. "I'm honored."

My stomach tightens. "Wait, where are we going?" I may not want to go back inside, but I'm not sure a joyride is a great alternative. Even though he's worming his way onto my list of "types," I don't really know him.

"Our first club outing."

He flips on the heat and throws the car into reverse.

"Wait!" I grab his arm. "I have to ask you a question first."

He shifts into neutral. "What?"

I'm not sure how to ask without offending him, but something he said inside sticks with me to the point of discomfort. "You wouldn't hit a girl, would you?"

His shoulders tense, and he grips the wheel tightly enough for his knuckles to bulge. "Those girls? My threat inside? That's all it was—a threat."

I lock my gaze to his. "You didn't answer my question."

He sighs and his expression softens. "Are you asking because you're afraid that's the kind of guy I am?"

I chew the inside of my mouth and think about how to respond. He definitely burns with an intensity I'm not used to, and his physical size and presence is intimidating even on a good day. I try to remember if I've ever seen him with a girl and come up empty. If he dates, he doesn't date anyone at school. I finally say, "I want confirmation that you're not."

He offers me his pinky and raises his brow. I curl my finger around his.

He tightens his hold and stares into my eyes. "I'll never hurt you, Kat. Ever. Better yet, I'll do whatever is necessary to protect you."

His words grip my heart and squeeze. I swallow, wondering what I've done to make him feel that way. "Okay," I whisper and nod my head.

"Hey," he whispers back. Something like pain flickers behind his gaze. "In case you really need me to say it: I don't hit women, and I'd hurt anyone who did. Pinky promise."

His answer and the intensity of his stare are more than enough to allow the relief I feel to take hold.

"I have an idea." He pulls our clasped pinkies to his mouth and nips mine lightly with his teeth before letting it go. A heated gleam sparkles in his stormy blue eyes, and suddenly I'm wondering what it would feel like to have his full lips on mine.

"What's that?" I ask as my brain short-circuits from the sizzle in his glance. Warmth rushes through me, wiping away any desire to do anything but go for a ride.

"I'm going to teach you how to punch that bitch back if she ever touches you again so I never have to."

I frown at him. "You said you don't hit women."

He gives me a crooked grin. "I don't. I think you missed my point."

I buckle my seat belt and we pull out of the parking lot. He flips on the radio. Cheap Trick's "Surrender" blares through the speakers.

I lean back into the bucket seat and listen to Robin Zander's vocals telling me to surrender and not give myself away. Wrapped in the comfort of John's varsity jacket, I realize that's where I'm headed. A small piece of me is already waving a white flag.

Kitty

I END MY story there and sit silent for a moment on the beach blanket, lost in thought.

"Don't leave me hanging! Where did he take you?" Jillian asks, her wide eyes aglow, staring at me. "Did he pass the test?"

I should've known the perils of telling my story to a romance novelist. I laugh softly. "You better never use any of this in your books."

Jillian smirks. "No chance of that. I only write stories with happy endings."

Her words unexpectedly lance my heart despite being true. My gaze drifts back out to the moonlit ocean, and I watch the hypnotic rippling water. "We ended up across town at Memorial Field on Ashland Road. He brought me out into the middle of the field and taught me how to distribute my weight and punch someone without breaking my thumb. Within about thirty minutes, I was throwing some good jabs. To this day, I can still throw a punch if I have to."

"So I take it John could hold his own in a fight?" Jillian asks, wearing a wry smile.

I nod. "He had an older brother, Ben, who was in the Marines by the time John and I met. He taught John everything he knew. I'd only seen John in one fight during high school, and trust me, that was one too many. Most days, his size and demeanor were enough to deter anyone from picking a fight."

Jillian hugs her knees. "Had? I've never heard him mention Ben."

"Ben died overseas during one of his tours when John and I were in our twenties. Before we . . . *reconnected*. That's probably why."

She presses her lips together and nods, then gives me a wicked grin. "Did you ever get to punch Karen Stark?"

I smile and shake my head. "Never had the chance, no. John appointed himself as my protector and would appear at my side to walk me to class. Karen and her friends avoided me after that."

"So . . . when did you start officially dating?" Jillian asks, resting her chin on her pulled-up knees.

I glance at her. "You sure you haven't had enough?"

"Are you kidding me?" she says, giving me the squinty eye. "Not even close. We haven't gotten to the good stuff yet. At least get me as far as your first kiss."

"Why do you want to know all this?" Other than morbid curiosity.

She clasps my arm and says more softly, "Because I want to know my big sister better. I feel like there's this whole part of you that I didn't know existed."

I sigh. Telling her more won't fix that part, or make me that girl again. "Well, if you want the entire story leading to that, I need to take a small detour first."

"Fine. But start with the test and work your way forward."

"Yes, ma'am," I say, and hope I'm not making a mistake.

Chapter 4

Kitty

November 1979 – Summit High School

I'M IN STUDY hall sitting next to Sue, cramming for an AP History exam, but my concentration is shot. Five more minutes until the bell rings and all I can think about is if John will be waiting outside to walk me to my next class.

Damn it. It's only taken a week since our little club outing to Memorial Field for the big lughead to weasel his way under my skin, and I'm not sure I like it. Mainly because I'm starting to like-*like* him, and he hasn't given me any indication whether he feels the same way.

Unless you count his hulking presence shadowing my every move. That's the only time I see him outside of our tutoring sessions. He hasn't tried to sit with me at lunch, and he's never hinted at seeing me outside of school. I just have to assume he's not interested in anything more. But damn him. For the first time ever, I'm tempted to go to a home football game to watch him play.

Either way, if I fail this test it's his fault.

Sue taps me on the shoulder just as the bell rings and waggles her eyebrows in a way that makes her look like Groucho Marx. All she's missing is a cigar and a moustache. "Think he'll be outside?"

He's shown up every day except for one since the Karen Stark incident.

I gather my books and shrug, trying to look nonchalant. "Probably."

"Has he asked you out yet?" she whispers.

I roll my eyes and play it off. "No, and I don't expect him to. We're just friends." *Liar.*

We walk out the door, and my heart skips a beat when I see the familiar rumpled brown hair and the ruggedly handsome face of the football player in question propped up against the wall, staring in my direction.

He flips his chin, pushes off the wall, and falls in step beside me. "Hey," he says.

"Hey," I say back as Sue takes furtive glances from my other side. Karen Stark and her minions give us a wide berth and don't so much as bat an eyelash in our direction as we pass. When the three minutes it takes to arrive at my next class are up, he mutters, "Later," and continues on without us.

"See ya," I say to his back, trying to catch my breath as he's swallowed up in the crowded hallway.

"Not much of a talker, is he?" Sue asks as she stares after him.

I shake my head. "Not really." I brace myself and walk inside, hoping I can pass this test.

A few hours later, I'm stationed at our usual table in the library, tapping my fingers on the polished mahogany, waiting for John. It's 2:55. Can't this boy tell time? He's already ten minutes late.

He strolls in thirty seconds later with an uncharacteristic grin on his face and plops his butt down in the chair across from me. There are a few pages of notebook paper rolled into a tube clasped inside his hand. "Hey."

"Hey yourself." I give him a stern look, unable to hide my annoyance. "Give me your wrist."

He narrows his eyes and his smile disappears. "Why?"

I raise my brows, a look he's come to know well. He rolls his eyes and sticks out his arms like he's expecting me to handcuff him. I push up his right sleeve, grasp his warm, thick wrist, ignoring the thrill I get from touching the light hairs covering his skin, and read the time on his watch.

"So it does work. Do you ever look at this thing? You're almost fifteen minutes late," I snipe and drop his hand.

His gaze takes on that stormy glare he gets when he's annoyed. "You done?"

I huff. "With what?"

"Your tantrum." He pushes out his chair and shakes the rolled papers. "Unless you'd like me to share my good news with someone else." Then I see a sliver of hurt and disappointment shining behind his glare, and it hits me like a blow to the solar plexus. I've just berated him like he's a big child.

I sigh and let my shoulders droop then give him a wan smile. It's his dime; he can spend it anyway he wants. "What's your news?"

"Wow. Could you be any less enthusiastic?" he snaps and rakes his gaze over me. If I thought he had a nice smile, the opposite is true of his frown. There's nothing sexy or appealing about the downward tilt of his lips when I'm the reason. He tosses the papers at me and gets up.

By the time I unroll them, he's halfway across the library. It's his geometry test. There's a big red 96 circled at the top.

I'm out of my chair and dashing after him. "John, wait!"

The librarian gives me a dirty look as I sprint past her. I throw myself in front of him and block the doorway, still clutching his test and sucking in breaths. "Wait . . ."

He's chewing his lip and staring at me like I've just let him down. The look on his face almost breaks my heart.

I put on the widest grin I can manage, because if it wasn't obvious before, it is now. My approval matters to him. "This is . . . stellar," I say between gasps, shaking the rolled pages. I look him straight in the eye and say softly, "I'm very proud of you."

His lips slowly tug up into a smile, and he nods.

Before I overthink it, I throw my arms around his waist and hug him. He hesitates for a moment before he pulls me close and rests his head next to mine. My body is encased within his embrace. Nothing has ever felt so right. The sheer size and warmth of him against my body makes me want things I've never wanted before. I hadn't realized how much I missed his touch from last week until now.

"That means a lot coming from you . . . ," he whispers into my hair. The heat of his breath makes my whole body quiver.

I pull away far enough to see his face, but he makes no move to let me go. "I think we need to celebrate . . . with another club outing," I whisper, not trusting my voice to do much more as I adjust to the fact that his face is only inches from mine and his lips are exercising a pull on me that's nearly impossible to resist. But I'd never be presumptuous enough to kiss him first, not knowing whether he wants to even kiss me at all. Especially not in the doorway of the school library.

A throat clears behind us. John drops his arms and we face the head librarian, who's eyeing us with consternation.

"Excuse me, but you're blocking the entrance. Maybe you should take your *conversation* outside?"

"Sorry, ma'am," John says. He turns his gaze on me and raises his eyebrow. There's enough heat blazing in his eyes that says he's not done with me yet . . . far from it. "Meet you outside?"

I nod and go to gather my things with jittery hands.

He's leaning up against the wall in the hallway, waiting for me when I exit.

"Would you be able to drop me off at home after we're done?" I ask.

"Sure. Where are we going?"

I give him a crooked smile with more confidence than I feel. "You'll find out."

He chuckles. "I hope so, I'm the one driving."

We stop by Marshall's locker on the way to mine. I slip a note inside telling him I have a ride and not to wait for me after band practice. Once we're at mine, I shove everything I'll need until tomorrow into my book bag, and then we stop at John's locker on the way to his car.

I'm buckling my seatbelt when he turns the ignition and says, "Now might be a good time to tell me where we're going."

I purse my lips. "Are you always this impatient?"

He snorts and looks into the rearview mirror. "Kat, you really have no idea. I'm the picture of patience."

"What's that supposed to mean?" I ask.

He gives me an eye roll and shakes his head. "Just tell me where we're going."

"Baskin-Robbins!" I say with what I hope is the proper level of enthusiasm. Too bad Magic Fountain is closed for the season, or else we'd be going there.

He breaks into an amused grin. "You're buying me ice cream?"

"Damn straight. Grades like that warrant at least two heaping scoops of ice cream . . . with sprinkles . . . and a cherry," I say.

He raises his eyebrows and I get one of the smiles I love that softens his edges. "And what kind of cherry would that be?"

I throw him a look of disgust and punch him in the arm. Not hard, but the way he taught me. "Pig." A flush rises to warm my cheeks.

He winces, but his smile only falters for a second. "You opened yourself up for that one. Like I said, I'm the picture of patience."

I suddenly feel out of my depth. He might be the kind of guy who expects more than I can give. I'd be stupid to think he's a virgin like me. If so, I doubt he wants to hold onto his virginity much longer. Still, I can't help but mumble under my breath, "You're not the only one."

AT BASKIN-ROBBINS, John chooses chocolate and vanilla swirl with hot fudge and a cherry. Who am I to question greatness? I order the same.

We take one of the two tables inside. It's early November, so it's not like we're competing for seats. As a matter of fact, the place is empty except for us and the guy working behind the counter.

John takes his spoon and tips it in my direction. "Thanks, Kat. This is worth the extra laps around the field later." There's a sweet and endearing look in his eyes. Vulnerability he hasn't often let me see. It does funny things to my stomach.

I blush and glance toward the calorie-fest in front of me. I eye the bright red cherry on top and pluck it off. Hot fudge drips from the bottom. I pop it into my mouth, lick it clean, then dangle it in front of John wearing a wicked grin. "Want my cherry?"

He nearly chokes on his ice cream. Covering his mouth with a hand, he swallows the bite he's working on. His face blazes red and he muffles a sound somewhere between a choke and a laugh. "Christ, Kat! Are you trying to kill me over here?"

My cheeks hurt from grinning as I swing the cherry by its stem. "Going once, going twice . . ."

He snatches it from my fingers. "You're gonna fucking destroy me with this cherry." I laugh as he leans across the table and lowers his voice to a whisper. "Don't offer your cherry to just any guy. Make sure he deserves it."

My laughter dies and I'm trapped in his gaze, utterly confused as my heart pounds. I blink. He dips the cherry into his mouth, bathes it with his tongue and hands it back to me. "Keep it safe."

My jaw hinges open and I can't decide if that was one of the sexiest or most disgusting things I've ever witnessed. I opt for sexy. Swapping spit on a cherry is the closest we've come to kissing. The longer I know John, the more enigmatic he seems. I'll confess, I want to taste his spit.

I take the cherry back and give him a pointed stare. "Am I supposed to eat this now?"

He shrugs, gives me an innocent grin, and says, "It's your cherry," before tucking back into his ice cream.

Damn, he's reached a new level of infuriating. I don't even think to lie and dispel his belief that I'm not worldly. His comment about deserving it niggles at me. Does he mean earning it first or not being deserving at all? I sure can't ask him.

Instead, I move into my comfort zone. "Do you play chess?" I ask, setting aside the cherry and taking another spoonful of ice cream.

"Not well," he answers and wolfs down a hunk of hot-fudge-covered chocolate-vanilla-swirl goodness.

"Want to learn?"

"Not unless I can teach you to play poker," he says with a sideways grin. "I've got to keep it fair."

"Deal. Shake on it." I offer him my pinky which he grasps and shakes. I enjoy even that small bit of contact.

We finish up, and as I'm about to dump my container in the garbage, John snatches my discarded cherry, pops it into his mouth, and chews. His throat bobs as he swallows and then the corner of his mouth lifts. "If you're going to throw it away, I'm not going to let it go to waste."

A shiver traverses my spine. I blink, unable to come up with an adequate retort, and let his comment pass.

We pull into the driveway at 3:45, fifteen minutes before I'm due at the grade school to pick up Jillian from after-school care. Luckily, it's only around the corner.

I unbuckle the seatbelt and scoop up my book bag. "Thanks for the ride."

John grabs my arm. "You interested in seeing the game this Saturday? It's the last one of the year. We're playing Somerville."

My lips threaten to part in surprise but I do my best to suppress a reaction. Despite the last bit of conversation over ice cream, I'd abandoned any hope that the incident in the library would lead to a first kiss.

"Shh-ure. That would be great," I say.

"I'll leave two passes under your name at the gate. Bring a friend if you want. Meet me on the field afterward. 'Kay?" he says. The look in his eyes is warm but without the earlier heat and tension.

This doesn't sound like a date, but maybe it's a step in the right direction. I hope. Marsh will be playing in the band, but I can probably drag Sue along under minimal protest. If all else fails, I'll go alone.

JOHN ESCORTS ME to classes on Friday. The level of conversation hasn't grown much, but there's a kinetic tension between us that wasn't there before. At least on my side.

Saturday morning couldn't come fast enough. I've never looked forward to going to a football game so much in my life. Sue couldn't be persuaded despite my best efforts. Probably better that she didn't since I'm having trouble hiding my budding feelings for John.

Picking out something to wear is agonizing. I finally settle on jeans, a turtleneck, and the classic Burberry pea coat Mom bought me at a consignment shop downtown. A scarf anchors the whole outfit. It isn't chilly enough for gloves, so I polish my short nails and spend extra time on my hair and makeup.

By the time I'm ready to leave, I'm satisfied with the end result. I'll never win a beauty contest, but I'm attractive enough if you don't mind curvy hips and nondescript brown eyes.

Dad lets me borrow the car so that I can drive myself.

True to his word, John has two tickets waiting at the box office under my name. Butterflies kick up in my belly as I head out to the small section of bleachers reserved for the players' friends and family per the note in the envelope.

I settle in on the hard metal bleacher next to someone's parents, feeling ill-equipped when I notice that other people have toted along cushions. The band plays a few warm-ups before announcing the players as they file onto the field. I swallow and catch my breath when they announce, "Number 34, John Henshaw," over the loudspeaker. In uniform, John makes my heart beat twice as fast as when he's wearing street clothes. Geez, football pants are the closest thing you can get to a guy in tights outside of the New York City Ballet. They hug John's hindquarters like a second skin. I try not to pant out loud.

Once he takes his position on the field, I watch him scan the crowd. Not wanting to look like a total geek, I don't wave or draw attention to myself. His gaze sweeps over my section of the bleachers but I'm not sure if he spots me.

The cheerleading squad does a cheer before kickoff.

My eyes don't leave John the entire game, including halftime. I'm tempted to wander down, but I don't want to distract him. Our team is winning and it seems like he's having a good game. He's been catching a lot of passes and taking the ball down the line. Even to my untrained eye, I can tell he's a great player. I'm as proud of him today as I was when I saw his math test score two days ago. There's no doubt he could get a scholarship with his skills.

Who knew football could be so exciting?

Who knew John Henshaw could be my new type?

The Hilltoppers crush Somerville 28 to 14, and I cheer as loud as everyone else, thoroughly enjoying myself.

After the last point is scored and the clock runs out, I abandon my seat in the bleachers and follow the crowd onto the field where the players and cheerleaders are milling about. My heart pounds as I weave my way through the throng of people until I spot John.

He doesn't see me as I approach from the side. I'm only a few yards away when, out of nowhere, a girl propels herself into his arms. I stop dead and stare, frozen in place.

"Oh, baby! You were fantastic," she says as she dangles from around his neck and puts her lips exactly where I want mine to be.

I can't tell if he's kissing her back because I'm too busy trying to repair the giant crater in my chest where my heart just went AWOL.

It's at that moment he lets her go and catches sight of me out of the corner of his eye. He blanches and shakes her off.

I turn on my heel and run before the tears in my eyes prevent me from being able to see at all. At least now I know why he hasn't asked me out or made any move to kiss me. . . . God, I'm so stupid! How could I think someone like him would ever be interested in someone like me as more than a friend?

I make it to the edge of the crowd before someone yanks me to a halt and spins me around.

John's out of breath and clutching my arms in his meaty hands.

"It's not what you think, Kat. I promise." His eyes are filled with regret and pain . . . but also heat and want.

My face flushes with embarrassment and I look away, trying to still my quivering lip.

"Please," he whispers. "Look at me."

"Why did you ask me to come here?" I squeak out, feeling hot tears blaze a path down my cheeks and hating myself for it.

He swallows and cups my face in his hands. "Oh God, Kat. I'm so fucking sorry. I'll explain everything. Just give me a chance," he whispers and wipes away my tears with the pads of his thumbs.

I hate myself for needing to hear his explanation. "When?"

"Later, I'll come by later this afternoon. Let me just deal with this mess first, okay?"

I nod and step back. "Why didn't you just say you had a girlfriend?" I ask. The question brings new tears.

"This isn't . . ." He swears under his breath and steps into me. He takes me into his arms, hugs me tight to his body, and kisses the top of my head. His piney, spicy scent is mixed with salt and sweat, but he's never smelled so good.

"I don't want to fuck this up, Kat. I'm glad you came. It means a lot to me. She's not . . ." He lets out a heavy sigh. "Please . . . hear me out later. Promise?"

I nod again, and this time I walk away in search of my dignity.

Chapter 5

Kitty

November 1979 – Post-Football Game

THE DOORBELL RINGS at three o'clock.

I've changed into jeans and a Summit Chess Club T-shirt, not caring that any kind of allure I tried to create earlier is gone. I've pulled my hair back into a ponytail and even scrubbed my face clean of makeup. I'm only wearing the barest of lip gloss.

The foolish feeling I've had is still with me as I open the door.

John, fresh and showered, stands on the porch wearing his varsity jacket and jeans. He tips his head toward his car. "Come for a ride with me?" He looks like he's holding his breath, and the earnestness in his gaze makes me forgive him just a little.

I nod. "Give me a second." I scratch out a note to my parents, who are across town at my Aunt Vera's with Jillian, then grab my jacket and purse off the hook behind the door.

He offers me his hand the moment after I lock up. I rest my palm against his and it envelopes mine in its warmth. He walks me to the passenger side of the car before he lets go to open the door for me.

Something has happened. Changed.

He slides behind the wheel and starts the car. We drive in silence until he pulls into the Memorial Field parking lot off Ashland Road.

It's a cool—but not too chilly—Sunday afternoon in November, and the place is empty. He takes a couple of thick picnic blankets and a thermos from the trunk of his car. We walk in silence out to the center of the field, close to where he taught me how to throw a punch.

He spreads one blanket on the ground and keeps the other folded next to us. We settle onto the soft, multicolored wool, the dormant grass making a nice cushion underneath.

He opens the thermos, pours out some hot chocolate, and offers it to me. I take a sip, hand him back the cup, and wait for him to speak. He finishes what I've left.

"Want more?" he asks; when I shake my head, he screws on the top and sets the stainless steel cylinder aside.

Not much has been said, but I already feel a little better. Just being with him makes me feel alive.

"What do you want to tell me, John?" I ask as gently as I can in hopes of coaxing out the conversation he's promised to have with me. "I should have never assumed —"

"Don't do that," he interrupts and shakes his head. Then he reaches for my hand, weaves his fingers through mine, and gently squeezes. "This is my fault. All of it. You didn't assume anything that I didn't want you to. . . ."

The feel of his hand around mine has me shivering in a good way, but I'm so confused I might self-combust if it doesn't mean what I hope it does. "I don't understand," I whisper.

He lets out a heavy sigh. "Remember I told you I repeated the eighth grade when we moved here from Bayonne?"

I nod.

"Carmela and I . . . we grew up together. My mom moved me and my brother here when I was fourteen. Carmela and I started dating for real when I was fifteen and she was old enough to drive. She's almost nineteen now. . . . Our relationship has been on and off for the last six months."

My heart sinks. So he does have a girlfriend. Someone he's been with for years. I can't look him in the eye, so I look down and nod, feeling tears well.

"But this funny thing happened," he says in a soft voice. "I met this beautiful girl who taught me geometry and asked me to join this club with only two members. . . ." He pulls me down on the blanket next to him, never letting go of my hand, and draws me onto his chest. He strokes my hair as a tear falls from my eye. His breath warms my scalp. "And all I could think about was how much I wanted to kiss her," he whispers.

I borrow into his jacket and sob with relief onto his shirt.

"It's all right. *Shhh*." He strokes my hair some more and I melt into his warmth. "I'm sorry. I didn't know Carmela was coming. I planned on ending it with her today either way. Because this girl I met, she makes me want things I never knew I wanted."

He cracks through every last defense I have as he says all the things I long to hear. Raw emotion, powerful and unfamiliar, rips a path straight to my heart.

I cry harder. They're happy tears. I can barely believe I'm with this boy who thinks I'm pretty and wants to kiss me.

I slide my arms around him and squeeze tight, taking one more shuddering breath against the wet patch on his shirt. Then I sniff and prop my chin up on his chest. His stormy blue eyes meet mine and he's wearing one of the smiles that I love.

"Really, all you thought about was wanting to kiss me?" My voice is a hoarse rasp.

He presses his lips together and nods. "Almost from the second I met you."

A smile pulls at my lips. "When do you think you'll get around to it? You know, kissing me?"

He breaks into a sweet grin and rolls me onto my back so that he's propped on an elbow, hovering over me. His warm body presses to my side. "Right about now."

He brushes a strand of hair away that's come free from my ponytail, and then he scrolls his gaze from my eyes to my lips and back again. He cups the back of my head in his palm and lowers his lips to mine until they connect.

My breath abandons me. I had no idea how soft his lips would feel. The kiss starts slowly but grows more insistent. He gently parts my lips with his tongue to explore and taste me. We breathe the same air as we kiss and I lose myself completely to his mouth, turning to jelly underneath him.

When we break apart, I'm drowning in the euphoria of our breath mixing as we pant, and he rests his forehead on mine. "God, Kat, I've been living for that kiss for weeks."

"Me too," I say, running my fingers through his hair, enjoying the softness of it. "That's what you meant by being the picture of patience?"

He nods. The rise and fall of his chest slows as he catches his breath. "I couldn't be with you until I settled things with Carmela. It wouldn't have been fair to either of you. When I'm in, I'm all in. Do you think you can handle that?"

His gaze grows more heated, to the point that it sears me. I swallow and say, "Some things we might need to take slower than others."

"Don't worry, Kitten. I have no plans to rush you." He lowers himself onto the blanket next to me and pulls me into his arms. I smile at the nickname. As close as it is to Kitty, no one has ever called me that or Kat. Just him. The discomfort I had around it has disappeared. I like it. I like him. He's more than my type now. He's someone I could fall in love with.

Kitty

"I THINK THAT'S enough for one night," I say, wiping away a tear before Jillian can see it. "Ready for the O'Connor's?"

Jillian doesn't say anything, so I glance over and see tears shimmering on her cheeks.

"What's the matter, sweetie?" I ask.

She reaches for my hand and squeezes. "That's such a beautiful story. I had no idea. You've loved each other forever, haven't you?"

I shake my head. "That was a long time ago. We're not those people anymore."

"How can you be sure?" Jillian asks with an earnestness that breaks my heart.

I sigh and speak the truth as I know it. "By the time you get to a certain point in your life, it's too hard and too late to change the past. . . ."

"God, I hope that's not true," Jillian says.

"It takes a level of courage and a series of circumstances that will never be there for me."

"Never say never, Kitty." Jillian stays quiet for a moment while I listen to the lapping waves. "I know you don't want to talk about how it ended," Jillian says finally, "but I really hope someday you will and that someday you'll find peace."

"Maybe someday." What I don't say is our relationship started with tears so it's fitting that it ended that way. Though, I can't deny that I've never loved anyone as deeply or with as much abandon as I've loved John. I can only pray that my sins of the past don't come back to haunt me.

Jillian unrolls the O'Connor's. I recover the cordial glasses and hold them as she pours that godawful stuff into each glass followed by a splash of Jameson.

We down two shots each. Raine was right. The Jameson did the trick.

"Do the honors?" Jillian asks, handing me the silver urn.

We roll up our pant legs to the knees and walk down to the water's edge. I break the seal on the urn, and together we pour eighty-two-years' worth of love, hopes, dreams, and secrets into the ocean.

Chapter 6

John

Same Night, August 2015 – Night of Vera's Memorial Service

"HEY, MIKE. POUR me a Bud?" I ask, and take a seat at the bar in Charley's Aunt, my favorite haunt in Chatham. It gets its fair share of regulars like me who've been coming here since high school before the drinking age in Jersey was raised to twenty-one. Complete with a Jack Benny movie poster of the same name, it's family-run and relaxed, with the best burger in town and good conversation if you want it.

Tonight, I don't want it. I still feel like shit from the last twenty-four hours of death and the delivery of bad news. On today of all days. Miserable excuse for a human being aside, to have to tell Raine at Vera's memorial service that his father's body was fished out of the Hudson River last night sucked. Big time. Though I left with the distinct impression neither Jillian nor Raine had any intention of sharing the news with the rest of the family. Given what Raine's father had done to him and how much Raine despised him, I don't disagree. No reason to sully Vera's memorial.

Pile on top of that errand a dose of Kat to make me feel things I'd rather not, and I'm ready for about ten of what Mike's pouring. But that'll have to wait.

Tony claps me on the back as I grab the frosty glass and welcome the chill of it on my palm.

"Sorry for your loss," he says, sliding in next to me onto the last open stool at the bar.

The mere mention of Vera's passing makes me flinch. Even when I couldn't bear to stay in touch with Kat, I kept my ties with her sister, Jillian, and their aunt Vera. Vera was like a mother to me. Her death hurt like hell, and the fact that Kat didn't care enough about my feelings to tell me . . . that hurt more.

Until I met her gaze at the funeral and the raw emotion in her eyes said the exact opposite, carving an even bigger hole in my chest. Fucking hell. Maybe someday I'll get my head out of my ass when it comes to Kat. It kills me that I can't.

"Thanks for coming," I mumble and take a long pull on my beer. Tony and I played football together back in the day. We both ended up in law enforcement, but in different branches. I came up through the NYPD and then shifted over to Jersey. He's been with the Feds for the last three decades, since college.

When I'm looking for a little off-the-record cooperation, he's usually willing to share, so I cut to the chase. "What can you tell me about the MacDonald case?"

Tony gives a snide laugh. "Nothing like starting with the hard questions." He flags down the bartender with a wave. "Mikey, get me a Stella?" Then he points to me. "Put it on Shaw's tab." He and a few of my high school buddies are the only ones who still call me that. There were three Johns on the football team, and we all answered to a nickname to avoid confusion on the field.

"This personal?" Tony asks, giving me a sideways glance.

Hell, yeah. "Kat's sister, Jillian, is dating MacDonald's son, Raine," I say.

Tony frowns. "Really? Isn't he a little young for her?"

I shrug. "Maybe, but he's a good kid." If you consider a twenty-four-year-old guy who's six-two and built like a brick shithouse a *kid.* If I wasn't convinced Raine truly cared about her, I'd be all over his ass. But I think the kid's feelings are genuine, and he treats her right. "Go easy on them this week, okay?"

"I'll do my best," he says and drinks down a quarter of his beer in one swallow.

I sniff and rub my nose. "Thanks. What can you tell me?"

Tony tips his head toward the tables, and we grab our beers.

"Kim," I call to the waitress and point to a back corner table. "Can we take that one?" There's no escaping the noise, but it will be quieter than the bar, with fewer ears.

She nods and grabs a couple of menus. Force of habit, we both grab chairs that keep our backs to the dark, wood-paneled walls.

"Bring us a couple of burgers, medium?" I ask. Kim scribbles down our order and walks away. "MacDonald's death, suicide or a hit?"

Tony takes a swig of beer then passes a hand over his face and sighs. "Hit. No doubt."

"Because of the money he owed?" I ask. Raine's father had gotten himself in deep with some dangerous people and racked up a gambling debt to the tune of two hundred grand that he couldn't repay.

Tony shakes his head. "I think they made him as our snitch."

Shit. Not what I wanted to hear. "Who did he rat on?"

"The Genovias."

A chill rattles my spine. That made sense, given the goon who posted his bail. Worry grips my gut for Jillian at the fallout this could bring. "What's his story?"

"MacDonald helped Genovias' Atlantic City contingent launder their money for nearly a decade when he was still in investment banking. Then he took their business private when he left Wall Street. If he hadn't snorted and gambled away his entire fortune, he could've been living large. It's the only reason we were able to turn him."

"What are the chances they come after his kid?" I ask, wondering how much of this could touch my jurisdiction and calculating how to protect the people I care about, Raine included.

My fucked-up Bayonne childhood gives me a soft spot for the kid. He and I are more alike than anyone knows. My father doled out the same kind of misery as his. The first time I met Raine, a few weeks ago, he'd been recovering at Jillian's after his jackwad father attacked him while he slept, beating him badly enough to land him in the hospital with a concussion and broken ribs. I know what that feels like only too well.

"Unlikely. His deal with us included protection for his son."

My brows spring up and the tension eases in my shoulders. "Really?"

Tony nods. "Still, given the incident at Jillian's house, we have to question them. I'll do what I can to buy her a couple of days."

"Thanks. Appreciate it."

Tony takes another swig of his beer. "I'm sorry we lost MacDonald. He was getting close to something big that could've connected the Genovias to the Cato conglomerate."

"The international shipping company?" I ask, not too surprised. They practically own the docks down in Elizabeth.

"Yeah. He was about to turn evidence when he was killed."

My brow furrows. "Shit like that's not done. Snitching on one family is enough of a death sentence, but two? That's absolute fucking suicide."

"Yeah. I know. That's why it's such a loss," Tony says and takes another draught of his beer.

With a huff and a head shake, I say, "I'd be happy just getting the drugs out of the middle schools." The Genovias were the major narcotics supplier in this part of Jersey.

"Wouldn't we all? As for this case, we've just taken two steps back."

The burgers arrive. As we chow down on red meat and fries, I digest all that Tony has told me. The odds are low that Jillian and Raine will need to worry after the Feds are done with the formalities, which gives me some relief.

"You mind if I deliver the personal effects to MacDonald's son when you're done?" I ask when we finish. It's the least I can do.

"Don't see why not."

My glass has gone warm in my hand. I flag down Kim with my empty. "Hey, doll, another round?" I point to Tony's glass. "Two of those fancy Belgian beers he's having."

She gives me a sweet smile and swings by for the empties. "You got it."

"Going to the Giants' preseason game tomorrow?" Tony asks.

I nod. "Yup. Looking forward to it." I've been a season ticket holder for twenty-five years with another buddy of mine. Between us, we have a block of four tickets. My one luxury in life. I still love the game even though my body let me down when it counted. It was just the first of many things. But no use holding a pity party over my fucked-up life. Wish I knew what I did to screw the pooch to deserve the hand I was dealt.

Tony and I shoot the shit over another beer and what's left of our fries until Kim drops off the check. Tony pulls out his wallet. "I've got to get home."

I wave him off. "No need. It's on me."

He stands and claps me on the back. "Appreciate it. I'll get the next one."

I move my tab back to the bar and wave Mikey down. "Jameson, no rocks."

He raises an eyebrow. "Is it going to be one of those nights?"

"I fucking hope not. This one's in honor of a friend." I think of Vera, and everything she did for me and Kat—especially me.

Mike sets the drink down on the bar. "Next one comes with you handing me your keys. We clear?"

I nod, pick up the glass, and swirl the amber liquid. "To you, Vee," I whisper and take a sip, letting the whiskey burn its way down my throat.

As much as I don't want to go there, I owe it to Vera to remember her. I just wish I could separate my memories of her from Kat.

Taking another sip, I stare into the glass and remember the first time we met. . . .

Chapter 7

John

November 1979 – Kat's House, Night of Our First Date

I RING KAT'S doorbell. Her house is in one of the "nice" sections of town; a perfectly maintained classic colonial that sits among similarly picturesque homes along a tree-lined street. Window boxes, shutters, manicured shrubs, the whole deal. Not a blade of grass out of place. It's a far cry from the rundown rental in East Summit where I live with my mom.

Meeting Kat's family has my nerves on edge. The minute anyone's parents in this town lay eyes on me, it's apparent I'm not from their social tier before I even open my mouth. Once I do, the Bayonne accent digs my grave. My size and protective cynicism don't do me any favors and only add to a perceived air of intimidation. My only saving grace is the varsity letterman jacket I'm rarely caught without. Football pride runs deep here, so wearing my numbers usually does a good job of gaining me enough cred with the fine residents of Summit and convincing them that I'm not a common street thug.

A woman, whom I assume is Kat's mother, swings open the door and leans into the jam. She's pretty; shorter than Kat's five-eight, with similar medium-length dark hair, unusual golden eyes, and a warm smile. Her clothes have the same cookie-cutter high quality as most of the moneyed women in this town, complete with a string of pearls.

"Well, aren't you handsome?" she purrs, running an appreciative eye over me in a way that feels uncomfortable coming from my girlfriend's mother.

My face heats against the chilly November air and I shift on my feet; the string on the Natale's cake box cutting into my fingers.

I clear my throat to get my voice back and hope it doesn't betray me. "It's a pleasure to meet you, Mrs. McNally."

Having dinner at Kat's house was a must before her parents would allow me to take her on a Saturday night date. In my car. Without supervision. I'm not sure if the dinner is to check out my suitability or to determine if I'm going to try to strip her of her virginity once I get her alone in the dark. Or both.

There's no denying I plan to strip her of her virginity . . . just not tonight. My mother taught me better than that. She taught me the meaning of respect.

This is the first Saturday since we started dating a few weeks ago that I haven't pulled a night shift at Shop-Rite. So here I am . . . for dinner. Our date's in two hours, or at least that's when the party starts at my buddy's parents' estate across town. Hopefully, I pass muster or our relationship could get a whole lot more complicated.

Her mom's gaze slides over me a second time with a glint of amusement. "Don't just stand there decorating the porch," she says. "Come in before we let out all the heat."

I draw a breath and step inside. Her eyes land on the box clutched in my hand. "May I take that?"

I hand her the cake and she nods at my jacket then the hooks on the wall filled with coats. "Just hang that wherever it fits."

Sliding off my jacket feels like removing a security blanket. Rather than scaring her parents by wearing the Saturday Night Fever black silk shirt I plan to slip on later, I have on a parent-friendly training jersey.

She eyes the Natale's label, lifts the box to her nose, and inhales. "Let me guess. Philly Fluff?"

It's the bakery's classic. A pound cake made with cream cheese that's been known to have an addictive quality for those who partake. I'm hoping it wins me some points.

"Do they make anything else?" I ask rhetorically and hint at a grin, pushing away any thoughts that she's sizing me up for herself. That would be messed up. On the upside, she let me in the door with no problem.

"Oh, and by the way... I'm *not* Mrs. McNally," she says, delivering the news with a wry smile. I blink. Then my shoulders loosen and my knees nearly buckle in relief that it wasn't her mother eyeing me up like beefcake. *Thank you, sweet Jesus.*

Before I can wonder who she is, Kat comes barreling down the stairs, dressed in jeans and a sweater, slightly out of breath but smiling. "Aunt Vera, stop flirting with my boyfriend. I could hear you all the way upstairs."

The corner of my mouth lifts at the word boyfriend. It sounds nice coming from her.

"Two thumbs-up, Katherine." Her aunt throws me a wink before disappearing down the hallway.

"Hey, babe," I whisper. Kat throws her arms around my neck as soon as we're alone, and I pull her close. "Shit, I thought she was your mom," I say, then home in on her lips and give her a deep but short kiss, not wanting any accidental witnesses.

I may be waiting patiently for Kat's virginity, but that doesn't mean I'm immune to her touch. The exact opposite. Having her pressed this close makes me half nuts with temptation. We've managed to sneak in a few make-out sessions between football practice and Chess Club, thanks to my Camaro, the Black Beast, but I've yet to take her back to East Summit. More out of concern for my self-control than embarrassment over my humble means.

She runs her fingers down my back and steps away. "Close. My mom's identical twin. She's a character and shameless when it comes to sexy men."

I wiggle my brows and give her a crooked smile. "Sexy men, huh?"

She glances nervously down the hallway, bites her lip and steps back into me. Her lips land near my ear. "Totally," she whispers, then trails a long, sensuous kiss along my jaw and down my neck.

Holy hell . . .

She tugs a soft groan from my throat then steps away with a flirty gaze. "Tease," I whisper and force my raging hormones back into submission.

The way her brown eyes almost melt when I smile does crazy things to my gut. I'm not sure she realizes how unbelievably beautiful she is. Even though her lips have some gloss, which I'm sure I'm wearing half of, she doesn't need makeup. I like when she keeps it to a bare minimum. But her curves are my undoing. She's tall with enough substance to hold on to, and everything I never knew I wanted.

She weaves her fingers through mine and pulls me toward the rattling of pots and pans in the kitchen. "Ready to run the gauntlet?"

No. I'm tempted to pick her up, carry her out to the car, and drive away rather than deal with the pressure of having dinner with her parents. But it's a small price to pay to win Kat's freedom for the night, and hopefully for many nights to come. "Yup." I swipe a wrist across my mouth to get rid of any excess lip gloss as she drags me along.

My heart picks up tempo as we walk into the eat-in kitchen. The smell of what's cooking awakens my stomach the moment we step over the threshold. The table is already set for six, and somewhere beyond the kitchen I catch the fading chorus of Olivia Newton-John crooning "Hopelessly Devoted to You" off the *Grease* soundtrack.

Kat's mother, an exact copy of her aunt down to the dress pants and silk blouse, takes the spoon out of whatever she's stirring, wipes her hands on her apron, and comes over to greet us.

She extends her hand. "John, welcome. I'm Vivian, Kitty's mother."

Shaking it with a firm grip, I take a second shot at my earlier greeting. "It's a pleasure to meet you, Mrs. McNally."

"Call me Viv."

My brows flick up. Where I come from, it's disrespectful to call parents by their first names. My mom is the exception, but she has a good reason.

I stay silent and give her a tight, closed-lipped smile.

She meets my smile with one of her own, but it doesn't quite reach her golden eyes. Rather than the playful warmth of her twin sister, there's cool assessment. Something about the way her gaze travels over me makes me feel like a package of ground chuck sitting among sirloin. I try to shove down the feeling that she's already judged me unworthy and that her offer of informality is merely a mask for her disapproval.

"Thank you for bringing a dessert. That was very thoughtful," she says.

It's already on the counter, sitting on a plate under a glass dome. "Least I could do." I say, disappointed that Aunt Vera isn't Kat's mother. Mrs. McNally's polite words don't do much to dampen my instincts, which have served me well and saved my ass on more than one occasion. Right now, they're sending up bright red warning flares as Kat stands next to me, apparently oblivious to what's going on between me and *Viv*.

I catch a twitch in Viv's brow and a satisfied gleam in her eye that confirms she's picked up on my discomfort and is enjoying it.

She glances at Kat on her way back to the stove. "Kitty, why don't you both join your aunt and sister in the family room until dinner's ready?"

Kat slips her hand into mine as I recover from her mother's slight. "Where's Daddy?"

A throat clears, followed by a deep chuckle. "Right behind you, honey." We swing around to face a tall, imposing man in the doorway.

"You must be John." He offers a hand that dwarfs even mine.

I shake and return the forceful grip with confidence. "Pleased to meet you, sir."

When Kat said her father was an accountant, I expected some meek guy with glasses, not someone who could kick my ass in a dark alley. He's built like a linebacker at six-six and weighs in at what I'm guessing is two-fifty under his conservative attire, but unlike Kat's mother, his smile has warmth. My chances may have just improved.

He moves past us to the refrigerator. "Kitty says you're one hell of a ball player."

I shrug. "I hold my own. You ever play?"

He nods. "Rutgers. Scarlet Knights."

"No kidding?" My eyebrows shoot up, unable to hide my surprise, wondering why Kat never mentioned it. I'm not sure how much she's told them about me, but a little voice in my head tells me to hold back on mentioning my courtship with his alma mater. They don't need to know it's the only way I'll be able to afford a college education, and I don't want to be tempted to tell them.

He shakes his head as he places the milk carton on the table. "Tore up my knee senior year. Haven't played since."

The smile slides off my face. Maybe that explains why it hasn't come up, and maybe that explains Kat's feelings about football when she met me. Who knows? Whatever the explanation, he just tapped into my biggest fear and my interest turns awkward. "Wow, sorry to hear that," I mumble.

Kat's gaze locks on mine and she gives me a reassuring smile. "Not everyone gets hurt, Dad. John's amazing. You should see him play." She grabs my hand and squeezes. I want to hug her in gratitude. Instead, I gather my wits and press on. "What position did you play?"

Kat's mom claps and comes over to herd us toward the table. "Why don't you boys sit down? Kitty, come help me." Less of a question, more of a demand.

Kat slides her hand from mine after one last squeeze and follows her mother back to the stove. Her father takes a seat at the head of the table and points at the chair next to him. "Running back. You?"

I clear my throat and join him at the table. "Tight end, but the coach wants to shift me between that and defensive end next season to strengthen my versatility."

Her father purses his lips and looks me over. "You're the right size. If you're as good as Kat says you are, that kind of versatility should make you real attractive to recruiters."

"That's what I hear." I drum my fingers on the table, working up my nerve, and then ask, "How did it happen? Your injury?"

He grabs the milk carton, lifts it, and tips his chin at my glass. I nod. He fills it and then his own. "Got tackled from two directions. I went one way, my knee went another," he says. "Dangerous and heartbreaking sport, football."

"Really, William? Why do you have to be such a killjoy?" Vera says as she sweeps into the room with Kat's little sister, Jillian, hanging off her hand. I hadn't noticed the music stop.

He glances at Vera wide-eyed and shrugs, "What did I say?"

Vera rolls her eyes, gives him a sour look, and shakes her head. She slips into the chair on his other side across from me, while Jillian slides onto the seat next to her.

Kat's little sister chews her nail and stares up at me with big, amber-colored eyes, the same shade as her aunt and her mother's. I stare back and she gives me a shy smile and then hides it behind her hand.

I get a twinge in the center of my chest and think of Denise. My sister was around the same age when she died. Her death is the reason I'm living in Summit. Irrational affection fills my heart for the little girl across the table, like she's stepping into the void vacated by my own blood.

"Hi." I smile.

She giggles behind her hand.

"He's charming, isn't he, Jillian?" Vera asks.

Jillian nods up at her aunt and then shoots me another shy glance.

Kat walks over with a bowl of mashed potatoes. "He's cute, too," she says and winks.

"What about me, aren't I cute?" her father teases, pointing at his chest.

"Of course, Dad, but in an old man sort of way," Kat says and heads back over to take a bowl of green beans from her mother.

His mouth falls open. "*Old?* Who are you calling old?" he says, taking mock offense.

"How about 'over the hill'?" asks Vera.

He throws her an offended glance. "You're not helping, Vee."

"Wasn't trying to," she says, flashing him a bright smile.

While Kat's aunt and dad continue to needle each other, Jillian leans toward me. "Can you sing?" she whispers, blushing and bashful.

I dip my head down to get closer to eye level and nod. "I can carry a tune." If there's another God-given gift I have outside of playing with pigskin, it's my singing voice. I don't use it much outside of church, the shower, and when I drive, but I do love belting out a tune.

"Will you sing 'Greased Lightnin' ' with me later?" she asks.

"Sure." It's a little higher than my range, but I can handle it.

Her gaze darts to Kat when she slides into the chair beside me. "You, too, Kitty. Will you sing with me?"

Kat smiles wide and squeezes my leg under the table. "That would be fun."

Her mother places the sliced pot roast in the middle of the table and sits at the opposite end, across from Kat's father.

My nerves haven't lost their jagged edge. I'm not used to sitting down for a proper dinner. Since my older brother, Ben, joined the Marine Corps, it's been Mom and me. She stopped making sit-down meals after we left Bayonne. I've never blamed her for not cooking after that. Shared meals were a trigger for violence, not tranquility, in my family. Now, most nights I fend for myself, or mom and I share a meal in front of the TV if she's home in time to cook.

Sitting here reminds me how different my world is from Kat's sheltered life. There's no amount of window dressing that can hide the fact that I'm an outsider. For a second, I feel "less." Like Kat is out of my league. Before I let my thoughts get carried away, I bury my insecurities behind the impeccable table manners I've forced myself to learn. At least that's something I can control.

Knives and forks clank against the dinner plates as everyone eats in relative silence.

Other than trading glances with Kat's little sister and the occasional reassuring squeezes on my thigh, I'm strung tight as piano wire as I focus on readying myself for questioning. The food tastes good, but I can't seem to ditch my discomfort enough to enjoy it.

Halfway through the meal the grilling begins.

Kat's mother dabs her lips with a napkin. "So, John, how long have you lived in Summit?" Her question is polite enough, but I suspect this is only the opener.

My mouth dries out around the bite of pot roast I'm chewing. I swallow it down while I still can. "Going on three and a half years."

She cuts a green bean and asks, "So where in Summit do you live?"

Here we go. I know where this will lead, because I've been down this road before, and it will likely unleash something Kat doesn't know about me. Something you wouldn't assume from the way I look since I take after my father more than my mother. But something that's triggered whispers from more than a few of my friend's parents. I hate that it does since it's nothing to be ashamed of.

I meet her gaze and name the street in East Summit where I live, preparing for a look of glazed judgment to slip into her eyes. I'm not wrong. I spot the second the look locks into place under the twitch of her brows.

Her mother tilts her head, "Isn't that the . . ." She stalls and then starts again. "Don't most people there speak . . . ?"

She's really going there. *Fuck it.* My jaw tightens and my gaze hardens. "*¿Hablo español? Si.*"

A blush spreads across her mother's cheeks and Kat stiffens next to me. "Mom," she grinds out.

I set down my fork and give her mother a pointed look. Prejudice be damned. Either she likes me or she doesn't. I'd hate to think her decision comes down to my accent or the composition of my blood. But rather than death by a thousand cuts, I lay it out for her.

"My mother came over from Cuba as a teenager. She works for a salon downtown, and my dad's a plumber." I leave off the part about him being a washed-up jazz musician. Before she asks, I add, "They're divorced. It's just the two of us since my brother joined the Marines."

Surprise, surprise. My blood's not blue, there's no Ivy pedigree, and parts of my family came over on a raft, not the fucking Mayflower.

The tension around the table is palpable. Kat's father stays silent, his gaze darting between us. Vivian smoothens the napkin on her lap and gives me a tight smile. "I'm sorry. I didn't mean . . ."

"Really, Viv?" Vera jumps in with an eye roll. "Yes, you did. Don't be such a snob." Kat's stiff fingers dig into my thigh under the table. At this rate, I expect bruises.

Vivian's head snaps back and her mouth presses into a thin line. "I'm no such thing."

"Ladies? Please . . . John is our guest," Kat's father says evenly, cutting his meat. He pops the bite into his mouth and chews, glaring between the two of them. When he's finished, he wags his knife at Kat's mom. "Vera's right, that was rude."

With a glance in my direction he says, "I apologize for my wife," and returns to his pot roast.

I nod. The exchange is more embarrassing than the slight. If I knew it wouldn't damage my cause and insult Kat, I'd get up and leave.

Vera turns her gaze to me along with a megawatt smile. "Ignore my sister. I think it's wonderful that you're bilingual with such a rich culture." She pushes her half-finished food out of the way and rests her head on her propped-up fist. "Honey, your mother must be so proud of you. Kitty tells me not only are you one of the best players on the Hilltoppers, but that you are one of the smartest guys in her class."

I take the lifeline but not without heat rising up my neck. I appreciate what she's trying to do. Rather than argue, I glance at Kat when she doles out another squeeze to my leg. She's glowing with a look of pride, nonplussed at my earlier admission. "Thanks, she is."

"What do you think about Gastineau? He's having a great season with the Jets, isn't he?" She winks.

The tension in my gut begins to ease. "Would you think less of me if I admit I'm a Giants fan?"

She clutches her heart and throws her head back. "You wound me, young man."

Kat's father holds a forkful of potatoes and chuckles. "Welcome to the club, son, I wound her, too. Go, Giants."

I laugh and survive the rest of dinner with Kat and Vera's help, ever aware of the disapproving stare from the far end of the table.

KAT AND I climb into the Camaro and I crank the heat. The strain of dinner wiped me out. Even that slice of Philly Fluff sits like lead in my stomach. How's that even possible?

I groan, rest my head on the steering wheel, and close my eyes. I'm desperate for an aspirin. "Holy God, Kat, your mother *hates* me."

A soft chuckle comes from beside me, and soft fingers run through my hair. I capture Kat's hand in mine and pull it to my lips. Her skin smells like moonlight and honeysuckle. I deposit a kiss on the back of her hand before letting go.

"No, she doesn't."

I straighten up and glance at her in dim light from the dash. "Yeah, she does. . . . I'm not what she has in mind for you," I say, trying to temper the bitterness that wells up inside me, knowing I can't compete with the wealthy kids in this town.

It's not Kat's fault. I know that. She still has no idea what kind of life I had before I moved here. How brave it was for my mom to leave everything behind in the middle of the night and take us away from my father. What it took for her to be dependent on the kindness of friends to help us start over after my sister died. What it took for me to crawl my way up academically and prove myself as an athlete. She has no idea.

Her amusement dies. "I don't care what she thinks. She's wrong," she says with no small amount of conviction.

"She's not wrong," I whisper through clenched teeth, unable to look at her.

"How could you say that?" Kat says, and sinks her fingers into my upper arm through my jacket. "You have nothing to be ashamed of."

A muscle twitches in my jaw as I clench the steering wheel. "It doesn't bother you that I check the ethnicity box marked *Hispanic or Latino* on standardized tests?" I don't want to be ashamed of my past or my heritage, but sometimes I am, and I hate that. I hate that her mother stripped away everything I've accomplished with a glance over the course of a pot roast dinner. My grip tightens and my breath hitches roughly in my chest. "You sure about that?" I say, not trusting myself to look at her.

"Positive," Kat whispers, and leans in close. "Look at me." She cups my cheek, and nudges my face toward her waiting gaze. She brushes her thumb across my lower lip. "You could be part Martian and it wouldn't change how I feel about you."

The tension in my shoulders eases back a bit. I should've known it wouldn't have mattered to Kat, but nothing makes up for hearing it. I drape my arm around her and pull her close enough to rest my cheek against her forehead. "Where have you been all my life?"

"Right here in Summit... waiting for you, ya big lug." She chuckles, tilts her head up, and nips my chin with her teeth.

Warmth fills my chest. "I guess I'm lucky I found you, then." Dipping in for a kiss and twining my fingers in her hair, I tease her lips open and make it count until we're both too out of breath to continue and my lips are sticky with her cherry-flavored lip gloss. My fingers itch to run over her body, but not while sitting in front of her house. "Let's go." I kiss her nose and release her, then shift the car into gear.

Instead of taking Summit Ave, I continue down Broad Street. "Wait, where are we going?" Kat asks.

"Home." I might as well throw it all at her at once. See if she truly meant what she said. Before I let this get any further, find out if Kat can see beyond the football hero to the guy from the poorer side of town who works almost every waking moment outside of school and the game to help pay rent and put food on the table. I'm lucky that the team funds my tutoring fees with Kat. "I want to change my shirt. You okay with that?"

"Sure." Her voice doesn't give away her unease. The wringing of her hands does that.

The two-family house is dark when we pull into the narrow driveway. Kat follows me to the porch lit by a single bare bulb, and I let us in the front door. I flip on the living room lights, exposing the threadbare carpet and the mismatched garage-sale furniture that decorates the place. Other than a few framed prints, the off-white walls are nearly bare. We might not have much, but my mother takes pride in keeping a clean house.

"This way." I lead Kat upstairs, not remembering the state I left my room in until I push open the door. The bedroom is small but mine, and has all the essentials: a twin bed with a crucifix hanging over it, dresser, desk, and a small secondhand TV on a stand. Ben's rack stereo and a milk crate filled with his albums sit against a wall. Football posters cover the cracks in the plaster and give me something inspiring to look at. Other than a few stray clothes on the rumpled but mostly made bed and some books spread across the desk, it's presentable enough.

Kat looks around and smiles. "This isn't bad."

I chuckle and shuck my jacket, tossing it onto the bed. Kat sits down next to it, and I head to the closet to find another shirt. The black one I was going to wear is still in the back seat of the Black Beast. My plan was to change in the car, but my decision to swing home forced me to come up with a backup.

I snort. "Admit it. It's not the gold-plated life you're used to." My words carry more of a sting than I intend as I sort through the hangers. It doesn't take long to realize my mistake.

"Are you kidding me?" Kat snaps. My spine straightens a moment before she snarls and shoves me from behind. "How could you even say that?"

My eyes widen at her sudden attack and my reflexes kick in. I spin, slipping into a defensive stance, and grab Kat's wrists as she comes at me a second time. "What the *fuck*, Kat?" I bite out as she struggles to free herself from my grip.

"What is this? Payback? You've had an attitude almost the whole way here. Are you doing this because my mother was a total bitch to you?" she screams. "You think we're so different? That my family has money? You're wrong!" She tries to break free but I hold firm for no other reason than I'm caught between shock and wanting to keep her close.

Unable to get loose, she kicks me in the shin. I suck back a wince and stay stoic, with her wrists securely in my grip, letting her rail at me.

"That house was my grandfather's. My father just got a new job after being unemployed for a year. He dishes out a chunk of money to keep his sister who is severely disabled in an institution because his parents are dead! My parents think I don't know that my Aunt Vera slips them checks a couple of times a year so they can make ends meet. My mother is an elitist snob who doesn't work and pretends to be part of Summit society. She won't clean her own house—she leaves that to me—and she keeps my sister in after-school care three days a week while she's volunteering and my father is stuck carrying the burden. So, don't tell me I live a gold-plated life! Far from it. I tutor because I need the money, you big idiot!" Tears stream down her face when she's done and I feel like an all-star jackass.

I drop her wrists and draw her into my chest, holding her tight against me. She shakes, and her tears soak through my shirt onto my shoulder. "I'm sorry, babe. I didn't know...." I whisper into her hair, feeling closer to her than I've ever felt to anyone.

"It doesn't matter where you come from or how much money you have.... I just want to be with you." She sniffles against me, and I fight back the overwhelming desire to unwrap her and explore every inch of her body with my tongue and teeth.

The upside of losing my virginity almost two years ago to a childhood friend was the ease we had with each other and the amount of practice and experience we managed to clock in twenty-four months. If there's one thing I'll always be grateful to Carmela for, it's that she wasn't too shy to teach me in every way she could think of, how to be a good lover despite being a teenage guy with out-of-control hormones. Between her experience before me with a much older guy and a stolen copy of the Kama Sutra, she taught me control and how to please a woman in imaginative ways. I was an eager pupil for those couple of years. But mind-blowing sex wasn't enough to satisfy my heart. The only thing that's come close is the girl wrapped in my arms.

Chapter 8

John

August 2015 – Later at Charlie's Aunt

"JOHN?" MIKE STANDS in front of me, wiping down the bar at Charley's Aunt. "Last call. You okay to drive home?"

"Huh?" I'm clutching the empty whiskey glass from my toast to Vera. The stools are all vacant except for mine.

"You've been sitting there like a statue for the last hour. How about a glass of water? So you don't feel like crap tomorrow."

I nod and stifle a snort. I already feel like crap. Worse. I had a feeling I couldn't revisit Vera without Kat taking over. Now that "Kat" is out of her bag, I'm having trouble stuffing her back inside. Who am I trying to kid? It started with the look she gave me today at the memorial service. The caress with her eyes.

I drink down the water when it comes and slap down enough cash to cover the bill and a nice tip.

Rather than heading back to my apartment, I pick up a bottle of Jameson at Bottle King before it closes and tuck the whiskey wrapped in brown paper under the seat of my unmarked county-issued Ford Interceptor. Not exactly a Camaro, but sleeker than the old Crown Vics.

I silence the scanner, pull out my phone and sync it to the playlist I save for rare occasions like tonight. I unpack all the songs that make up the soundtrack of my early and later years with Kat.

The opening lyrics of "Any Way You Want It" blast out of the speakers, and I let my voice rip alongside Steve Perry as I hit the gas and head over to Memorial Field to drown my sorrows.

Stars and a full moon light the sky over the large, manicured field surrounded by a residential neighborhood. I park in the dark, empty lot. Chances are my Summit brethren will patrol through here at some point. Given the car and my plates, they should grant me some professional courtesy and ignore my presence.

I snag the Jameson, my phone, and a blanket from the trunk. Everything else, including my duty sidearm, stays locked in the vehicle.

The August night is a comfortable seventy-five with minimal humidity. The mosquito bites will be worth it. A pang hits my chest the closer I trek to the center of the field where Kat and I spent many a night lost under the stars, talking, drinking, and on a few bold occasions, making love. A place of hopes and dreams shared and lost.

Before Kat, this was my place to escape. The surroundings fed my need to find a better life than the one I had, and its open space gave me a sense of peace and freedom. A place I could dream. A place I didn't want to share with anyone else until the day I saved Kat from the bullies our junior year. The need to protect her and share the sense of freedom offered by the field had nearly split me open.

I spread out the wool blanket and drop to the center. Not as easy as it used to be with my knees and the extra bulk around my middle. At some point, I'll need to get busy and haul my ass off the path to fat slobbery. Another battle for another day.

I hit RESUME on the music app with the sound lowered, crack open the seal on the Jameson, and take a deep swallow, letting it burn a path to my gut.

Releasing a breath, I take another long swallow, recap the bottle and lie down, losing myself in the music and my memories of Kat.

November 1979 – After school in East Summit

"WHAT'S THE DIFFERENCE between sine and cosine?" I ask, sneaking up behind Kat as she does homework at the desk in my bedroom. I wrap my arms around her small shoulders, bury my face in the warm skin of her neck, and inhale moonlight and honeysuckle.

There's something I'd rather study than the trig section of my math book. I kiss a path to her ear and nibble on the shell.

She giggles and shrugs her shoulder up to protect herself. "I knew this was a bad idea," she says, putting down her pencil.

Her ponytail tickles my neck as I whisper into her hair. "Can I talk you into a study break?"

With football practice over for the season, we've been almost inseparable since the night of the party. Tomorrow's the last day of school before Thanksgiving break.

"Perhaps..." She pries my arms away and slides out of the chair.

I head to the stereo to tee up *Frampton Comes Alive* for some background music and then remove my books from the bed.

She wears a shy smile as I take her and pull her down so she's lying beside me—exactly where she belongs—and resting her head on my chest. My index finger slips beneath the elastic holding her hair and I slide the band down the length to free it, letting the soft, dark-brown strands cascade over my arm. It's become our routine, me letting her hair down. I slide the band over my wrist so I don't lose it and hum along to "Show Me the Way."

"Sing to me, *Shaw*."

The hum dies in my throat, and the corner of my mouth tugs up. "Shaw?" I like the way it sounds when she says it, like a caress.

She idly traces a pattern over my heart with her fingertip. "That's what the guys call you at school, isn't it?"

"Just the guys on the team... too many Johns. Gets confusing on the field." I cover her hand and lace my fingers through hers.

"Is it okay if I call you that?" she asks, biting her lip.

"I guess it's fair, since I gave you a nickname that first time we met," I say, untwining a finger and pressing it into the tip of her nose.

She crinkles it then nips my finger with her teeth. "Sing to me?"

The idea of singing to her gives me an unexpected thrill. I chuckle and sing along to the last chorus and the next two songs.

"You have an amazing voice," she says, her fingers back to tracing circular paths over my chest and making me want to purr. "Jillian hasn't stopped talking about you since you sang for her last weekend."

I groan with the memory of last Saturday's dinner, but can't suppress a smile over the compliment and the memory of Jillian's delighted face.

After the meal from hell ended and we were readying for a hasty departure, Kat's sister had come running down the front hall. "Kitty! You promised to sing with me!" The look of distress on her cute little face nearly killed me. Kat and I shared a glance. "Okay, one song," Kat said, and we followed Jillian back to the family room. I channeled my best Travolta for a performance of "Greased Lightnin'," which triggered an encore duet with Kat of "You're the One That I Want." After we took a quick bow, we hightailed it out of there.

"She's a sweetheart," I say, squeezing Kat.

"You were really good with her. You'll make a great dad someday," she whispers.

Her innocent words trigger a complex response. I go rigid and press my eyes shut. The secret fears I have growing up poor and in an abusive household rip through me. I've seen what poverty and desperation can do to people. The question I fear most: "Will I take after my father?"

I didn't lie to Kat that day in the car when I said I'd never hit a woman. Consciously, I know I wouldn't. I'd cut my own arm off before I ever touched Kat that way. But that doesn't mean I'd be a fit parent. Neither Ben nor my mom ever blamed me, but it's my fault Denise is dead.

I release a long exhale and open my eyes. "Someday, babe, but not for a long, long time. Maybe when I'm in my late twenties." That seems long enough for me to get my shit straight.

Her finger stops tracing, and she lifts her head from my chest. "I don't want to be an old mom."

My muscles loosen and I sniff. "You don't want to be a young one either. My mom was eighteen when she had Ben, and she'd be the first to tell you how important it is to enjoy your life before having kids." I leave out the part where my mother's strict Cuban parents disowned her for getting pregnant.

I run my fingers through Kat's hair and stare into her dark brown eyes. "No doubt you'll be the best mom ever, but I want to get established and know that I can provide for a family before I have kids."

She rests her head back on my chest, her breath warms me

beneath the fabric. "That's fair. . . . Does it have anything to do with your sister?" she asks softly.

I tense a second time. I've never given her any details. She only knows that Denise died young. I don't want my family's ugliness to touch her, taint her. "Some." I leave it at that.

She's silent for a moment then asks, a note of hesitation in her voice, "Do you think . . . that when you do have kids . . . it might be with someone . . . like me?"

The question slaps me upside the head for making her doubt herself. We may be young and have more than our share of obstacles ahead, but that doesn't make this any less real. "Kat . . . look at me." She lifts her head, her gaze glistening. "I can't imagine having kids with anyone *but* you," I say, and take her mouth with mine, letting the heat of our kiss ignite my senses. My body reacts immediately with a tidal wave of blood shifting south and leaving one hell of an erection in its wake.

Other than rounding second base and tentative touching through clothes, Kat and I haven't gotten much further. Mostly because our alone time has been limited to parking in the Camaro.

But I want to. . . . I'm just not sure if she's ready to do more.

Until she runs her hand over the front of my jeans. I close my eyes and bite back a groan at the welcome friction.

"Kat . . ."

"I want to learn . . . how to satisfy you," she whispers.

My eyes fly open and I look down into her wide stare. My heart picks up steam and I tread carefully. "What do you mean?"

"With my mouth." She nibbles her lip and blushes.

I expect to do some teaching, and as incredibly tempting as her offer is, I'm thinking we might need to start with something simpler.

For one, I've got nothing to be ashamed of in the size department, which makes oral a challenge for a novice. For all of Carm's experience prior to me, none of it extended to giving a good blow job—something she had wanted to rectify badly. Early memories of Carm and me assault my senses and make me shudder. Teeth grazing sensitive skin as we fumbled through a few sessions of the ignorant leading the clueless. Ranks right up there with catching myself in a zipper.

For another, I want Kat to like sex—no, I want her to freaking love it—enough to want to do it a lot and only with me. That's going to take some trust, self-control, and emotional investment for both of us. That part I definitely learned from Carm.

Her eyes widen in expectation. "Will you teach me?"

I nod and kiss her nose. "Let me ask you something first."

She licks her lips. "What?"

"Have you ever had," I clear my throat and wrestle down my discomfort, "an orgasm?"

She squints and presses her lips together like she's thinking. Then she runs her finger over my chest again. "Not . . . *personally.*"

I try not to laugh. "*Hmm.* That's the only way you can have one."

She pouts and gives me a halfhearted sock in the arm. "Don't make fun of me."

"I'm not, I promise." I give up suppressing a smirk. "Okay . . . let me try another one. Have you ever seen a guy . . . without clothes."

She snorts. "Yes!"

My head jerks back. I'm not sure what I expected, but it wasn't the surge of jealousy that burns bitter in my throat. "Really? When?"

Her brow quirks up. "Jealous?

"Fuck, yeah! Who? Anyone I know?"

A smile spreads across her face and she nods.

A frown etches deep and heavy into my brow, and I'm ready to hunt the guy down and beat him to a pulp. I sit up and lean back on the headboard. "I can't believe you're enjoying this."

Her grin gets wider.

Anger wells up in my chest. "Kat, I'm serious. Who?"

"Marshall."

Shock washes over me and my jaw drops open. "The geek who takes you to school?" I shake my head and try to get up, but she grabs my arm and chuckles, clearly having fun at my expense, and says, "When I was five."

"When you were *five?*" I relax back onto the bed.

Her eyes dance with amusement. She covers her mouth and laughs. "Oh my God, you should see your face!"

The tension drains out of me and I feel like an idiot. Skimming unsteady fingers through my hair, I laugh with her. "How did you see Marshall's five-year-old pecker?"

She throws her arms around my neck and kisses my cheek. "Kiddy pool."

I tackle her onto the bed and hover over her on my elbows. She stares up with wide eyes, and I brush back a strand of her hair. "I want to keep you for myself," I whisper, and kiss her gently. She goes still under me then runs her fingertips over my cheeks. "Then teach me how to . . ." She waggles her eyebrows and touches the front of my jeans again.

I nod slowly. "Yeah . . . I'll teach you." Just not today.

A voice calls from downstairs. "Juan! *Estoy en casa.*"

"Shit!" I roll off her and catch a glimpse of my watch. It's not even six o'clock. "My mom's home early." I say a small prayer of thanks that we're still clothed.

"Is that bad?" she asks, straightening her clothes.

"I'm not allowed to have girls in the house when she's gone."

Kat's brow pops up. "Really?"

I glare at her. "Like you don't have the same rule?"

"Good point." She stuffs her books into her backpack. "What are our chances of making a clean escape?"

I turn off the stereo and grab my keys. "Low."

Kat turns serious. "Will you be grounded?"

"No, but I'll have to listen to an hour's lecture on birth control in Spanish, along with a trip to the confessional." I slip on my sneakers and grab my coat. "You ready?"

Her coat's on and her backpack is slung over her shoulder. "Ready when you are."

I touch a finger to my lips, motioning for Kat to be quiet. I hear the rustling of pots in the kitchen, and we creep down the stairs. I pass Kat my car keys and crack open the front door to let her out, then wink and head to the kitchen.

"I have to run out. I'll be back in fifteen minutes."

My mom cocks her head. Her long, dark hair falls over her shoulder, and she gives me a piercing look as she taps her high-heeled foot. "I thought I heard someone upstairs." She's sharp and could've done well in college if she'd had the means and hadn't had a baby slung on her hip the moment she left high school— something she's had no qualms or embarrassment about educating me against.

At thirty-seven, my mom has an obsession with tight clothes and can still turn heads. Which she does, frequently. I'm just glad she doesn't bring any of her boyfriends home. Keeps me from having to pound them into dog meat.

"TV." I dip in to give her a kiss and head out.

I crawl into the car and kill the interior light, nearly crumbling in relief. "Shit, that was close," I say, jamming it into reverse and taking off down the street to safety.

We ride in silence for a few blocks. "The party Friday night? You think your mom would let you stay at Sue's house?"

"Why? Isn't this another football meathead gathering complete with bubble-headed cheerleaders? Sue's not invited to the party."

I shake my head and blow out a breath. "You're missing my point, Kitten."

She lays a love tap on my arm. "So we're back to small furry animals again?"

"Hey, be careful not to leave a bruise." I chuckle. "So? Would she let you stay? At Sue's?"

She shrugs. "I guess. If Sue was going to the party . . . but I don't want to stay at Sue's. Where is this leading?"

I throw my head back and roll my eyes. "Jeez, Kat. For one of the smartest girls I know . . . sometimes . . ." That earns me another love tap.

"Just spit it out, ya big lug."

"My mom is leaving to see her cousin on Friday afternoon. She won't be home until Sunday. Is this starting to make sense?"

"Ohhhhhh . . . Why didn't you just say so?"

I say a silent prayer in Spanish for patience—the one my mom usually says for me—then ask, "Stay with me Friday night?"

Her hand warms my thigh. "Okay . . . I'd like that."

If she's ready to explore her boundaries, far be it from me to deny her that chance.

Chapter 9

John

November 1979 – Night of Matt's Post-Thanksgiving-Day Party

"PICK ME UP at Aunt Vera's house," Kat says.

I squint at the phone. "Why?"

She ignores me and says, "Oh, and we're taking Marsh and Sue to the party."

"*What?*" I snap, taking the receiver in a death grip. Matt will have a hemorrhage if I bring uninvited guests, especially Kat's nerdy friends. Not only will I never live it down, but this could get me excommunicated from my crowd. I've already taken my share of shit for dating Kat, but if they so much as glare in her direction they're dead. But extending that courtesy to her friends is pushing it, even for me.

"You heard what I said. Marsh and Sue are coming."

"Kat . . ." I say, a warning lacing my tone.

"Shaw, don't 'Kat' me. Just get your butt over here. Oh, and don't *ever* mention to Marshall that you know I saw his ding dong." *Click.*

I stare at the phone, listening to a dial tone. *Fuck.* She hung up on me.

Unbelievable.

I laugh, not in amusement but out of total goddamn frustration, and grab my keys. If nothing else, tonight will be interesting.

I drive to Vera's for the second time this week. We did a movie night there on Wednesday.

The door glides open and Vera takes in my leather jacket, unbuttoned-to-my-pecs black shirt and jeans, and gives a low whistle. I don't have the Tony Manero gold chains, mine are silver, but I'm looking less Summit and more Bayonne.

"Hey, handsome. My niece sure has fine taste in men."

I smile wide and flirt back now that I know she's all talk. "Hey, yourself, gorgeous." I dip down and give her a peck on the cheek.

She winks and gives me her usual follow-up line. "If I were twenty-five years younger, you'd be in trouble, young man."

"You're good for my ego, Aunt Vera," I say and step inside her Northside mansion. Another tidbit in Kat's twisted family history. Vera's husband left her more than well-off when he passed away two years ago. You wouldn't know she liked younger men based on his age. He died at seventy-seven. Talk about robbing the cradle. He was approaching retirement when she married him in her twenties. Kat swears they were madly in love and that her aunt barely got out of bed the first year after he passed.

"Oh hell, son. Don't make me feel ancient." She waves a hand then plants it on her hip. "When you are going to stop with the 'Aunt Vera' BS and just call me Vee?"

"When I'm fast enough to outrun my Cuban mother who would kick my butt for disrespecting you," I say.

She frowns and closes the elaborately carved wooden door. "Oh, *pshaw*. Can we agree that by the time you hit twenty-one, you'll call me Vee?"

"Deal."

I glance around the elegant foyer that looks more like a museum than a house. Even though this is my second visit, I'm still amazed at the beauty and size of this place. Classical music plays somewhere down the hall. "So where's my girl and her friends?"

"Come with me. They're in the den."

I trail after the small, energetic woman down a hallway that seems to last forever and leads into the back of the house, which ends in a wall of glass overlooking the back lawn.

Hushed voices hit me a second before I walk into the den.

"I'm still not sure about this. . . ." Marshall says with more than a little trepidation. I snort, thinking how right he is if he's talking about the party.

"It's for Kitty—" Sue stops short as I pass over the threshold into the room, and she gives me a nervous, braces-filled smile. "Hi, John."

I nod and tone down the surly look brewing on my face. "Hey." They're nice enough—Kat's friends. Not that I have anything against nerdy, smart kids. Kat's sort of one of them, though she doesn't really look the part. She could blend into almost any crowd. Dress her up and she could blow away those airhead cheerleaders any day.

"Where's Kat?" I ask no one in particular.

Vera answers. "She'll be down in a minute. Make yourselves comfortable. There's some soda in the bar."

Marsh and Sue wear twitchy smiles and stand there, shifting on their feet, looking uncomfortable. At least they dressed to passable standards. Marsh is up to his eyeballs in Izod, the brand of choice for half the team, and Sue's wearing a dress. If it weren't for the glasses and braces, she'd be kind of cute.

They head to one of the two large sofas to sit down while I head to the bar, tempted to steal a nip of something stronger, but knowing Matt, the party will have its share of spiked drinks. Plenty of opportunity for liquid help getting through the evening later. I pop the top on a cola. "Anybody want anything while I'm here?" I ask.

"No, thanks," they say, almost in unison.

Marsh speaks first. "Uh . . . thanks for taking us along."

I turn and catch Sue elbow him in the ribs. "What?" he murmurs.

The words barely dislodge from my throat. "No problem." I still want to throttle Kat. I'm not sure how this change in plans happened or how it helps us.

I'm sipping from my soda can, facing the door, when Kat makes her entrance. I almost spit out my cola. I'm stunned silent.

She's wearing a black dress that hugs her curves in all the right places. The right combo of sophisticated and sexy without a hint of slutty. Her hair is down and curled in soft waves, and her makeup is subtle yet dramatic. It makes her look older and, for any guy with eyes, qualifies her as a walking wet dream.

The knowing smile on her lips lights her face and then I understand why she asked Marsh and Sue to come to the party. She needs protection . . . probably from me.

I blink a few times and shake my head as we walk into each

other's arms. "Holy crap, Kat." I push her away from me and scan her from head to toe. "You look . . . wow . . . freaking . . . just wow."

She does a little twirl in front of me. Sue covers her mouth and titters as Marsh sits there practically cross-eyed. His brows knit and he nods. "John's right, you look stunning, Kitty." Then he glances at Sue and gives her a shy smile. "You look really great, too, Sue."

Sue's cheeks flare bright pink before I shift my gaze back to Kat. I'm tempted to skip the party and take her straight home.

Kat twines her fingers through mine and casts a glance at Marsh and Sue. "Are we ready?"

I release a breath and count to ten in Latin. It's the best I can do, short of a cold shower.

"You all look wonderful," Vera says, and herds us back to the front door. Marsh and Sue grab their coats from the closet by the door and step outside first. Vera intercepts Kat as she reaches for her coat and raises a brow. "May I have a word with both of you?"

I signal to Marshal over Vera's shoulder. "Let's take both cars." He nods and escorts Sue toward the driveway.

Vera glances behind her and waits until they're out of earshot, then splits a hard look between us. "Katherine has a key. I don't get up before eight a.m. I'll be sure to check the guest room not a minute after eight . . . and not a minute before. I expect to see Katherine's body in that bed when I do. Am I making myself clear?"

I swallow and open my mouth to speak.

She cuts me off with a glare. "Not one word, young man. Only a warning: be smart and be *safe*. I was young once, too. I haven't forgotten what it was like."

Kat gives her a hug. "Thanks, Aunt Vera."

"Don't thank me yet. Your mother isn't stupid — a victim of her own hubris, maybe, but not stupid. Keep your story simple. Now go have fun. . . ." She shushes us out the door and gives us a sly wink as she closes it.

I pull Kat to a stop on the porch. "Will you please explain what's going on?"

She leans in to drop a kiss on my lips and then pinches my cheek. "You really should learn how to play chess." She gives me a smug smile and click-clacks toward the car in her heels.

Jeez freakin' Louise. What the hell? I catch her and thread my arm through hers, escorting her to the car and then tucking her inside.

Marshall's waiting in his shiny new BMW for me to back out. I slide into the driver's side of the Camaro and throw the car into reverse. It's not until we're heading down the street that I say, "Enlighten me, O Great Chess Mistress."

She blows on her nails and buffs them against her coat. "Simple, Grasshopper. This game needed three pieces to work and to provide Sue with plausible deniability." She takes a pause and cracks her knuckles. "Ready?"

"As I'll ever be." I half laugh, preparing for what I'm sure is Kat's brand of convoluted brilliance.

"All right. . . . Sue's mother said I could sleep over. I told my mother that I'm sleeping at Sue's. I have no intention of sleeping at Sue's, and every intention of staying with you. So when Sue wants to leave later, I'm going to tell her I want to stay at the party and that I forgot my stuff at Vera's. I'll tell her I'll just stay there, since I have a key. Because . . . Isn't it fortunate that Aunt Vera said I was welcome to stay there if it got too late and Sue wanted to leave early? So, when Sue goes home without me, she'll tell her mother I decided to sleep at Vera's—and she will be telling the truth as she knows it. If my mother calls her mother—not very likely—but if it happens, she will tell her the truth as she knows it—that I slept at Vera's. Because no matter where I sleep, I will be in the guest bed at Vera's by eight a.m. If my mom asks Vera if I slept at her house, Vera will tell her the truth as she knows it—yes, I was sleeping in her guest room when she checked. There you go, plausible deniability. This way, no one is lying except me, and I can live with that."

"How the hell is that simple?" My head feels like it might explode from her explanation. "I can't even pretend to follow what you just said . . . but I think I like it. Except for one thing . . . you left your stuff at Vera's."

"Ha! Ye of little faith. It's in your trunk. My dramatic entrance had a dual purpose. I snuck out to your car while you were in the den. Lucky for me, you only lock your car when it's in your own driveway. Bad habit, by the way. Cars get stolen in rich neighborhoods, too."

I glance at her and shake my head, not quite sure if I'm confused or impressed. Regardless, her plan has merit. I only wish it didn't involve the Bobbsey Twins in the car behind us.

She stares back at me, wearing a grin from ear to ear, and says, "Checkmate."

I chuckle. "All that counts out of that twisted plan of yours is that I have you for the night." Not that I'm planning on letting her get a minute of sleep between now and eight a.m.

She leans over as far as her seatbelt will allow and attacks my earlobe with her tongue. A shiver travels up my spine and I bite back a moan.

"Maybe I'll be the one having you . . ." she whispers.

Heaven help me.

MARSH AND SUE are huddled up behind us when I ring the bell. I'll be surprised if anyone hears it over the racket inside. The place is teaming with cars that will have to be cleared out of here by two in the morning or else the town cops will have a ticketing smorgasbord. Matt's parents are in Europe for the month and his live-in housekeeper went home to spend the holiday weekend with her family . . . so, party hardy.

Matt's girlfriend, Sandy, whips the door open and nearly spills out along with the disco tunes playing inside. "Oops," she giggles and runs her gaze over me, ignoring Kat, then flashes a salacious smile. "Hey, John. Looking good enough to eat."

Kat tightens her fingers around mine. I don't have to see her face to feel her glare.

"You gonna let us in?" I ask, as patiently as I can with someone who is already well lubricated.

Matt's head pops out from behind the door, and he steps behind Sandy and gives her a kiss before she slips back inside. "Hey, Shaw . . . Kitty." His mouth drops into a frown when he spots our tagalong guests. "Who are they?"

Before I can open my mouth, Kitty smiles brightly and steps forward. "Matt, I hope you don't mind. John and I had plans with Marsh and Sue tonight, but we didn't want to miss your party, so I asked them to come along."

She opens the handbag she retrieved out of the trunk on our way in and pulls out a bottle wrapped in brown paper. "A gift."

Matt's brows shoot up. He accepts the bottle and peels back the paper to reveal an expensive bottle of vodka worth at least half a week of my Shop-Rite salary.

A smile spreads across his face as I stand there dumbfounded. He opens the door wider. "Thanks, Kitty. Come on in and make yourselves at home."

I'm still speechless as I follow Kat into a foyer that rivals Vera's, with Marsh and Sue trailing behind us. They all dump their coats on a pile in the dining room while I hold onto my leather for fear of never seeing it again, and we travel deeper into the house toward the source of the beat.

"Nice move. I'm impressed. How'd you get it? Sticky fingers and a blind eye?" I ask close enough to her ear so that she can hear me over the pulse of the music as we travel down the hall.

"Nope. Vera gave it to me for Matt's parents. Figured it would help smooth things over for bringing Marsh and Sue."

I snort. "They'll never see that bottle."

She grazes her lips over my cheek and holds tight to my hand. "I know, and I suspect Vera knows that, too. Like I said, plausible deniability."

I'll hand it to Aunt Vera, she's got a bead on how our errant teenage minds work. Part of the reason I like her so much. Not many adults I know would be so accommodating, but I'm not going to question it. Having her to counterbalance Kat's mother is a godsend.

I'm still shaking my head over Kat's smooth move as we walk into what looks like it had been a family room before its transformation into a disco. Rolled rugs sit pushed against the walls along with all the furniture, exposing the hardwood and freeing the center of the room for a generously sized dance floor. A guy manning turntables flanked by large speakers spins discs in the corner. Matt had even rigged up a mirrored disco ball that hangs from the ceiling.

Nice production.

Bodies fill the space in the near darkness, writhing to the music. A couple of the girls I know from the cheering squad are attempting to coax two guys from the team into something that looks like the Hustle.

Another guy from the team squeezes by with his girlfriend. "Hey, Shaw. How's it hanging?"

I nod and clap him on the shoulder as he passes. Heat pulses around us from too many people, and I'm thinking drinks might be in order before we join the madness on the makeshift dance floor. I motion Kat and her friends toward the adjoining hall that leads to the kitchen.

There's a tapped keg on the counter and a game of quarters going on at the table with more guys from the team, complete with Karen Stark draped over her boyfriend, Mike Ryan, our quarterback, and two of her minions hovering nearby. She gives us the evil eye as we walk in, and Kat goes rigid at my side. Karen hasn't said "Boo" to Kat since the day I put her in her place, and she better not start now.

"Yo, Shaw! You want in?" someone yells over.

"No, thanks," I yell back and focus on the beer keg.

"So who are your little friends?" Mike yells over. Taking a deep breath, I prepare for him to be the total douchebag he usually is and shoot him a glare without missing a beat on drawing our beer.

Marsh and Sue look around like two skittish colts caught somewhere between fear and fascination. At some point, Marsh must have slipped his hand around Sue's, because he's holding it in a white-knuckled grip.

"You get stuck with babysitting duty?" Mike asks and bounces another quarter that misses the red plastic cup.

My jaw tightens. "Shut it, Mike," I say, and assess our chances of us getting out of the kitchen without this turning ugly. I hand the first two beers to Marsh and nod toward the door. He takes the drinks and catches my drift as I fill Kat's and hand it to her.

They're out the door when Karen eyes Kat then leans in to whisper something into Mike's ear. He gloats and mumbles just loud enough for me to hear, "So she's a geek? At least she's *white* pussy."

Kat gasps next to me, and I crush the cup I'm filling. Of all the things I expect, that's not one of them. I've caught a few slurs behind my back but never to my face. I can't decide if it's the sexist or the racist overtone that makes me snap first.

Fury blazes a trail outward from the center of my chest and before they can see me move, I'm around the table with Karen shoved aside and my arm cinched around Mike's neck, pulling him back and choking him enough to see panic rise in his eyes.

One by one the rest of the guys around the table push their chairs back, some my friends, some his. They all hang back, trading glances, probably debating if they should jump in. One thing I learned early on, most guys in this town can't fight worth a fuck, and the ones who've seen me in action won't be stupid enough to take me on unless I'm on the verge of killing Mike, which, as tempting as that is, won't happen. I won't jeopardize my future by landing in jail.

I say, low and menacing, into Mike's ear as he claws at my arm, "You better fucking apologize for disrespecting my girlfriend."

Karen beats on my back with her fists, and I shove her off me with my free hand.

"Let me go," Mike croaks.

"Apologize," I bite out.

"I'm . . . sorry."

"To Kat . . . I'm sorry, Kat," I whisper.

"I'm sorry . . . Kat," he grinds out.

Good enough. I release my grip and shove him into the table. "Don't say anything like that again unless you want me to kick your WASP-y ass from here to Milburn."

Everyone moves back to let me pass as I stride over to Kat, who stands frozen, clutching her beer and wearing a look that's a mix of shock and awe.

I fill a cup for myself then take Kat's hand and gently steer her out of the kitchen.

"Well, that was something," Kat says as we navigate our way back to the family room. I can't tell from her tone what she means by that.

I raise a brow. "Assholes. Sorry about that, babe." She still looks a little shell-shocked. I drape my free arm over her shoulder and kiss the side of her head, suddenly worried. "I hope I didn't scare you."

She snugs in closer and shakes her head. "He deserved it. But he should've apologized to you, too. That put-down was for both of us."

It's not the first time—obviously—that I've come up against prejudice in this predominantly WASP town. I hate that she had to witness it. " 'S okay, baby."

As we get closer to the dance floor, the music drowns out any further attempt at conversation. Donna Summer sings about "MacArthur Park" melting in the dark and a cake in the rain. I spot

Marsh and Sue looking cozy on the edge of the dance floor, swaying to the beat. His arms are wrapped around her and she's staring up into his eyes. I'm unexpectedly warmed by the sight. *Way to go, Marsh. Hope your ding dong is more impressive now than when you were five.*

"Dance?" Kat mouths. I nod, wishing we could just leave. Then I hatch a plan of my own and head over to whisper in Marsh's ear.

Chapter 10

John

November 1979 – My Place, East Summit

MISSION ACCOMPLISHED. WE'RE back to my place by eleven. I thought Marshall was going to shed tears of gratitude when I suggested that if he wanted to leave with Sue, I'd take Kat back to Vera's for the night.

Seems like I'm not the only one who wanted to peel a dress off of someone, though I think my chances are a lot higher.

I slip the key in the door and escort Kat to my bedroom. All I can think about is spending some quality time with her in a state of undress. We trek up the stairs with her overnight bag slung over my shoulder and our hands clasped together.

She carries her pumps in her free hand and giggles. I'm hoping that glass of spiked punch she had after sipping and then discarding her beer has set her at ease but hasn't plowed her under.

"Shaw?"

"Yeah, Kat?"

"I can't wait to see you naked," she whispers in a voice that's more sing-song than it should be. Crap. The punch was definitely a bad idea. We barely make it through the door when she's on me. Lips, hands, her body pressed to mine. Tugging at my clothes — shirt, belt, pants.

It's all I can do to suppress a groan after leashing my primal impulses all night. Let's face it, ever since I hit puberty I've been a walking hard-on, but my two years with Carm taught me a little about control and what's important to a girl you care about. I'm light years ahead of the guys on the team when it comes to women. I take pride in that. Especially after watching my father disrespect my mother all of those years. I want to be exactly the opposite of that bastard, even though I'm petrified I won't be.

That said, I don't want this to go further than it should. I'm not stupid, Kat's not ready. If it happens too soon, I have no doubt I'll live to regret it. So my stash of condoms will remain untouched for tonight.

"Babe . . . let's slow it down," I whisper, capturing her wrists gently in my hands. "Just a little."

She stares up into my eyes. "But I thought . . ."

I pull her into me and kiss her deep, sliding my hands down the black crepe-y fabric of her dress and the curves underneath. She tastes like fruity rum punch. I press my forehead to hers and trade breath with her.

"*Hmm*. You thought right . . . but I want this night to be perfect. Let me do that for us?"

She nods and drops onto my bed. "All right."

I cue up a mix cassette with some of my favorite make-out tunes taped from Ben's album collection in the milk crates.

Nudging Kat over, I lower myself down beside her. "Come here," I say to the opening chords of Lynyrd Skynyrd's "Simple Man."

She tucks herself into my chest, and I thread my fingers through her hair. I sing softly and enjoy the feel of her warming my side. She trails a hand over my abs and along my thigh. My eyes slip shut. I think about the significance of the song and the memory it triggers. My mom with tears in her eyes, telling Ben and me to grow up to be men who would always be proud to look ourselves in the mirror, and to value a woman's love and show her respect when the time came. There's no doubt Kat has mine.

She shimmies out from under my arm and unbuttons my shirt the rest of the way. Her lips land on my mouth as she works the fabric off my shoulders.

I let her, shifting around so that she can slide the shirt down my arms and pull it out from under me. She runs her hands down my bare back, her fingers hesitating over the lumpy scars under my shoulder blades. Then she backs up and feels them again, tentatively touching and prodding.

"How did you get these scars?" she asks, shifting down alongside me.

I'm not drunk, but I've had enough to let my guard halfway down. That must be why I open my mouth and spill some of my secrets when all I should be focusing on is making the most of this rare opportunity to get naked with Kat and explore her soft skin.

I squeeze her against me and let out a long exhale. "My father beat my mother. . . ." I whisper. "That's why we left Bayonne. She ran in the middle of night and took us with her."

She stops caressing my thigh and raises her head from my chest. The look in her eyes almost breaks my heart. "What about you? Did he . . . ever beat you?"

Slowly, I nod. "Yeah. Ben, too."

"Is that . . ." She swallows and tries again. "Is that why you have so much . . . anger?"

Her question surprises me. It's no secret that I come off as intimidating, and yeah, it's motivated by self-preservation, but I don't consider myself angry. Rightfully pissed off at times, but not angry.

"I'm not sure angry is the right word," I say, hugging her. "But it's why I learned how to protect myself and the people I care about."

Except Denise. The one person I couldn't.

She brushes her palm back and forth over the light hair covering my chest, sending chills across my skin. "Where's your father now?"

I shrug. "Don't know. Don't care."

"Does he know where you are?"

"Nope. This is the last place he'd look. My mom doesn't have any family ties here, only a friend who was willing to help us when the time was right."

"Are you worried he'll find you?"

I shake my head. "God help him if he does." Carmela will never tell; her family was instrumental in our escape.

Kat runs her finger absently over my skin. "Shaw?"

"Yeah?"

She lifts her head and rests her chin on my chest with a gleam in her eye. "Kiss me?"

Thank God. I'm ready to leave that conversation behind, but I'm glad I had it. It feels good to unburden myself and know she accepts me for who I am and doesn't judge me for it.

I smile, cup her face in my hands, and take her mouth. Kissing her deep in a dance of tongue, lips, and teeth until we're both breathless and panting. I shift her on top of me so we're a mass of tangled hips, legs, and hands caressing, kneading, and finally, stripping each other of the clothes covering us.

Everything lands in a pile next to the bed until I'm in only my boxers and she's covered by nothing but a black lacy bra and matching panties.

Kat licks her lips and runs her palm over the erection I have no hope of hiding. I groan, pressing my head back into the pillow, nearly coming undone at the feel of her hand rubbing the cotton covering me. Before I can stop myself, I bow my hips up hard against her palm.

"You promised . . . ," she whispers, "to teach me . . ."

I release a breath.

My eyelids stay half shut, and I cover her hand with mine, pressing it onto rock-hard but sensitive skin. I guide her hand up and down, along my length. "Let's use your hand first," I whisper, still a bit squeamish about unleashing her untrained mouth on my dick. Getting past the gag reflex alone will take some work. Right now, I want to give her a win-win and manage the shock of that first. If she's never seen a guy naked, she's never seen one come either. I'll be the first to admit, it's not the prettiest sight.

"Okay," she says, and works her hand in tandem with mine. I let her take the lead but add pressure when needed.

"Don't be afraid . . . to press harder," I whisper, meeting her eager gaze. "Glide it, like this." I take her hand and show her what I mean.

It feels so fucking good having her touch me, better than touching myself by far.

"Like this?" she asks.

"Yeah," my voice comes out a rough whisper as my breathing gets ragged.

"Faster . . . ," I whisper, and she speeds up her pace. My body catches the wave before my brain has a chance to register the orgasm about to grip me. "Kat!" My back arches into the bed and I squeeze her hand in place as I fucking shatter and unload what feels like a lifetime of hot desire inside my boxers.

I hug her close and turn to mush, letting myself rest for a moment and enjoy the feel of her next to me as I let my heart rate decelerate. I kiss her.

My eyes crack open, and there's a radiant smile on her face. "That was good?"

I pant. "Holy shit, Kat. That was really, really good."

We rest for a few minutes until I can't take the cooling stickiness pooling underneath my hips. "I'll be right back," I say and take a quick trip to the bathroom to clean up. I drop my underwear into the hamper and head naked into the bedroom, dimming the lights as I enter. Kat's eyes go wide when she sees me. I crawl onto the bed and collapse down next to her.

I run my fingers over the lacy cups covering her breasts, pulling a gasp from her. "My turn now, Kitten. But first... let's get rid of this." Sliding a hand beneath her, I unhook her bra on the first shot, work it down her arms, and toss it to the floor.

She swallows and licks her lips.

"You nervous?" I ask.

"A little," she breathes.

"Relax, babe. I'll do all the work," I say, and slide down to the edge of the bed, hooking my thumbs inside her panties and sliding them down her thighs and off until I have a full view of her virgin flesh.

I say a silent "thank you" to Carm for breaking me in and giving me a clue how not to be a fucking Barbarian like so many of my friends — if what they talk about in the locker room is even half true. The idiots think porn and Hustler are the gold standard. Leads me to believe they're all full of shit with relationships limited to a girl named *Palmala* or just suck in the sack. My screwed-up youth has aged me in more ways than one, this being the best of them.

I kiss a path up her inner thighs until I'm lying between them. Her legs tense around my ears. "Relax...," I whisper, and her legs fall back an inch. Gently, I explore her with feather-light touches until I find the sweet spot I'm looking for. With the soft tip of my tongue, I glide over her core and she lets out a soft gasp. I stop and check in. "Does that feel okay?"

"Yes... it does," she says, licking her lips.

I suppress a smile and resume my play. Giving her a soft circular massage with my tongue, I free my hands and try to raise a reaction in her breasts. I'm not disappointed when she moans softly and her tips pebble under my thumbs.

She arches up and I pick up my pace when she swells in my mouth. Patiently, I coax her first orgasm to the surface. She digs her fingers into my shoulders. "I feel something," she says, breathlessly. My mouth is too busy to stop, and rather than tell her what's happening, I focus on making it happen. I continue to caress one breast then reposition my pinky at her slick opening without missing a beat on my circular rhythm. Slowly, I sink my smallest finger inside her, working it back and forth. Kat hits the edge and cries out.

"Oh God. Shaw!" She squeezes her thighs around my face, and her body shatters around my finger and in my mouth. I ride out her climax with her, not moving until her entire body stills and she's drawing in heaving breaths.

She lifts off the bed and stares at me with parted lips. "That was the most amazing thing I've ever felt."

I collapse down between her legs and wipe my mouth. I laugh with sheer, unadulterated delight. "Told you."

I crawl up next to her, already standing at attention and hoping for round two.

This time, she wraps her hand around bare skin. "Shaw?"

"Yeah, baby?"

She tugs gently on my dick and shakes her head. "This is much, much larger than Marshall's."

I laugh. "Hell, I hope so. I'm thinking he's much larger now than the last time you saw him." I nuzzle her neck and wiggle my eyebrows, "But he's probably still not as big as me."

She giggles and flinches her shoulder up to protect her neck. "Shaw?"

"What, babe?"

"I'm glad we're going to wait to, you know — do it."

"Why's that?"

She glides her hand up my length. "It's going to take me awhile to work up the nerve to fit this inside my body."

I chuckle and squeeze her tight, enjoying the excitement of her touch. I can wait for as long as it takes. As long as she touches me like this — a lot. "I told you, Kat. I'm the picture of patience." I kiss her then, my heart beating in a contented rhythm, enjoying every moment I spend with her more than the next. As much as it terrifies me, I can't imagine a day without her.

She kisses my chest, still gripping me firmly in her hand. "John Henshaw, you're going to be my Kryptonite."

John

August 2015 – Memorial Field

ECHOES OF THAT long-ago night fade away, leaving me staring up at the stars on Memorial Field. My back cushioned by summer grass beneath the blanket, I sing along to the last lines of Jefferson Starship's "Find Your Way Back" as it melts into 38 Special's "Second Chance." I gaze at the night sky, knowing Kat's somewhere under it with me, just separated by time and space. What I'd freaking give for another chance to do it right. To hold her like I used to . . . to fix all our broken dreams.

My voice wrings out the melancholy tones. I hit the high notes, remembering the touch of her fingertips trailing over my chest as I sang to her all those years ago. The song ends and leads into "Show Me the Way."

Propping up on an elbow, I unscrew the top on the whiskey bottle and add my vocals to Frampton's. My head swims in a good way as I revisit some of my happiest memories. To a love I didn't know how to fully appreciate until it was gone. To a love I let slip away not once but twice.

I take a long pull then fumble with the cap, trying to get it back on. For some reason it's monumentally harder than the last time I tried. I lie back down, rest my hands on my chest, and stare at the pinholes piercing the night sky.

The stars above me blur in a watery haze. "God, Kat, I was such a jackass. Forgive me, babe . . ." I say with a shuddering breath.

Someone once asked me what I'd tell myself if I could go back in time. I wouldn't say anything. I'd be too busy kicking my own ass from here to kingdom come for making the wrong choices. For thinking life would always be as good as it was when I was eighteen. Not realizing I sat on the top of the world with only one direction ahead — down.

Vee tried to cushion my fall on the descent. For that, I'll be forever grateful. Raising the bottle, I salute the heavens. "Love you, Vee," I say, my voice a thick whisper, before taking one last drink in her honor and packing my memories up tight.

Chapter 11

Kitty

One Year Later, August 2016 – Jillian and Raine's Wedding Night

"WHAT ARE YOU doing out here?" asks a low, familiar voice behind me. Missing is the gruffness it has acquired over time, in its place a gentle crooning quality that seems to be reserved just for me.

God, not him, not now.

My traitorous heart flutters as I sit draped in darkness, rocking my eight-week-old niece in my arms and enjoying what had been—a moment ago—solitude. Rather than face John, I keep my gaze fixed on the glimmering ocean view from a chair on the hotel balcony in Spring Lake.

"Trying to give everyone a little peace," I answer. Peace. Something I can't seem to find for myself. "She's finally asleep." I cradle the blanketed bundle, taking comfort in her reassuring warmth.

The wedding after-party in the bar ended hours ago. By now, any sane person is either deep in REM sleep or locked in a passionate embrace somewhere. Hopefully, that's true for the bride and groom, since babysitting Rachel was one of my gifts to them. Jillian and Raine deserve a perfect, unencumbered wedding night.

"What are you doing up so late?" I whisper.

"Couldn't sleep." His hand brushes a quick swathe across my shoulders, and he pulls up a chair close enough so that it's almost touching mine. I shiver, but not from the night breeze. Even what feels like a lifetime later, his touch still connects with a well of need buried deep inside me.

He holds out his arms toward his godchild. "May I?"

I let his voice wrap around me like a distant dream and hand Rachel over. Jillian and Raine had chosen John and Brigitte, Jillian's best friend, to serve as Rachel's godparents. My husband, Bob, was mildly offended, but a wise choice given recent events.

John's expression softens in the moonlight the moment the baby settles into the crook of his arm. "She's so beautiful," he whispers.

A pang of raw emotion hits my chest for more reasons than I can name as I watch John cradle Rachel.

Being chosen as her godfather is the closest John has ever come to claiming a child of his own. After a short, failed marriage in his thirties, he never remarried. His childless state saddens me for more reasons than I care to admit. Despite his long-ago misgivings, he would've made a fine father.

Before I can stop myself, tears well in my eyes and I look away. That's been happening a lot lately. Secrets can do that to a person. Rip away at the fabric of who you are.

I'm not out here breathing in the night air only to put Rachel asleep. The events that started last summer after Vera's death are finally coming to a head, along with decisions that need to be made. I needed a place to think. A place to escape from my room and the man lying in my bed.

Having John here provides too much of a temptation to lean on him and unload the burden resting inside my soul. The tiny part I kept for myself after I fell in love with him in high school. The part that's held me prisoner for half my life.

His close proximity triggers a combination of pain and raw aching need inside me. That's a hard thing to reconcile while married to someone else.

I don't realize my shoulders are shaking and tears are streaming down my cheeks until a warm hand clasps my shoulder.

"Kat, what's the matter?" There's an ache to his voice that slices straight into my heart.

I brush at my eyes and glance over my shoulder.

Stupid, stupid thing to do.

Worry shines in his eyes and creases his brow as he searches my face. Holding Rachel snug to his broad chest with one hand, he reaches the other to tuck back a piece of my hair with large, gentle fingers. "Tell me what's wrong, babe?" he whispers.

My breath catches and I lean into his touch, yearning for more. The intimate tone of his gruff voice flows like lava over rock. It's been so long since anyone's called me babe, or since I've felt like a woman and not some invisible nonentity.

I regret my transgression and freeze as his hand remains resting on my shoulder and my skin sizzles beneath his fingertips.

Squeezing his eyes shut, he pulls away. "Sorry, Kat. I didn't mean . . . "

He misunderstands, but rather than try to explain what can't be explained, I say, "It's okay," and fight the urge to reach for his hand, craving his warmth so much that it's painful. He doesn't understand what he does to me, and I can't tell him.

Tonight's the first time we've seen each other alone since he caught me in the hallway at the hospital the day Jillian gave birth to Rachel.

I'd nearly told him that day. Everything. Well, maybe not everything, but at least why I'd asked him for the name of a private investigator . . . for a friend. True to form, he respected my privacy and didn't ask any questions though I'm sure it killed him not to. I'd be insulting his intelligence to assume he didn't suspect there wasn't a friend.

The hardest thing about letting him go was losing my closest confidant. In the early years of my marriage, it was impossible to even consider a friendship. Over time, we've met on some tentative middle ground that doesn't require disclosure on my part and is largely one-sided. I hate that's how it has to stay, at least for now. But anything else would be selfish and unfair.

We sit quietly for a few minutes, breathing in the briny ocean air.

"I know I said I wouldn't ask again . . . ," he says quietly. "You sure you won't come to our thirty-fifth reunion? Marsh and Sue will be there."

Guilt gnaws at my stomach. I've done a poor job staying in touch with my best friends from high school. They're just another casualty in this mess I call my life.

I ache to say yes, but October is still two months away. He has no idea that everything's about to change. I shove down the images hidden inside of the manila envelope that's locked in my file cabinet.

If I say the wrong thing, his detective brain will pull at the threads of my answer until he unravels what I'm trying to hide.

I glance at his timeworn features in the moonlight, softened by the way he looks at me, and I give him a different answer than last time. "Maybe . . . I'll think about it."

He nods. "All right." There's a sliver of hope and relief packed into his near-silent exhale.

I lift myself out of the chair and grab the empty formula bottle sitting on the wooden deck.

Rachel looks at home sleeping soundly in his arms. I hate to take her, but I have to leave. Now.

"You're going?" he says, doing nothing to hide a crestfallen look of disappointment.

I nod. "Yes." A twinge grips my chest. He has no idea how much I want to stay, but being around him makes me vulnerable and weak.

John Henshaw, you are still my Kryptonite.

He stands and lays a kiss on Rachel's head before handing her back to me. His arms graze mine in the transfer. I take a deep breath, hoping to get a bit of the spicy-piney scent he's worn for years. The scent that's so distinctly him.

" 'Night, Kitten," he whispers, his breath close enough that it warms my cheek. I press my eyes shut and shove down the yearning inside of me.

" 'Night, Shaw," I whisper back, and walk away from the man I should've spent my life with.

Chapter 12

John

Spring Lake Hotel Balcony

DAMN IT.

I grip the arms of the chair and grit my teeth, cursing myself after Kat takes the baby and leaves. I've let this situation ride for too long. But if she wanted me to know what was going on, she'd tell me, and knowing her, she'd never fucking forgive me if I interfered. Her track record has proven that.

From my view, her misery has been palpable for over a year. I'd almost told her what I found out a few months ago, ready to take whatever heat she gave me, but then she asked for a good private investigator. I'd almost dropped to my knees in relief that she'd given me an out. So, instead of telling her, I gave her Rudy's number.

Still, if she ever finds out what I know, she'll grind me up and spit me out for keeping it from her. But that kind of news coming from me, of all people, would not end well.

I clutch my head in my hands.

It's a fucking no-win situation. But if something doesn't happen before the reunion, I'm forcing it. The thought of . . . my stomach roils whenever I think about him. . . . *Fuck!*

I wish I could erase what I saw during that raid down on Route 22, about what I know that she probably doesn't but hopefully will soon. And then maybe . . .

Three Months Earlier – Wayfarer's Club Raid

"WE READY?" I ask the team as we prepare to rush the Wayfarer's Club. We have a group of eight officers geared up and ready to go.

Tonight's the night we're going to take down part of an organized crime ring in a coordinated raid with the Feds. After months of surveillance, we're targeting an upscale members-only gay club while another team surrounds a warehouse in Newark. The club is legit but acts as a cover hiding a sophisticated weapons exchange with a suspected illegal cache worth millions.

Our undercover team managed to get a bead on the layout. Given the exterior size of this place, there was a lot of hidden ground to cover.

Front-room access gets you a fine dining experience complete with white tablecloths and candlelight. Behind the dining room is a private 'after dinner' section with velvet-draped alcoves filled with cushioned banquettes and moveable drink tables that allow for privacy and all the accoutrements for a different kind of dessert.

From there, colored wristbands allow entry into a few eclectic sections that cater to some kinkier shit. We plan to go past that into the interior depths of the building.

We make our move. Our team breaks off to cover the exits. I count to three into the earpiece and my unit files through the front door, badges visible.

Fanning out, we quietly empty the place of patrons as we move deeper into the club. There's not a woman in sight, not even on the wait staff.

I'm the first one to hit the curtained after-dinner section with my partner, Curt, at my back.

When I tug the curtains aside on the first two alcoves, I startle the guys, but lucky for me, they're still clothed. They don't hesitate to gather their things and head swiftly toward the front door.

"Dining room's clear," I hear in a low voice through the earpiece as I pull the third curtain.

My luck runs out. A guy is on his knees with another guy's dick in his mouth. The guy seated on the banquette is moaning low, enjoying the ride, with his head thrown back, eyes closed, and hands clutching the other guy's head between his palms.

Days like today I wish I was in another line of work.

"*Psst*," I say through my teeth to get their attention.

Their eyes flash open, and the guy on his knees looks up, red-cheeked. I flash my badge with a finger to my lips for them to remain quiet. "Get dressed and head out the front door," I whisper.

They give me vigorous head nods, wearing looks of embarrassment. The guy who's seated hurriedly stuffs his junk back in his pants while the other one gets off his knees as I move on to the next booth.

I pull back the next curtain more cautiously this time and breathe a sigh of relief when it's two guys, fully clothed, making out on the cushioned bench. I'm staring at the back of one guy's head, which obscures the other guy's face. I snap my fingers to break up the party.

They separate with a gasp and face me.

My eyes lock on the second guy. When our gazes connect, my jaw drops and he turns as white as a sheet.

It takes my brain about three frozen seconds to cut through the shock. Something primal awakens inside me and shuts off all conscious thought. I lunge over and haul him to his feet by the collar.

"You fucking prick," I say, holding back the urge to pummel him because if I did, I might not stop. I shake the man who's married to the only woman I ever really loved and spit in his face. "How could you do this to her?" With an uncontained growl, I shove him backward.

Bob's startled lover, a well-preserved older guy, catches Bob before he hits the ground.

Swiping an arm across his face, Bob replaces his glasses and avoids my gaze as his lip trembles.

"We need to go," Curt whispers, and tugs at my arm. "Deal with this later."

"Get the fuck outta here," I say to Bob, clenching my fists. If I wasn't in the middle of a goddamn raid, I'd take him out back and beat the shit out of him. Happily.

Bob seizes my arm. "I'm sorry. Don't tell Kitty, please ... ," he begs, boldly holding my gaze.

"I won't, but you fucking better." I grit my teeth and let the curtain fall back into place. My hands shake while the image of Bob and that guy tortures my retinas.

There's never been any love lost between me and Bob, but there's always been a minimal level of respect. That respect just dissolved into disgust and rage on Kat's behalf over what he's done to both her and their daughter, Jenny.

Top that off with anger at myself for stepping back when I should've fought for Kat... *afterward*. Instead, I let her marry this prick while I went off to lick my wounds. I sacrificed my happiness for hers, thinking that's what she wanted. Maybe she did. But if this is how it ends, the sacrifice wasn't worth it. That's a bitter pill I'm not willing to swallow . . . and now maybe I won't have to.

For the first time in decades, a spark of hope reignites in my withered soul, and I take a breath.

Chapter 13

Kitty

Spring Lake Hotel

I SLIP BACK into the hotel room after delivering Rachel to Jillian. A text from Raine woke me at six forty-five a.m.: *J showering. Asked if you could bring Rachie up. Forgot pump. Needs to let down some milk.*

The door latches behind me with a soft *snick*. Bob's head of dark hair stirs on the pillow and the blankets rustle as he changes positions. His familiar movements fill me with an aching loneliness.

"Kitty, you there?" he asks in a morning rasp brought on by a few too many drinks the night before. If I hadn't been watching Rachel, he wouldn't have been drinking alone.

"Go back to sleep, it's still early," I whisper, keeping my tone pleasant and coaxing. I've gotten better at playing along and so has he. He's done everything I've asked, including keeping our problems quiet until after the wedding. I love my sister and don't want our drama to overshadow her well-deserved happy day.

Bob and I have had a passionate enough relationship over the years. But at its core, our marriage had been rooted in a deep friendship with a steady comfort to it. That comfort's gone, and in its place is a hollow echo of what once was.

Jenny will be the first to hear our news later this morning.

The timing works out well. Last week, Jenny and her fiancé Devon signed a lease on a new apartment. They move in this coming week—on the same day Bob agreed to move out. This way

Jenny wouldn't be tempted to change her plans or experience our home without Bob. Somehow, that seemed important.

Despite everything that's happened, Bob is a good father and a caring companion to me, even now. He's a good man.

We've made it through the last eight weeks with our secret intact.

But I never expected it would end like this... with a slow burning anger that simmers under the surface of my skin... with everything we had shattered to pieces by a few glossy eight-by-tens.

Two Months Earlier – Meeting with the Private Detective

IT'S SATURDAY AFTERNOON. Bob's picking up a car part in Pennsylvania for one of his classic beauties.

"I'm sorry," says Rudy, the private investigator I had hired on John's recommendation. There's sincerity in his words and a regretful gleam in his eye. He slides the unmarked manila envelope across my kitchen table.

I take a deep inhale before opening the clasp and grasping the edges of the photographs. Sliding them halfway out, the glossy, black-and-white eight-by-tens show enough skin to confirm my suspicions, but it's not until I extract them fully from the envelope that I gasp and drop them like they're on fire. This wasn't quite what I expected.

My vision wavers, and nausea hits me. I lunge for the kitchen sink in time for the bile to burn up my throat and make a sickly splash onto the stainless steel.

A man. My husband is cheating on me with another man. I give myself a few minutes for the shock to recede, but there's no recovering from something like this.

I recognize my husband's lover, Carl Robbins. He's one of Bob's classic car buddies; a wealthy Summit man who lost his wife to cancer last year.

A tear slips down my cheek, followed by another as I struggle to take in enough air. I don't know which emotion to tackle first: betrayal, anger, or revulsion. I can't decide which is worse, an affair with a man or a woman? Then again, an affair is an affair. Should it really matter?

If his lover was a woman, maybe we could've survived with

some therapy. But not a man. That's a need I can never fulfill. And it sure explains why we haven't been intimate in almost two years.

I don't see Rudy leave but vaguely remember him muttering a goodbye. I sit for what feels like hours, staring into a void inside my kitchen. The one place I've found joy during my twenty-three-year marriage is now tainted by a shattering truth that overshadows all the happy memories.

The long months of wondering and worrying are over . . . and so is my marriage. In this moment, my house no longer feels like a home.

I write on a pad in the fading light, not sure when I grabbed a pen and paper. When I'm done, I have a list of to-dos, our joint assets, and what I want from our long years together.

It's all surprisingly simple.

I spread the lurid photographs across the kitchen table and place my list alongside the glossy pictures. Then I throw back a scotch and wait.

I'm not sure how much time passes before the key turns in the front lock.

"Kitty?" I hear from the hallway.

My heart pounds.

"Back here . . . In the kitchen," I say in a voice that's so brittle it's unrecognizable to my own ears.

Bob's footsteps approach and he flips on the overhead light. "Kitty, why are you —"

My bespectacled husband freezes and his mouth drops open. His big blue eyes — Jenny's eyes — widen when he sees what's on the table. Then he clamps them shut as if that will block out the truth.

His shoulders slump and he quietly comes apart in front of me, collapsing against the doorjamb and sliding down until he's sitting crumpled on the floor.

"I want a divorce," I whisper as my vision blurs and my heart aches with wild abandon.

He doesn't try to fight me, which only digs the knife deeper. He removes his glasses and cries softly into his hand.

My ire rises when I realize he has no intention of begging for forgiveness. Not that I would've given it, but don't I deserve even the pretense?

Brushing away my own tears, I release the true Kat who doesn't hide behind a pleasant façade. A woman whose strength I've kept long buried. My voice turns hard and cold. "I'll call the lawyer on Monday. You'll make this as easy as possible so that we can get this over with quickly . . . or I'll destroy you." Not a threat, a promise.

I shove back my chair and head for the doorway.

"I'm sorry," he whispers through his tears, reaching for me with no real conviction.

"Fuck you," I seethe, kicking his hand away.

"Fuck me?" He staggers to his feet and wipes a hand across his face as I shove past him and keep going. "What does it matter anyway? You still love him. You've never stopped loving him," he says with a bitterness I've never heard before.

I whirl back to him. "How dare you!" My scream is shrill as I launch myself at him, and land a punch to his jaw the way John taught me when I was a girl. He collapses back to the floor and I ignore my throbbing hand.

"I've never cheated on you! I gave you a daughter. I've been a good wife. You fucking bastard! How dare you say that to me . . ." I say, looming over him.

He clutches his reddened jaw and stares at me, wide-eyed. "You hit me," he mutters like he didn't believe I had it in me. We've never struck one another in all the years we've been together.

But I ache to do it again, so I put a safe distance between us before I lose my proverbial shit and really hurt him. Because I want to. Badly. I really do.

"So how long have you been fucking Carl? And why did you wait twenty-three years to come out of the fucking closet? Did you ever love me?"

He covers his face as I scream each question, and his shoulders shake. He slides down until he's lying prone on the Persian hallway rug.

I sink to the floor with him as I expend my rage. Hurt replaces anger, leaving me exhausted and wholly bereft.

"Kitty, I do love you . . . you're my best friend." His voice is broken and vulnerable. He meets my gaze with equal pain in his red-rimmed eyes. "I didn't mean for this to happen . . . I'm sorry."

That he's sorry for hurting me and not the affair hurts even more.

"How long?" I bite out.

"Two years," he whispers. "Before you ask, he was the first and only."

I release a heavy sigh and lie down on my side to face him, drained. "Are you in love with him?" I ask softly as our cheeks rest on opposite ends of the Persian's soft wool, and we stare at each other across the seven feet that separates us. It might as well be an ocean.

He nods. "Yes."

His one word sinks the knife the rest of the way home. "Does he love you?" I whisper in utter defeat. His eyes fill with tears again and the corner of his mouth lifts. "Yes."

A sense of stillness settles over me. My anger turns to jealousy, not that Bob loves someone else, but that he's found something we no longer have together. With that comes the realization that I chose the wrong fork in the road all those years ago. That all my actions led me to this moment.

This is my fault, but I'm not the only one to blame.

That honor is shared with my mother.

Chapter 14

Kitty

Spring Lake, Breakfast Later That Morning

"WHAT'S WITH ALL the cloak and dagger, and why couldn't I bring Devon?" Jenny asks with trepidation as she slides into a seat across from us at the restaurant down the street from the hotel. It's fancy, upscale, and most of all, quiet.

I glance at Bob, who clears his throat. We've agreed that as the wronged party, I should open the conversation. We're hoping if we approach this as a united front it will lessen the blow. The last thing we want is to hurt our child. Logically, this isn't complicated. Jenny is an independent adult. But emotionally? Who knows?

Bob agreed to my one stipulation that Jenny gets the whole truth. No hiding, short of sharing the lurid photographs. Even I wish I'd never seen those. Images I'm likely never to forget.

Jenny's bright blue eyes widen in alarm when I reach across the table and take her hand. "Mom... what's wrong?" Her voice quivers. "Neither of you are sick, are you?"

Bob lets out a breath. I try to smile, then squeeze her fingers and say as gently as possible, "No, honey. Daddy and I are getting a divorce."

Jenny blinks. Then blinks again and screws her face into a quizzical frown. "Wait, what?" her gaze travels between Bob's face and mine.

"I'm sorry, sweetheart," Bob whispers. "It's my fault. I'm leaving your mom..."

I grit my teeth and resist the irrational urge to slug him. Oh, now he's leaving me? Last I checked, it was me who showed *him* to the door.

Jenny's lips part before her fingers fly up and cover her mouth.

"What your father's trying to say," I say calmly, taking the high road for Jenny's sake, "Is that he fell in love with someone else."

She uncovers her mouth and frowns, a look of incredulous disbelief shining in her gaze. "You're leaving Mom for another woman?"

Bob removes his glasses and passes a hand over dampening eyes the color of Jenny's, then shakes his head. "No, Pumpkin . . ." He swallows hard and says in a bare whisper. "For . . . a man."

Her mouth drops open then snaps shut. After another flurry of rapid eye blinks, she grips the edge of the table. "Oh my God. But . . . ? Oh my God, I don't know what to say." Jenny presses her eyes closed then cradles her head in her hands. Her silky brown hair cascades around her hands curtain-like, obscuring her face.

"You don't have to say anything," I whisper. "We filed the paperwork on Friday, and we're putting the house on the market. Daddy's moving out this week, too." Since it's uncontested, we should both be free by Thanksgiving, but I keep that part to myself.

When Jenny looks up, her eyes glisten. "How could you do that to Mom?" she asks Bob, her tone more sad than accusatory.

Bob's lip trembles and he brushes at his cheeks. "I'm sorry, I didn't mean for this to happen. I love your mom." He glances at me. "I hope she'll forgive me someday."

Resentment flares inside me. God, I can't even look at him. He's making me the bad guy? *Unfair. Very unfair.* I let out a slow breath. Forgiveness? That will take a while. Ignoring his comment, I ask her, "Will you be all right?"

Her brows bunch. "Forget about me. How are you? Will *you* be all right?"

"I'll be fine, sweetheart," I say, not sure if it's the truth. Bob leaving forces me to confront things I've allowed myself to avoid. "Despite what happened between me and your father, we both love you very much."

She wipes away the tears trailing down her cheeks, and pushes her hair behind her ears. After a deep exhale, she says calmly, "Who else knows?"

"You're the first," I say. "I'll tell your aunt Jillian tomorrow."

"What about grandma and grandpa?" she asks, meaning Bob's parents, since mine are dead.

Bob stiffens next to me. "No, not yet . . . soon," he says simply, with more control than I expect. The prospect of his very conservative Catholic family finding out has been one of the reasons he's hidden his affair for so long. That he cared more about their opinion than my feelings still sticks in my craw. For now, I've agreed not to tell them.

Jenny shakes her head and stays silent for a moment, then asks, "Who's the guy?"

Bob clasps and unclasps his hands, then swallows. "Carl . . . Remember? From the last Summit car show?"

Recognition flashes across Jenny's face, followed by a look of discomfort. "Oh, yeah. He's . . . nice." Squinting, she adds, "Doesn't he have a family, too?"

Bob licks dry lips and nods. "He's a widower. His kids are older, married." Carl is ten years older than Bob.

Jenny sniffles. "Were you always . . . *gay?*" The last word seems to stick in her throat.

Bob shakes his head vehemently. "No . . ." He leaves it at that. Though when I'd pressed him, he admitted that he'd once been attracted to a man in college, but that it had never gotten physical.

Jenny's gaze drifts to her hands and she asks in a low voice, "Are you moving in with Carl?"

Bob nods and reaches for her. "He lives across town. I won't be far. This shouldn't change how much I see you."

Liar. I grind my teeth at his comment, as if life can just go on unchanged. Impossible, since I have no intention of dropping by Carl's for dinner. That's the only way he can see her as much as he always did without her seeing me less. Selfish idiot.

Her gaze turns to me and her voice turns brittle. "Where will you go after you sell the house?"

I force a smile. "I'm not leaving, either. I plan to buy something small in Summit."

"I can't believe it," Jenny whispers, shaking her head. Then she glances my way, "Here, all this time . . ." Her voice drifts off.

"What?" I ask. Anger and betrayal well up inside me. She isn't seriously insinuating that she expected me to be the one . . . ?

She shakes her head again and wipes her eyes. "Nothing."

By the time the waitress is brave enough to approach the table and take our order, my appetite has fled. Then again, I haven't had one since I saw those photographs.

The food comes and we eat in tense silence. For me, eating consists of pushing food around on my plate with next to none of it reaching my mouth.

Tomorrow, I'll break the news to Jillian that her favorite nuclear family is on its way to Splitsville. Then after that, I'll do my best to repair what's left of my life.

Chapter 15

John

September 2016 – Morris County Police Department

"SHAW, CAN YOU talk?" Tony asks over the phone. The sound of his voice has me thinking about Kat's daughter, Jenny, and the reason we connected in June. As for Kat, I haven't seen her since Jillian and Raine's wedding in Spring Lake four weeks ago. I'm keeping the faith that she'll show up at our thirty-fifth high school reunion next month.

"Hold up." I press the cell to my ear and shut the door. From the tension in Tony's voice, this doesn't sound like a social call. Friend or not, I frown and wonder what precipitated a call from the Feds. Tony and I traded a few phone calls after I called in a favor for Jenny—one I'd rather forget—the night of the Memorial Hospital Gala hosted by her fiancé Devon and his family's foundation.

The door latches, rattling the glass pane. "Go on."

"Remember that connection between Genovia and Cato I mentioned to you last summer after the memorial service? The one MacDonald was about to make before he got killed?" Rather than return to my chair, I pace in front of my desk and rub a hand across the back of my neck to settle the prickling hairs. "Yeah."

"We made the connection.... Makes that favor you did for Kitty's daughter a little more interesting."

Shit. My favor for Jenny was on someone else's behalf. That someone else was Devon's twin sister, Leticia, and her boyfriend— Howard Cato III, heir to the Cato Shipping conglomerate. The same

Cato Shipping conglomerate that Raine's father died trying to tie to the Genovias. I'd almost crapped when Jenny asked. She had no idea who Howard was when she'd made that call, or the unwanted heat it would bring down on me afterward. Not that I would've denied her. I'd do anything for her. Or her mother. Or Jillian.

"We're forming a new task force. You want in?"

I silently consider it. Half of me wants to yell, "Hell, yeah," while the other half wants to run in the opposite direction. A coil of dread winds around my throat and tightens, leaning me toward the "hell, yeah." I eye the mound of paperwork sitting next to a mug of late afternoon coffee. A change of pace might be nice, but not the additional workload. "I'll talk to my captain."

"Already done. He's on board."

My eyebrows pop up. "That was fast." Then I ask him the million-dollar question, "Why me?"

Tony pauses. "Your connections, expertise . . . because I trust you. Pick one."

I grunt.

He lets out a long sigh. "Listen, Shaw, I'm hand-picking the team. This might last a while. There's a lot to unravel. This network is complex. Taking down the major players will take time."

"How long do I have to decide?"

"Tomorrow morning. We're setting up shop down by Newark Airport."

Fucking great. "I'll let you know tonight."

"Good enough."

I hang up and blow out a breath, already knowing my answer. Protecting the people I love is a personal obsession directly tied to my very early failure. I don't need a shrink to tell me what losing my baby sister did to me. I've lived with that guilt since I was a teenager. It makes me hell-bent on protecting what I consider mine — whether they know it or not.

Unhealthy? Maybe. But there are far worse things than choosing to exorcise my demons through a profession in law enforcement for the same town that holds some of the best and worst memories of my screwed-up life.

If this task force can help keep Jenny's and Devon's families safe from the Catos, then I'm in. The only thing holding me back is an odd sensation that I might not come out alive.

Chapter 16

Kitty

September 2016 – Intervention

"TIME TO GET up!" Jenny says a moment before she rips off my warm blankets, leaving me to lie exposed on the king-size mattress in knit sleep shorts and an old white T-shirt.

Says, who? I groan and fumble blindly for the covers, refusing to open my eyes.

"Oh, no you don't!" she says and tugs me by the arms until the mattress disappears from beneath me, and I fall—butt first—onto the floor.

Well, that's an eye-opener.

"What are you doing?" I snap, angry at the intrusion, staring up into Jenny's lovely face framed by her dangling long, silky hair. She's wearing yoga clothes. Unless she forgot to change when she got out of bed, this can't be good.

She breaks into a wide grin. "You're not sleeping all day again. Upsy-daisy."

The front door slams shut downstairs. With half the furniture gone, a hollow echo reverberates up the stairs. "Hello!" Jillian's voice booms louder than it should.

Great, just great. Maybe I should take back my keys. Not that it matters. Four weeks from now, I move into my new home across town after closing on this one, and I'm keeping all the keys.

Jillian took the news of my impending divorce better than I expected, and to Jenny's credit, after her initial shock wore off, she's been supportive and doing her best not to take sides.

Other than his classic car collection, Bob moved all his stuff out last month after Jillian and Raine's wedding. He's now comfortably ensconced in Carl's house across town.

Before Bob left, he said something that utterly shocked me. . . .

He takes my hand in both of his and whispers, "Kitty, look at me."

I blink away tears and meet his eyes. There's kindness and love there. It hurts me more than if we were at odds. "What?"

"John . . . Give him a chance."

I rip my hand from his. "You're pushing me off on another man?"

He lets out a soft chuckle and shakes his head. "Stop lying to yourself. This marriage has always had three people in it. . . . I want you to be happy, even if it's with him." He bows his head and swallows. "He loves you, Kitty. He always has. And you still love him. For crissakes, even Jenny can see it."

I hate that Bob said that, all of it, and I hate that he's happy when I'm so broken. He may think John is what I need, but it's not so simple. And it never will be.

Jenny bounces to the doorway and yells. "We're up here!"

Jillian's steps pound up the stairs toward us. She's also wearing yoga garb.

"Why are you both here?" I whine, crawl back onto the bed, and hug the pillow. Why can't everyone just leave me alone?

Jenny heads to my closet. "This is an intervention. We're taking you out." Hangers screech and clash together as she looks through my clothes.

"In pajamas?"

Jenny rolls her eyes as Jillian chimes in, looking too perky for a mother of a three-month-old, "No. Bar Method."

"Bar *what*?"

Jenny huffs and points at me. "Aunt Jill, would you mind?"

Jillian's smile spreads and she heads toward me. "Come on, Kitty. Up, up, up!" I let her drag me to the edge of the bed, pull me onto my feet, and shove me in the direction of the bathroom.

"After Bar, we're taking you for a makeover and shopping for new clothes," Jenny says as she disappears halfway into my closet. Clothes fly out in a colorful arc behind her, landing in a messy pile.

I frown. My feet hit the cool marble tile and I shamble over to my toothbrush, feeling like the walking dead. "What's wrong with my clothes?"

"Pretty much everything," Jenny says from inside the closet. "Some of these things weren't in fashion even in the '80s." Maybe, but they've served as good camouflage, according to my therapist, Dr. Graham.

I plod through my morning routine. When I emerge, there's an exercise outfit laid out on the unmade bed.

"What's that?" I ask Jillian as Jenny takes a pair of jeans out of the closet, holds them up, and then discards them onto the mountain of clothing on the floor.

Jillian's sitting on the bed with an amused shine in her clear amber eyes. She points to the outfit. "That's the first step to finding your new body."

The frown I'm wearing deepens.

Jenny shoots me a look from across the room. "Mom, you're starting to look like a concentration camp victim. You've lost a ton of weight since spring, especially since Daddy left. Now you've got to firm up what's there and get your game on."

My brows pop up. "Get my game on? Are you seriously suggesting I date?"

Jenny pulls out a shirt and looks it over with an assessing frown, then she shrugs and tosses it on the bed. "Yeah, maybe you'll find a hottie like Raine."

A blush heats my cheeks. "I'll do no such thing!"

Jillian smiles, hands me the clothes on the bed, and sends me back toward the bathroom. "Don't knock it until you've tried it."

Now it's my turn to roll my eyes. "When hell goes on holiday," I mutter.

Before I know it, I've shimmied into a pair of yoga pants, a sports bra, and a T-shirt, and they're ushering me into Jillian's car, with a change of street clothes in hand.

Thirty minutes later, sweat is pouring down my back as I'm doing some sort of thigh exercises while gripping a ballet barre and hoping I don't die of a heart attack. By then, I've figured out at least a dozen ways to kill my kith and kin in the parking lot.

I haven't followed much of a workout routine in over a decade. There's no escaping that I'm out of shape. But the most shocking part is looking at myself in the mirror. Gone is the rosiness and fullness in my cheeks; replacing it is a gauntness that makes me look ill. My clothes hang shapeless on my body after losing close to forty pounds in the last sixteen weeks. I guess that's what a steady diet of stress, depression, and coffee will do for your waistline.

By the end of the class, I feel like I want to die . . . enough that I plan to come back tomorrow. Having something kill me is easier than starving myself to a slow death. Maybe it will lift my mood and give me something to strive for. I haven't been a size eight since I was in college, and it would be nice to have some muscle tone after hiding any muscles I've ever had under a layer of fat.

The class ends with a deep breath and my hands clasped at my heart center. Jenny and Jillian sidle up to me as we're putting away our mats.

"What did you think?" Jenny asks, a hopeful look in her eye.

I glare at her and growl low in my throat.

Her eyes widen and she nips at her lip. "It gets easier."

Jillian suppresses a chuckle and has the good sense to keep her mouth shut.

"Great job, Kitty!" says the overly friendly instructor. "You did awesome for your first class." I give her a tight smile and try to ignore the fact that I'm saturated and most assuredly going to wake up crippled tomorrow. "Thank you."

When we get into the locker room, Jillian hands me a bucket with shampoo, soap, and a towel, and shoves me in the direction of the nearest shower stall. I yank it defiantly from her hand without a word.

It's official. Kitty has left the building and Kat is in the house.

"You'll thank us tomorrow," Jillian calls after me.

"Doubtful," I mutter. Maybe I'll thank them next month, but not tomorrow.

The hot water pelts my skin in a steady shower of punishing drops. I let the rivulets cascade down over me, hoping the water can wash away my bad mood.

By the time I'm dressed in normal clothes and done with the blow dryer, I feel closer to human.

"Peace offering." Jenny wears a sheepish grin as she hands me a glass of hot apple-spiced tea from the small station in the lobby that provides beverages and protein bars.

I offer a small smile in return. Jillian and Jenny check their phones while I sip my way through the tea and refrain from any further grumbling. They barely broke a sweat and look like fresh-cut flowers in their stylish weekend wear.

I hate them.

An alarm goes off on Jenny's phone and she pops up. "We've got our first appointment in fifteen minutes at Neiman's."

I groan and ditch my cup. "Do we have to?"

"Yes," they say in unison, and once again herd me toward Jillian's car. To think I could be home doing bills right now. They sing an overly joyful version of Katy Perry's latest song from the front seat on our way to the Mall at Short Hills. I can't decide whether traveling in the back seat makes me feel more like a toddler or "Driving Miss Kitty."

Katy Perry gives way to a new party tune blasting through the speakers that sounds like it should be played at a nightclub. Jillian and Jenny seem to know all the words . . . something about cake by the ocean or on the beach, or something blah, blah, blah. Shit, the only song I know that mentions cake is "MacArthur Park," God rest Donna Summer's soul.

Okay, fine. I admit it. My comfort zone hovers between the '80s and into the '90s with music, clothes, and almost everything else. Jenny says I'm like a modern-day Miss Havisham. Maybe because that's where I froze Kat in time, where she died and Kitty survived.

As far as my wretched wardrobe, as Jenny likes to call it, I still find comfort there. Keeping up with fashion and attracting admiring glances became unimportant to me after she was born. Whether from apathy, self-loathing, or self-preservation—take your pick—they're all partially true. At least that's what I've figured out in therapy.

The not-so-easy question: Did I ever suspect my husband liked both women and men? *No. Yes. Maybe.* I don't know, but in retrospect I'm not sure I'm completely surprised. I think the bigger question is: Do I really care? I'm still working on that one.

"How's the new place with Devon?" I ask over the music, making my first attempt at polite conversation since the J and J duo stormed my house and dragged me out of bed.

I haven't seen Jenny's new apartment since the day I helped her and Devon paint the place with Devon's sister, Lettie, and her boyfriend, Howard Cato III, some shipping magnate who looks more like a football linebacker.

My fault, not Jenny's. Getting divorced and becoming an empty nester all at once has been a major shock to the system and has decimated my routines. I've split my time between work and depression since Bob and I announced our split to the family after Jillian's wedding. Jillian and Raine—more accurately, Raine—has taken over hosting the family dinner on Sundays at their house. The only bright spot in my week.

Even harder has been the inadvertent tug-of-war between me and Bob on Jenny, creating another source of irritation at my soon-to-be ex-husband. When Jenny didn't ask him to help us paint, he had no problem sharing his annoyance with me.

Jenny notches down the volume and twists in the passenger seat to face me. Her vintage engagement ring dazzles in the light. "The new place is great! Devon set up his painting studio in the second bedroom. I can't wait for you to see what we've done with it since that last time you were there. Come for dinner next week?" she asks with a hopeful gleam in her eye.

"Sure . . ." I'm happy that Jenny found Devon and decided not to marry Russ, her high school boyfriend. She's made some decisions over the past year I haven't agreed with, but she's also grown a lot and made me proud.

Her change of heart makes me wonder how things would've turned out if everything had gone according to plan after graduation for me and John. Would it have turned out as it did for her and Russ? Staying together but growing apart? Or would it have been like we'd dreamed, a happy-ever-after despite a few changes of plan?

Jillian parks under the covered deck across from Neiman-Marcus. We pile out, and Jenny hooks her arm through mine as we walk toward the entrance. "I can't wait to see what Naomi picked out for you," she says with a bounce in her step.

I give her *the eye* and try not to scowl. "Wasn't she the one who sold you and Devon the dress for the gala that cost a fortune? I'm not made of money, sweetie. Especially with the divorce. I can't afford a bunch of high-priced clothes."

Jenny rolls her eyes. "She's not pulling from the couture boutique. I told her to stay modest. Just some casual stuff you can wear on weekends, some clothes for work, a dress for the reunion, some shoes, and lingerie."

"*Lingerie?*" I say as we step onto the escalator.

"Uh, *yeah*. Those high-waist cotton granny pants have to go." She snaps her fingers like a magician making a rabbit disappear into a top hat. "You don't want to get in a car accident and have them cut your clothes off to find *those*."

Jillian chuckles to herself while Jenny taps a finger to her lips. "*Hmm*. On second thought, maybe we should go to Victoria's Secret for undies." Then she wiggles her eyebrows. "Maybe throw in some thigh-highs for under the reunion dress."

"Good idea." Jillian fist-bumps her in a Raine-style gesture.

"Oh my God, Jillian. Between Jenny and your husband, you're turning *millennial*," I mumble, proud of my Boomer roots.

"Lighten up, Kitty. Don't be such a grump." She hip checks me and says to Jenny, "And a couple of thong bikinis."

Jenny's eyes light up. "Yes! Brilliant!"

"No!" I say, horrified. "And who said I'm going to the reunion?"

They trade a glance and ignore me.

As we approach the personal shopping area, I follow like a prisoner in a chain gang. How does anyone find this fun? Not to mention the dent this will leave in my credit card.

A well-coiffed and waiflike saleswoman greets us outside the private dressing area, and Jenny makes the introductions. "Naomi, this is my mom, Katherine Lynch, and my aunt, Jillian MacDonald."

Naomi flashes a bright smile and hugs a clipboard as if she's getting ready to coach a sporting event. "Wonderful. I've set up a dressing room filled with a variety of clothing off the list that Jenny provided."

Jenny claps and makes giddy sounds.

I shove down the passing desire to throttle her. I hate shopping. More than I hate Brussels sprouts, and I'd consider eating a plate of those just to get out of doing this.

"Come on, Mom. This will be fun," she says and takes up residence on the Louis XIV–style French settee next to Jillian.

"Follow me. I need to take some measurements before we begin," Naomi says, removing a measuring tape from around her neck.

I huff and plod after her into the oversize dressing room. As the door closes, Jenny gleefully exclaims behind me, "We should've brought popcorn."

A frown dents my brow at the amount of clothing stuffed inside the dressing room. Hangers are ten deep on every hook, and there's an entire rolling rack that's crammed. "You can't seriously expect me to try all this on."

Naomi gives me a patient smile. "I've pulled three sizes of each, so no, you won't have to try them all on." She points and spins her finger in the air. "Down to your underwear, please."

I huff again and reluctantly remove my clothes.

"What size bra is that?"

"38B, why?"

She comes at me with the tape measure and circles my bust. "*Um-hum*, as I suspected. You're wearing the wrong size."

My face contorts into a look of disbelief as she jots something on her clipboard. "What are you talking about?"

She touches the pencil eraser to my bra strap. "See how the strap cuts into your shoulders? You're really a 36C. I'll pick out some bras while you get started. Begin on the left." She points her pencil at a section of jeans and slacks. "Start with the middle size, the eights, and we'll flex up or down if needed."

I scowl. "Three sizes, right? I'll start with the tens. Maybe bring a few in a size twelve while you're out there."

Her gaze travels over me from head to toe. "You're not a twelve," she says and walks out the door.

I'm officially not having fun. This feels more like torture. I snatch the first pair of jeans from a hanger in a size ten and put them on. They're too big. Screw it. I drop them to my ankles, step out and kick them aside as I grab the eights.

Better.

"Mom! Come out and show us what you're wearing."

"I can't. I'm in my bra."

"Throw on a top for Pete's sake and come out," Jillian says.

What am I? A show poodle? I roll my eyes, throw on a random shirt from the mountain of clothes, and open the door.

Jenny breaks into a grin. "I vote yes."

"Yes to what?" I ask.

"Yes to the whole outfit." She elbows Jillian. "What do you think?"

Jillian squints and taps her lip. "A possibility."

I catch my image in the three-sided mirror. True. The jeans are more flattering than any I own, and the top is updated and make me look younger.

Jenny motions for me to spin. "Double yes."

I shuck off the clothes, put them back on hangers, and start a "maybe" section in the dressing room.

Naomi pops in with a few bras, and I try them on. Not bad. Okay. She's right. These are much better. They give a whole new meaning to the phrase, "lift and separate." Instead of monoboob, they give me cleavage. Nice, sexy cleavage. I keep on the one I like best, and attack another outfit.

An hour later, my yes and maybe piles are overflowing, and I'm hungry enough to eat a side of beef. We're finally down to a dress for the reunion. It's a formal affair, but not black tie—thank God. I stare at the variety of cocktail dresses Naomi has hanging for me to peruse.

All jewel tones: purple, green, sapphire, except for two in black. I gravitate to the black dresses first. I slip the first one on. It's short-sleeved with a round neck and a belt. I amble out in a pair of black heels to show the peanut gallery.

Jenny shakes her head and gives me a sour look. "You might as well pick out something from the funeral section of your closet. Not sexy at all. . . ." She waves her hand toward the dressing room. "Off with it."

I plod back inside and slip on the other black dress. More like a slinky black glove. It's sleeveless, dips down to show off my new cleavage, and clings to my hips in a way that hints I left my underwear at home. I blush looking at my reflection and my pulse quickens. There's something transformative about the dress.

I look good. Better than good. *Sexy.*

This time when I make my entrance, Jenny and Jillian sit up straighter and a glimmer of approval shines in both pairs of eyes.

"Now that's what I had in mind," Jenny says, slapping her leg.

"It's perfect." Jillian nods her approval, then whispers behind her hand to Jenny. "Definitely needs a thong."

"Screw the thong. Can we eat? I'm starving. . . ."

"Great idea! Skip the underwear," Jenny snickers at my retreating back, leaving me wishing for the days when children thought it was gross for their parents to have sex. She whispers to Jillian, "Let's schedule a bikini wax."

"No!" I yell over my shoulder and stomp back into the dressing room. I'm not having the hair ripped off of my crotch, and that's final.

I abandon the rest of the dresses. As annoyed as I am, I'm not stupid. The dress looks spectacular, like Cinderella but a whole lot sexier. If I decide to go to the reunion, that's the dress I'll wear. So I add it to the pile. Then I look at the avalanche of clothing that has made the cut and cull it down to something reasonable so I'm not living on cat food for the next two months. Fitting, since my future prospects could be limited to a new family of felines.

Naomi knocks on the door, and I give her my final choices.

"They'll be wrapped and waiting when you get back."

Jenny grabs me in a hug. "You picked out some great stuff, Mom. I'm so proud of you."

"Thanks, sweetheart." In an odd way, I feel accomplished. Maybe this is a breakthrough of sorts.

"After lunch is your makeover. I'm so excited!" she says.

Well, that makes one of us. Maybe it won't be so bad. I don't remember what I look like in makeup. I haven't worn it for years.

"Time to give up the cherry lip balm," Jillian whispers next to my ear.

"Never," I murmur. As I say it, I realize it's another vestige of my past with John. I'm fashion-conscious enough to no longer wear roll-on lip gloss like I did in high school, but the flavor of cherries has never lost its appeal.

I opt for a glass of wine with my pasta over lunch at Paparazzi. Shopping took over two hours and I'm already exhausted. How am I going to make it a few more?

Jillian pokes at her food and averts her eyes, "So . . . you're going to the reunion, then?"

I let out a breath and give her a warning glare before swinging my gaze to Jenny, whose lips part to speak. I notch up the glare with a deeper frown. Her mouth snaps shut and she slumps back in her seat. "I'm still deciding," I say.

"Fine." Jillian throws up her hands. "Don't be so hard on your cheerleading squad. We love you, we want you to be happy, and we think that when two people still love one another . . . they should be together."

Two pair of eyes — one set blue and one set amber — bat at me in unison.

Is John paying you both to say this, or has everyone just gone insane? I want to snap, but I know John well enough to suspect he'd be as mortified as I am. More likely they're insane.

I blow out a breath, set down my fork, and steeple my fingers like I'm leading a business negotiation. "I love you both. Very much. But stop fixating on me and John. Life isn't a romance novel. Not everyone gets a happy ending."

Jenny intakes a sharp breath and shakes her head. "Mom, Devon used to believe that, too, and now look at him. Look at us." She reaches across the table and grabs my hand, toppling my steeple.

My future son-in-law would've died had Jenny not done everything in her power to save him. I may have disagreed with her methods, but not her commitment or sacrifice. I'm so very proud of her strength.

My expression softens and I squeeze her hand. "I know, sweetheart. Your happy ending and Devon's are well deserved."

Jillian smiles and grabs my other hand, eliminating the barrier that I've attempted to erect between us. "Don't forget about mine. Wasn't it you who told me on the beach last summer that you admired me for seizing my second chance at love with Raine?"

I chew the inside of my mouth and remain silent.

There's a beseeching look in her eye. "Your story isn't over . . . you still have time to write the ending. Don't waste your chance like I almost did."

"John loves you, you know," Jenny whispers.

I pull out of their collective grasp and hide my hands on my lap. "Jenny . . ."

"This summer . . . the day after the Gala when John drove me home from the hospital . . ." She swallows.

My gaze hardens on her. God, I hope she didn't mention anything to John.

She looks away and draws on the tablecloth with her finger. "I may have asked him . . ." she looks up, squinting with her nose crinkled, "if he still loved you."

A flush burns its way clear up to the tips of my ears. "Oh, Jenny! You didn't. Did you?" I twist my napkin in lieu of my daughter's neck.

Her nose stays crinkled. "Sorry . . ."

"And what? He told you he loved me?" I snap, knowing John would poke his own eyes out before he'd admit that to my daughter. If there's one thing I can guarantee about the man I love, loved, *whatever*, it's his strong code of honor. He would never admit such a thing about a married woman to her own flesh and blood. Ever.

"No . . . he got angry and shut me down when I brought up your relationship, but when I got out of the car, I *may* have let drop that you still loved him. His car sat in the driveway for a full five minutes after that."

I cover my eyes with my hand and shake my head. Desperate for some oxygen, I breathe deeply through my nose, trying to reconcile my embarrassment with a glimmer of hope. Probably explains why he's been so hell-bent on getting me to attend the reunion. At least he held true to form and didn't volunteer any information. Still, sounds like Jenny rattled him.

"Please . . . let's drop it, okay?" I beg.

Jillian leans forward, the pain of old loss shining in her eyes, and says gently, "Just promise . . . when you're ready . . . you'll consider the *possibilities*."

I nod. "But please stop pushing me. Whatever is meant to be will happen."

And that's what I'm afraid of . . .

JENNY AND I wave to Jillian as she pulls out of the driveway, and then she helps me carry all of my purchases—capped off with four hundred dollars of creams and makeup from the Clarins counter—into the house.

We hike everything up to my bedroom and plunk it on the floor.

Jenny takes her keys from her purse and shifts on her feet. "I have something to ask you."

I half sit, half collapse onto the bed and sense another uncomfortable question on its way. "Oh?"

She nibbles on her lip as she formulates her question, then releases a breath and meets my gaze. "Will you be mad if Devon and I do the car show with Daddy next weekend downtown?" I vaguely remember them making those plans months ago.

My spine stiffens. "Alone?"

She looks away and says in a low voice. "With Carl."

I'm not sure why it feels like she's run me through with a broadsword. But it does. And I know it's not fair to put her in the middle. This is going to happen a lot. She'll split her time between us, and not at the exclusion of the man who makes her father happy. She loves us both, and I wouldn't change that for anything.

"It's all right. Have a good time, sweetheart," I say, pasting on a smile and waving a dismissive hand. Realizing, as I do, it's one of the passive-aggressive gestures my mother used most. One that I despised with a passion. I promise myself to be more mindful. Lucky for Jenny, I'll never meddle in her life the way my mother meddled in mine.

She comes at me with open arms and pulls me into a hug. "Thanks, Mom. I love you. This is hard, you know?" Her voice cracks. "I hate that you're alone and he's not."

"I know. Life's not always fair. Don't worry about me. I'll be fine." I squeeze her tight. "I love you, too, sweetheart."

I wave to Jenny from the porch as she pulls out. On the way inside, I spot the invitation to the thirty-fifth reunion sitting in the tray on the table next to the front door. Creamy card stock and fancy script beckon me to confront what I've worked so hard to ignore.

There's a fierce tug-o'-war between desire in my heart and fear in my soul battling it out inside of me. I want to take Jillian's advice and finish my story, but what she doesn't understand is that it might not have a happy ending.

Chapter 17

Kitty

September 2016 – Dr. Graham's Office

"MUST WE TALK about my mother?" I ask my therapist, Dr. Graham, from the plush couch on the other side of her desk. I tuck myself into one of its corners, needing the added sense of security given by the solid arm against my side. The office is sleek and modern, with large framed photography, except for the sofa where I've taken refuge.

Resistance floods my veins, making me cranky and irritable.

In fairness, my mother's the root of all my dysfunction, and this *is* therapy, so why not? I've burned out on examining the disintegration of my marriage.

At first I questioned whether sharing a therapist with my daughter was such a good idea, but she did wonders for Jenny's anxiety issues, so I decided to try her.

A ghost of a smile passes over my attractive, thirty-something therapist's lips. "She's the one you blame the most." *Understatement.*

I huff, rolling my head and eyes along with it. I can't argue. She's right. I concede. "Fine. Where shall we start on my laundry list of bizarre behavior, control freakishness, and vicious sabotage?"

She leans back in her leather chair behind the desk, pen poised to take her unique form of shorthand, which I've occasionally caught a glimpse of. "How about the episode you hinted at last time? The one about cleaning the house?"

My brows flick up. Oh, that one. That falls closer to the sabotage category with a strong dose of control freak thrown on top. "Sure."

119

My relationship with John made my mother half insane. At first it was just small things, nothing more than minor annoyances like failing to pass on phone messages, not wanting to meet his mom, strapping me with babysitting duty on a Saturday night—all things John and I mitigated through teamwork and creative solutions. Eventually, she escalated to things such as sabotaging our junior prom plans.

Much to our benefit, my mother continually underestimated our ingenuity. She failed to realize her tactics to keep us apart pushed us closer together, and as a result, every second we spent in each other's company was precious, appreciated, and *thoroughly* enjoyed.

It wasn't until after this incident that she realized she had finally lost control of me.

October 1980 – My Mother and Her Meltdown

"WHERE DO YOU think you're going, young lady?" my mother snaps.

My hand freezes on the car keys sitting in the dish next to the garage door. I whirl to face her, frowning. "Out. Why?"

Kickoff for John's Saturday home game is in fifteen minutes. The Rutgers scout is supposed to be there today, and I don't want to miss seeing John play for anything in the world. Least of all because of one of my mother's bullshit sabotage tactics. Worst comes to worst, I'll walk.

She jerks her chin up defiantly and passes a hand down the side of her perfectly coiffed hair. "The bathrooms still haven't been cleaned. You know the rules. Chores first, fun later."

My blood heats to a slow boil. She's not doing this to me today. I won't let her. I spent the entire morning cleaning this house from top to bottom, but ran out of time to do the bathrooms.

"I'll do them tomorrow," I say with forced patience. Tension pulses through my body, readying it to bolt out the door.

"No, Kitty. You'll do them now," she bites, and something close to malicious pleasure gleams in her eyes. She's doing this to prevent me from seeing John—she wants me to miss his big game. My powers of manipulation fail me. Instead, my rage surges and boils over. Without my usual finesse, I meet her head-on and let her have it.

My fist tightens around the car keys. "I'm not your slave! You want the bathrooms clean? Do them yourself. What's your excuse anyway? It's not like you work for a living. Or is it just beneath you to clean your own damn house?"

The slap comes swift and sharp across my face. My mouth drops open in shock as my hand flies to cover the heated sting on my cheek. Tears of frustration well in my eyes.

"How dare you! I give my heart and soul to this family!" My mother's face flames a bright crimson, her amber eyes bulging with rage equal to mine. She shakes a finger at me. "You selfish little bitch! You think you have it bad? You have no idea what bad is . . . what I gave up to give you this life," she says, clenching her jaw. Tears fill her eyes, too, as her rage collapses into a look of hurt and pain. She wipes them away and takes a ragged breath. "I want you to have more choices than I had. We've sacrificed more than you'll ever know to position you for success. I want only the best for you, but all you want to do is throw it away on that low-class thug!"

That again? I'm sick to death of hearing her refer to John that way. My teary eyes narrow. "He's an honor student!"

She grits her teeth, shakes her head, and snarls. "He'll be your undoing, Katherine."

"He's not Daddy!" I scream before I even realize the words have left my mouth. For what purpose other than to hurt my mother, I don't know.

A second slap cracks across my face. "Don't ever imply your father is anything short of the saint he is," she says in a low hiss. "That man has stood by me and this family during the most trying of times. If you love him, you'll remember that." She snatches the keys from my hand. "Now go clean the bathrooms."

The print of my mother's hand burns on my cheek, while my insides mingle in a combination of shame, defiance, and rage.

I stare into her eyes and say in a low, steady voice, "If that's true, then you'll understand why I'm leaving. John's the same kind of man."

She gapes at me as I walk around her and leave through the front door.

One of the pleasures of being eighteen: legally, she can no longer stop me.

Dr. Graham's Office

I PAUSE UNTIL Dr. Graham finishes taking notes. She looks up when she's done and asks, "Did you ever find out what your mother meant?"

I give her a blank stare. "About what?"

"What she gave up . . ."

A frisson of anxiety passes through me. Yes, I knew exactly what she gave up, but I had yet to discover what it was back then. Without missing a beat, I answer, "A career as a principal dancer in the New York City Ballet."

Her eyebrow quirks up. "Why?"

I tell her the truth, but I'm not ready to disclose the whole story. "To get married and have children." She takes another note.

We have thirty minutes left in our session.

Taking a deep breath, I redirect her to a topic I hope she'll find more interesting. "My family staged an intervention this weekend."

"Really?" She cocks her head, wearing a mildly amused smile, and leans forward over tented hands. "Tell me about it."

"They invaded my house, dragged me out of bed, and then forced me into an exercise class, a new wardrobe, lunch, and a makeover," I say, folding my arms across my chest.

Most of my purchases are still in bags on my bedroom floor, except for one of my new bras and the pants I'm wearing. There's something to be said for clothes that don't slide off your hips without a belt.

Dr. Graham's gaze brushes over my posture. "How did that make you feel?"

"Bullied . . . but with the most loving intentions," I admit and don't quite frown. It's taken me two days to get this close to forgiveness.

She nods. "Any positives? Sounds like there could be a few."

I pout and offer a shrug. "I've signed up for an unlimited month of Bar Method. Jenny says I look like a concentration camp victim. I figure if it doesn't kill me, it'll make me stronger and take the sag out of my muscles. The endorphins won't hurt either. Better than sleeping the weekends away, I guess." I mumble the last part.

"Good. That's one positive. Any others?"

I chew my lip and stall for a moment, assessing the can of snakes

I'm likely to open. *To hell with it.* I peel back the top and let them spring free with a sigh. "I bought a dress for the reunion."

Her eyebrow arches. "So you've decided to go?"

Another shrug.

Dr. Graham takes a note on her pad and comes around to the front of the desk, her modus operandi when she's hit on the topic she wants to go deeper on for the rest of the session.

She takes a seat in the chair catty-corner to the sofa, removing the desk as a barrier separating us.

"This feels like a breakthrough. What made you decide to go? Are you ready to confront your feelings for John?"

Hell, no.

I hold my head high. "Because I want to see my friends." I ignore her second question.

"*Friends* or John?"

"Does it matter?" I ask in a brusque tone.

She smiles. "Obviously."

"Marsh and Sue will be there. I haven't seen them in ages," I counter in my defense.

"And John? He'll be there, too."

Of course, he'll be there! I want to scream, but that doesn't mean I want to confront him, screw him, or do anything else with him, does it?! Instead, I slip back into Kitty politeness. "Yes, we were all friends in high school."

Her mouth shifts sideways into that odd half smile she has, and she shakes her head. "No, Kitty. John was much more. He's one of the reasons you're here. He's the epicenter of the event locked up in your shared past. The one you refuse to confront. How about you share a bit of your story in the time we have left?"

Locked up in our shared past. Accurate. I nearly growl as she approaches my no-go zone. That chunk of time I refuse to discuss — the one she's been prodding me toward for months. Why won't she just help me focus on fixing myself without going there? If I had to choose, I'd rather talk about my manipulative mother.

I brush nonexistent lint from my slacks. "Depends."

"Pick something safe then."

I give her a tight smile. "You mean *safer*." Not much about me and John is safe. There are only pieces easier to tell.

"Pick up where you left off the last time then, and choose a happy milestone. One that shaped your relationship in a positive way."

Relief washes some of the tension from my shoulders. A happy milestone I can do. The early years were the easier years. Both to remember and to relive. More than revisiting my time with John, I like reacquainting myself with Kat. The more I go there, the sorrier I am that I left her behind.

Maybe it's the new clothes, but I feel her float to the surface more easily. Not as a negative reminder of my relationship and buried past, but as a piece of my soul struggling for rebirth.

I drag in a deep breath and let it out slowly, one of the techniques we use to start from a place of calm. "That would've been the night of our junior prom."

Dr. Graham gives me a warm smile. "Perfect."

A derisive snort escapes before I can stop it. "Why don't I start with how my mother sabotaged it first?" What she did sent our relationship into a death spiral from which it never recovered. "The prom incident happened a full five months *before* the bathroom cleaning argument."

Dr. Graham's eyes light up. "Even better."

"Fine. Buckle up for your ride into the land of crazy. . . ." I slouch back into the corner of the couch and hop back in time.

Chapter 18

Kitty

April 1980 – Riding the Crazy Train

"WHAT'S WRONG WITH you?" I scream, holding my hairbrush and staring at my mother like she's lost her mind. "How could you do that?"

"But Kitty, Marshall is the perfect date and he likes you. . . ." She follows me around my bedroom as I stomp back and forth across the floor.

I stop short and shake the brush at her. "I'm not going to the prom with Marshall! I have a boyfriend, remember? The one who you make feel like crap on a regular basis!"

She frowns and holds her arms wide, palms heavenward in that sermonizing pose she takes when she's trying to tell me she's doing something for my own good. I'm sure there's a Jesus complex buried in and among all her crazy. "Honey, I have nothing against John, but you shouldn't get serious with him. I told you that."

I glare at her with my mouth hanging open. "Where have you *been*? We've been *serious* for months now." Not to mention that he's already bought the prom tickets, and that we're going to Matt's parents' house at the shore with friends afterward (still need to negotiate this one).

"But I promised Marshall's mother that he could go as your date," she snaps, and plants her hands on her hips.

It's finally happened. My mother has slipped and fallen off the edge of sanity.

"Then un-promise her! You had no right," I seethe through gritted teeth. "Why would he want to go to the *junior* prom anyway? He's a senior!" Okay, so it's a combined junior/senior prom, but that's not the point. "Admit it. You're doing this because you don't like John and you're trying to break us up."

Mom's mouth drops open, and she has the audacity to look offended. "I'm doing no such thing. It's only one event," she says, and swishes her hand like she's batting away a horde of insects. Apropos, since that's how she categorizes John, as some biting insect that won't go away.

Thank God he hasn't broken up with me for all the crappy things my mother has done to him, or because of my crazy gene pool in the event I can convince him to have kids someday.

"Yes, but it's an important event. For me and *John*." I throw my arms up, still clutching my hairbrush, tempted to whip it at my mother's head. "How could you even *think* this was acceptable?"

She gives me a hard look. "Katherine, this thing you have with that boy will end when you go to Stanford and he trots off to play football at Rutgers. You should date around. Keep your options open before he *expects* something from you."

I cock an eyebrow. "*Expects* something from me? Like what? A blow job? Sex?" I spit out.

My mother gasps and clutches her chest. "Don't talk to me that way."

"What way? Are you afraid I'm going to get knocked up? A disease? What?" Am I really having this surreal conversation? I storm over to my vanity, drop onto the stool, and run the brush through my hair in angry strokes. I catch a glimpse of my mother hovering behind me, arms crossed over her chest and feet rooted to the carpet.

"Fine. I'll say it. He's not good enough for you. You can do better. Someone in a higher social class with a guaranteed future."

Like Marshall? Marshall who was accepted to Yale, and drives a BMW, Marshall? What is this, a throwback to arranged marriages?

My jaw clenches and I whirl around. I'm too angry to address her jabs at John's worthiness. Instead, I kick her where I know it will hurt. "I'm not going to Stanford. I'm going to apply to East Coast colleges." At least that's my plan.

A flush rises along her neck. "Over my dead body," my mother grits. "You won't waste your grandfather's legacy like that. And you won't waste your life on *him!* You're too young to know what you want." She snatches the Judy Blume book sitting wedged open on my bed and shakes it at me. "Didn't you learn anything from reading *Forever?*"

Obviously not; I'm only halfway through. Do Katherine and Michael break up? *Shit.* "I'm not breaking up with John, so get over it." Anger knots my stomach and raises bile in my throat as I turn back to the mirror and grab my makeup.

Her voice is low and icy. "You're not going to the prom unless you go with Marshall." She slams the door on her way out, and I fling the hairbrush with all my might at the closed door and scream in frustration.

What's gotten into my mother? Brava! She's achieved a whole new level of crazy. This is low, even for her. I hate that she goes out of her way to do shitty things to John behind my back. I get it. He's not rich. So what? Neither are we. So he talks with a Bayonne accent? So he's half Cuban and lives on the wrong side of town? So-the-fuck what? His future is as bright as Marshall's and mine. He's also good to me, smart, funny, respectful, and makes my heart beat faster than anyone else on the planet . . . and I think he loves me. I *hope* he loves me, because I love him.

Frustrated tears trail down my cheeks as I curse the woman who gave birth to me. Fine. She wants me to go the prom with Marshall. Nothing says I have to go as his *date.*

A large picture of Shawn Cassidy as one of the *Hardy Boys* smiles down at me from the poster next to my bed. One of these days I need to take that thing down and replace it with a life-size poster of John in his football uniform, not just for me, but to piss off my mother.

I pick up my pink princess phone and dial Marsh's number. "Hello?"

"It's Kitty."

Thirty minutes later, I've laid out my plan with Marsh as my willing accomplice.

Chapter 19

Kitty

May 1980 – Prom Night

"SMILE!" MY MOTHER says with too much enthusiasm while I stand locked in Marsh's arms on the front steps, wearing a smile that's half a lip curve away from a snarl.

My mother lowers the camera and glowers at me. "Kitty, give me a better smile than that. You look slightly . . . *psychotic*."

Maybe that's because I can almost feel the smooth wood of Jack Nicholson's ax handle against my palm, like the scene in his new movie, *The Shining*. The arms warming my waist on this perfect balmy May evening should belong to John, not one of my best friends.

Marsh hugs me closer and coaxes sweetly, "Come on, Petal, smile for your mom."

Petal? I cough to cover elbowing him in the side, and give him credit for keeping his flinch to a minimum. The big ham.

My mother frowns and grits a warning, "*Kitty* . . ."

"What?" I ask, giving an innocent shrug.

Marsh clears his throat and digs his fingers painfully into my hip, a reminder that he's got something riding on tonight, too—his dream date with Sue. "Mrs. McNally, I want to thank you for this evening. Ever since we were kids, I've dreamed of taking Kitty to the prom. You've made my dream come true."

I roll my eyes and try not to gag.

My mother brightens and showers him with one of her classic

128

adoring smiles, reserved for people she's trying to impress. "You're very welcome, sweetheart." Then she glances my way and her smile falters. "Try to look more cheerful for the last couple of photos."

In keeping with my act so she doesn't get suspicious, I paste a saner smile on top of an expression that's a cross between bored and annoyed. I'm not sure how long it will take to forgive her for this or for making me lie to my baby sister about my prom date.

"Johnny isn't your boyfriend anymore?" Jillian asks when Marsh walks in, her amber eyes round and distraught as she clutches the stuffed rabbit John gave her for Easter. Her question batters my heart. I say hello to Marsh and let my mother gush all over him while I pull Jillian into the living room and crouch down for an eye-level chat.

"Johnny is still my boyfriend. He couldn't take me tonight, so he asked Marshall to take his place so that I could see my friends," I whisper, hating every word out of my mouth, but hating my mother more. "Don't worry. Johnny said to tell you he's sorry he couldn't see you tonight, and that he loves you." At least that's true.

A smile blooms on Jillian's sweet face and she hugs the floppy pink bunny to her cheek. "I love him, too. Will you marry him someday?"

My smile is unstoppable but so is the prick behind my eyelids. I gently pat the corners of my eyes and pray my mascara stays put. "I hope so," I whisper.

JOHN'S CAMARO, the Black Beast, is parked in Vera's driveway when we pull in.

I slip Sue's corsage off my wrist, place it back into the clear plastic box, and hand it to Marsh before getting out of the BMW. I had bought a pair of boutonnieres for the guys, leaving John's with Vera earlier so we don't screw up the official pictures later.

"You were great with my mom. A little overplayed, but great." My mother snapped close to a hundred pictures before we escaped. I snatch my overnight bag from the back seat. Closing the door with a hip check, I duck down to give Marsh a quick once-over through the open window. He's traded his glasses for a pair of contacts, and his thick hair is less lopsided than usual, dampening the Gumby effect. "By the way, you look handsome."

"Thanks." He blushes. "Hey, sorry about the Petal thing. It just kind of slipped out."

I shake my head and chuckle. "Don't worry about it. Go knock 'em dead, Tiger."

Marsh gives a wave and pulls out to pick up Sue. My mother thinks she's going to the prom with one of Marsh's friends—not a complete lie just a stretching of the truth.

I didn't feel guilty lying to my mother or manipulating her into letting me stay out all night after what she's put me through. Her ill-gotten victory made her magnanimous, and I took shameless advantage of her double standard of providing permission when the guy is Marsh and not John. All she requested was a phone number for Matt's parents in case of emergency. Easily provided. She didn't say that they had to be in the country. Marsh will sleep at Vera's tonight to cover for me then meet us at the shore tomorrow.

I totter over to John's car in my heels, drop my stuff in his trunk, and head up the front walk to ring the bell.

Vera, dressed in her usual silk blouse, slacks, and pearls, opens the heavy wooden door. I can't tell if her delicate exhale is pride or delight. A smile grows on her lips and lights her amber eyes as she takes me in. "You look beautiful, Katherine."

I do a quick twirl in my knee-length sapphire blue dress before entering the foyer and giving her a hug. "Thanks for saving the day yet again."

Having Vera to subvert my mother and support any rational decision I make has been a godsend. In some ways, she may be as nuts as my mom, but I can live with her brand of insanity.

She squeezes me tighter and mumbles, "I've been where you are, sweetheart. I was young and in love once, too."

I loosen my grip and lean back with a quizzical smile. "Really? Do tell."

A look of regret accompanies a clipped head shake, telling me the subject isn't open for discussion. "I'll tell you about him someday, but tonight is about you." She flashes a pained smile that carries the weight of understanding behind it. "Listen to me, Katherine. Your mother's tactics might not seem to make sense, but I know she's coming from a good place. Hard to see sometimes, I know. But she loves you."

"She's got a funny way of showing it. I hate that she's disrespectful and downright cuckoo when it comes to John." I scowl and make a mental note to pump Aunt Vera for info about her mystery man when we have more time.

Vera's expression softens. "You're lucky I'm a hopeless romantic and that John's a fine young man." She tips her head toward the library. "He's waiting. I'll join you with my camera once Marshall and Sue arrive."

I give Vera one more squeeze, then practically float down to the library where John's no doubt pacing a groove in the glossy hardwood floor. A flutter of anticipation tickles my ribs. Even after seven months, I'm amazed at the effect he still has on me.

My breath hitches as I cross the threshold and see him in a tuxedo. Wow, he cleans up well. Not classically handsome, he has the rugged, square-jawed good looks of someone who's strong, protective and capable. Not radically V-shaped like a bodybuilder; rather, he's tall, broad, and solid like an immovable object. His suit-jacketed finery barely contains his intimidating bulk. If I didn't know him, I'd never believe he was young enough to be in high school, especially wearing a tux. Maybe it's the old soul that peeks out through his eyes, or the awful things he's lived through. There's nothing soft about John until he smiles. His smile is like sunshine cracking through storm clouds after a summer rain.

His gaze shifts in my direction, and he stops pacing. The side of his mouth lifts in a lopsided grin, which does the trick to soften his rough edges. "Wow." He opens his arms and I propel myself into his embrace.

Our lips meet and he kisses me with tempered abandon in an exchange of minty breath and shared oxygen. With tentative touches, we're both careful not to undo all the work that's gone into our prom preparation.

He presses me into his warmth. The sleeve of his fine wool jacket brushes across my bare arms as his muscles flex underneath. Closing the kiss, he leans down to rest his forehead on mine. I catch the heady scent of his spicy, piney cologne and inhale deeper. His face loses focus this close, and all I see is a blob of blue-gray merge with the bridge of his nose. "You look gorgeous," he says.

"So do you," I say in a breathy whisper, excited but nervous. We've decided tonight is the *night*. After six months of fooling around and what amounts to a serious apprenticeship in foreplay, we're going to do *it*. Yup, tonight I'm serving him my virginity on a naked platter.

And I'm not doing it to take revenge on my mother for ruining the plotline of *Forever*, or for holding my prom hostage. I'm doing it because I'm nearly eighteen and I'm finally ready.

John has been the picture of patience as he once claimed and has never pushed. Not that he's had to. I've learned how to keep him satisfied in other ways.

Surprise, surprise. The thought of giving a blow job is no longer disgusting. I may have taught him some geometry, but he's returned the favor in spades. He's been a patient and generous teacher, and he's let me drive the lesson plan. Not to mention, he's done it all without making me feel weird or grossed out. Who knew a guy could teach me so much about my own body? Although I hate that Carmela taught him most of what he knows, I'm grateful he was such a good study.

Better yet, he only has eyes for me. As much as I don't want to admit weakness, he's become my world. My center. My everything. I hope I'm his.

He slips his hand in mine, steps away, and pulls me over to one of the couches. "How'd it go with the pit viper?"

I grunt. "*Pit viper?* Fitting." I snuggle under his arm. "Fine. Marsh is a wonderful sport."

"I owe him one," he says.

I rub my palm over the pleated white shirt covering John's abs. "I owe him and Sue about twenty. Same with Aunt Vera."

He presses his mouth to my stiffly coiffed updo. "I can't wait until later," he whispers.

A flutter tickles my belly along with a shot of warmth down below. "Me too." I shimmy away from him to get access to the sensuous mouth I've come to love.

As I lean in, he taps a finger to my lips to hold me at bay, and whispers, "Not yet." Instead, he reaches for the clear plastic box on the coffee table with a purple orchid wristlet inside. "Your corsage." He pops the box open, removes the exotic flower, and slides the elastic over my wrist.

I run a quick fingertip over the white rose on his lapel, and with an imperceptible nod, he whispers, "Now." Then he bridges the gap between us, hovering his lips a hair's breadth from mine. I close the distance and we share a tender kiss, before Vera, Sue, and Marsh stream through the library door, interrupting our beautiful moment with the click-clacking of heels and a cleared throat.

Sue looks amazing in the pink prom dress I helped her choose at Bloomingdale's. It complements her dark hair and light eyes that can now be seen without cola-bottle obstruction. After months of begging from Sue, her mother took her to get fitted for contacts last week when her braces came off. So tonight, she looks every bit the swan. Here's hoping Marsh finally kisses her.

"Come, come," Vera claps, a camera hanging around her neck. "Let's go to the garden for a nice backdrop."

Twenty minutes later, after Vera's given my mother a run for her money in the picture-taking department, Marsh glances at his watch. "We need to go. The limo should be here."

"What limo?" John's jaw tightens.

Marsh wears a smug smile. "My treat." Then he glances at Sue and his gaze gets all starry. "It's a special night."

I smile and give John a pointed look, emphasized with some added pressure to his fingers, to wipe the scowl off his face. "Thanks, Marsh. What a wonderful surprise."

John catches the hint and exhales a defeated huff. "Thanks, Marsh. Appreciate the gesture." I'm happy we're getting better at reading each other's signals, a necessity when we're around my mother.

We trail behind on the way out of the garden. John pulls me aside and waits until everyone is out of earshot before he runs agitated fingers through his hair. "So I shouldn't offer to pay half the bill?"

Even if I said yes, he doesn't have the money. I know without asking that he's spent his savings on tonight. Money has always been tight for him . . . for both of us. Aunt Vera slips me cash every few weeks, which helps. I'm happy to take it if it means I can do something nice for John. I'm not proud, but I can't say the same for him. He refused to speak to me after I offered to pay for our prom tickets. For a full day. Silly male pride.

A few months ago, he finally explained why he'd failed geometry last fall and ended up as my tutoree. His mom had hurt her ankle and couldn't work for a few weeks. John had to give up sleep and studying to keep food on the table and make rent by working double shifts at Shop-Rite. Her medical bills were covered, but in a business driven by working for tips, she has no disability plan or paid sick leave. All the money John makes pays for gas, food, football-related expenses, and rent contribution. If there's anything left over, he'll spend it on me rather than himself.

That's why I take the cash. I sneak in creative extras he can't typically afford: surprise take-out when I come over, a little gas in his tank whenever I borrow his car, a new shirt I know he has his eye on to celebrate some accomplishment, the latest Bruce Springsteen or Rolling Stones album that he wants but thinks is mine . . .

He's pacing with his mouth set in a hard line and his brows drawn into the contemplative look he gets when he's working on a problem.

"No, you don't need to offer." I grab his arm to still him. "In a way, I've already paid thanks to my mother buying Marsh and Sue's prom tickets. Stop. Let him think he's doing something nice. Don't ruin it."

"It feels weird," John says, his cheek twitching from that grinding thing he does with his teeth when he's perturbed.

"Would it feel weird if it were Matt?" I ask.

He frowns. "Hell, yes! We pull our own weight for team social stuff, and a lot we do is cheap or free. Like later. Other than twenty bucks for the party bus, some food and a six-pack, we're not paying for our luxury accommodations." He runs a hand down his face and tips his chin toward the house. "It bugs me that I'm not set up like your friends, or mine."

His angst carves out a small piece of my chest. I extend my hand between us and wait. My lips curve up at the sides and I lift a brow. "If you had money on top of being so gorgeous, you'd be insufferable."

There's a hint of a dimple in his cheek when his expression softens into a closed-mouth smile. He takes my offered hand and pulls me into him. His heart beats steadily against me, and he whispers into my hair. "You're the only one who knows the truth about my past, and that my mom and I just scrape by. Matt and everyone else only know what I've told them, which isn't much."

"Damn. You mean I'm the only who knows that you're sexy, smart, talented, an amazing singer, and have Latin rhythm?"

He chuckles softly and kisses the side of my head, his arms

circling me in protective warmth. "I love you, Kat McNally."

The breath stalls in my lungs. I squeeze my eyes shut and tighten my grasp around his waist, savoring his declaration. "Say it again," I whisper and hold my breath, hoping my ears hadn't deceived me the first time.

He pulls back and I get a full view of stormy blue. He runs a finger down my cheek to my lips. "I said, 'I love you.' "

A lump rises in my throat and I pat at a tear in the corner of my eye before it fully forms. "I love you, too, Shaw."

The full force of smiling sunshine brightens his face before his lips descend on mine in a kiss to end all kisses. Lipstick be damned. I don't know what it feels like to kiss someone else, and I never want to find out. It would only end in disappointment, because in this moment, the synchronized tango of our tongues, fit of our mouths, and my sizzling awareness of his body is so perfect. His hands slide down my sides until they're cupping my backside and pulling me closer.

I press into the gentle nudging of his growing desire against my stomach, a promise for later.

He moans low in his throat. "You're killing me, babe."

"In a good way?" I ask, and trail a kiss along his jaw.

"In the best way." His hands slide back to my hips and he eases me away from him. He tips his chin toward the garden behind us. "We should go before I take you behind that oak tree over there and peel off your pantyhose with my teeth."

ONLY MARSHALL WOULD hire a Rolls-Royce limo to drive us the paltry two miles to the Short Hills Hilton for the prom, and only John would be unhappy about it. Extravagant and a waste of money, if you ask me, but I fully support Marsh's desire to impress Sue.

On our way over, we drink glasses of sparkling cider to the mellow strains of romantic ballads, probably left over from a wedding event. John's tension-filled arm drapes around my shoulders, but he stays scowl-free under my watchful eye while Marsh and Sue sit hip to hip with excited blushes spread across their cheeks. By the time we get there, Sue's hand is cradled securely in Marsh's palm, and he's grinning like an idiot. A very happy idiot.

He's not the only one. I'm still flying high over John's declaration in the garden.

We file out of the car one at a time. "Meet you inside, before the photo line," I say as John and I take our bags, which we retrieved from the Black Beast before leaving Vera's. We need to switch dates again for the pictures and hope no one wonders why. Any official photographic evidence needs to support the story I told my mother.

I follow John through the crowd milling around in the lobby over to the bellhop desk next to reception. We hand over our bags to store until later when we take the party bus to LBI. Marsh will meet us at Matt's tomorrow and give us a ride back to Vera's.

John pockets our tickets. "Ready?"

I nod and hook my arm through his.

The lobby is mobbed with promgoers in their tuxedo, ball-gown, and short poufy cocktail-dress finery. We join the flow of the crowd toward the photo area, our only mandatory prom stop before entering the ballroom.

"Hey, Shaw!" Tony, one of John's teammates, yells through the crowd. We step aside and wait for him and his date to catch up. They're sitting at our table, along with Matt and his new girlfriend. Marsh and Sue round out our table of eight. From what John told me, Tony and Matt were less than enthusiastic about sitting with any non-football brethren, but John laid out the situation and they fell into line without complaint.

"Hey, Tone." John breaks into a half grin and they do the team's signature combo shoulder-bump, hand-grab, back-clap move. "You guys drop the food at Matt's?"

He nods. "Got it covered." Tony glances at me. "Hey, Kitty. Nice dress. You know Mel?"

I wave at Melanie, Tony's date. She's in my AP History class. This is the first time I've seen them together. Not surprising. Tony changes girlfriends as often as most people change underwear.

Of all John's friends, Tony and Matt are the closest. The more I've gotten to know them, it's become obvious they're the most decent of the meathead lot. Nothing like Mike Ryan and his asshole clique of jockstrap idiots.

I wave to Sue and Marsh, and we jump in line behind them for a quick switch of dates and corsages and more "death by photo." My mother may be drunk on victory, but she's not stupid or unobservant. God forbid she notice that I changed wristlets between the prom photo and her snap festival in the front yard. Marsh and I will buy the photographic evidence to support our ruse, while Vera makes sure John's mother, Rosita, gets the real ones in her batch. Sue's mother already took the real ones with Marsh. Bless Sue's heart, she'll conveniently forget to buy hers from the school.

After we're done, Marsh and Sue go on ahead of us while we stay behind and wait for Tony and Melanie to finish their shoot. A few forced smiles and awkward hand positions later, we're giving our names to the announcer as we walk through the door.

Popular music pulses over the speakers in the ballroom as we walk the promenade down the red carpet in the semidarkness. John clutches me to his side. I savor the feeling, glowing next to him, knowing he loves me as much as I love him.

The prom committee chose a "Party like a Rock Star" theme. Giant glittery guitars, colored lights, and hanging star-shaped fixtures decorate the stage area while clusters of helium balloons in maroon and white, our school colors, float suspended over each of the round, numbered tables covered in white linen, glitter, and floral centerpieces. Rock music plays over the speakers as the band sets up.

Excitement swells in my belly with the pulsing music.

"You want a cola?" John asks, elevating his voice over the chatter and music.

I nod. He and Tony head back into the crowd toward the nearest beverage station while I claim the two seats next to Sue and Marsh, who are already seated with drinks in their hands. Melanie takes the ones next to those.

No sooner does my butt hit the chair than I'm back on my feet and cursing my bladder. Sue giggles at something Marsh whispers in her ear.

I tap Sue's shoulder and nudge my chin at the exit. "Tell John I'll be back." Unfolding my napkin, I drape it over my place setting.

"Bathroom? You want me to come?" Sue asks.

I shake my head. "I'll be fine." I don't buy into pack mentality when it comes to using the ladies' room for real business. Gossip and boy talk, a definite yes, but not the genuine need of taking a pee.

I escape toward the first bathroom I can find. A line of girls in sparkles, poufy tulle, and taffeta extends halfway down the hall. My bladder objects to the wait, so I head toward the lobby's stairwell.

Sneaking past the velvet rope barrier, I creep down the carpeted stairs toward the spa and hope the bathroom isn't locked, or worse, swarming with a bunch of other rule breakers clogging up all the stalls.

The lower level is quiet and empty. My shoulders slump in relief when the bathroom door yields to my touch. I push inside, turn on the light, and take the last stall.

My body relaxes into a state of empty-bladder satisfaction. I reach behind me to flush when the door cracks open and two sets of clacking high heels enter along with the sound of someone sobbing.

Instinct freezes me in place. I'm not sure why I do it, but I shimmy my underwear back into place and pull up my feet, resting them on the back of the door so the stall looks empty. Whether it's to save the girl from embarrassment or to satisfy my curiosity, I don't know. Probably a little of both.

"*Shh*, it'll be all right," a girl says softly, though her tone doesn't sound very convincing. I hear tissues being pulled from a box. "Here."

The other girl blows her nose, then asks thickly, "Will you come with me?"

"Yeah, I'll come. How far along are you?"

A shiver skitters down my spine as I listen, suddenly regretting my decision.

The crying girl sniffles a few times, then responds in a calmer voice. "A little over two months, maybe."

My breath catches and my stomach rockets to the floor with recognition.

Holy shit.

Karen Stark. No. *Pregnant* Karen Stark.

I breathe in shallow breaths and stay silent.

"What did Mike say?" asks the other girl, who I'm now guessing is her best friend, Pam.

"He doesn't know, and if you tell him I'll kill you," she whisper-snarls with a vehemence that only half shocks me. "You're the only one who knows, so if anyone finds out I'll know it's you."

"Your secret's safe with me. I'd never tell anyone!" the other girl answers in a tone that's both offended and filled with hurt.

My mouth dries out as I hover with my heels pressed to the back of the fine mahogany bathroom door, frozen.

A few more minutes pass as they talk about the logistics of Karen's impending abortion. When they're done, I hear the snapping of a compact and rummaging in what I imagine is a makeup bag. With a *click-click-click*, they head to the exit and flip off the lights on their way out.

Drawing in deep breaths to ease the throbbing behind my left eye, I drop my cramped legs to the floor and sit draped in darkness as I tremble. The gravity of Karen's situation hits me like an unanticipated blow, and I promise myself three things:

One, I'll never have sex without a condom.

Two, I'll never take a life.

Three, call it maturity, but unlike last fall when I announced Karen's parking lot blow job to half the junior class, this time her secret is safe with me.

Halfway upstairs, I can't remember if I flushed the toilet.

After dinner, as the band comes onstage for their second set, John leans in close, worry darkening his eyes. "You all right, babe?"

I can't shake the conversation I overhead in the bathroom, but I don't want it to take away from our night, so I revisit our time in the garden and smile brightly. "Totally fine."

A few seconds later, the band rips into the driving beat of "I Was Made for Lovin' You" by KISS. One of John's favorites.

"Yeah!" Matt punches the air and pulls his date to her feet. "Come on, Shaw, Tone. Let's show 'em how it's done." I suppress an eye roll. Matt's idea of dancing is closer to a fantasy concert of air guitar.

John shoots me a look and a smile. Most guys would rather crawl under a rock—like Tony, who looks like he's on his way to the gallows—than willingly dance, but not John. No air guitar for him. He has amazing rhythm, and for a big guy he has some pretty smooth moves. As for me, all those early years of jazz dancing my mother forced me to take before age eleven have paid some dividends besides securing me a place in the SAA dance show this year. Together, we can hold our own on the dance floor.

I smile back and lay my hand in his, letting him lead me out to dance with the others. We squeeze onto the floor and dance close enough that we are touching in all the right places.

Next, the band covers Journey's new single, "Any Way You

Want It." Matt and Tony grab John and break into poor Steve Perry imitations. John shakes his head and snorts. The music's loud enough that we're reduced to hand signals and lip reading.

Matt cups his hand over John's ear. Irritation passes over John's face but quickly morphs into a look of wicked delight. He nods. Matt and Tony disappear with their dates into the crowd.

Before I can ask what's going on, John winks and gives me a crooked smile. "Gotta go." He kisses my hand and then disappears into the crowd. I'm left standing there, bewildered.

Rather than ripping into the next tune when the song ends, the band goes silent and the lead singer, a guy with dark hair longer than mine, puts his lips to the microphone. "Summit High School, Class of '80 and '81! Great to be here tonight. Everyone having fun?"

Hoots, whistles, and clapping echo in response.

The lead singer nods to someone standing in the crowd below. "So, I hear we have some talent in the room. We're going to hand the mike over for a couple songs to a few of the guys from your varsity football team. Come on up, guys."

Matt, Tony, and John jump up onto the stage. More hoots and hollers.

My heart skips a beat and swells with pride and excitement. Sue and Marsh grab me, and we propel ourselves to the front of the crowd.

John grabs the microphone. The opening notes of Cheap Trick's "Surrender" bleed out of the speakers, and the crowd goes nuts. John takes lead vocals while Matt and Tony do backup, and the whole audience joins for the chorus. John usually downplays his talent in public, saving it just for me, but he shines on the stage with a presence very different from his usual intimidating self.

I sing along, clapping and dancing with Sue. When the song ends, Matt and Tony jump off the stage but John stays put.

His gaze travels over the crowd until he finds me. "This next one . . . is for my Kat." His lips tug into a sideways smile, and he points at me with the opening line of Cheap Trick's "I Want You to Want Me."

The crowd catches on with catcalls and whistles. Then all eyes, not just John's, are on me. Heat rises in my cheeks as my boyfriend tells half the school how much he wants me to want him.

Not a problem. Tonight, I plan to show him just how much.

Chapter 20

Kitty

May 1980 – Prom Night

BY THE TIME the ten of us pile out of the bus at Matt's parents' oceanfront house on Long Beach Island, it's close to 1:00 a.m.

We huddle in the chilly, salt-laced air as the driver grabs our bags from the storage compartment under the bus. The thin sweater I'm wearing doesn't do much to protect my gooseflesh-covered skin against the gusty wind rolling off the water. Tomorrow should be sunny and much warmer, enough to play volleyball on the beach.

Matt and John each take a handle of the large cooler filled with contraband beer and food for breakfast, while the rest of us grab the overnight bags and trudge up the steps into the expansive modern structure.

Less than ten minutes later, John and I are ensconced in a guest room on the far side of the second floor overlooking the beach.

I kick off my heels and perch on the edge of the bed, pulling my sweater tight around my shoulders and wishing the heat would hurry up and chase the chill from the room.

But the shiver running over my skin is about more than the temperature. Sudden anxiety grips my middle at the prospect of John merging a sizable part of his body into mine.

Leaving our bags by the door, John loosens his bowtie. His lazy grin falls into a frown. "You all right, babe?"

I shrug, trying to push away any shyness. "I'm fine. A little cold, a little nervous."

He tosses the bowtie onto the bed then holds out his hand. "Nothing to be nervous about. It's just me." I nestle my palm against his and he pulls me to my feet. "We go at your pace, remember?" he whispers, wrapping me in a warm embrace.

Gratitude and relief ease the anxious fluttering. I rest my cheek on his lapel and breathe in his familiar scent. We hold each other, and I squeeze him tighter to the muted crash of waves against the surf. He feels so right pressed against me. He always has. I want to do this. I want to know what it's like to have him inside of me.

We linger a moment longer in silence before he leans back and brushes away a strand of my hair that's come free from my updo. He tips his head toward the bathroom. "How 'bout we get out of these clothes and take a shower first . . . or a bath? Your choice."

I nod with more enthusiasm than I intend. The thought of warm water surrounding my body sounds heavenly, if for no other reason than to thaw out. John kisses my nose and tugs me toward the bathroom under a draped arm.

The bathroom, decorated in pink and mauve, is as large as a small bedroom, with a Jacuzzi and a shower stall big enough for two.

Slipping behind me, he eases down the zipper on my dress with sure fingers. "What'll it be?" he asks in a low voice, and gives my neck a playful nip.

I let the dress fall to the floor, turn, and rest a hand on his shoulder. "Bath." I meet his heated gaze, letting it slide over me. A bath sounds nicer and gives me the option of keeping my hair up and avoiding hairpin hell until tomorrow.

"You got it." He steps away and toes out of his shoes before striding over to the Jacuzzi to turn on the taps.

We make quick work of stripping down to our underwear, discarding our clothes into a heap on floor. John's left standing in his boxers, while I'm in matching black bra and panties. His eyelids lower halfway and his smile turns sexy. "Come here . . ."

Smiling, I step in and circle my arms around his neck.

Anxiety turns to anticipation as he presses me against his bare chest. The same chest I've charted every Tuesday and Thursday evening between six and eight p.m. for the last four months, thanks to his mother adding two late nights to her schedule. Four months of uninterrupted study time. And study I have—every millimeter of

John's hard, muscled body, with both fascination and reverence. I've spent countless hours skimming my fingers over the fine, dark mat of hair that covers his pectorals and tapers down the front of his torso into a narrow trail that disappears inside of his boxers. Hours tenderly touching the knotty scars created by his father's hand that dot his back. Hours gliding my fingertips along the hollow of his spine and over the birthmark above the swell of his left glute. Add to all that time the hours I've spent stroking and licking his most intimate parts, and one could say I've excelled in the study of John Henshaw's anatomy.

That's equal to at least a marking period in biology, isn't it?

Thank God for Sue. I've let my mother believe that we've forged an intense study partnership to explain my sudden absence until eight-fifteen two nights a week. It's been perfect.

John's lips melt onto mine. We share a kiss to the sound of water splashing on porcelain and the warmth of steam collecting in the air.

A low moan rises from his throat as his hands travel up and down my back before settling on my hips. The gooseflesh on my skin retreats as the heat from his lower body seeps through his cotton boxers, along with a stirring that reminds me of what we plan to do. Anxiety resurges in my middle.

Am I ready? I hesitate for only a second.

Yes, I'm ready.

He closes the kiss and pulls away. There's a roguish look in his eye and a tilt of his lips to a near smile. "Kat?"

"Yeah?"

"First bath together . . ." The unnaturally small-size tub in his mom's rental has never presented an opportunity.

I smile. "Yeah . . ."

He unhooks my bra with one hand and I let it fall to the floor. His gaze darkens and takes on a sizzle. He passes his thumbs over my nipples, pulling a pleasure-filled hum from my throat.

He leans in and whispers into my hair, "You're so . . . beautiful," then he slides his hands down my sides, peeling away my panties as he goes. They tumble down my legs, and I kick them away. Repaying the favor, I hook my thumbs under the waistband of his boxers and slide them down, springing him free. My pulse quickens as I shimmy them down his hips.

He leads me over to the Jacuzzi tub and waves his hand through the water as it fills.

"It's good." He climbs inside and gingerly eases down into the hot water. I position myself between his muscled thighs and settle back against his chest. The water displaces to surround us and heats my skin like liquid heaven. A warm fog hangs around us, and once the water covers us to my collarbone, John turns off the taps and starts the jets.

The bubbling water draws the tension from my body, and I relax inside John's embrace, his chin resting on my shoulder.

"Still nervous?" he asks and drops his lips to my neck.

"I guess it's normal, right? Even though we know each other so well?"

He nods and his hair brushes mine. "Yeah . . . I'm a little nervous, too."

My brows rise. "Really? But you've done this before."

His arms tighten around me and he whispers into my neck. "But not with you. . . . I feel like shit knowing what should feel good won't. Not tonight. Not the first time."

A shudder passes through me. I don't want to ask how he knows that, but if I had to guess, it's the same source that helped hone his skills. My nerves erase any jealousy over his past with Carmela. None of my friends have done *it* before, so John's the only one who can set my expectations. And he's a guy. Still, I'll take what I can get. "But it'll feel good for you?"

"Yeah . . . it will, and I hate that, too . . . for tonight."

I swallow. "I can live with that. It should feel good for one of us."

He lays another tender kiss on my neck. "I'll warm you up first, then I'll go slow and stop if you want me to."

I brush the hair on his arm just beneath the water's surface back and forth with my finger. "You meant what you said in the garden? That you love me?"

His breath heats my hair as he says, "So much that it hurts, babe. I swear it. On a stack of Bibles." My whole body warms from the inside out.

"I love you that way, too," I say, looking over my shoulder and finding his lips to seal our words with a kiss.

We sit for a moment, silent, just wrapped in an embrace inside the bubbling tub. I memorize the moment, the significance of it, and realize I want to crawl even farther inside of him.

"What do you dream about, Shaw? How do you picture your future?"

He huffs a laugh. "Where do you want me to start?"

I shrug against him. "Besides playing football, what do you want to study in college? What major?" I know he wants to go to Rutgers, but until now, everything else has seemed too far away to think about.

He strokes my belly in a languorous rhythm. "*Hmm.* I haven't decided yet. I like law but hate the idea of that much school. Maybe criminal justice or business."

My mother would like law best. "Criminal justice?"

"Yeah, you know . . . FBI, CIA, local law enforcement. I'd like to do something about assholes who hurt kids . . . like my father." The muscles in his arms flex and tense around me.

A shiver skitters across my skin at the thought of him putting himself in danger, but his desire to help people also makes my chest swell with pride.

"Your turn. What about you, O lovely Chess Mistress?" He grins against my neck and nibbles. I let out a girly shriek and wiggle away when he hits my ticklish spot. He chuckles and pulls me back inside the dual columns of his arms.

"Okay, but don't tickle me," I say, shrugging up my shoulders to protect my sensitive neck.

"Deal." Instead, he snickers and circles my nipples underneath the water lightly with his fingers until they peak.

"Torturer," I moan and savor his touch for a few beats as I formulate an answer. The plan, for as long as I can remember, has been to attend Stanford under the special endowment my grandfather set up for me before he died. Molecular biology and curing disease had been my predetermined destiny . . . until I met John. The thought of leaving him now has me reassessing my options. Not as much in careers as in schools. Suddenly, the last thing I want is four years and three thousand miles separating us.

"I'm waiting . . ." he says, continuing to tease me with skillful fingers.

"You're making it hard to think," I breathe.

He nuzzles my nape and drops his hands to my waist. "Fine."

"Accounting," I blurt, saying the first thing that comes to mind, and then add, "or maybe something in the sciences. Biology, maybe.

I haven't decided yet." Safe options. Both. And most East Coast schools offer them.

"Good choices," he says, and then lowers his voice to a rough whisper. "I know it's a lot to ask, but I don't want to lose you, Kat . . . when we go to college."

"I don't want to lose you, either." Or cut out my own heart. Or stop breathing.

"Make me a promise?"

"If I can," I say.

"We'll do what we can to be together, even if we don't go to the same school?"

My heart does a little dance that we're thinking the same thing, as if it could be real and actually happen. "I promise," I say, finding his hands in the water, and ask in a dreamy voice, "Where do you want to live, you know, when we're older?"

He lets out a contemplative breath. "That's a tough one. Will you rough me up if say I'd like to live as far away from your mother as humanly possible?"

I give him a blind, half-hearted elbow to the ribs.

"*Oof.* Watch that elbow, McNally."

The truth is, I'd follow him anywhere, but I'd prefer to stay close to the people I love. "What about your mother, my father, Jillian, and Aunt Vera?"

His shoulder rises in a shrug behind me. "I'm open to compromise. Maybe the city. I've always wanted to live in New York."

"Perfect!" Then I brace myself and ask, "Are we still waiting until twenty-five to have kids?"

"Thirty," he whispers and then trails kisses down my neck and across my shoulder.

His answer furrows my brow and a sliver of disappointment slices across my heart. That felt close to an indefinite postponement. I take hold of his forearms and loosen his hold on my waist. "Do you even want kids?"

He releases an exasperated sigh behind me. "We've talked about this, Kat. I had young parents, and it was ugly." His rough tone softens to a gravel-filled whisper. "I don't ever want to be like them, and I don't ever want a kid of mine having the childhood I had."

I turn in his arms. "But we're not your parents. We wouldn't be like that."

His jaw twitches. There's pain and a hint of fear shining in his eyes. "How do you know? How do you know I won't be just like him?" he whispers, his gaze holding mine.

My mouth dries out. "Why would you say that?"

He swallows and looks away. "My mom says my father wasn't always like that . . . that they were happy. Then something snapped in him after they were together a few years, after I was born. He lost his job and couldn't provide. That's when it started . . . the heavy drinking, the abuse." He sweeps his gaze back to mine. "What if . . . I have that same thing buried inside me and I don't know it? I want a career, a paycheck, a future before that happens. I've got to know that I can provide before I have kids." He cups my cheek. "I've got to prove that I'm not like my father. Understand?"

I nod, unsure what to say. I can't imagine he would ever be like his father, but he's the one who needs to be sure.

He presses a soft kiss to my lips. "Still love me, even though I'm screwed up?" Sadness hovers inside his naked, vulnerable gaze.

"Yes," I whisper and kiss him back with the full force of my passion. Sliding my tongue between his lips and tangling my fingers in his hair, I brand him as mine until I'm not sure who's moaning louder.

He slides his mouth away and clamps my hips in his hands. "Babe?"

"*Hmm*?" My breath hitches, thinking of all the things I want to do to him.

"I'm pruning up back here. What do you say we take this party into the bedroom?"

THE BEDROOM IS warm enough by the time we leave the sanctuary of the tub, wrapped in terry robes we found on hooks behind the door.

I close the curtains over the sliding glass doors facing the ocean and dim the overhead lights, while John takes out a cassette tape, pops it into the stereo, and sets the volume on low.

I slide naked between the sheets and smile when I hear the opening chords of Boston's "More Than a Feeling" and John's voice as he softly sings the first two lines. It's one of our favorite make-out songs.

He strolls toward me, opening his robe. It drops to the floor halfway to the bed. As much as John doesn't like to draw attention to the scars on his back, he's never been modest about flaunting his assets. His attitude has gone a long way to ease me toward releasing my own sense of modesty. Still . . . There's something overwhelming about all that naked male muscle coming at me that sends a shiver down my spine. Especially when it's paired with that hungry gleam in his eyes and a sensual smile filled with promise.

He dips down to retrieve a small box from his overnight bag and drops it on the night table next to him before he crawls under the blankets with me.

"Let's get this party started," he whispers, and dives underneath the covers. He slides into position between my parted thighs.

Like so many times before this, he plays me with his probing tongue and gentle fingers in a symphony of pleasure. I throw back the covers as heat fills my veins and rushes to all the right places. I dig my fingers into his firm shoulder muscles, and his gaze slips up to catch mine from where he lays nestled with my legs wrapped around his upper back.

"You taste fucking amazing, Kat," he says in a hoarse whisper. I moan with the mounting pressure, and he slips a finger inside. The added sensation throws me over the edge, triggering that amazing thing my body does. Like catching a wave that pulls me to shore, only it drops me over and over from one exhilarating peak to the next in pulsing harmony.

I release him and clasp the comforter, gasping and letting the power of my climax wash over me.

John pauses for only a few seconds before continuing to stroke, coax, and probe until my body understands there's more to give. It's only after I hit my peak a second time and recover that he crawls up beside me wearing a satisfied half grin.

"Good?" he asks, with enough confidence that I suspect his question is rhetorical.

I nod anyway, panting and trying to regain my breath. He flips onto his back and my hand drifts to his groin for a little unnecessary coaxing of my own. He's silky steel against my palm. I slide my grip up his length.

He groans and grabs the small box off the nightstand. Ripping it open, he dumps out the square foil packets and tears one off.

"You ready?" he asks.

I nod in the dim light. He opens the packet with his teeth and rolls the latex over himself. It's a tight fit and compresses his skin underneath, but it's the only way to ensure our safety. After what I overheard earlier tonight, I'd be too afraid to take any chances.

He positions himself on top of me, nudging my thighs apart gently with his knee. Then he settles his weight in between, a position we've only practiced.

The muscles in my thighs strain to open wider. Although John's lean, he's broad and a lot of guy to wrap my legs around.

He hovers over me on his elbows and stares into my eyes. "I love you.... Let me know if you want me to stop." Swallowing, he gives a wry smile and adds, "Fair warning, I probably won't last long."

I arch up to kiss him, tasting a residual saltiness, and put my finger to his lips. "Stop talking."

He pulls my gaze to his and holds tight. The heat of his tip nudges me open. He sinks in an inch before I flinch and he stops, giving me a questioning look. My muscles clench and there's a small ache but not enough pain to change course.

I nod. "I'm fine."

He eases in farther. The muscles in his arms ripple and shift.

I swallow, catch my lip in my teeth, and nod again.

His hips press forward, pushing deeper. Other than a small cramp, I'm still fine. His brow knits in intense concentration. I run my hands along his waist, then dip them down until they're cupping the finest tight end this side of Barnegat Bay. I take a deep breath and pull him toward me with all my strength.

His eyes widen as he thrusts all the way in and stills. "Damn, Kat! What happened to going slow?" He lifts off me with trembling arms, amusement filling his half-hearted glare.

I give him a coquettish smile and chew my lip. "You looked like you were in more pain than I was." Other than a sense of utter pressure and fullness, I feel... fine. I slap his ass. "Now move, damn it, so I can see what all the fuss is about."

He chuckles, lowers back onto his elbows, and tucks his head into my neck. "You kill me, woman, but, God, you feel unbelievable...." With that, he rolls his hips in a tentative thrusting rhythm. I'll admit, it doesn't feel as good as his tongue on my soft center, but it doesn't feel bad, either.

My gaze shifts downward, and I watch as his body moves in and out of mine, fascinated by the sheer biology of it.

I close my eyes and relax into the undulating motion, trailing my nails up and down the hollow of John's spine, over the knotty scars, across his rippling shoulders. I decide it's more than biology, it's sheer love that makes me want to do this with him. I already know once won't be nearly enough.

He runs a finger over my lips, his breath growing ragged above me as moisture beads on his forehead. "Last chance for me to stop," he says in a hoarse whisper.

"Don't you dare," I whisper back.

His eyelids close and he thrusts faster. I clasp my hands tight to his sides.

"God, Kat..." His head arches back and his body shudders above and inside me in wracking tremors. He rides it out with a loud groan and finally stills.

He eases himself out, holding the condom in place, and then collapses next to me, dragging me onto his chest. I run my fingers through the damp curls over his pounding heart as he regains his breath.

"How do... you feel?" he rasps.

"Not too bad... a little sore," I say. All right, maybe a lot sore. But I didn't notice it until he pulled out.

He looks slightly crestfallen. "You sure?"

I crawl up to kiss him. "I'm sure."

"It'll be better the next time. Promise."

I run my fingertip over his eyebrow to smooth it out, down the bridge of his nose, and over his bottom lip. "I love you, Shaw."

A smile ghosts across his lips. "Love you, too, Kitten."

Then I give him a wicked grin. "You did a fantastic job deflowering me."

He laughs, and pulls me closer. "How about a repeat performance in the morning?"

"I can be persuaded."

"Glad to hear it." He untangles himself and swings his legs over the side of the bed, and glances at his groin. "Let me take care of this."

"Will you teach me how to put those on you?" I ask his retreating back and fabulous tight end.

He chuckles. "I'll be sure to add it to the lesson plan."

On his way back to bed, he stops to kill the music, and then dips into his bag for another box. A small gold one this time.

"What's that?" I ask, pointing to his clasped hand as he slips back between the sheets.

Delight gleams in my favorite landscape of stormy blue. "It's for you," he says and hands me the gold box.

I remove the lid. The air flees my lungs. A silver, heart-shaped locket sits on a cloud of white cotton.

"Open it," John whispers.

I gently pry it apart with my fingernails. Inside is a small cutout picture of us that Vera took on Valentine's Day. I don't know what comes over me, but tears well in my eyes when I see the inscription: *Forever, my Kat. Love, John*

He freezes when he realizes I'm about to cry. "What's the matter?"

"I love it," I squeak. Pulling his face to mine, I press a kiss to his lips and pray he didn't jinx us.

I haven't had a chance to tell him that I finished reading the book and that Katherine broke up with Michael in *Forever*. That no one could really promise forever. Not even us.

Dr. Graham's Office

I'M EMOTIONALLY EXHAUSTED after finishing the story. I glance over at Dr. Graham. She's taking copious notes on her pad.

By the time she puts down her pencil, we've gone over our session by fifteen minutes.

I shift forward and prepare to get up.

"Stay a minute longer. I don't have a patient for another thirty minutes."

I relax back onto the leather.

She grabs her chin and furrows her brow. "Do you still have the locket?"

I shake my head, wishing I did. "No."

"Where is it?"

Pressing my eyes shut, I shake my head again and answer her as honestly as I'm willing. "I don't know."

Chapter 21

John

September 2016 – Jillian and Raine's House

MY GRUNTS JOIN Raine's as we finish our last set of free weights in his home gym. I eye the mirror. I'll never have the kind of bulging muscles that cover Raine from neck to calves, but I'm finally at a point where I'm not embarrassed to remove my shirt.

The spare tire I've been packing for years around my middle has flattened into submission and given way to more than a hint of abs and a V-shaped torso I haven't seen since my thirties.

Between my workout schedule over the last five months and Raine's cooking lessons, I'm on my way back to health and fitness. A freaking miracle after years of apathy and neglect. But I'd be lying if I said my sole motivation was avoiding the Type II diabetes path I was on.

The tat over my heart winks out at me in the mirror. "KAT," written in lacy script and embedded inside the dagger and feather mural that covers my chest. A reminder of a promise I made to myself. A promise I hope someday to keep, now that—

Raine thrusts a water bottle at me. The corner of his mouth lifts in amusement. "Admiring your handiwork?"

I blink and it takes me a moment to realize he's talking about my slimmer look and not my ink. My frown melts away and I take the water. "Nope. Just thinking 'bout something."

Raine wipes his face with a towel and drops down onto one of the weight benches. "Talk to Kitty yet?"

I let loose a deep breath.

So we're finally going there, are we? I've wondered how long Raine could hold out on asking me that.

Right after Jillian and Raine's wedding I spotted a FOR SALE sign on Kat's front lawn and assumed the shit had hit the fan. But it wasn't until I showed up for my next workout with Raine that Jillian took me aside afterward and shared the news about Kat's divorce.

One month. Raine held out from asking for a whole bloody month. Good man.

I bury my face in a towel to buy a second to school my face into nonchalance, and then use the soft cloth to rid myself of the dampness covering my neck and chest. "Not yet," I murmur.

Raine raises his eyebrows and tilts his head. "What are you waiting for? A silver-plated invitation?"

Exasperation and hope have me in a chokehold I can't wiggle out of. I settle on the weight bench across from his and rest an elbow on my thigh as I pass a hand over my face to erase the grimace I know is there.

Once I'd let my guard down with Raine at the hospital when Rachel was born in June, there was no going back. Surprised the shit out of me that it felt kind of good. So I've slowly let him in.

After years of having no one to relieve the strain Kat has exerted on my soul, telling Raine even the little I did released some of the pressure I didn't realize was eating me alive. Not that I've turned into a gossipy girl since then, but having a friend—even one young enough to be my son—has been a lifesaver.

I hang my head, shake it, and release a breath. "It's too soon. I tried to call. Left her a message. She hasn't called back." *Hey, Kat. It's me. . . . I heard. I'm really sorry. I'm here if you want to talk.*

Something resembling sympathy fills Raine's eyes and he purses his lips. "How long you going to let it ride?"

Blowing out a breath, I stare at my scarred and calloused hands, trying to shove down the sliver of hope that someday I'll get to run my fingers over her skin again. "She said she might come to our thirty-fifth high school reunion. It's next month." My jaw twitches with self-doubt. "It's been a lot of years, kid. There's a good chance I've been imaging that I'll have another shot."

He snorts and says, "Are you fucking blind?" Then he shakes his finger at me with a lifted brow and a sardonic grin. "You think she's not gonna want some of that? The way she looks at you? I'd lay down good money that once she recovers from the blow of losing her husband—God, forgive me—to another *dude*, she'll be on your doorstep."

Fucking hell.

I haven't felt like this since I was in high school. Heat creeps up my neck and fills my ears. "You're good for my ego, you know that?" I give him a sideways glance and half a smile.

He shrugs and fist-bumps me. "That's what friends are for, old man." He smiles back, his white teeth shining in a face much younger and prettier than mine.

I throw him a glare. "You better stop calling me that, or I might take you a few rounds."

Raine's smile falters and he lifts himself off the bench. "Ha! You might want to rethink that. I've been boxing since I was fifteen. How do you think I survived that bastard who called himself my father?"

A pang hits my chest and the bitter memories of my own father reach up and grab me. Too bad my boxing lessons didn't come until years after a few broken bones and the belt buckle scars now hidden underneath the ink on my back. "Sorry, that was insensitive."

He claps me on the shoulder and tosses his towel into a basket halfway across the room. "Nah. It's all good."

Even though his father sucked as a human being, there was one redeeming thread. He asked the Feds to protect Raine. If nothing else, I'll give him a shred of respect for that. "You sad he's dead?" I ask in a low voice.

Slowly, he shakes his head and meets my gaze with an intense blue stare. "No. I'm relieved. Dead, he can't hurt my family or me ever again. I'm glad my mom wasn't alive to see what went down, though I wish . . ." He rolls his lip between his teeth. "I wish she could've met Jillian and Rachel."

I nod, and the corner of my mouth lifts. "She would've been proud."

His gaze softens. "Thanks."

That's another thing we have in common—our mothers were good women. Mine still is. Though she stayed too long in a situation that cost my sister her life. It wasn't until adulthood that I truly understood Battered Wife Syndrome. What counts is she left my father and took me and my brother with her before one of us was next. She's retired now, living down in Miami with my stepdad, José, a retired doctor. A great guy. Treats my mother like gold. As for my real father? Like Raine, I'm not sad he's dead. I've made it my life's work to put people like him away.

The door cracks open, followed by a gleeful gurgle from my godbaby. A grin slides onto my face. I haven't gotten over the thrill of being a godfather.

"Are you guys decent? May we come in?" Jillian asks.

I lunge for my T-shirt. I'm not usually one for modesty, but something about Jillian seeing me half naked doesn't sit well.

Raine throws me a wink and heads toward the door. "Hey, baby, give John a minute to cover his hairy chest. You sure you want to come in? It's a sweaty dude zone in here." He's not wrong. The place smells like a mixture of heated sweat and rubber floor tiles.

A chuckle sounds from the hall. Raine gives me a quick once-over before letting the girls in and greeting his family with carefully deposited kisses.

"Morning, Jilly," I say on my stroll over.

Jillian offers me a cheek. I drop a peck on her and another on the cooing cutie pie in her arms. "Early feeding?" I glance at the clock on the wall. It's six-twenty.

"Yup. The princess insisted on a bottle half an hour early," she says, bouncing the baby in her arms and wearing a glowing smile. "You guys want tea and coffee before your shower? It's ready."

Raine glances at me and smirks. "Not sure who I smell, but I'm thinking a shower first might be a good idea for everyone involved."

I resist the urge to do a pit check. I'd bet Raine and I smell equally offensive right now. "You're an angel, but I have to agree with your husband. Give me ten minutes?" The thought of coffee gives me a shudder of anticipation.

"I'll take my tea to-go, love. I have a 7:00 a.m. train to catch." Raine brushes a kiss over Jillian's lips then claps me on the shoulder. "Good workout. See you Wednesday."

I nod as he slips by Jillian and disappears.

"Join me for coffee upstairs after your shower?" Jillian asks a moment before Rachel's tiny fist clocks her in the collarbone. "Hey, missy, watch it with that right hook." The baby gives her a gummy smile and gurgles in amusement before trying to swallow her hand.

"Sure." I don't need convincing.

I'm halfway to the bathroom that's hiding behind a pocket door in the gym, when I hear her from down the hall. "Don't forget to bring your towel up!" I snort a laugh at her domestic request. Raine's one lucky bastard. It's kind of nice having someone give a shit where I leave my towel.

I strip down and stare into the mirror. Raine's right. I'm not as hard on the eyes anymore. I feel worthy enough for Kat to see me now. That thought alone awakens my sleepy groin . . . until my gaze catches on the thick, pink scar under my ribcage.

An old bullet wound.

A wound that cost me Kat.

JILLIAN HANDS ME the creamer and sits down across the table with the baby monitor.

She takes a sip from her mug, closes her eyes, and lets out a low, satisfied *mmm*. "This is the best part of not breastfeeding anymore. I can't believe how much I've missed coffee."

With an amused half chuckle, I inhale the deep, rich aroma. "I'm scary enough *with* coffee; you should see me on a day without it."

Jillian looks at me over the rim of her mug as I drink down a quarter of the hot Columbian brew. Her stare sticks.

"What?" I ask, feeling an immediate jolt from the caffeine.

She shifts in her seat and chews the inside of her mouth like she's measuring her words before she speaks. Shit. That could only mean one thing.

My eyelids sag under the weight of my frown. Setting down the mug, I brace myself for what I anticipate will be a line of Kat-related questioning. "Just ask, Jilly."

"Are you going to call Kitty?" *Bingo.*

I blow out a breath and rub a hand over my eyes. "Why?"

She shrugs. "She could use a friend?"

As much as I've been forthcoming with Raine, I'm not sure how comfortable I am airing my feelings with Jillian though I love her like a kid sister. She's one step closer to Kat, and my biggest fear is that I'll look pathetic or appear too eager. It's not like I haven't been down this road. Even after my divorce from Carmela, as bad as that marriage turned out to be, I still needed time afterward. Rushing into things too soon usually spells disaster for the first person post-breakup. After waiting all these years, I sure as shit don't want to end up as a casualty on Kat's road to recovery.

"She knows where to find me, if and when she's ready," I say, and give Jillian a thoughtful look. "I appreciate what you're trying to do, but I don't want to push her. She needs time to grieve her marriage."

Jillian nods and clutches her cup. "You're right."

I take another gulp of coffee, fight the urge to ask about Kat, and lose. "How's she doing?" I finally whisper.

Jillian's brow twitches up and she rubs her thumb back and forth over the mug handle. "I've never seen her like this before."

"How so?"

"Depressed. She's lost an unhealthy amount of weight since the beginning of summer. But it's more than that. I can't explain it. She's been fragile, brittle even, ever since Vera died last summer. Something's been wrong since way before their break-up." Jillian clutches her mug with both hands and shakes her head. "I don't know . . . something else. More."

I shrug. "I haven't been around her enough to be sure, but I know what you mean." I've seen it too, but I haven't been in a position to do squat about it. I feel another frown coming on. I'd been so worried about the issue with Bob that I'd tamped down my instincts. *Maybe I should stop by . . . just check in?* The decision settles to an affirmative.

A sad smile spreads across Jillian's lips. "Last summer, the night of Vera's memorial service, she told me how you both met in high school. That's the first time she's ever mentioned the early years. You both seemed so right for each other."

A pang of longing grips me. After meeting Kat, my junior and senior years of high school were some of the best years I've ever had. Her innocence gave me a chance to renew mine. Between her and the football scholarship, life was shiny and new, filled with hopes and dreams. I should've known I'd never be able to hold onto it all.

I stare into my coffee and mumble more to myself than Jillian. "We were kids. What did we know?"

She reaches across the table and clutches my forearm. Hard. "You came back right after Drew died, you saw the aftermath of what that did to me. How could you say that?" There's sadness so deep in those golden eyes of hers that I draw in a breath. I remember that first time seeing Jillian after Kat and I got back together. My heart tore open for her, because, yeah, it resonated. Chafed old wounds that never really healed.

"We may have been kids, too, but we knew . . . Knew what it was like to love deeply . . . My love for Drew and his loss affected most of my adult life. You can't deny that it wasn't the same for you and Kitty. You forget, I've borne witness to your relationship since I was six years old. You can't tell me your love for each other didn't color your whole lives."

My knuckles turn white as I choke the coffee cup. Jillian might as well have just flayed off a layer of my skin. I shut down my expression and press my lips into a hard line. I don't want to go there. Admitting it is the same as telling her what a failure I've been. Something I want so fucking desperately to come back from.

Her fingers tighten and dig deeper into my arm. "Drew *died!* That's what ended us. That's the *only* thing that separated us. Thank God, neither of you have that excuse, but you both walk around with enough pain as if you do. Tell me . . . Tell me why neither of you will ever talk about it. What happened that was so bad it made your whole relationship off-limits for discussion? I love you both. I want to help. Please . . . let me help." Her tone has turned from pleading to desperate.

I swallow what feels like a pound of rocks. Discomfort crawls over my skin like an army of biting insects in the sandy trenches of Kuwait. No matter where I've been, I've never run far enough. The accumulated pain from all the years of starts and stops with Kat without an opportunity for closure has taken its toll. Unfinished business has left a black, gaping hole in my soul whose maw isn't satisfied with anything I've tried to fill it with that isn't Kat. Kat is my unfinished business. Kat is the hole. Kat represents everything I ever was and ever wanted to be . . . and everything I lost.

I drop my head into my hands and rub my palms over my face, then look into Jillian's desperate eyes. Some I'm able to tell, some I'm not.

"Please . . . ," she pleads.

I mumble a curse. After a few beats of serious contemplation and several deep breaths, I decide to break my silence. "You win . . . June 1981, you were eight . . ."

Chapter 22

John

June 1981 – High School Graduation Day

"I'LL KEEP THAT safe," my mom says, liberating the diploma from my hand and placing it with care inside of her purse. "I wish your brother could be here. I'm so proud, *cariño.*" She stands on tiptoe and wraps her arms around my neck. My cheeks heat with the attention while the hot sun sends sweat rolling down my back underneath the black nylon graduation gown.

She throws herself at Kat next, smiling broadly. "You too, *chica.* Your parents must be so happy." Clutching her diploma, Kat squeezes my mother tight and beams. We both graduated with honors, me by sheer luck and Kat because she's smart.

"Thank you, Rosita," she says, bending down into the hug. Hearing Kat call my mom by her first name feels somewhere between nails down a chalkboard and getting caught naked in public. Normally, my mother considers it disrespectful—enough to slap me upside the head if she heard me do it—but she refuses to use my father's name because she hates him, and avoids her maiden name for fear that the fine people of Summit will think I'm illegitimate. She'd anglicized my name and Ben's when we moved to Summit so that we could blend in. So Rosita it is.

I slip my arms around the two most important women in my life and steer them through the milling sea of black-robed graduates and parents looking for their offspring. It's a miracle my mom found us on the field so quickly after the ceremony.

159

We just clear the fence onto the dusty track when I spot Kitty's father towering over the crowd and glancing in our direction.

I whisper into Kat's ear. "Three o'clock."

Kat looks to her right and waves frantically at her dad above everyone's head.

"Kitty!" He smiles and waves back.

My shoulders tense the closer we get to Kat's family. In the year and a half we've dated, my mom has never met her parents. I'd be delusional to think it's due to anything other than a lack of interest and respect based on all the crap her mother has pulled since Kat and I met. Forgotten phone messages, after-the-fact invitations, misinformation, ruined holiday and birthday plans . . . generally making our lives miserable. You name it, she's tried it. All because my half-Cuban blood will never be blue enough for her daughter.

Vera peels away from Kat's parents. When she reaches us, she wraps my mom in a warm embrace. "Rosita, so good to see you! Do you believe these two are off to college next year? Where does the time go?"

My mother laughs softly and tosses her long, dark hair over her shoulder. "Stop, you're making me feel old."

Vera gives her a wry look. "You, old? Never." Then she pulls me and Kat into a group hug. "I'm so proud of you two! Johnny, are you and Rosita coming to the house later?"

"Huh?" I frown, caught off guard.

She narrows her eyes and her gaze shifts to Kat. "The party?" Kat flinches and I can feel fury at her mother rise with the tightening of her fingers around mine. But in typical Kat-style, she does an elegant job of spinning the truth. Not to protect *her* mother, but to protect the delicate feelings of *mine*.

Her free hand flies to her mouth and she gives me that look, the signal to play along. Part of our secret language. We've used it dozens of times. Then she speaks, "I thought—Didn't I—? I just assumed—*Oh my God*. I'm so sorry. You can both come to Vera's later, can't you?" Kat says, delivering a stellar performance.

My mom glares at me. "*Juan?* You forgot to tell me?" Rather than blaming Kat—in typical Mom-style—she blames me. According to her, it's never the woman's fault. Then she slips into rapid Spanish and tells me what she really thinks—for a smart boy I have a lousy memory and she hopes that I don't have a brain tumor.

Suppressing an eye roll, I stand there and take it. "Sorry."

Vera shoots me a look that says she knows exactly what's going on and covers for her bitch of a sister with a winning smile. "Seven o'clock, my place?"

My mom blushes, no doubt embarrassed and feeling more than a little uncomfortable as her gaze travels to where Kat's parents are chatting with another family.

Vera has hosted several dinners on babysitting nights with only the five of us, including Jillian, but never with Kat's parents. It's been no small chore making excuses for Kat's mother's rudeness over the last eighteen months. Instead, Kat's hinted to my mom in hushed tones that her mother is mentally unbalanced, spends most of her time medicated, and can't be trusted in polite company.

"Of course. *Gracias*, Vera." My mom arches a reproachful brow at me and says, "We will be there."

I nod and press my lips shut. My sour expression gives way to a smile as Jillian runs full tilt toward me and launches herself into my arms. "Johnny!"

I hoist her up and kiss her nose. "Hey, princess."

"I saw you walk to the stage."

"What am I, chopped liver over here?" Kat asks, tugging on Jillian's arm.

Jillian giggles. "No, Kitty. Liver is disgusting."

"Daddy," Kat says as her father arrives and enfolds her in a hug.

"Congratulations, baby girl."

After a prolonged squeeze, she steps out of his arms and he extends a hand to my mother. "Ms. Henshaw, I'm Kitty's father, Bill McNally."

My mother gives him a polite smile. "Rosita, please."

He smiles back. "Rosita." Then he offers his giant mitt to me, and there's a genuine look of pride as he shakes my hand. "Congratulations, John."

I flush, warmed that he made the effort even though Kat's mother hasn't so much as cast a glance in our direction.

"See you at the house at seven," Vera says.

"Give this to my mom?" Kat asks, handing Vera her diploma. Vera nods then departs in Viv's direction, where she's holding court fifteen yards away with someone's parents.

Kat squeezes my arm, giving me another signal. "Dad, tell Mom

I'll be home to change before the party. We're going to say hello to some friends."

"See you later, princess," I say to Jillian and set her back on her feet. I glance at my mom. "Be home later to shower and pick you up for the party."

"*Sí, cariño.*" She leans in for a kiss and then turns a polite smile to Kat's father. "Very nice to meet you, Bill."

He takes her small hand a second time. "See you at dinner."

My mom shoots me a quick glance filled with something close to dread before she waves and totters off in her heels toward the parking lot.

Kat tugs on my arm. "Later, Dad."

"Say hello to your mother before you run off," Mr. McNally says, wearing a stern frown, before ambling back with Jillian to rejoin the pit viper as we linger behind.

As soon as he's out of earshot, Kat groans and mumbles, "Gird your loins."

"Ha! As if that'll help," I mumble back. A sound of disgusted agreement rises from her throat. She threads her fingers through mine and tugs me toward her mother to fake polite conversation. My stomach sours with every step closer.

Well-coiffed and looking every bit the snobby socialite in her pink designer suit, Vivian McNally runs her slithery, bug-squashing gaze over me. It takes less than a second for her to throw down the gauntlet. "Congratulations. Nice to see you graduated," she says, capping her comment with an arctic smile.

Bitch.

Vera gives her a sideways glare laced with disgust.

"Mom, please," Kat grinds out.

My smile doesn't falter. "Amazing, isn't it? Graduated with honors, just like your daughter."

"Yes . . . amazing."

I keep smiling and wonder how it's possible for someone who's ten inches shorter to look *down* her nose at me. It's like being trapped inside the M. C. Escher lithograph of Penrose's impossible stairs on the cover of my math book.

Kat gives her mother a quick hug. "We'll see you later." We make our escape and lose ourselves in the crowd before the pit viper can respond. My shoulders slump with relief as soon as we're out of striking distance.

I spot Matt up ahead and wave. "Mad Dog!"

He turns and reverses course through the flow of bodies.

Looking as sweaty as I feel, he's dragging a hand through his dark hair to unplaster it from the side of his head as he walks up. "Hey, Shaw. Freaking boiling out here."

"No shit." We do the bump-slap-hand-grab move all my teammates use to greet each other.

"Hey, Kat. Happy graduation." They trade a loose hug, and then he slaps my shoulder. "You ready for tomorrow?"

I wish the team's annual beach party wasn't a guy-only thing. Matt's hosting it at his parents' LBI shore house, and bringing girlfriends was voted down by the team for the third year running. Not that it will kill me or Kat to be apart for a day, but it would be much nicer with her there.

At least Kat and I have a couple of days before I report to Rutgers for the football clinic this weekend. After that, we have most of the summer ahead of us until I leave in August for pre-semester football training.

Deciding on colleges this year ended in a grudge match of epic proportions between Kat and her mother. Kat wanting to go to NYU so that we're in commutable distance from each other, and her mother insisting on Stanford to take advantage of some endowment set up for Kat between her dead grandfather and his alma mater. Endowment or not, with her grades Kat had no problem getting accepted. Although we both graduated with honors, Kat was at the top of the spectrum while I barely clawed my way in.

No doubt Viv had two reasons to lobby hard for Stanford: a free education compliments of Kat's grandfather and enough distance to put a major crimp in my plan with Kat to stay together. Kat ultimately won with Vera's help, but not without collateral damage—the relationship with her mother.

"Nine a.m., your house, right?" I ask.

"Yup," Matt says. "We'll take Steve's van and convoy down to LBI with the rest of the team. Can you pick up a few six-packs?"

I nod. "See you then."

We get a few yards away and Kat lets loose on me. "Your teammates are lunatics. Please be careful and promise me you're not going to start drinking at nine in the morning."

I snort a laugh and give her a playful side eye. "We may be lunatics but we're not idiots. The beer is for the beach volleyball tournament." She grumbles a response I can't make out. I let it go.

We stop for hugs and chats as we drift through the masses until I've reached my limit of congratulating, back slapping, and broiling in the unrelenting sun. I pull Kat behind the bleachers in search of shade and a moment of peace.

Brushing a wave of curled hair behind her ear, I cup her face in my hands and kiss her like it's the last chance I'll ever get. Despite the oppressive heat, I pull her close, needing to breathe in her scent as I yearn to feel her body underneath me. It's been a couple weeks since we've spent any quality time together, and it's killing me. I'm hot, bothered, and more than a little horny.

I give her a crooked smile. "I can't wait to celebrate after all the celebrations."

She runs her hands down my back until she's clasping two handfuls of my ass. Her lip catches between her teeth and there's a wicked gleam in her eye. "You have no idea what I want to do to you right now," she whispers.

Screw the heat. A shiver hits my spine, and my groin awakens with a vengeance. "Does it have anything to do with your hot mouth?" I ask, rough with need.

"Maybe," she says, and grinds her hips into mine. My eyes nearly roll back in my head.

"Tease." Two can play this game. I casually slide my hands along her sides until I'm close enough to swipe my thumbs over the center of her breasts.

She moans and shifts away. "Now who's the tease?"

"Pretend it's my tongue."

She narrows her eyes and runs her hand over the hardening bulge in my pants. "Same here."

I jump back and laugh low in my throat. "You're an evil woman, Kat McNally."

She snakes her fingers through mine, reels me in closer, and lays a gentle kiss on my lips. "Only when it comes to you, ya big lug."

"Sneak out at eleven and meet me down the road? We'll have a little celebration over on Memorial Field?"

Her eyes light up. "I'll see if I can find a bottle of something to bring."

My brows rise. "You're going to raid Bill and Viv's liquor cabinet?"

She shrugs. "They don't drink much and the cabinet's packed. I'll find something I don't think they'll miss. Easy peasy."

I shake my head and run my fingers through her hair, damp from the heat. "I like the idea, but don't do anything that will give Viv another excuse to make our lives miserable."

"You only live once, Shaw," she says, and plants a kiss on my lips.

"Yeah, well, we'll have plenty of time to live once we're out of here. In the meantime, I want to spend every minute with you and enjoy whatever freedom we have this summer without the Dragon Lady examining our every move."

Too bad we both have to work to save for school, and in my case, help my mom, too. Kat dumping the Stanford deal made it necessary to get some financial aid to pay her way. Vera's helping, but Kat's on her own for spending money.

She kisses my lower lip. "As much as I'd love to make out with you on the freaking hottest day of the year under the school bleachers, I could use a shower before dinner at Vera's."

I nip her nose with my teeth. "Me too."

A cold one, and for more reasons than the blistering heat.

"Kat, what is this vile shit?" I ask after taking a swig out of the bottle Kat pilfered for our celebration on Memorial Field. I knew I should've picked up something extra at the liquor store. If I hadn't been so low on funds after buying the six-packs for tomorrow and filling the Black Beast with gas, I would've done just that.

Kat answers in the darkness from where she lies on the blanket next to me. "O'Connor's Irish Crème de Menthe. Vera's favorite. My parents hate it, but they don't have the heart to tell her, so they just shove the bottles to the back of the cabinet and pretend they drank it. Guaranteed they'll never know it's gone."

"*Ugh.* No wonder. It's fucking awful." I gaze at the stars and try to clear the taste from my palate.

"Gimme." She wiggles her fingers in the silvery moonlight.

If tonight had been any other phase of the moon, I wouldn't have had a chance at doing a successful handoff without a flashlight. I hand her the bulbous bottle. "Here."

She takes a gulp and smacks her lips. "*Hmm. It's* not that bad . . . in a pinch. Desperate times, desperate measures, and all that." She hands the bottle back to me.

Fuck it. I groan and drink some more.

We're down to half a bottle before I cap it and set it aside.

"That stuff tastes like crap, but damn it if I'm not nursing a healthy buzz." I find Kat in the dark and wrap my arms around her. She giggles and liberates the hem of my shirt from my jeans. I shift my hips so she can get at the back.

"Admit it . . . you like that slice of minty heaven just a little."

My lips stretch into a smile. "Definitely not my definition of heaven, but consumable in a crisis."

"Ingrate." She finds the ticklish spot on my side.

I laugh and squirm away from her, clutching my elbow to my body for protection. "Don't fight dirty." I roll on top of her, pin her underneath me, and trail a path up her neck with my tongue.

"Shaw!" she shrieks, and writhes against me, dissolving into a fit of laughter and trying to free herself. I'm not the only one with a wicked ticklish spot. Hers is always worse when she's on her back.

Eighteen months of intimate experimentation have provided ample time to explore each other's landscapes and map out weaknesses.

Not only that; Kat's been a sponge, absorbing everything I've taught her — including how to give a stellar blow job — while adding her own imagination to make it even better.

I've never trusted anyone as much as I trust Kat, and I know I have her trust in return. The guys on the team go through girls like six-packs, but not me. There's no one else for me but Kat. She's had my heart since the day I met her. The thought of being without her is the only thing sucking the joy out of going to college. But it's also a good thing for my focus on the game.

She stills under me. "You okay?"

I shake my head to clear it. "Just going to miss you come fall," I whisper.

Her eyes shine. She cups my cheek and passes a thumb over my lower lip. "Me too. I'm going to miss you, too, but we'll see each other on weekends when you have home games and on breaks. It'll be fine."

I collapse down next her and pull her back onto my chest. "At least your mother behaved tonight at Vera's. Maybe there's hope for the holidays yet."

She gives a derisive sniff and runs her fingers in lazy circles over my pecs. "I'm sure her behavior was tempered by Vera's threat of expulsion if she insulted you or your mom." I'm not surprised.

"You and your mom talking yet?" I ask.

"Outside of today? No . . . not really."

"Sorry about that," I murmur, painfully aware that I'm responsible for Kat's choice in schools. Up until she met me, she'd been working toward that acceptance at Stanford.

"Don't be," she murmurs, and kisses my chest through the shirt she'd started to remove before we ended up on a tickle tangent. "I'd choose you over Stanford any day. NYU's a great school. So stop apologizing."

I rest my lips on the top of her head and stroke her hair, letting the soft strands caress my palm. "I love you, Kat McNally. I want to marry you someday."

Her fingers pause on their slow, soothing path, and she lifts her chin so that she stares into my eyes. "I love you too, Shaw. . . . May I ask you something?"

I nod. "*Um-hmm.*"

She hesitates and chews the inside of her mouth. "You sure you want kids someday? When we first started dating . . . the thought seemed to scare you." Her gaze locks on mine, and for the first time, I see concern. "If we're going to be together, I need to know."

I press my eyes shut and decide it's time to tell her about Denise, hoping like hell it doesn't change her opinion of me. It's still true that I'm fearful of becoming my father—not out of choice, but rather, due to genetics. But that's only the tip of the issue. It's always gone deeper than that. Bone deep, no, make that soul deep.

I smooth her hair with my palm. "Kat . . . I . . . ." I try again. My brow knits tight and I try to whisper the words I've never said out loud. They travel over the lump in my throat and make a tenuous exit. "It's my fault that Denise is dead."

"What do you mean?" she asks softly but without a hint of judgment.

"My mom had a late shift at the salon, and Ben had to work his convenience store job after school. It was my turn to watch her. I should've been home when the bus dropped her off after school." I shake my head. "I wasn't . . . I was at Carmela's."

She lifts her brows. "And?"

My pulse quickens. Images bear down on me of my sister lying in a small heap at the bottom of the stairs with her neck broken, and my father crying over her lifeless body. Her dead eyes staring at the ceiling but not seeing. I swallow to loosen the words caught in my constricted airway. "I found her . . . dead at the bottom of the stairs," I whisper. "My father said it was an accident, said she tripped . . . but I know he pushed her."

Kat's frown deepens and she caresses my cheek. "How's that your fault?"

"I wasn't home to protect her." My jaw clenches. "If I had been home on time, she'd be alive."

She cradles my cheek in her hand, presses her lips together, and shakes her head. "You can't know that."

"Can't I?" There's nothing anyone can say that will ever ease my guilt.

She shakes her head. "No, you can't. It's not your fault, Shaw."

I capture her hand and pull it away from my face. "If I had been there when she got home, my father would've never gotten near her."

She releases an exasperated breath and gives me the look she reserves for times when she knows she can't win an argument. "So what happened to your father?"

"The police took him for questioning, then dropped the investigation," I mumble.

Kat leaps back from my chest, her eyes flashing. "Are you kidding me?"

I shake my head. "Nope. My dad may have been a lowlife, but he had some strong ties on the police force."

Her shoulders droop and she lies back down next me. "Is that when you left Bayonne?"

I nod. "Yeah. The night of the funeral, my father went out to get tanked and my mother took us and ran with the help of a friend."

"How come it took her so long?"

"She didn't have any means. My dad took her paychecks. Her friend who owned the salon helped with our escape. He shaved money off her wages and gave her two checks every week for a year.

One she gave my dad and the other she socked away in the bank under her maiden name."

"God, I'm sorry . . . about all of that," Kat says.

I pull her close and release a long breath. "It sucks, but it is what it is. So, it's not as much having kids that scares me as losing them . . . like I lost Denise." As I say the words, I know it's the truth. There's something therapeutic about my admission. "Do you think that's nuts or what?"

She goes back to doodling on my chest with her fingertip. "Not nuts at all. You're lucky to be alive and safe. . . . Shaw?"

"Yeah?"

She rests her chin on my chest. "You'll make an amazing dad." She smiles. "Someday."

The corner of my mouth lifts. "Someday . . . As long as you're the mom," I say and mean it.

"I want that," she whispers and then scoots up and hovers her lips over mine. "You're my Kryptonite, John Henshaw. You make me weak."

"And you're mine, Kitten," I say, diving into her minty-tasting mouth and putting my mark on the one person who could ever bring me to my knees. I explore, probe, taste, memorize the feel of her lips and the way her tongue caresses mine as my hands run up and down her sides. I kiss her until the lack of oxygen leaves me breathless, then I slide her on top of me, giving her control.

"I need you, Kat . . . now."

She kisses one corner of my mouth and then the other. "Be patient for me, Shaw." A spark dances in her eyes and she shimmies down my body, unbuttoning and sliding down my jeans along the way. Air hits bare skin a second before Kat's hot mouth slides over my length and consumes me.

Holy hell.

A loud groan escapes from my throat before I can stop it. My hips shift up and I fist the blanket on either side of me. *Damn.* Give the teacher an apple and the student a gold star. I taught her well.

My eyes clench shut and my breath hitches as her fingers hit all my hot buttons and her tongue bathes me in liquid heaven. But if she keeps this up, it's all over.

Just when I think I might lose it, she pulls away and I hear a condom wrapper rip open. She sheaths me in rubber before straddling my hips and getting into position on top of me. I clasp her waist, thrust deep, and groan as my nerve endings fire.

She plants her hand on the center of my chest and I let her ride me hard, doing my best to hold on while she warms up on her path to release.

We hit an urgent, rocking rhythm and she purrs deep in her throat, stroking me with her tight heat. I shift my focus and pull her close enough to push up her shirt and free her breasts to occupy my mouth before I lose my mind in the only form of mental insanity I care to indulge in.

She runs her fingers through my hair and cradles my head as I stay busy teasing her toward climax. Her body tightens in a caressing handshake as she cries out, and her nails scrape down my sides. That's all I need to crest my own wave and unload in a sharp, pulsating surge that bows my spine. I shudder one last time and lie back. Kat collapses on top of me and drapes herself over my chest. Damn, we're amazing together after a solid year of practice.

Panting to catch my breath, pinpricks of light, brighter than any stars, dance behind my eyelids. It's only when Kat gasps and clenches her knees into my sides that I crack open my eyes . . . into a flashlight.

Fuck me.

A throat clears. "Nope. Not a bear. Just two teenagers," the cop says over a hand radio before clipping it to his belt. He picks up the bottle of minty madness and kills the light.

"I'll give you three minutes to pull yourselves together. Meet me by the bleachers with your IDs."

I cover my face with my hands and try not to die of embarrassment. At least Kat's skirt is covering most of the view. "Yes, officer."

He ambles away. Kat rolls off me and squeaks in a hushed whisper, "Holy shit! We're in trouble."

"Don't panic," I whisper back as she makes quick work of disappearing the condom and wrapper. God bless Kat for always being prepared. Lucky this isn't our first rodeo.

We readjust our clothes and pack our things, then trudge to the bleachers like convicts on our way to jail while I assess the potential charges. *Fuck.* This isn't going to end well. Bastards raised the drinking age a year ago, and Kat's still two months shy of her nineteenth birthday.

Summit's finest already has his flashlight on as he writes up what looks like a ticket.

"IDs," he says without looking up. Kat and I dig out our driver's licenses and silently hand them over.

The officer, who looks like he's in his early twenties, glances at us in between writing. "Graduate today?"

"Yup," I say, my teeth grinding behind my cheek.

"As a graduation present, I'm not going to include public fornication, trespassing, or public intoxication, but I *am* citing you both for having an open container in public. Not a big issue for you, Mr. Henshaw, since you're nineteen and legally an adult." He finishes scribbling, rips off the ticket, and hands it to me.

"But for Miss McNally here," He holds up Kat's license, "who is still considered underage until August, she gets a free ride to the police station and a phone call to her parents along with the fine."

My fists clench at my sides and I fight for whatever control I can find. If I thought we had problems with Viv before, this will make it ten times worse. But before I can open my mouth to speak, Kat beats me to it.

"No, please! Don't call my parents. They think I'm home in bed," Kat pleads.

"Sorry, Miss McNally, no can do. You're both first-time offenders, so a little embarrassment and a small check will make this all go away." He rips off another citation and hands it to Kat, then stands and grabs the flashlight.

"And kids, find someplace else to drink and fuck. We patrol here a couple of times a night and the neighbors walk their dogs fairly frequently. Generally, we won't bust your balls if we find you out here fully clothed without alcohol, but when we get a call-in, like tonight, and I find what I find?" His brows quirk up and he gives a flat-lipped head shake. "I patrol here most Wednesday and Sunday nights." He shoots me a glare. "Catch my meaning, Mr. Henshaw?"

I sigh. "Yes, sir." Keep my dick in my pants and the juice at home, at least on Wednesdays and Sundays.

"And because I'm a generous kind of guy and have a soft spot for this park, I won't mention any unnecessary details to Miss McNally's parents outside of what's in the citation."

I almost drop to my knees in gratitude. "Thank you."

He's right, he did us a favor, but I doubt Kat's mother or mine will see it that way, even without the fornication charge. We've been lucky for over a year coming here and doing just that, drinking and, well, fucking . . . though with Kat I'd rather call it making love.

"Are you going to cuff me?" Kat asks in a small voice.

The officer chuckles and waves us toward the parking lot where I left the Black Beast. "No, Miss McNally, not unless you commit a more serious crime on the way to my cruiser."

Chapter 23

John

Jillian and Raine's Kitchen

WHEN I'M DONE with my trip down memory lane, I realize that I probably shared a tad too much detail, but you'd never know it from the mesmerized look and grin on Jillian's face.

"No wonder Kitty hates O'Connor's. I can't believe you and Kitty got caught having sex on Memorial Field!" She giggles like a giddy schoolgirl.

My neck flushes hot and I shake my head. "Sorry, I should've filtered some of that."

"Oh my God, I'm so glad you didn't! I would've paid good money to hear these stories." Resting an elbow on the table, she leans forward and props her head on a raised fist, staring at me with those big, golden eyes of hers. "So what happened next? Did my parents have a cow or what?"

I cross my arms over my chest and rock back in the chair. "Yeah. Total shit storm. We tried to reach Vera but couldn't, so Kat called your dad and he came to the station to get her. He was surprisingly cool about it, but we didn't have a prayer with Viv. Kat got grounded for sneaking out and stealing the O'Connor's. By the time I got home, your mom had already called mine. And whatever she said had my mom in tears."

Jillian sighs, her brows knitting into a frown. "My mother wasn't a nice person, was she?"

"Not to me," I say. But what happened after made me

173

understand her a little more and hate her a little less than I did that night.

Jillian's gaze softens and she reaches across the table for my hand and squeezes. "I'm sorry she was so awful to both of you. All my memories from back then were fond ones of you and Kitty. I didn't realize any of that."

I squeeze her back, then slide my hand away. "I know, Jilly. You were just a kid. Be glad you and Kat aren't like her."

Jillian's smile turns thoughtful. "I like that you call her Kat. No one else has ever called her that."

I shrug. "That was who she was to me. Brave, strong, smart, loving . . . my Kat." Speaking the words triggers a wistful pang of longing in my chest.

"Is that the incident that tore you apart?"

I raise an offended eyebrow. "Jeez, Jillian. Do you think that little of me? Or Kat? That wouldn't have been enough to keep us apart." I shake my head and my gut clenches as I think about what came after. My role in it, and the part that's baffled me for thirty-five freaking years.

"Then what was it?"

"That's just it . . . I can tell you what *happened*, but I can't *explain* it—because I don't know. It's been a goddamn mystery to me ever since it went down. Even ten years later when Kat and I reconnected. Nothing. No clue. Just a waltz around the truth."

Jillian narrows her eyes. "What happened?"

After a deep breath, I start my descent into the hellish days that followed. "Our bad luck that night turned out to be the bellwether for everything that followed."

June 1981 - Day After Graduation

"UGGG . . ." I slap the alarm clock next to my bed and try to ignore the pulsing behind my eye sockets. *Fucking O'Connor's.*

Memories of last night at the police station come rushing back in a deluge.

I give Kat's dad credit, he could've taken me out back and slapped me around or ripped me a new one, but he didn't do either. Instead, he seemed sympathetic and more put out from being woken up in the middle of the night than by the actual crime.

Since I met Kat, he's always stepped in if Viv pushed too far in his presence, and he's never made me feel unsuitable for his daughter.

I seriously consider bailing on the shore trip and trying to see Kat. But her father told me to lie low for a week and let things shake out with her mom. He's a good man and has my respect, unlike my own father. So, I'll consider taking his advice. At least he let me kiss Kat goodnight before he took her home.

What I'll never forgive? Viv making my mom cry last night. Mom won't tell me what transpired with the pit viper, but whatever she said had to be truly offensive to trigger my mom's protective defenses rather than her wrath. Other than a short diatribe about the *puta loca*, I got nothing.

Screw it. I might as well go to the shore.

I roll my ass and throbbing head out of bed and trek toward the shower.

The Black Beast rolls into Matt's driveway at a few minutes before nine. I park next to the other cars tucked at the end of the driveway. A few aspirin and a pair of sunglasses minimize the damage from last night's minty brew.

Looking at the rest of the crew, I'm not the only one who had a rough night. I greet my six teammates with no more than a grunt. They do the same as we pack the van and pile in.

I sleep most of the way down.

As usual, the day is filled with too much food, too much sun, way too much alcohol, and more than the usual show of testosterone on both sides of the volleyball net. I'm sort of glad we had to leave the girls behind after what went down last night. Saved me from having to talk about it.

Still nursing a hangover from the O'Connor's cordial disaster, I stick to beer and plenty of water.

The salty breeze keeps the insects at bay, and the cool water feels good after an afternoon of excess. I lose myself in the crashing waves and float on my back in waist-deep water, enjoying my escape from the rowdy shouting and chest thumping on the beach.

In a moment of self-reflection, I stare at the sky and thank God for delivering me from hell, giving me a future, and for Kat. I decide to get past this coming weekend's football clinic before I force my way into Kat's house. Hopefully, four days is enough cool-down time for her mother.

I hope our incident in the park doesn't screw up our summer. But I'm not going to panic. As Kat and I have proven throughout our relationship, where there's a will, there's a way.

By the time the bonfire on the beach is over and we've packed our gear in the van, I'm more than ready to hit the road and go home.

It's almost midnight when we get off the island and down the causeway to the Garden State Parkway. My world still feels off-kilter, like it's slipped off its axis. The only cure I can think of is to sleep my way into tomorrow. Steve, one of our defensive linemen who got accepted to Tulane, puts on some Pink Floyd, and I doze in the back.

The seatbelt snaps tight, cutting deep into my middle. I'm jolted awake straight into a nightmare. Screeching tires, panicked screams, and a deafening crash of twisted metal. I don't even have time to react before my head slams into the side panel with a solid *thud* followed by what feels like a herd of elephants coming down on top of my leg before a body slams into me.

The van flips.

I free fall, then lights out.

FRENETIC ACTIVITY, SHOUTS and the ear-splitting buzz of a chainsaw chewing through metal. Screams of agony. Red and blue pulsing lights. The taste of blood. Pain so intense I slide back into unconsciousness to escape.

"CARIÑO?" MY EYES flutter but don't open.

"I think he's waking up." My mother's relieved whisper among the beeps, whooshes, and whirs that make it sound like she's talking to me from the bottom of a tin can.

My eyes open to slits, but the intensity of the overhead lights almost blinds me, forcing my eyes to shut again. My head feels like it's swathed in cotton and my mouth tastes like a dry gym sock. The closer I get to consciousness, the more I feel like I've been run over by a Mack truck. Twice. *Screw it.* Three times.

Someone squeezes my shoulder with strong fingers. "Hey, *hermanito.*"

"Ben?" I rasp and try to keep my eyes open this time. "When did you get here?" I'm not really sure why I ask, but I think it's the right question. I feel weird, disconnected, and as close to an amnesiac as you can get. Must be the drugs. The last time I felt this way I had a concussion.

"Two days ago. I took emergency leave the day mom called." That was fast. Last I heard he was somewhere in the Middle East. "Sorry to drag you home."

He hovers over me, takes my hand, and clutches it. He looks good. Takes after my mom with brown eyes and skin that bronzes in the sun, while I take after our blue-eyed, light-skinned Anglo father. Ben's high and tight haircut and the dog tags dangling around his neck on top of a tight black shirt are the only signs giving him away as military.

"I'm the one who's sorry... for missing your graduation." A dimple dents his cheek when he smiles. Still hate that he's better looking than me. "I see you're taking good care of my Camaro."

I give a half-hearted sniff. "Mine. You gave it to me, remember?" I croak.

He releases my hand and retrieves a glass of water from the table near my head. I take a sip. The water trickles down my throat in a cool path straight to my stomach. I drink some more then give him the glass. "What happened to me?"

He sets aside the water, sits in the chair next to the bed, and rests his elbows on his thighs. Hanging his head, he blows out a breath before he's willing to look me in the eye and answer. "There was an accident on the Parkway. The guy driving your van fell asleep at the wheel. He hit three cars then rolled the van down an embankment. They had to cut you out.... All of you are lucky to be alive."

Holy fuck.

My brain catches up with everything he's said and the heart monitor goes wild. "Wait, how long have I been out? The clinic..."

He trades a heavy glance with Mom, who's been standing silently next to us stroking my hair.

I rub my eyes. "I missed it, didn't I?"

Ben nods. "The coach will be by later," he says quietly and avoids my eyes.

My stomach dives to my feet as unbridled fear claws at my chest. "What aren't you telling me?"

His gaze travels to the bottom of the bed and mine follows.

The sight of my left leg suspended from the ceiling with weights and pulleys shakes me out of my medicated fog. My lungs seize and I can't breathe.

I gasp for air, clawing the sheets and trying to get away from my own body. My mother bursts into tears and runs for the door as Ben's hand clamps onto my shoulder to hold me in place.

He shakes his head. "Breathe, *hermanito*. Don't panic. I'm here." Ben uses the same words he would say when we were kids and I'd wake from nightmares after a beating. The times those beatings ended with a cast.

My reaction is swift and brutal.

I break down and shake uncontrollably from a deep-seated panic triggered by seeing white plaster cover one of my body parts.

"*Shh* . . ." He presses my head into his chest, and I'm ten years old again. Except this time, the price of the plaster is much higher. I don't need a visit from the coach to know that I've lost my first-year scholarship . . . that I've lost my future.

I half sob, half scream into Ben's shirt as reality grabs me by the balls and twists. He holds on hard and says soothing things in Spanish.

Everything I've worked for is gone . . . lost . . . forfeited.

Twenty minutes later, I've cried myself out. I'm left feeling empty and bereft. "Where's Kat?" I ask in a lifeless monotone.

One corner of Ben's mouth lifts into a half smile. "She's pretty, your Kat. You were unconscious the last time she came. She'll be here in a little while."

Kat. I have nothing to give her now.

I'm nothing now.

Nothing.

For the first time since I met her, I don't want to see her.

I turn away from Ben, close my eyes, and let myself drift off to sleep, hoping I never wake up.

"SHAW? CAN YOU hear me?" Kat says, running her hand over my hair. I keep my eyes shut and pretend to sleep. It's the second time she's been here over the last two days, and the second time I've avoided her the only way I know how.

Coward. I'm a worthless coward. She deserves better.

I don't react as she strokes my hair and holds my hand.

The doctor delivered the news before the Rutgers coach dropped by to confirm what I suspected. Not only was my leg broken in two places, but it twisted in the crash, tearing my ACL. Fucking football injury without the benefit of going out in a blaze of glory on the field. Surgery is scheduled for tomorrow. I'm looking at eight to twelve weeks of recovery before I can start physical therapy. I'll never be what I once was . . . my football career is over before it even started, along with my shot at college.

To say I'm bitter and resentful is an understatement. Beyond angry? Too mild. What's happened has left me hungering for violence.

Kat drones on. I'm barely listening.

"The job at the Y is turning out to be pretty good," she says tentatively, clutching my hand and making small circles on the back with her thumb. "Mom and I are talking again. . . ."

She pauses and I hear her sniffle. Her voice has a brittle quality I've never heard before. "Come back to me, Shaw." She pulls my hand to her lips and kisses the back, crying softly. "I need you," she whispers. Her words cut my heart to ribbons, but there's nothing I can do to help myself, much less her.

I hate myself as I listen to her cry while I do nothing.

She sits for a little longer, then kisses my lips softly and leaves.

The moment the door shuts behind her, tears leak from the corners of my eyes, and I let them trail down the sides of my face until I fall asleep for real.

KAT VISITS TWO days later, right after my surgery. I can no longer fake unconsciousness. I can't fake much of anything, partially due to the drugs and partially due to my life falling straight into the shitter since the accident. At least I'm out of traction. *Whoopee.* I still have a catheter up my dick.

But I can no longer keep people at bay. I've suffered through a few well-meaning classmates who've stopped in on their way to see one of the other guys. Steve, Matt, and I took the brunt of the collision on our side of the van. We're all still here. Matt and Steve get discharged today: Matt with a broken jaw after recovering from a head injury, and Steve with a broken arm, a punctured lung, and one less kidney. None of their injuries will keep them out of the game. A bitter pill I can't bear to swallow.

"Shaw!" Kat's face lights up when she sees me awake. My smile is limp at best. She doesn't seem to notice as she runs full tilt toward the bed and throws her arms around me. Her lips hit mine and I do my best to return her kiss, but I fail miserably.

She pulls away and swallows, suddenly at a loss for what to do with her hands. "I came by, but you've been sleeping. I've been so worried about you." Doubt, fear, and panic mix in a strange brew behind her eyes, and she looks like she might come apart.

There's nothing I can do to help her. Every emotion I have is dead on arrival. She's the collateral damage in the firestorm raging inside me, charring my insides to bitter ash.

"I know," I say in a listless monotone. "I'm sorry."

"Why are you acting like this?" Her voice comes out breathy and one step from escalating hysteria.

"Acting like what? Like my fucking life is over before it even started?" I scowl, unable to stop myself from unloading all the rage inside of me on the only available victim. It's beyond unfair, and I know it as the words travel through my lips and it's too late to take them back. "Like any future I had is gone? I've got nothing, Kat, nothing!"

Blinking back tears, she says, "You have me. Isn't that worth something? Aren't I worth something?"

I intake a sharp breath; her words are like an ice pick to my heart.

Then her tears turn to fury, and she socks me in the arm and stalks away to pace. "You're worth more than your goddamn leg! So you can't play football, so what? You'll do something else, just like my father did. You're more than that damn game!"

My molars grind, sending a vibration through my jaw as she rages at me, and I snap. "That damn game was going to buy my future, our future!" I flail my arm at her and seethe. "Admit it, Kat. You're not going to spend your life with a guy who's making minimum wage at the fucking supermarket!"

She narrows her eyes and bites back, "Stop the fucking pity party, Henshaw. So you take a year off and get your act together?

Rehab your leg back into shape, then you get loans and you go to school. Even if you have to work at the same time. There's no shame in that, John. It will be hard, but so-the-fuck what? What else have you got to do? You're nineteen-fucking-years old. I'll be by your side. Won't that make it somewhat bearable, you big lughead?"

My eyes widen at Kat's flagrant use of the f-word. As a rule she rarely swears. I easily cover the quota for both of us. "Jeez, Kat... when you put it that way," I say, giving her a menacing stare.

She strides over and gives me another shove. I'm lucky she doesn't dislodge any of the tubes. "I'll hate you if you give up on yourself... on us. Fight, damn it. You're not dead. You're not paralyzed—you'll walk again, and run." She shoves me a third time for good measure and collapses onto the bed, letting her shoulders fall forward. "Shaw, that first day . . . when you were unconscious, I was so scared." She sniffs and wipes her eyes. "I just wanted you to wake up." Her voice breaks and my heart breaks with it.

I pull her into my arms and tuck her head under my chin. She clings to me as I rock her in my arms. I hum, and she shatters against me into wracking sobs.

"I love you," she chokes out.

"I love you, too," I murmur into her sweet-smelling hair, and close my eyes. All I want is to fade into oblivion holding Kat and forgetting what happened along with the pain-filled ache in my leg. She's right. A future with her is better than one without her.

If I fight, it will be for her.

Chapter 24

John

August 1981 – Losing Kat the First Time

"BUT IT ITCHES!" I yell, swiping at Kat as she steps out of my reach and hides the coat hanger behind her back. I'm lying on the sofa in my living room with my good leg hanging off the edge and the other one propped up on a pillow.

She throws me an evil eye. "The doctor said you're not supposed to be using this in your cast."

I pound the cushion with my palm and grumble. "I don't care. I'm dying over here! It feels like a swarm of mosquitos are feasting on my leg."

"I brought my blow dryer," she says. "Either that or you can take the antihistamine."

I press my head back into the arm of the sofa and whine, "It makes me sleepy."

Her brows pop up and she heads for the tote bag she left by the door. "Blow dryer it is, then."

I make fake crying noises and whine some more. "It's too hot. . . ."

She clucks her tongue and rolls her eyes. "You are the *worst* patient ever. I'm going to set it to cool, ya big baby."

I've been lying around in the house like a beached whale for five weeks, with another three weeks to go before the cast comes off and I start physical therapy . . . *if* I start physical therapy. Without a private medical policy, the only two doctors in town covered by the insurance from the accident settlement are booked solid. If I have to walk around on crutches any longer than necessary waiting for a PT opening, I'm going to lose my mind.

Kat's been spending all her free time outside of her summer job keeping me company. She's whipped my ass at chess at least six dozen times, but not as quickly as she used to. We've watched a boatload of movies and nonstop videos on a new music channel called MTV, played Scrabble and Trivial Pursuit with my mom and Vera like there's no tomorrow . . . and squeezed in some quality naked time while my mom's been at work. All in all, not the worst summer, but far from the best.

The one thing we haven't done is talk about what happens when she starts school in the fall and I'm left behind to finish recovering and figure out the rest of my *not-as-miserable-as-it-was-a-month-ago-but-still-sucky* life.

My football coach offered to help me fill out and file the paperwork to defer matriculation until spring and apply for traditional student loans. The thought leaves me cold but I'm starting to warm to the idea. If it helps me and Kat stay on track, I guess I can learn to suck it up. One upside to my leg being immobilized and encased in a million pounds of plaster — no chance I'll tax my ACL before it's fully healed. Part of me is nursing the hope that I'll be able to play again.

Kat shoots cool air into the top of the cast. A satisfied hum travels up my throat, and I collapse in relief.

"Marsh and Sue want to know if you're interested in hobbling to a movie tonight. They want to see *Arthur* with Dudley Moore and Liza Minnelli," Kat says. Before I can answer, she turns off the blow dryer and adds, "My treat."

Resentment wells in my chest. I had to let go of my schedule at Shop-Rite until I'm off crutches. I hate that I'm living on next to no cash. Having Kat pay for things makes me crazy and punches a dent in my pride.

She catches the passing scowl on my face and gives me one of her own. "Let's not go there again, Shaw. I'm not keeping count. Relationships are about support. I'm sure there will be a time when you're the one supporting me . . . so stop, okay?"

I frown and plant my arms across my chest. She shoots me in the face with a stream of cool air from the blow dryer and chuckles. "I said, stop it, ya lughead. Let's go. It'll be fun."

"Funny." I grab her, pull her down on top of me, and attack her ticklish spots until she's a mass of shrieking giggles and squirmy arms and legs.

"Not fair!" she screams and attacks me back. "Stop! Or I'm going to draw a giant penis on your cast while you're sleeping."

It's been our running joke, Kat threatening to draw lewd pictures on my cast whenever I give her shit.

"And let the world know my secret?" I tease.

Her shin strikes the plaster and pain shoots down my leg.

"Ow! Careful, that hurt." I laugh and loosen my grip on her.

She takes the opening, rolls off the sofa and onto the ratty carpet, laughing. "You're an evil boyfriend," she says, her eyes gleaming with a look that says otherwise.

"At least I'm good with my tongue," I say, making a rude gesture with my mouth. That earns me a Kat love tap to the shoulder.

Then her expression softens. "So, is that a yes? Will you go to the movies with us?"

My smile wavers. "Planning on going without me if I say no?"

A guilty look flashes across her face, answering my question. As unjustified as it is, I'm hurt that she would. The ache that hits the center of my chest is swift and painful, releasing a torrent of anger that's been lurking quietly under the surface, waiting for release. Anger more at myself and my situation for feeling insecure and inadequate than at her. Anger for the vicious reminder that she'll be leaving me at the end of August.

A grimace drags down my brow and when I speak my words are icy and bitter. "Then go without me." I'm being unfair. *Again.* And I know it.

Kat's head snaps back like I've struck her. She's been sympathetic and patient with my outbursts of self-pity since my release from the hospital. I've made an effort not to direct my frustration at her. But sometimes I can't help myself.

She jumps to her feet and tears form in her eyes. "Is it too much to ask for a change of scenery? We need a break from this," she waves her arm at the dingy living room walls. "I need a break from this."

I grind out my next question. "Do you need a break from me,

too?"

"That's not what I said!" She swipes at a falling tear. "Don't put words in my mouth. I want to go out. I want to see friends before we all leave."

My jaw twitches and I turn surly. "*We* all, you mean *you* all. Me? I'm not going anywhere. I'm stuck right here on this fucking couch. Go. Have fun. I'm going to hang out here."

Kat finally loses her patience with me and lets loose. "Fine! Mope in front of the TV, play solitaire, play with your dick, I don't care! I'm going with Marsh and Sue to see a movie, eat popcorn, and enjoy some fresh summer air." She snatches her blow dryer and storms to the door. "I've been here for you all summer, every step of the way, and you can't do this one thing for me? See you tomorrow . . . if I've forgiven you by then."

My stupid male pride lets her leave. Fucking idiot. I hear her car pull out of the driveway. I throw my hands up and let out a frustrated growl.

By the time I change my mind and call Kat's house, the pit viper reports with more than the usual amount of glee that Kat just left to meet Marsh and Sue at the movies. If I hadn't broken my clutch foot, I would've driven over to the Beacon to meet them.

Instead, I sulk and watch the tube, wishing I'd kept my big mouth shut.

THERE'S A KNOCK at the front door the next afternoon. "Come in!" I yell from the couch, expecting it to be Kat even though it's an hour earlier than she usually comes on Thursdays. After a miserable night of bad TV and a heavy dose of self-pity, I have my "I'm sorry" speech all lined up.

"Hey, handsome," Vera says as she swings in, carrying a brown paper bag that smells like there's a cheeseburger and fries hiding inside. My stomach rumbles with the prospect of a lunch that holds more appeal than last night's leftover red beans and rice.

Shoving aside the crossword puzzle I'd been working on, I stare at the bag and drool like one of Pavlov's dogs. "Aunt Vera, *please* say that's for me," I almost beg.

She breaks into a wide grin. "Of course it's for you, sweetheart. Did you think I'd bring this for myself?"

"Not really," I say, unable to rip my gaze from the bag.

"Let me get you a plate." She disappears into the kitchen and comes back with the feast arranged on a dish and a large glass of milk.

"I love you, Aunt Vera," I say, my eyes glued to the food.

"I guess that's better than hello." She chuckles and sets the burger, fries, and milk on the TV tray as I haul myself into a sitting position.

"Sorry, hi, but this smells like heaven after weeks of my mother's cooking — no disrespect to her — but I miss red meat," I say, ready to dive in. "May I?"

She nods and sinks into the cracked leather chair across from me. "Be my guest."

"Thanks for coming by," I say after devouring my first mouthful.

Her humor slips into a look I'd expect to see from my mother. "This isn't just a social call."

My eyes flicker from my food to where she's sitting. I finish chewing and swallow. "What's the matter? Kat tell you we got into a fight?"

She shakes her head and stares me down. "No, she told me the physical therapist may not be able to fit you into their schedule until Christmas."

My shoulders slump at the reminder. "Yeah. It's true."

"Sweetheart, that's not acceptable to me," she says softly.

I rub my hands together and stare at the fries, beating back a hint of despair. "Nothing I can do about it, Aunt Vera."

"Yes, but there's something *I* can do."

I'm not sure I like where she's heading. "What do you mean?" I grab some fries and pop them into my mouth.

"I've hired a personal PT to work with you the minute that cast comes off to get you back to your fighting strength."

I nearly choke on the fries. "How . . . ? I can't . . . You can't . . . pay . . ."

She's comes over and clutches my arm. "Johnny. Look at me." Her expression hardens, and when Vera puts on her business face, I pay her the same respect I'd give my own mother and meet her gold-colored eyes.

"This is not up for discussion or negotiation. Sven will be here the day after that cast comes off. Forget about the money. I have more money than I can spend. This is a gift because I love you as much as I love my niece. Do you understand me?"

A lump rises in my throat, and I can no longer hold her stare. I nod and drop my gaze, tenting my hands in front of my mouth to hide the quiver in my lip. That she'd do this blows me away. Outside of my coach helping me get in front of the Rutgers football scout, no one has ever done anything this big for me before.

She crouches down beside me and her voice softens. "Make me a promise?"

Damn it. My eyes water as I fight to hold it together. I nod again.

"Fight, sweetheart. Fight as hard as it takes to get your life back on track. Sven will work you hard. Let him. Don't ever settle for anything but your best self . . . your best life."

I lose the battle and tears silently drop onto my tented hands. Vera stands and wraps me in her arms.

The well of pain I've tamped down all summer spills out, and I choke out the root of my angst, "But I'll never play . . ." She strokes my hair and I unleash my broken dreams onto the fancy blouse caressing my cheek and sob with abandon for the first time since the hospital and the second time since I was ten. She holds me tighter, kisses the top of my head, and lets me unload.

"You will, darling, you'll play again. Don't lose your love of the game, whether you can use it to fund your future or not. It wasn't the game that let you down. Remember that." No, it was my own body.

I sniff loudly and pull away. My neck burns from the embarrassment of my breakdown. She hands me the napkin next to the plate and I make good use of it. "Sorry about that," I mumble.

"There's nothing to be sorry for, unless you plan on drowning in defeat."

I wad the napkin in my fist and give an imperceptible nod. "I'll do my best. I promise."

She waves a hand at the food in front of me. "Eat before it gets cold."

I give a last sniff then grab the half-eaten burger, not having the heart to tell her I'd lost my appetite.

She takes a seat until I finish and then clears my plate. When she returns from the kitchen, she sinks back into the oversize armchair. Her expression turns melancholy. "There's another reason I came today."

I position a pillow behind my head and try to get comfortable. "What's that?"

Vera smiles, the smile she uses to soften the blow before delivering bad news. *"I'm sorry, kids, Bruce Springsteen is sold out,"* or, *"They were out of rum raisin ice cream at the store,"* or, *"Viv's coming with us."*

"I won't be here to hound you about Sven," she says, trying to make light of the news. "I'm leaving for a few months. But don't get any ideas. Sven will provide me with frequent reports."

The sick feeling of abandonment hits the pit of my stomach. "You're going back to work?" I ask, trying to prevent the grimace that's working its way into my brow. Vera gave up her design business when her husband died, and she's been a lady of leisure ever since.

She glances at her hands before her smile slips back into place. "I've grieved for Harold long enough. It wouldn't be fair of me to ask you to get on with your life if I couldn't do the same. An old client contacted me to help with a new project near and dear to her heart. The timing isn't the best, but I've accepted."

"Where's the project?" I ask, not that it really matters. Gone is gone.

Her smile tightens and she can't quite meet my eyes. "Rhode Island."

Might as well be Siberia.

I nod. "Thanks . . . for Sven. I appreciate it . . . and everything else you've done for me . . . *Vee*." Contrary to my mother's rule and how I address her twin in my head, in Vera's case, I use her name to show my respect.

Her expression softens and she rises. "Calling me Vee a couple of years ahead of plan? There's hope for you yet, handsome." She winks, grabs her purse, and comes over to give me another hug. "It's my pleasure to help you, sweetheart. You take care of yourself and make me proud."

"Will do. . . . When do you leave?"

"Tomorrow morning. Tell your mom I said goodbye. I'll see you both when I get back."

With a wave, she's gone. But the ache in my chest stays rooted in place.

The afternoon ticks by and still no Kat.

By dinnertime, I'm edgy with worry that she's still mad from yesterday. I try calling her house, but still no answer after the third attempt.

Where the hell is everyone? If all else fails, Jillian usually picks up the phone when none of the adults are paying attention. Nothing.

By eight o'clock, I'm sulking, convinced that Kat's still pissed. She said she'd come over today if she'd forgiven me. Damn it. Guess she hasn't. I really must've screwed up this time for her to be mad enough to skip a day. She's never done that before, no matter how much we've pissed each other off.

Friday comes and goes. No Kat. I've tried her house a dozen times and still no fucking answer. My worry has taken a different turn and I'm wondering if something bad has happened. Vera would know, but she's already gone.

My mother gives me the evil eye after I tell her why I'm acting like a lunatic. "For a smart boy, sometimes you are *estúpido*." Of course, she blames me and agrees that Kat is probably mad. Our argument ends with me in a huff and watching more boring shit on TV.

I set a limit of noon on Saturday. If she doesn't show up by then, I'm calling a cab to take me across town, since my mom's working. In preparation, I reacquaint myself with a razor and, thanks to a black plastic garbage bag, I manage to navigate the shower.

I'm sitting like a zombie glued to MTV, one step away from unhinging if I have to listen to "Video Killed the Radio Star" one more time, when the door cracks open thirty minutes short of my deadline and Kat slips inside. The breath seeps from my lungs in relief.

I'm not sure if I want to hug her or scream at her for leaving me hanging for almost three days without so much as a phone call. It's not until she looks up and I see she's been crying that I fall down on the side of hugging her.

"Babe, what's the matter? Where've you been? I almost went out of my mind. . . ." I stop. Something's wrong. She doesn't say a word. She just comes over and crawls into my lap. I wrap her in an embrace and breathe in the floral scent clinging to her hair.

Inside, I'm unwinding, not sure what to do. I press my cheek to the soft strands. "Talk to me, Kat."

"I'm sorry," she whispers from underneath the hair draped over her face like a curtain.

I squeeze her tighter. "I'm the one who's sorry. For being an ass. I've been trying to call you for days. Where have you been?" I whisper back.

She doesn't answer.

A sliver of fear cleaves me open the longer she stays quiet. "Kiss me, Shaw," she says so low it's almost inaudible. I brush back her hair in search of her face. When I find it, I tip up her chin but she avoids my eyes.

I take her mouth with tentative licks and caresses, running my hands down her back and pressing her close. We're midway through the kiss when she comes alive and gives back everything I'm giving. There's something desperate and frantic in her touch. Rather than alleviating my anxiety, it adds to it.

I capture her wrists as she runs them over my torso.

"Stop." I breathe into her hair. "What's going on?"

She stills in my arms and rests her head on my shoulder. "I love you, Shaw. . . . I'll always love you."

I grasp her shoulders and peel her off me. "Kat, what the hell?" The fear inside me spreads and I shudder.

Her eyes glisten when she finally meets my gaze. "I'm . . ." She swipes at her face and her lip quivers. "I'm leaving."

Her words land like a punch to the gut and my fingers dig into her skin. *"What?"*

"Stanford . . . I'm going to Stanford," she whispers and catches her lip between her teeth.

I push her off me onto the sofa. The pressure behind my furrowed brow is immediate. "What? What are you talking about?" I say, choking out the words. "You're going to NYU." My mind has trouble grasping the message.

She's staying with me, not leaving. *Right?*

Something breaks inside me, snaps my emotional spine. My voice is hollow. "We're going to make this work. That's what you said."

Her voice comes out a breathy shadow of a whisper. "I can't . . . not now."

I hear but don't understand. I blink and blink again as the shock takes hold.

"What did I do?" I ask over the lump in my throat, pressing my eyes shut. I must've fucked up bad. I've never cried in front of Kat, and I don't want to start now, but the despair of living without her opens up and swallows me whole.

She brushes her tears away. "Nothing. You didn't do anything wrong."

"I don't understand," I say and fight with everything I have to keep my blurry vision in check. I can't lose Kat on top of everything else. I just can't.

She kisses her fingers and then presses them to my lips. "I'm doing this for you."

Before I can protest, she runs out the front door.

I grab my crutches and hobble after her as fast as I can, but I can't navigate the stairs in time to catch her before she pulls the car out of the driveway and drives away.

By the time the cab picks me up and I get to Kat's, no one is home. After dinner, Matt picks me up when he gets off work and I try again. He waits in the car while I go up and ring the bell.

This time Viv's car is in the driveway and she answers the door. Gone is the condescending glare I've come to expect, and in its place is a sad but genuine smile. The first ever. She steps aside to let me in. "I figured you would come."

"Where's Kat?" I ask, afraid I already know the answer.

"Gone. She left this afternoon."

Anger, hurt, and betrayal overshadow my need to pursue this further. I turn to leave, and Viv clasps my arm. "Stay . . . Let's talk," she says softly, her voice bordering on kind.

I'm tempted to tell her to go to hell, but the rational side of my brain wants some answers. I nod, my mouth set in a grim line, and follow her into the kitchen.

She pulls two colas from the fridge and pours them into glasses. For a moment she looks like Vera. Ever since I met Viv and Vera, I've been amazed how easily I could recognize the difference between them from the soul that lives inside. Today, I have trouble making the distinction.

I clench my fists and cut Viv a glare. "What happened? Why did Kat leave?"

Viv takes a breath and runs her finger over the condensation on the glass. "Did you know that Kat wanted to be a molecular biologist before she met you?"

My eyes shutter to half-mast. "Yes." *Kind of. No. Not really.*

"Did she tell you that Stanford has one of the best programs for that in the country?"

I shake my head and leave the cola untouched. She definitely didn't tell me that. She talked up Stanford, but mentioned molecular biology only in passing. "Doesn't matter. She decided to go to school for business."

"No," Viv says quietly but without malice, "she didn't. She decided to give up her dream and stay home to be with you. A dream her father and I traded pieces of our souls to secure for her."

Her words hit like an unexpected blow.

"She wasn't staying here just for me...." Even as the words leave my mouth, I'm not sure if they're true. She never told me the endowment meant that much to her.

Viv chews her lip, much like Kat when she's pensive, and says, "Bill and I met when I was in high school. I had dreams of dancing in the New York City Ballet." She gives me a sad smile and nods. "He was a football player with hopes of going pro, just like you."

I swallow and shift in my seat, suspecting where this conversation is headed. My jaw clenches and I look away.

Viv grasps my wrist. "I found out I was pregnant during Bill's senior year in college, right after I was selected as a principal dancer—and right before his football career ended in injury. It's bad enough when one person loses their dream, exponentially worse when they both do... I didn't want that for Kitty... and I don't want that for you."

I slump in my chair. "People can have new dreams," I say in our defense.

She shakes her head and wrings her hands. "You're both even younger than Bill and I were, and it was *hard*, very hard. I warned Kitty about falling in love in high school...." Her voice trails off and her eyes gleam with unshed tears. "It was never personal, John, me pushing you away. I just wanted Kitty to have a better life and more choices than I had."

My jaw clenches. "And what? I couldn't possibly give her that? Because my blood isn't blue enough for you, *Viv*?" I ask, my disrespect intentional.

She gives me her full-on gaze. "That was only a convenient ruse.

You're a good person, John. I see that. I've always seen that. That's never been the issue. Not really."

Her response knocks me back and rips the rug out from under me. I'm left speechless.

She grabs my hand and squeezes. "Get some life under your belts and find each other again in a few years. If you love each other as much as I believe you do, you have time on your side. Love doesn't disappear. It's a golden chain around your heart. For some, a chain that can never be broken."

I suck in a ragged breath and pull my hand away, trying to keep a lid on my emotions as guilt gnaws at my gut for my selfishness. For my weakness.

"If you truly love Kitty, let her go. Don't let our sacrifice be in vain. Let her have her dream. Come back and give her more dreams once you're able. Be strong and get stronger." Her eyes gleam. "I won't get in your way ever again."

I hate that there's a twisted logic to what she's saying, and that it's true I don't have much to offer Kat right now. Instead, I'd drag her down. Vee's offer suddenly makes sense, and I'm left to assume she knew this would happen.

I get up and Viv gets up with me. "How do I get in touch with her?"

Viv gives me a tight smile. "I'm sure she'll be in touch when she's ready."

Why am I not surprised that she won't offer a way for me to contact Kat? Then again, she wouldn't throw a bucket of water on me if I was on fire.

I leave without looking back or saying goodbye, and everything inside me goes numb as I hobble out the front door on my crutches, shell-shocked.

After all Viv said, there are a couple of things I can't reconcile as I reach Matt's car. What kind of sacrifice did her parents make? Even more important, what did Kat mean when she said she was doing this for me? By all that's holy, I can't imagine how breaking my heart was for my benefit.

The ache that takes hold inside my chest is almost unbearable, but I love Kat enough to let her have her dream and not stand in her way—even if that doesn't include me. The realization settles in and I shut down all communication with the muscle that beats to keep me alive.

From this moment forward, I'm on my own, minus a limb called Kat.

John

Jillian and Raine's Kitchen

I CLUTCH THE empty coffee cup and stare at the rim. "Whatever I could've given to her was taken away. After that, rather than fight for her, I went to the extreme opposite. I made choices she wouldn't have approved of. Took chances that pushed her away because I was angry and bitter . . . undeserving of her love."

When I finish, Jillian frowns with an unfocused squint as she glides a finger back and forth across her bottom lip. "John?"

A heavy frown drops onto my face and I start to panic that my sob story upset her. "What's the matter?"

The look in her eyes is pensive and guarded. "Kitty is a CPA . . . she never became a molecular biologist. . . . And what happened to the baby my mom had at twenty-one? Kitty wasn't born until eight years later when Mom was twenty-nine." Her gaze locks on mine. "I was a surprise. She didn't have me until she turned forty."

Shit. I blink a few times and give my God's honest answer. "I have no idea. At the time, I assumed . . . I'm not sure what I assumed." I shrug. "Probably that she was talking about Kat. My mom had my brother at eighteen, so I never questioned it." Through my teenage eyes, I couldn't reliably guess a woman's age if my life depended on it. And it's not like Viv and Vera looked much older than my mother, or that I had a reason to do the math.

"Do you think my mother lied to you? About the baby?"

I swipe a hand across my chin and shake my head. "Don't know. Want me to do some digging?"

Jillian shakes her head as if to clear it. "Not yet. Let me think about it first?"

I nod but decide to do the research anyway, because now I want to know. As much as I'd like to think Viv manipulated me that day, my natural-born instincts — the same ones that make me good at my job today — would've bet against it.

"Makes me wonder about the molecular biology story, too," Jillian says and pushes away her coffee mug.

I shrug. "Dunno. Never made sense to me either. Then again, I bailed on college. So who the hell knows? I was too fucked up and pissed off at the time to look beyond the fact that she left me."

Jillian taps her fingers on the table. "Weird... So, what happened after that?"

I scrub a hand down my face to erase my grimace. "Sven showed up a couple of weeks later and, true to Vera's word, he kicked my butt every day for three months. By Thanksgiving I was able to run two miles a day."

The corner of Jillian's mouth lifts. "Sven, huh? Was he anything like Raine?"

I snort. "Not nearly as pretty or as forgiving. He was in his forties, first-generation American, full-blooded Swede. Former medic in the army. Tough as nails and could drink me under the table. Which he did. On more than one occasion at the height of my misery."

Jillian chuckles for a second before her frown reappears. "Did you hear from Kitty after that? What happened?"

I shake my head. "Not much. She sent a short note that September without a return address. Other than that, no contact. I figured that's what she wanted."

"What did the note say?"

"She missed me, she was sorry, and she loved me."

Jillian shakes her head and brushes a knuckle across her lips. "If this were one of my suspense novels that note could mean anything."

I have a flash of regret for oversharing and give Jillian a pointed stare. "Promise me you're not going to put any of this in one of your romance novels. This stays in the family. Agreed?"

She huffs. "Like I told Kitty—I only write stories with happy endings." She lets out a breath. "I'm sorry that you haven't found a happy ever after... with or without Kitty."

My mouth tips up in a half smile. "I'm not dead yet, Jilly."

"That reminds me. I have a bone to pick with you." She folds her arms over her chest and pouts underneath a recriminating golden glare. "Kitty wasn't the only one you left behind; you left me, too, you know. I loved you like a big brother. I didn't see you again until

I was in high school."

An image of Jillian as a cute eight-year-old flashes through my mind. I hang my head between slumped shoulders and take it. Way to drive a stake through my heart. Deeper still is a sharp reminder that she's not the first little girl I let down. "I'm sorry, doll. I loved you, too. At the time, I couldn't see a good way of staying in touch. Forgive me?"

Her pout turns up at the corners and her gaze warms. "I'll think about it."

"Best I can hope for." I rest my elbows on the table and rub my eyes. "I'm not proud of what I did afterward, but I was too messed up to think straight. She cut me off without so much as a second glance after that one note. I just couldn't believe it. It hurt worse than anything I've ever experienced in my life." *Until the next time it happened.*

"What did you do after she left? Is that when you enlisted?"

I nod and press my lips into a grim line. "After my rehab with the mad Swede, I gave up on the thought of attending Rutgers if I couldn't play ball. I could run, but my knee couldn't handle the punishment of playing on a first division team. Going there would be a constant reminder of what I'd lost, and somehow it meant less without Kat. . . . But I didn't want to be around stocking shelves when Kat came home on break from Stanford and run the risk of knowing for sure she didn't want to see me. So I left. Followed Ben's footsteps and joined the Marine Corps. I was gone before Christmas. Before Kat or Vera came home. Part of me didn't want to be found. I wanted Kat to think I didn't care."

Jillian's golden eyes fill with empathy. "I'm sorry, John." No stranger to loss when it comes to love, she reaches across the table and takes my hand. "Thanks for sharing your story with me."

I nod and deal with the residual emotions my recounting has churned up inside of me. But this chunk is only one piece of the giant puzzle that makes up my history with Kat. A jigsaw with pieces only Kat can supply. Pieces I'm not sure I want to find.

Rachel releases a tiny wail through the baby monitor, cuing me to glance at my watch. I'm thirty minutes late for work. "Gotta go." I push back my chair.

She comes around the table to give me a hug. "I'm going to think on this mystery and help solve it. I'd like to hear more next time."

Warning bells clang between my ears. "I'm not sure Kat would be happy if she knew I told you even this much. Let's keep it between us. Okay?"

"Don't worry, I won't say anything." She waggles her brow. "But that doesn't mean I can't ask questions."

"I guess it doesn't," I say, scooping up my gym bag on my way out. But if Jillian wants the next installment, she'll have to ask Kat. Revealing my secrets is one thing; revealing Kat's is another.

In the meantime, I have a stop to make on the way to work and some research to do. I'm turning the knob to let myself out the front door as Jillian heads up the center stairs. "Jilly?"

"Yeah?"

"When does Kitten close on the new Pine Grove house?"

"Next month. Why?"

I glance back and shrug. "Got the number?"

The corner of her mouth tugs up. "I'm not sure, but the sign's still up. It's on the Ashland end."

I nod and tack a detour onto my already packed agenda.

Chapter 25

Kitty

September 2016 – The Visit

DING. DONG.

I flinch, stop typing, and rub my temples before glancing at the Tiffany desk clock. 9:05 a.m. Too early for the postman or UPS. I contemplate ignoring the door, but my client's business valuation is putting me to sleep. I've been working on it since seven, and I could use a breather. Even if the person at the door is Mrs. Nelson about her perpetually missing cat. I push away from my desk.

Rather than the bell ringing a second time, there's a soft rap on the door that echoes off the newly bare walls.

"Hold your horses," I mumble, and pad out into the hallway, hobbling more than walking past the stacks of boxes lining the wall. Thanks to my new exercise regimen, every step between my office and the front door reminds me that muscles I never knew existed are, in fact, present and accounted for.

Hopefully, whoever is knocking doesn't have a keen sense of smell since they're catching me in the T-shirt and yoga pants I wore to my 5:30 a.m. Bar Method class.

I fumble with the sticking lock and give myself a reminder to dig up the WD-40 before swinging open the door.

My breath catches and I blink.

John fills the doorway, his face unreadable, his stormy blue eyes assessing me with a combination of sharp vigilance and a hint of worry.

His gaze travels over me like he's evaluating me for injury, pausing for a second on my lips before landing on my eyes. "Hey," he whispers.

We haven't spoken since August on the hotel deck, the night of Jillian and Raine's wedding. I've avoided answering or returning his calls the numerous times he's attempted to reach me. I didn't know if I could trust myself around him. I still don't. Seeing him dead-on, in full daylight instead of draped in darkness, does a whole different thing to my insides.

His dark brown hair is evenly threaded with salty gray, while experience and age give his face lines and character. What was once rugged in youth is now craggy in middle age. His workouts with Raine have paid off; he's in the best shape I've seen him in since his thirties. Never classically handsome, he has appeal that comes from knowing him on the inside, and seeing the younger man I loved so desperately peeking out from behind his eyes. To me, he's still the most handsome man in the world.

My pulse comes alive, and for the first time in forever I wish I was wearing something nicer and smelled a whole lot better. "Hey," I say with a breathy exhale.

He looks past me and tips his chin. "May I come in?"

I nod and step aside, making way for him to pass. I catch the familiar scent of spice and pine, and my heart beats faster. How can one human being represent everything I want and nothing I can have?

"Would you like some coffee?" The words come out of my mouth before I realize I've spoken. The door clicks shut but I don't remember closing it. The decision to keep my distance was sound. I can't think straight when he's this close.

I join him in the center of the foyer under the crystal chandelier. Once my pride and joy, I've sold it to the new owner.

He scratches the back of his head. "No, thanks. Had too much already." He releases a breath and takes a step closer. A crisp, crackling energy fills the air between us and threatens to pull me into his orbit.

He tucks his hands casually into the pockets of his khakis; the tension in his shoulders tells me he's fighting to keep them under control. "Just checking in. I wanted to make sure you were all right." His voice is a gentle croon.

I nod, unable to manage more than a wan smile. "I'm fine."

My hands tremble at my sides, aching to reach out and touch him. Unearthing my stories for Dr. Graham has cracked open the sealed vault to my past, leaving me vulnerable.

Tender feelings I've buried rise to the surface and struggle to break free. I remind myself that it's dangerous to confuse the past with the present. What existed very distinctly in the *before* no longer exists in the *after*.

"I'm sorry . . . about *Bob*," he says with a twitch in his jaw and a probing detective stare. A look he uses to cloak his protective anger when I'm the object of his protection. The subtext, an unspoken question wrapped in an apology.

I'm assuming he's heard the truth from Jillian, so I skip my mental rolodex of socially acceptable responses to the disintegration of my marriage. Those don't apply to John. He's not someone who would be satisfied with something so trite or prepared, especially from me. He's also not someone I can lie to, unless it's by omission . . . and an absolute necessity.

I meet his stare and lay it bare, Kat-style. "Thanks for Ray's name and for not asking any questions. I suspected an affair, just not one like that." I shake my head with gritted teeth. "I'm so damn angry and hurt I could spit, but I'm working through it and doing my best to dig myself out of the depressing place I'm in."

That does the trick to diffuse the tension bunching his shoulders and stiffening my spine.

He nods and presses his lips together in a closed-mouth smile. "I've been there. I remember. If you need to talk . . ."

A jealous and shame-filled pang hits my chest. "Carmela?" I ask tentatively, knowing I caused him just as much pain, or more, during the course of our lives. Knowing he ended up back in the arms of his first girlfriend after I left the second time still sticks in my craw, despite my not having a right to feel that way.

His eyes shutter. "Yeah." He slides his hands from his pockets and glances around. "Jillian mentioned you're moving in a couple of weeks. . . . I drove by the house on Pine Grove. It's nice."

"Thanks," I say, slightly taken aback but not surprised that he would want to see it.

Then he raises a brow with a hopeful gleam in his eye. "Need any help moving?"

The corner of my mouth lifts. "Thank you," I say, hugging myself to occupy my hands and prevent them from developing minds of their own. "But I've already hired a mover."

He gives a nod and doesn't press further. "I should go . . ." His gaze runs over me again, this time like he's memorizing every detail, before it stops and lingers on my face. No. My lips. "You look good, Kat," he whispers.

Damn it. Why is he such a master at stealing my breath?

My gaze slides to his lips before returning to the stormy blue windows into my past and I whisper, "So do you, Shaw."

The energy resurges and fills the gap separating us, drawing my soul dangerously close to being sucked into his gravitational pull.

He steps closer and runs the backs of his fingers down my cheek, then says, "You take care, 'kay? Call if you need me?"

I nod and follow him the few feet to the door. He clears the threshold and turns. He opens his mouth as if to speak, then closes it and shakes his head.

I glance at the invitation in the tray next to the door and smile. "I'm still thinking about it."

He huffs a laugh. "Am I that predictable?"

I cross my arms and lean into the jam, feeling my smile radiate up to my eyes. "Only to me."

He doesn't move. Rather, he swipes a hand across his mouth and clutches his chin in a contemplative look before giving me a sideways glance. "Can I ask you something?"

I trot out the answer I give to Dr. Graham for the same reasons. "Depends."

He squints and asks, "Did you have an older sibling?"

My heart almost stops. I freeze the relaxed smile I'm wearing and squint back, holding my casual expression with every shred of control I have, hoping like hell to escape his intelligent, probing gaze. "What do you mean?"

He studies me with an equally worry-free smile and waits a beat before shaking his head. "Nothing."

My smile doesn't waver. "Thanks for stopping by. . . . It's good to see you." And it would've been if I could erase the last sixty seconds.

He winks and gives me a roguish, confident grin. "See you at the reunion, Kitten." My knees weaken for all the wrong reasons as he turns and swaggers toward his sleek, county-owned car.

It's not until I've closed the door and slid down the wall onto the foyer floor that I realize my mistake and the choice I have to make. Sooner, rather than later.

Chapter 26

John

In Transit to FBI Task Force Meeting in Newark

"LISA?" I SAY over Bluetooth to my contact in records as I hightail it from Kat's place to the task force office in Newark. "It's John. Do me a favor?"

"Sure. What 'cha need?"

I do some quick calculations. "Pull a marriage cert for me. William McNally, spouse, Vivian. Get her maiden name and check birth records between 1953 and 1957. Run 'em both and see what shakes out."

"What are you looking for beside the obvious?" she asks.

"Hunch."

"You got it," she says over the sound of keystrokes in the background.

"Thanks, doll. I owe you."

"Your tab's already sky high," she scoffs. "If I was single, I'd take it out in trade."

I chuckle at our running off-color joke and disconnect before merging left onto the Route 78 express lanes.

What are you hiding, Kat?

She may be better at chess, but I'm better at poker. Whatever Viv mentioned that day, Kat knows something about it. That much was evident from her reaction. But even if she knows, it's obvious Jillian doesn't. Not a surprise given Kat's history and her secretive side. One thing's certain, whatever happened wasn't common knowledge, which makes me wonder if Viv kept the child. She mentioned the pregnancy and that it destroyed her dreams, but not whether she had the baby. Abortion was tricky in those days. My bet's on a live birth.

Shit.

I swipe a hand down my face, trying to chase away the jitters after seeing Kat. Damn the effect that woman has on me. Even in workout clothes and looking like she hasn't slept in days, she's still the most frigging desirable woman in the world.

As tempting as it was to take her into my arms, I recognize the place she's in. That shitty, post-divorce, five-stages-of-grief mindset that sours you on anything and everything. Still, I'm not blind. I wasn't the only one fighting for control.

Here's hoping my visit and presumptive parting shot nudge her decision to make an appearance at the reunion. If I get her there, in our element, I'll have a better playing field to reestablish some contact . . . at least that's my plan. But what worked once might not work again. Kind of like the stock market—past gains don't indicate future performance. Something like that.

There's no denying the wedge of time that separates us, or the stew of old hurt, resentment, and lies by omission. But I have to believe what we had—what lies beneath—is strong enough to weather any past hurts as long as we give it our best shot this time.

There's no reason not to . . . at least on my side.

But this go-round, I'm not going to let her bury the past.

If she can't trust me now, then we have no hope for a future and it's time for me to retire from the force and move to Florida.

This is our last chance, and I don't plan to screw it up.

My thoughts spiral around like a whirlpool being sucked down a drain for the entire twenty-minute commute to Newark.

"Where the hell have you been, Shaw?" Tony snaps, glaring at me over a pile of paperwork the moment I walk into the war room. "You missed the meeting."

I glance at the scattered seating and abandoned coffee cups. Doesn't look like Tony's been alone for long. I cock a brow, not really giving a shit. "Had to take care of some personal business. What did I miss?"

A large conference table sits in the center of the command center. Marker-filled whiteboards and corkboards with networks of red string and push pins connecting photographs and notes cover one wall. Major players, dates, times, and suspected linkages are organized in columns, all pieces of the crime syndicate operations puzzle we're attempting to fit together and then dismantle. Drugs, guns, murder, prostitution rings, a cornucopia of illegal activities all happening here in central Jersey under the noses of federal, state, and local law enforcement.

Tony runs a hand through his hair. "Big shipment due into the port. All our contacts close to the Genovias are telling the same story. More product being smuggled under a fine arts manifest from Italy using Cato Shipping."

I glance at the boards. New push pins and string connect the Genovia and Cato columns. "When?"

"In a few weeks." He takes a deep breath and sizes me up. "Give any more thought to questioning Leticia Soames?"

My hackles lift. I grind my teeth and give him a flat, "No."

Last thing I want is to involve Jenny's future sister-in-law, Lettie. I get it. Her boyfriend's father owns Cato Shipping, but so far Howard has come up clean. Having worked with Lettie as part of Devon's case this summer, I have a lot of respect for her. She's as sharp as they come. We'd be better off having her on the team than trying to pump her for useless information. But she's got better things to do, like taking her uncle's board seat at Kingsbridge Industries, one of the world's largest privately held conglomerates, after her twin brother Devon is sworn in as CEO next month when he turns twenty-five.

Tony huffs. "Why not? What do we have to lose?"

I drop into one of the scattered chairs and rub my eyes. "Not a good idea, Tone. Not unless you want to draft her ass. Minute we tip our hand, we've got Nancy-fucking-Drew on our tails, and that's saying something. She's the best damn hacker I've ever met. No way she's going to let me ask her questions about the guy she's with and not do some homework afterward . . . You want to bring that on?"

He chews the end of the pen he's holding and shrugs. "Might be worth it if she can get us closer to the son."

I shake my head and spill what's really bugging me. "Devon's like family. I don't want Leticia ending up dead like MacDonald. I want her safe. We should be able to do our damn jobs without her help."

He levels me with a stare and says with forced calm, "I'm asking out of courtesy. I can get someone else to do it."

Son of a bitch. "You're really going to play that card with me?" I grit my teeth.

"I've let it sit long enough out of respect, but she's a link we can't ignore. I get that it's personal for you, but she's also the straightest line between two points. We need to find out what she knows . . . with or without you."

Aggravation spikes my blood pressure, and I want to lunge for his throat, but I know he's right. "Fine," I snarl, and get to my feet. "I'll talk to her, but she gets protection, or I'm out."

Tony's mouth pulls up into a smug smile, full of himself as if he's just scored a touchdown for the opposing team. "Done." He tosses the pen on the table and checks his watch. "Call me at noon. Let me know what you find out."

I sneer, flip him the bird, and head for the door.

"Love you too, Shaw." He laughs and yells after me, "You're still a sore loser."

"And you're still a prick," I mumble under my breath and hit the exit release next to the outside door.

Twenty minutes later, I ring the bell of the Soames' mansion on Summit's north side where the big money lives. Running my fingers along the back of my neck, I shift on my feet, not happy to be here.

The door swings wide. Barefoot and dressed in jeans, Lettie, all pale blonde ponytail and broad smile, leans into the jamb. "Detective! Let me guess? Wicked craving for my blueberry muffins?" she asks in a playful sing-song paired with a coquettish twist of her lips and a vigilant sparkle in her light blue eyes.

China-doll-petite and wearing no makeup, Devon's twin looks like a doe-eyed teenager. The only tip-off she's not fourteen is the in-your-face set of double Ds. Lettie may look cute and harmless, but anyone stupid enough to underestimate her does so at their own peril. She's usually two steps ahead and has no qualms about stealing your ass and handing it back to you on a silver platter before you even know it's gone.

My kind of girl. Doesn't hurt that she has a wicked sense of humor. Heavy emphasis on *wicked.*

I smile despite myself and lean in to give her a peck on the cheek. "Let's just say, if you're offering baked goods, I won't turn you down."

She smiles wider and steps aside with a sweep of her hand. "You're in luck. I have a batch coming out of the oven. Part of a care package for Dev. He and Jen are coming for dinner."

I follow her as she pads down the hall to her fancy kitchen. It's large enough to go out for a pass. The aroma of fresh muffins hits me and reminds me I skipped breakfast.

"Have a seat." Lettie grabs two big oven mitts that look like crab claws. My mouth waters when she pulls out the steaming muffins.

"So . . ." Lettie waggles a good-humored blond brow and places the pan on the stovetop. "Is this visit family business, muffin lust, or something else entirely?" By family business she means the court case pending against some of her relatives for their nefarious activities involving Kingsbridge and their part in endangering Devon's life.

"No family business today. Eighty-twenty something else and muffin lust," I answer, giving her a crooked grin, cottoning on to her double entendre. But it's only affectionate teasing between Lettie and me. When it comes to "muffin," there's only one woman on my lust list, and I'm positive Lettie's interest in smoked sausage doesn't extend to me.

She gives me a playful wink, grabs a plate, and carefully extracts one of the steaming muffins from the pan with a pair of wooden tongs. "Let me satisfy your lust first, Detective. I promise, these little goodies are better than sex."

I laugh and shake my head, unable to argue her point given the current state of my love life. "You're an evil woman, Lettie Soames."

Her delighted smile turns full Cheshire Cat. "Why, thank you, Detective. That's kind of you to say."

Before I can sink my teeth into the hot, spongy cake, she pours a tall glass of cold milk and slides it in front of me. "For the full experience," she says.

I take a bite and hold back a groan. Yeah, it's true, I feel like I might've just died and gone to Heaven. "Fuck, these are good," I mumble as I devour the last piece and a second one hits my plate.

"I love a man who enjoys a good muffin," she says with a teasing smile and her head propped on her hands. I let that comment slide, because I can't deny it's true whether she's talking baked goods or one woman in particular.

"Admit it . . . they're better than sex, yes?"

"It's a tie." I take a milk break and hold up a hand to stop her from offering me a third.

Her smile broadens. "So now that I've satisfied your twenty percent, what's the other eighty?"

I push aside my plate and wipe my mouth with a proffered napkin.

"I've got some questions about Howard."

She scoots her stool closer to where I'm sitting and taps her fingernails on the granite. "What about him?" she asks, resting her cheek on her other hand and looking only mildly curious.

I lean back and cross my arms. "What do you know about his family?"

She shrugs. "Never met them. Besides owning Cato Industries, what's there to know? The company made a smidge over $27.4 billion last year, offices in 125 countries and twenty-five thousand employees around the globe. Howie oversees worldwide ops."

"I'm thinking more along the lines of questionable connections."

She arches a brow and a cocky grin slides onto her lips. "You mean like the extra $20 billion of undeclared revenue from his father's smuggling operations for the mob?"

I choke out a snort and try not to fall off my stool. That thing about her being two steps ahead? She doesn't disappoint. "Yeah. That's what I meant. How do you know that?"

She shrugs again. "Not much gets by me, Detective." Grabbing a muffin, she takes a bite. Her eyelids lower as she chews, and she lets out a moan. "*Mmmm.* I outdid myself this time." It takes her a couple of seconds to refocus. "To answer your question, I investigated his company when I first met him eighteen months ago. You'll be happy to know, Kingsbridge uses another shipping company."

"Your boyfriend involved with the smuggling?"

She shakes her head. "Nope, but I won't claim he's entirely unaware."

"He ever talk to you about it?"

She gives me a wicked smile. "Howie and I don't spend a lot of time talking, if you know what I mean. He's a man who loves his muffin . . ."

I snicker at her comment and move on. "But yet you investigated him. You've never talked about it?"

Her humor dims and her shrewd eyes narrow. "What are you looking for, Detective? And how can I help?"

I shake my head. "Ongoing investigation. I don't want to get you involved."

"Why not? You're the one sitting in my kitchen asking questions. Besides, I have a little spare time between now and Dev's appointment in October. Sounds like you need me." She gives me another eyebrow wag.

I sigh. "You going to roll on your boyfriend?"

"Howard's a good guy. He's not the problem, it's his father. I'd like to know that not everything is going to be seized by the Feds when the time comes," she says matter-of-factly.

"What have you got so far?"

She waves a finger at me and shakes her head. "Nothing you can use, Detective. You know my methods. Anything I have is ill-gotten and can't be used without violating a take-out menu's worth of laws. But draft me proper and sanction my activities, and I'll see what I can dig up for you," she ends with a smug smile.

I get a sick feeling in the pit of my stomach, blow out a breath, and give her a hard look. "I really don't want to involve you, Lettie. If I do, they'll want more than that. They'll want you to go inside. You could jeopardize your position at Kingsbridge, but more than that. . . . These people are lethal; if they catch you snitching, you're as good as dead." I reach for her small but capable hand and squeeze it. "I couldn't live with myself if anything happened to you. Understand?"

Her gaze softens and she bites her lower lip, looking fourteen again. All pretense gone, she leans over and kisses my cheek. "Thanks, John. You've been a good friend to me and Devon. But I'm happy to help, if I can."

Damn it. That's what I was afraid of.

I don't say anything for a moment, just nod. Then I clear my throat. "When I came here today, I had wished to God you didn't know anything. But, yeah, I'll take it back and let them know." My brow drops into a heavy frown. "But you don't agree to anything until they guarantee full protection and immunity past, present, and future. Got it?"

Her lips lift to the side. "Got it, Detective."

I slide off my stool.

"Wait! Let me pack a muffin to go." She trots over to a drawer near the fridge and pulls out a zip-locking bag. She stuffs another baked treat inside and hands it to me.

I graciously take it with thoughts of saving it for tomorrow. My waistline has reached its limit of sugary carbs for the day. "Thanks, doll." I give her another peck on the cheek and pray I didn't just sign her death warrant. "I'll be in touch."

My cell rings the moment I hit Springfield Avenue, on my way to the Morris County office where I start my real day job. "Henshaw."

"John, it's Lisa."

My interest piques. "What did ya find out?"

"Baby wasn't born in Jersey, she was born in New York. Beth Israel Hospital. 1956. Birth cert lists both parents. Wife is listed under her maiden name. No first name on the child, but interesting, they gave the kid her father's last name. She's listed as Baby McNally. Female. No death cert. Trail ends there."

My hunch was right. Live birth. Now the million-dollar question: What the hell happened to Kat's big sister?

Chapter 27

Kitty

October 2016 – Thirty-Fifth Reunion Day

"WHERE DO THESE go?" Jillian asks, holding up a pair of what looks like a cross between an eggbeater and a feather duster.

I squint across a sea of boxes in my new dining room at the out-of-focus objects in her hands and promise myself a visit to the ophthalmologist. Age or fatigue, who knows? I can't see an everloving thing anymore. "Heck if I know. What are they?"

Jillian frowns with pursed lips and studies them more closely. "I'm not sure."

"What does the box say?"

She squats and reads the side of the large cardboard cube. "Jenny's Room."

We share a glance and say in unison, "Basement." Per my warning to Jenny, she has exactly three months to sift through her worldly belongings before I haul them to the curb.

A Nantucket-style cottage, this place is half the size of our old house and perfect for exactly two people and maybe a small dog or two cats. Or ditch the second person and make it two large dogs or four cats.

Bottom line, all nonessentials must go. I made a conscious decision not to be anyone's storage unit. Whatever Bob, Jenny, or I didn't want in our new homes, I either sold or donated—including the bed from the master bedroom. I bought a new queen-size bed from Pottery Barn and claimed the guest room furniture for my second bedroom. The tiny third bedroom is a perfect home office.

Jillian blows an errant wave of hair from her face and plants her hands on her hips. "May I make a suggestion? Since the bedrooms, bathrooms, half the kitchen, and living room are passable, let's quit for today and get you ready for the reunion. The rest of these boxes can wait until tomorrow, and, frankly, some of them can wait forever."

I survey the dining room and nod in agreement.

Definitely not the best plan to move the Thursday before the long-awaited Thirty-Fifth Summit High School Reunion. Long-awaited by someone who's not me.

My middle knots with an unhealthy mix of excitement and dread. I haven't had time to mentally prepare for tonight. Between the disarray of moving and the jarring impact of new living arrangements after twenty-plus years, I've been too overwhelmed to think straight.

Not wise when it comes to John, especially after our last conversation.

Of course, Dr. Graham did her best to ready me by attempting another drive-by into my no-go zone. We reached an impasse when I informed her that John deserves to hear it first, regardless of any clinical necessity. Thirty-five years overdue is better late than never. I had more bravado than conviction at the time and failed to produce a plan for delivering the news.

Now here I am, thoroughly unprepared.

I've protected the people I love for so long that time has compressed what I've hidden into a grenade of lies and lost opportunities. Once I pull the pin, I expect the shrapnel to hit everyone close to me, with John at the epicenter.

But I've come to terms with my decision, accepting that the cost of honesty could be, very possibly, losing John forever and alienating my family. Funny thing, *that*, about redemption—it's not usually synonymous with a happy ending. But what I've learned? Sometimes there are no good choices. Only a series of bad ones from which to choose the best.

I nod and wipe the perspiration from my brow. "Let me take a shower, then I'm putty in your hands, dear sister."

Jillian claps and beams with a delighted smile that borders on giddy. "I can't believe Jenny is missing this."

Humph. I can't say *I'm* sorry. Not tonight. If their intervention last month was any indication, they would've been downright annoying with their matching Cupid's bows. Jillian will be insufferable enough, a pitfall of having a sibling who writes romance for a living.

I shrug. "It's for a good cause. Devon's CEO induction dinner for Kingsbridge is tonight in New York." The thought warms me. After all my future son-in-law has been through, this is a huge milestone for him and his family. I couldn't be happier for him and Jenny.

Jillian sighs and looks swoony. "I know. Devon's a gem. I love them together." Then she squints and arches a brow. "Now if I could knock some sense into her mother regarding men. One tall, handsome detective in particular."

Did I mention *insufferable?* I paste on a smile. "Knock yourself out, but don't for one minute suggest I wear a thong."

Her smile dampens. "Why not? What about the thigh highs?"

I glare in answer.

She rolls her eyes. "Fine, but no 'granny panties,' as Jenny calls them, or I'm out of here," she says, her thumb pointing toward the door.

I snort. "Fine." Like anyone's going to care.

"And no orthopedic shoes!"

If it wasn't so ridiculous, I'd be offended. "I don't own orthopedic shoes."

"Or flats."

I huff. "Do you want me to tower over everyone?"

This time she glares back. "You're wearing heels with that dress, Kitty. No lip. I don't care if you're as tall as RuPaul, you're wearing them."

I lock my arms across my chest. "Really? You're comparing me to a six-foot-four drag queen?"

She rubs her temples and presses her eyes shut. "John's six-two; you have some room."

"You're doing it again, Jillian. Stop shoving me off on John. I knew other people in high school, you know."

Exhaling an exasperated breath, she closes up the box she'd been unpacking and shoves it aside. "Why do you go out of your way to make everything so hard on yourself when it comes to him?"

"Hard on me or hard on you?" I retort, losing patience.

Her eyes narrow and she shifts her hand onto her hip. "Are you, or are you not, planning to sit with him, Marshall, and Sue?"

I grind my teeth. "So?"

She raises her brows and stays silent.

"What?" I shrug.

"The dress. You didn't buy that dress for Marshall and Sue," she says, and gives me a challenging amber-hued stare. "You bought it for John."

"I bought it for *me*," I snap. How do I explain what took me almost eighteen months of therapy to discover? That I've spent the better part of twenty-five years trying to stay invisible, hiding behind my weight and out-of-fashion clothing? Not because I thought I looked good, but because I knew I *didn't*.

Wearing that dress is a large step for me. Sexing it up steps over the line and *makes* it for John. That's asking for trouble and equal to letting Kat out of her bag.

In my heart, I want that. But Kat can't be trusted not to minimize the damage without a plan. And right now, I'm one plan short.

Jillian hangs her head, shakes it, and looks back at me. "Putty in my hands, remember? That was our deal."

I release out a long, frustrated breath. Why did I agree to this? Oh, yeah! That's right! She bribed me. Her help with the move for the privilege of playing Fairy Godmother to her old, dowdy sister on reunion night—as if she didn't trust me to get ready on my own. If I didn't know better, I'd think that this is a conspiracy. I take that back . . . it probably is, led by my absent, darling daughter.

"Fine," I say, barely suppressing a growl.

She flashes a smug smile that sets my teeth grinding. "Take pity on the man for once and look your best. Unless he goes blind between now and then, he'll ask you to dance. Wear heels." Then she waves me off. "Chop, chop. Go take your shower."

My shoulders slump in defeat, and I grumble all the way to my new master bathroom.

Chapter 28

John

October 2016 – Thirty-Fifth Reunion Day

MY IPHONE TRILLS with a bing-bongy tune as I finish toweling dry in the bathroom. I secure the towel around my hips and walk to the dresser, praying the call isn't work-related. I'll freaking quit before I'll miss tonight's reunion.

Mom blazes at the top of the screen. I heft a sigh of relief and answer on the last ring.

"Hola mamá, ¿cómo estás?" I say with heartfelt warmth. "I was going to call you tomorrow. Everything okay?" We usually chat on Sundays.

She chuckles softly. "Tonight's your class reunion, *sí?*"

My spine stiffens a little. I smell a pep talk coming. My mother may be seventy-four, but she's still as feisty as ever. Whatever qualms she has don't extend to nagging me about my love life or lack thereof. She harbors hope that someday I'll miraculously supply her with grandchildren, which usually comes in the less-than-subtle form of, "*You know, cariño, men can father children well into their seventies. A grandchild would make my life complete.*"

José worships my mother, and for the last thirty years he's given her all the things she so richly deserves, but nothing can ever make up for losing two children and the shitty life she had before. Or for not having grandchildren, obviously.

"Yeah," I answer cautiously, preparing for a full-frontal assault.

"Is Katherine going?"

I let out a breath. "Don't know. I hope so."

"Did you send her flowers like I told you?" she asks with less patience.

I roll my eyes and grit my teeth. "No." For fuck's sake, she needs to give me some credit. I know she means well, but she doesn't get the nuances. Flowers would be a wrong move if there ever was one. Too aggressive, too soon. Nope, need to play this one cool, and leave it in the good Lord's hands that Kat will show up tonight.

She curses at me in rapid Spanish. "*¿Por qué no?* Women love flowers."

Last thing I need right now is my mother chewing out my fifty-four-year-old ass for not taking her advice like I'm still a teenager. I pass a hand over my eyes and suppress my frustration. "Pushing her won't bring her back. Her divorce isn't even final yet. Flowers would only make it worse."

A sigh filters over the phone. "It's been so long. You deserve happiness."

"Maybe . . . maybe not," I mumble.

"*Cariño . . . ,*" she says softly, "Why do you always sabotage yourself? Enough time has passed. You need to stop blaming yourself."

I stiffen and snap to attention. "For what?"

"You know what—your sister's death. That was your father's fault, not yours. Stop punishing yourself."

Her words take root deep in my chest and I blink. I wish I could deny it, but whenever I take a hard look at the shit that's happened to me, I can't escape the guilt that maybe I'm paying the cost of messing up the day Denise died. "Why would you say that?" I ask in a gruff voice.

"I'm your mother, I know these things," she whispers. "It's in your eyes every time her name comes up." No question I inherited my mother's intuition, but being the object of hers isn't pleasant. Makes me pity my perps.

Feeling exposed, I swallow back a lump and stay silent.

She continues on, "You've never been like your father. You're a good man, Juan, and I'm so proud of you. Remember what I told you when you came back from Kuwait, before the ten-year reunion? You weren't going to go, remember?"

Pressing my eyes shut, I nod as the lump chokes me. "Yeah . . ."

She'd told me that the only time she'd ever seen the light of happiness shining in my eyes was when I looked at Kat. That if I couldn't try to find that again for myself, I should do it for Ben and Denise. I needed to live my life, since they couldn't live theirs.

"If you love her, fight for her," my mother says with renewed passion. "She's worth it."

"I know," I choke out.

"And this time, *cariño*, don't do it for the dead—do it for the living. Do it for you."

Chapter 29

Kitty

October 2016 – Thirty-Fifth Reunion Night

FRESH FROM A shower and dressed in a fluffy white robe, I stare into the mirror in front of the master bath vanity where Jillian and I set up a chair.

Jillian drags a brush through my shoulder-length hair with one hand and blows it dry with the other.

The house may be small, but the last owner spared no expense making the master bathroom an oasis, which sealed my buying decision.

When my hair is almost dry, she takes a flat iron from her bag and works some style into it—more than I've had since my wedding a lifetime ago. Between that and my trip to the salon to have my hair colored, I look ten years younger. I barely recognize myself in the mirror.

My lips turn up in a smile, despite myself. "Thank you for doing this."

"I'm happy to." She meets my gaze in the mirror and smiles softly. "You look beautiful."

My cheeks flush at the compliment. I'd never be bold enough to consider myself beautiful, though I'll admit I haven't looked this attractive in decades.

She pats my shoulder. "Let's turn the chair so I can do your face." I lift my butt and we tug the chair a quarter turn. Jillian gathers my new creams and makeup, selects a moisturizer, and unscrews the top. "May I ask you a question?"

Uh-oh. "Sure."

She squints, dabs moisturizer up my neck and over my cheeks. "What's the significance of all things cherry-flavored?"

Warmth flares again in my face. Of all the questions. "Why do you ask?"

She caps the moisturizer, pulls my lip balm out of my makeup bag, and holds it up. "This—exhibit A." She sets it on the counter and dips her hand inside a second time. Plucking out my new *Bountiful Cherries* lipstick, she sets it beside the lip balm. "And this— exhibit B. They're both cherry-flavored. You're the only adult female I know who purposely wears flavored lipwear. Worse. All in cherry."

I scowl and mumble, "So I like cherries. *Arrest me.*"

Her brow quirks up. "I knew it had to do with him."

"What? *Ppth,*" I sputter. "I didn't say that."

Jillian pouts and stamps her foot. "Come on, Kitty. You promised more stories tonight." For a second, I'm a seventeen again and she's my baby sister.

I roll my eyes then give her a warning glare. "Jillian, if you ever repeat this to Jenny, I'll never forgive you," I say, shaking a finger for emphasis. "And! Don't ever let me see anything I tell you in one of your romance novels. Promise?"

"I wish people would stop saying that," she murmurs, and then slips on a grin and claps her hands like a giddy teenager anticipating juicy gossip. "Promise!" God, as much as I love my sister, I don't quite trust the mischievous flicker in her eyes.

Jillian's still grinning wide as she positions the dark, smoky-colored pencil next to my eye. "Now, look up and hold still so I don't poke you in the eye with the liner."

I wait until she finishes, trading the sharp pencil for a spongy wand, and moves onto applying eye shadow before I reveal the story behind my cherry lipwear. "Remember the story I told you last summer, the night we spread Vera's ashes in the ocean?"

She snickers. "Which one? You told a few."

"The one where I took John to Baskin-Robbins to celebrate his grade on the geometry test, and he teased me about my *cherry?*"

"Oh, yeah," she says, her smile gleeful.

The memory of my naïve boldness still sets fire to my cheeks and elicits an embarrassed smile. "I promised I'd give him my cherry when I was ready. Then, I tortured him with every cherry-flavored kiss." My smile fades. "I guess I never really stopped . . ." Torturing him, or letting go of the reminder that somewhere in my soul I was his.

Jillian's expression flattens with mine. "He was the *one*, wasn't he?"

I smile again and nod as she covers my skin with sheer foundation. "You know," she says, "most of my memories of you and John were from the second time you dated . . . after you got back together at your ten-year reunion. I remember loving him like a big brother when you both dated in high school, but I was too young to understand or remember much."

I glance at her, wondering where she'll take this. "You used to call him Johnny. He was crazy about you."

And he was. His soft spot for Jillian ran deep. A dichotomy of love and remorse. Jillian was as much a substitute as a reminder of the sister he lost. My mother would've been apoplectic if she knew that John was my co-babysitter all those nights at Vera's during high school.

"You and John seemed so happy that first summer I came home from Villanova after . . . ," she stammers and clears her throat. "Drew died." Her first summer without him after the accident the August before. All these years later, my heart still aches for her over his loss.

She sets down the blush brush, furrows her brow, and asks in a whisper, "What happened, Kitty? By Christmas, you had broken up with John and returned to California. Granted, I was coming out of a year-long depression over Drew's death, but what did I miss?"

Why did she have to start with the hard stuff? I release a slow breath and assess how much to disclose. Her losing Drew lies at the root of why I never told Jillian what came next, mostly to preserve mental ground she'd finally regained.

"It's complicated, Jillian," I say, unable to meet her eyes.

Her lips press into a hard, exasperated line. "I know. You've been telling me that for years." She sighs and gentles her tone. "John told me a little bit . . . about your time in high school. But he said I'd have to ask you about the second breakup."

Of course he did. I specifically made him promise not to tell her what happened after she returned to Villanova that next fall, and I'm not inclined to confess to hiding it. At least not tonight, since one question most likely will lead to more uncomfortable ones that I'm not ready to answer.

"Will you at least tell me about how you got back together at your ten-year high school reunion?"

Considering her request, I nod slowly. I can do that. I've already churned through the memories when I decided to attend this reunion. Releasing a deep exhale, I ready myself to begin.

But before I can speak she picks up the blush and says, "Suck in your cheeks." I pucker like a guppy and she dusts my cheekbones with feather-light strokes.

Leaning back, she sweeps an assessing gaze over my face, swirls the brush over the compact, and adds a touch more to my left cheek. "Before you start, tell me what happened after you left the first time. Did you have any contact in between that and the reunion? John ended his story with you at Stanford and him joining the Marines."

As she reaches for the lipstick, I take a second before answering her question, avoiding my no-go zone. "I sent a couple of letters after I left, but they went unanswered." Okay, so I didn't include a return address and maybe it was only one letter. "When I came home from Stanford in February, for winter break, John was already gone."

I remember only too well the thread of bitterness and the overwhelming ache in my heart when his mother told me he had enlisted in the Marines. A new plan that had no room for me. A new plan that unwound all of *my* plans.

"Why didn't you come home for Christmas?" Jillian asks, eyeing my mouth with the lipstick poised between her fingers.

"I had to take a class that conflicted with my normal schedule. It was that or a longer summer session."

I hold still until she finishes painting my lips, then resume my story. "After college I took an audit job with the old Andersen Consulting, now Accenture, in California. I traveled a lot until Mom got sick," I say, taking a momentary break to rub my lips together and spread the gloss. "Then I transferred to the East Coast and came home when you were thirteen."

More accurately, I caved to my mother's emotional blackmail to protect the secrets that had been forced upon me. But as far as my father knew, I returned to bury the hatchet with my mother before she died. Vera's support was invaluable in helping me find forgiveness for the woman whom I resented and despised.

"I remember that. Where was John when you moved back?"

I shrug. "I'm not sure. His mom, Rosita, had already met her second husband and moved to Miami. Vera had a military postal address for him that indicated he was stationed somewhere in the Middle East. Other than that, I didn't know where he was or see a point in trying to reach him."

"Did you still love him?" she asks in a tentative whisper.

"Of course . . . ," I say, feeling the remembered ache. "But there was too much to say, explain. A letter or phone call would never suffice. By then, he knew how to find me. I just assumed he didn't want to."

Jillian turns me around to face the mirror. I gasp at the stunning woman in the white robe staring back at me. "Jillian," I whisper, "You're a miracle worker."

"I had good clay." She smiles. "So you didn't see him again until the ten-year reunion?"

I nod, still astonished by my reflection. "That's right."

She leans back and boosts herself onto the granite countertop next to me. "I remember you traveled a lot for work before you met John again."

"Yes. The senior partner who I'd worked for in California asked me to take on a two-year project—the project where I met Bob. After that, I split my time between the two coasts. By the reunion, we were about a year into the project."

Jillian cocks her head and squints. "Were you and Bob . . . ?"

"Already involved when I met John again?" I press my lips together and nod slowly. "We were and we weren't. Things started to get hot and heavy between me and Bob about four months before the reunion. When you live, eat, and breathe work together on a project like we did then, it was easy to get attached and let things happen. But as the reunion drew closer, I took a step back, wanting some distance." Shaking my head, I admit the truth. "I put a hold on my relationship with Bob to regain my freedom before I came home."

She arches a brow. "So what happened at the reunion?"

"My whole world turned upside down." I close my eyes and

revisit 1991 and my ten-year high school reunion — the first time I'd seen John in a decade.

Chapter 30

Kitty

October 1991 – Summit High School Tenth Reunion

"Suuuue!" I squeal and propel myself into my friend's outstretched arms. I squeeze Sue with every ounce of strength I have, her basketball-size belly wedged between us. "I've missed you so much. Why didn't you tell me you're expecting?"

Sue giggles. "Surprise!" Her face holds a healthy glow.

I loosen my hold, step back, and gawk at her middle. "When are you due?"

She rubs her palm over her midsection in a slow circle and rolls her eyes. "Christmas week, if the dodo-bird doctors are right this time. Our first two came three and four weeks early, so we'll see."

I swallow and paste on a smile. "You and Marsh have sure kept busy."

At the mention of his name, Marsh wraps his arms around Sue from behind and rests his chin on her shoulder. "Hey, Kitty! I see you two found each other."

Marshall has aged nicely. Gone are the glasses and gangly frame. Even his hair has been tamed into symmetrical submission. His geeky image has transformed into handsomeness with a hip haircut and a lean, muscular build wrapped in expensive custom tailoring. Goodbye, Gumby. Hello, sexy California millionaire. Lucky Sue! Wow, who knew besides my mother?

"I'm so thrilled for you guys," I say.

Sue narrows her eyes. "So when are you coming to visit us in San

Jose?" I shift on my feet, feeling more than a little guilty. She's been after me to visit ever since my project started in San Francisco last year. Shamefully, I've hidden behind the pathetic excuse of work to avoid visiting.

"Yeah, Kitty, what's the deal?" Marsh chimes in with a teasing smile. "Do I need to stoop to kidnapping? It's been four years. I can't believe we have to come all the way home to see you."

I sigh. I'm a crap friend. I should go see them. But spending time with them is a raw reminder of how much I gave up . . . how much I lost. Finally, I throw up my hands and cover my embarrassment with a laugh. "All right! Stop shaming me. I'll come for dinner in the spring."

"Dinner? Heck, no!" Sue whines, "For the weekend, Kitty. The *whole* weekend. The nanny can watch the kids and we'll have some fun. I'll need some girl time by then—" Sue gasps and her eyes go wide as she stares over my shoulder.

I freeze and my heart instinctively pumps faster as Marsh straightens and breaks into a grin. Without moving his lips, he says, "Kitty, the eagle has landed."

Shit, shit, shit!

My hand trembles and I'm left feeling faint after the hasty exit of oxygen from my lungs. I lock my knees to keep from collapsing.

I'm thankful for the dress I chose and the makeup I applied with near perfection. On the off chance that John would be here, I prepared with the intention of showing him what he's missed and to make him regret that he's stayed away.

That was the idea until ten seconds ago.

When I left him the summer after high school, my plan was to come back . . . not to stay away forever. He was the one who made the more permanent choice to leave for a place I couldn't follow, never to return.

My spine stiffens. I don't have to turn around to know he's standing right behind me. Besides the prickling sensation running rampant over my skin, it's written on Sue and Marshall's faces. Taking a deep breath, I press my eyes shut for a second as I pivot.

I let the shock pass through me.

The man standing there is an older version of the boy wearing a cast who I'd abandoned on his sofa ten years ago. He stands tall and rigid. He's more muscled now than when he played football, and his hair is shorter and more severely cut. Shaved tight at the sides and bristled on the top, the style screams Marine. His face has hollowed and become more handsome with age. My gaze locks on his eyes and the quiet reserve inside the stormy, blue-gray pools. He's statue-still except for the twitching in his hands, which hang at his sides.

My lips part, but no words come out as I soak him in to the pounding of my heartbeat in my eardrums. The din of the room recedes into the background, and my world shrinks until it contains only the two of us.

His gaze caresses my face and his Adam's apple bobs as he swallows. "Kat," he whispers.

"Shaw . . .," I say on a heady exhalation. Everything and everyone else is forgotten.

Thump, thump, thump.

Oxygen returns to my lungs and I blink. Then my gaze latches onto his and my hand rises, trembling, to touch . . .

His gaze shifts to my hand and hardens from fire to ice.

I freeze, my fingertips falling short of reaching him. Pain slices through my chest sure and swift, shattering my heart into tiny shards that rain down like tinkling glass. I draw in a sharp breath as tears sting my eyelids. On reflex, I sprint around him and across the dance floor until I'm running blindly out the front entrance into the chilly night.

Halfway into the parking lot, a large hand clamps onto my arm with an iron grip and jerks me to a stop.

I gasp through my sobs as the momentum swings me around into a warm and familiar muscled chest.

John's lips are on mine before I can react, his hands cupping the sides of my face. Muscle memory takes over and my fingers dig into his hard biceps as I pour a decade's worth of pain, longing, and desire into the mouth I've craved for just as long.

I don't want the kiss to end. I'm crying, laughing, and dragging heaving breaths in and out all at once when he pulls away and tucks my head under his chin. My body is flush against him, absorbing his warmth and inhaling my favorite scent of spice and pine mixed with the distinct scent of his skin.

"Jesus, Kat . . .," he whispers, his heart thundering under my ear.

Questions clog my throat, aware that he deserves answers more than I do. Instead, I just spill what's in my heart. "I've missed you so much," I whisper back, wrapping my arms around his waist and locking my hands at the small of his back. My waning tears soak into the cotton next to my cheek.

His lips rest on my crown, his breath warming my hair. "Come back inside."

I'm afraid to move and shatter the moment. "Hold me for a minute?" I ask, on the verge of begging if he refuses.

Instead, his embrace gets tighter.

I close my eyes and savor the feel of him in case this is all there is.

He kisses the side of my head. "It's freezing out here. Let's talk inside." His voice is rough gravel.

Talk. I don't want to talk. I want to make love to him and forget that ten years have passed. That mistakes and choices have been made. That he's no longer mine.

Silently, I shift into position under his draped arm and we walk back toward the entrance. Instead of heading back to the ballroom, he steers me toward the Hilton's hotel restaurant.

I stop in the Ladies' room on our way to splash cold water on my face, repair my makeup, and gather my wits.

He's leaning against the wall across the hall when I come out, like he used to do in high school when he would walk me to class.

On second glance, I notice the dog tags around his neck over his tight black T-shirt, the cargos, and boots. A dive watch replaces the one he had when I knew him last. All in all, he looks amazing. Mouthwatering. Tempting . . . way too tempting.

He extends his palm and quirks his brow. I slide my hand into his and watch it disappear in his grasp. We walk in silence straight to the restaurant's bar and take the two stools in the far corner. He calls the bartender over and glances at me. "What are you having?"

"Tanqueray and tonic, twist of lime, please," I say, trying to keep the tremor in my hands out of my voice.

"Talisker. Neat," he says and hands the bartender his credit card. "Start a tab." He shifts on his stool and turns his stormy blue gaze to face me. He lets out a deep breath and shakes his head. He gives me a crooked smile. "You're going to be the death of me someday, woman."

I return his smile and hope that's not the case for either of us. "Same here," I whisper.

He pushes back a piece of my hair that's fallen into my face and his eyes soften. The bartender sets the drinks on the bar. John hands me mine then takes his.

"Toast?" He holds up his glass.

I nod and touch mine to his.

"To old friends."

I take a sip of my drink and try to ignore the pang of disappointment that jabs my heart. The reserved sparkle in his eye is painted with the unmistakable feeling of his retreat.

"Did you just get back?" I ask, taking a guess but not really knowing if that's the right question.

He nods, cradling his drink in his hands. "Been transitioning out since Desert Storm ended this winter and I got back from Kuwait."

My heart quickens. "So you're coming home for good?"

He gives me a sad, lopsided smile. "Where's home? My mom's in Florida now with my stepdad. Ben's gone, so there's really no place I can call home."

I'm your home! I want to blurt, and then I realize what he's said. I seize his forearm as my stomach drops. "Ben's gone?"

His shoulders slump and he scrubs a hand over his face. "Sorry. I forget you didn't know. Yeah. He died five years ago. Training accident."

"I'm sorry," I whisper, but that doesn't seem sufficient. I'd only met Ben those couple of times after John's accident. But I knew they were close.

A stoic look slides over his features. He sips his Scotch. "Thanks."

"When was the last time you exchanged letters with Vera? Does she know about Ben?" They've been in touch for years. She won't share his news unless I ask, and I stopped asking after he signed up for his second tour without trying to find me. But this . . .

He dips his head and shakes it. "No. It's been a while."

I study my drink as he avoids my gaze and revisits his glass. "So . . . what are your plans?" I ask, breaking the silence and selfishly hoping he won't be leaving again.

"NYPD Police Academy. Started this month." I nearly drown in a flood of relief, though I'm not sure I like the risks associated with his choice. Then again, the man came back from a Middle East conflict less than a year ago.

I take a large gulp of my gin and tonic in the most ladylike way possible, praying the alcohol hits my bloodstream. Anything to settle my jangled nerves. "Are you going to get a place in the city?" I remember that's where we talked about living "when we grew up," all those years ago in the Jacuzzi tub at Matt's shore house after the junior prom.

He nods and gives me a small grin. "Yeah. I got a studio in the West Village. Where are you living now?"

"I live in a couple of places," I say, keeping my voice casual as I play with the edge of my cocktail napkin.

A quizzical look creases his brow, paired with a hard, wary stare—John's version of veiled jealousy. If I'd moved in with Bob before we "took a break," John's reaction would've been warranted. A sparkle of hope reignites and glimmers in the distance.

I sigh and explain. "I live at home when I'm in working in New York, and I have a small apartment in San Francisco where I stay two weeks a month—for a long-term project with a West Coast client."

He gives a derisive sniff. "*Home?* How's Viv?"

"She died four years ago. Breast cancer," I whisper.

His brow furrows, his expression unreadable. "I'm sorry. I didn't know."

I give the only acceptable answer. "Thanks."

John throws back the rest of his drink and signals the bartender for refills. He clasps his hands loosely and gives me the full weight of his stormy stare. "So, you seeing anyone?"

Given the present situation with Bob, I answer guilt-free. "Not at the moment. You?"

He shakes his head. "Nope."

Warmth invades my chest along with that renewed glimmer of hope. Our kiss in the parking lot was ten years of pent-up emotion, I understand that, and even if I was still with Bob—I would've done it anyway. But any decision to attempt a second kiss needs a little more consideration . . . on both sides. At least relationships with other people won't be a factor.

As if on cue, he slides a finger down my cheek and whispers, "I've missed you, too, Kat. You look great."

My eyes close and I lean into his touch. "So do you."

His lips touch mine before I have time to react. So much for consideration. His tongue is soft yet insistent, and I melt into his mouth, tasting scotch mixed with gin. Need floods my soul as I grip the soft cotton covering his torso and sink my fingers into the warm muscled flesh above his hips.

We're breathing heavily, sharing the same air when we part.

"John Henshaw, you're still my Kryptonite," I murmur.

He pulls my barstool close enough so that I'm seated between his thighs. All I can think about is taking him in my mouth and running my fingertips over the birthmark above his glute as he's yelling my name at the height of ecstasy.

God, I've never needed a man like I need him right now.

"Shaw?" I ask, my breath labored.

"Yeah?" His stare is fixed on my lips.

"Let's get a room," I whisper without a moment's hesitation.

His eyes dilate and darken. He leans in close enough for his lips to touch my ear, and whispers, "Patience, Kitten. Later. I've waited ten years. I want to dance with you first." He trails a kiss down my neck to my collarbone, sending a shiver along my spinal column. Then he continues his trail of soft kisses up the opposite side of my neck, resting his lips beside my other ear, before saying in a throaty growl, "Then I'm going to break the Guinness Book of World Records for using the most condoms in one night."

This time the shiver doesn't stop until it hits the juncture of my thighs and I gasp. He huffs a laugh and slides off his stool.

I'm panting as he closes the tab. On our way out, he twines his fingers in mine and pulls me in to lay a kiss on my forehead. "Let's do this." And then we stroll back to the ballroom.

Kitty

Thirty-Fifth High School Reunion Night

I STOP MY story there, aware that I'm already late. If the heat in my cheeks is any indication, I'm probably beet red. I glance at the mirror. Yup. Bright crimson.

Jillian stares at me with a wide grin then giggles into her hands. "Oh my God! I love it!"

"Can we save the depressing breakup part for another time?" I beg.

"Deal. After that story? I wouldn't want to ruin the moment! You need to recapture *that* tonight. Who knew John had it in him?" she says with a delighted twinkle in her eye. "One question, then I'll let you go."

I brace myself, suspecting what she's going to ask. "Depends."

"How many condoms did you use?"

I fail miserably at suppressing a wicked smile. "That night? Or including the next morning?"

I've never seen my sister wear a wider grin.

"Both."

I stare at the ceiling and pretend to count even though I've never forgotten the number. "Five."

She squeals and does a little dance. "Kitty, you're my hero! Wait here. Don't come out until I tell you."

My face drops into a suspicious frown. "Why?"

"No questions!" she closes the door behind her.

I drum my fingers on the counter for what feels like an eternity before I hear, "You can come out now!"

I crack open the door. Jillian's gone. My dress is laid out on the bed with a pair of high heels on the floor. Next to it, a thong and a pair of thigh highs.

Oh no, she didn't!

I race to my underwear drawer. It's filled with bras, thongs, and nothing else.

Son of a bitch! Next stop is my closet. All of my flats are gone.

"Jilliaaaaaan!" I scream at the top of my lungs.

"Call me tomorrow! Settle for four, he's not as young as he used to be! Good luck!" she says a moment before the front door slams.

By the time I get downstairs, her car is halfway down the street.

I plod back upstairs and snatch the dress off the bed.

Two boxes of condoms are hidden underneath. I roll my eyes and growl through gritted teeth as I take the scrap of fabric Jillian left behind and shimmy into what's no more than a triangle and some string, cursing her, my daughter, and every dead person responsible for my plight.

Chapter 31

John

October 2016 – Thirty-Fifth Reunion Night

"YO, SHAW? THAT you?" The question comes with a touch of good humor and a slap on the back that sends a ripple over the top of my beer.

When I turn, Matt Ferguson's wearing a crooked smile and a good thirty pounds more than the last time I saw him.

I set down my beer on the nearest high table and pump his hand. "Mad Dog! Good to see you, man." And it is, if for nothing else than the satisfaction that after all my hard work with Raine I won't have the future that's standing in front of me. Unlike my friendship with Tony, Matt and I didn't stay close after I enlisted. A few beers over the years, but not much else.

His small, blonde wife stands next to him flaunting some serious cleavage. She was a sophomore when we were seniors. Her name escapes me even though it shouldn't. Not a surprise. I'm crap with names but never forget a face. It's forced me to come up with a few creative solutions over the years.

I reach for one now as I lean in and give her a peck, "Hey, gorgeous. Beautiful dress."

She giggles and wags her eyebrows. "Hey, John. You're looking pretty fine yourself."

I flash a tentative smile, hoping Kat will agree.

I'm certainly not the twenty-nine-year-old guy I was at our tenth reunion, the last time we did this. Not to get ahead of myself, but at fifty-four, there's not a hope in hell I'd be able to get it up five times in twelve hours. Even back then, I'd chalked that miracle up to pure adrenaline and a decade's worth of pent-up desire. I'd wind up in the ER if I tried that shit now. If the opportunity arises, I'd be grateful for a solid double play. *Just saying.*

"Thanks." I clear my throat, noticing his wife's hot, roving gaze. *Not a chance, honey.* I glance at Matt, "You guys still living in Vegas?" Last I heard, they owned a staffing agency that supplied casino workers.

"For now. Matty Junior moved to San Diego with the wife and grandbabies, so Mandy and I are thinking about getting a rental for the summer when school lets out. We can work remotely from there." He glances at my left hand. "What about you? Wife? Kids?"

"Nope." I grab my beer and take a swig.

"You still talk to Kitty?" Matt asks, draping a protective arm around Mandy.

Tension fills my spine behind a relaxed, mildly amused smile. "We keep in touch. I'm godfather to her sister Jillian's daughter, Rachel." I leave it at that.

"She coming tonight?"

Fuck, I hope so . . . in more ways than one. I shrug. "Last I heard, yeah."

Matt points to the bar. "Get you a refill?"

I shake my head and clap him on the back, ready to make an exit. "I'm gonna hit the men's. Catch you later?"

He gives a nod, so I head into the crowd and expel a relieved breath. Ten minutes and I already want to leave.

There's only one reason I came and she hasn't arrived yet. I catch my reflection in the mirrored walls and say a silent prayer, thanking our class president for making this a formal event. Not my usual gig, but with a new suit that Devon, Jenny's fiancé, helped me select—a month's paycheck, gone—a fresh haircut, and a close shave, I'm at my finest. If Kat doesn't bail, my bet's on her wearing a dress—something I haven't seen in decades.

Across the room, Marshall and Sue stroll in. A smile slides onto my face and I relax for the first time since I arrived. Fine, maybe there are two reasons I'm here. I head in their direction. We plan to share a table.

Looking at Kat's best friends now, you'd never know they were the class geeks. Sue's a corporate lawyer, and for a woman in her fifties, she's hotter than hell. Tall and slender with a knockout smile from all those years wearing braces and unencumbered by soda-bottle glasses after Lasik, she's just as beautiful on the outside as she is on the inside. Something I never noticed or appreciated in high school.

Sue dangles off Marshall's arm in a sexy red dress and high heels, waving frantically and wearing a big grin. Still one of the tallest guys I know, Marsh filled out nicely once he exited puberty. He made a mint on a start-up in Silicon Valley, enough that they took their private jet from California. Even though they're own-your-own-jet kind of rich, they're still as down-to-earth as they come.

We've kept in touch over the years; it's been nice. I've always welcomed Sue's care packages when they came during my time in the service. Every Christmas like clockwork, there would be something special waiting.

"Johnny!" Sue yells and throws herself at me.

My smile widens as I catch her. "Hey, Suze. Good to see you, beautiful." She slides away and I seize Marsh's hand and pull him into a man hug. "How's it going? You just get in?"

"A couple of hours ago. We stopped at my parents' first, and we'll see Sue's parents tomorrow before we go back." He shakes his head. "No rest for the weary."

Sue latches back onto his arm and squeezes. "Don't let him fool you, he loves the insanity."

He gives her a crooked smile and his eyes dance with merriment. "She's right. I can't complain." Then his gaze sweeps over me. "You weren't kidding about working out. You look good. Whatever you're doing, keep doing it."

"Thanks. I plan on it. How are the kids?" I ask.

Sue lights up. "Great! We're expecting our third grandchild. Crazy, huh? Everyone's coming home for Christmas, so it should be absolute mayhem. I love it!"

Not having kids never bothered me as much as it has recently. Ever since Jillian and Raine asked me to be Rachel's godfather. That baby cracked open something inside of me and provided a grim reminder of how badly I'd fucked up with Kat the second time. After we got back together. Whatever it takes, if I have another chance, I won't be that stupid again.

"Kitty here yet?" Sue asks.

I shake my head. "Not yet. You hear from her?"

She frowns and purses her lips. "She sent a note last week and said she might come, but hasn't answered my emails since. I tried calling, but her cell mailbox was full and the home number I had is out of service."

A classic case of Kat-like avoidance. "She moved into the new house on Pine Grove this week," I offer.

Sue crosses her arms. "No excuse. I'll hunt her down tomorrow and give her hell if she doesn't show up." Sue won't be the only one on the hunt.

Marsh points at a table. "Hey, why don't we grab seats before the tables fill up?"

We stake out a prime spot near the dance floor with a full view of the front entrance. Out of habit, I sit where I can see the door. Matt and Mandy join us, and I wave Tony and his wife over. I get a sudden flashback of our table at the junior and senior proms—same cast of characters, only a lot more life behind us now.

Tony and I trade a glance after I give Maria a hello kiss.

"Save my seats," I say to Sue over my shoulder as I follow Tony away from the table. She winks and places open napkins in front of both my seat and the one I've saved for Kat. Here's hoping I don't end up sitting alone all night and looking like a chump.

Tony and I hit a quiet spot along the ballroom wall. "The raid moved up. They're going in tonight," Tony says in a low voice.

I fight back the sudden urge to punch something. "Are you fucking kidding me?" I grit my teeth, my hands fisting at my sides. Of all the goddamn nights. "Lettie said the delivery wasn't happening until next week." I'm still less than thrilled that she joined Tony's task force as a snitch after our tête-a-tête in her kitchen last month.

Chewing his lip, he shakes his head and won't meet my gaze. "She's wrong."

After a quick glance around, satisfied we won't be overheard, I stare him down. "How the fuck could she be wrong? She's never wrong."

"Got word from another informant. Someone on the inside. Don't worry, I know tonight is important. You won't get called unless it breaks bad."

"Good. Make sure it doesn't," I grumble and stalk away to get some air. Damn right tonight is important, and work better not screw it up. Still, Tony's news gets under my skin. Something feels off. I duck out of the ballroom and find a quiet alcove down the hallway to call Lettie. I'm dumped straight to voicemail. *"You've reached Leticia Soames. Leave a message."*

Shit. That's right. Devon's induction is tonight. Chances are she's with Cato's son. I hang up without leaving a message and sneak back into the ballroom through a side door.

I'm halfway to the table when Kat walks in. I grind to a halt and nearly drop to my knees. Blood thunders through my veins in a mad rush and sends my heart slamming against my ribs.

My gaze rakes over her with hunger and longing while my lungs forget to breathe. The black dress she's wearing clings to her slimmer new curves and bares more cleavage than she's ever shown in public. In high heels, her legs look like they go on forever.

Holy hell. I'm blown away. I haven't seen her in makeup for over two decades and the effect is . . . *Sweet Lord.* I'd bet every dime in my bank account on the flavor of her lips. A flavor meant to torment me. She's so fucking gorgeous I can't do anything but blink like an idiot. Once. twice. A dozen times.

A smile grows on her face as she spots Sue, who's waving frantically to get her attention. Forcing some air into my lungs, I manage to uproot my feet from the carpet and walk to our table.

I approach from behind and wait as she and Sue squeal in a delighted embrace. Déjà vu slams me when Sue's gaze catches mine and she whispers something to Kat. Her spine stiffens, and she slowly turns to face me.

I slide a hand into my pocket and school my expression into relaxed male appreciation as I fight like hell not to press her against me and bury my tongue and part of my lower anatomy into two very different parts of her. *Heaven help me.*

Our gazes meet and a hint of a smile plays on her lips. I lean in and drop a kiss on her cheek, catching a whiff of cherries. The scent that meant she was mine.

"You came," I say in a hoarse whisper, fighting a head rush and thankful my voice doesn't come out as a croak.

The corner of her mouth quirks up and her eyes sparkle. "I came *here . . . yes."*

My eyes press shut for a second and heat rises up my neck as I remember the lines of teasing banter we used to trade back then—the last time we were together . . .

I open my apartment door, drag her inside, and latch onto her neck. "You came." I growl and kick the door shut.

"Not yet, but I'd like to," she says in an urgent whisper between heated kisses. She runs her hands down my back and under the top of my jeans until she's cupping my bare ass.

"Give me a minute, and I'll see what I can do about that." I shove aside her blouse, past her bra, until my teeth and tongue are wrapped around her nipple and I'm tugging a moan from her throat. Without missing a beat, I hoist her up with her arms wrapped around my neck and her legs around my waist, and I carry her in the direction of my bed.

Maybe I should leave the room and gather my freaking wits before I eat my shoes all night. Or worse. I clear my throat and add, "No pun intended."

Her smile softens and I see a glimmer of my old Kat behind her eyes. "None taken . . . yet."

Fuck. It's going to be a long night. I untie my tongue and point at the chair next to Sue. "We saved you a seat. You want a drink?" I ask, and scratch the back of my head, hoping to step away and down a shot to settle my nerves and dampen my libido. Erectile dysfunction? Not a problem.

She nods.

"Tanqueray G and T, twist of lime?"

She nods again and gives me a soft smile.

I take Sue's and Marsh's drink order and leave in search of a slice of sanity. After two quick shots of premium Scotch, my hands stop shaking and I recover what's left of my mind. I make my way back with everyone's drink orders.

Dinner slides by with a lively discussion around the table and a good amount of old stories and laughs. Even though Kat didn't come as my date, it feels good—natural—to have her at my side.

But as dinner wears on, I feel less and less confident that I'll be ending the night with Kat in my arms. She's been friendly but distant, and doesn't seem nearly as affected by me as I am by her.

The DJ plays a mix of '80s and '90s music, some songs more danceable than others. Mandy and Matt head out for a dance, while the rest of us stay and chat over coffee.

I'd be lying if I said I wasn't disappointed, enough that I withdraw from the conversation, going from participant to observer. Being this close to Kat and not being able to touch her makes me feel like I'm dying of hunger in front of a locked refrigerator.

A few notes play from "The Flame" by Cheap Trick, the first song we danced to at our tenth reunion, and I'm on my feet before my brain has a chance to catch up. My heart pounds as I offer Kat my hand. "Dance with me?" I whisper. The gravel in my voice barely travels past my throat.

Her lips part and her wide, brown eyes meet mine with a watery gaze. She's more beautiful than I've ever seen her, and I can't wait another second to test my chances.

She nods. "Yes . . ."

My heart skips a beat and I swallow. Slowly, she raises her hand and rests it in my palm. I twine my fingers through hers and let the buzz of her touch travel over my skin as I lead her to the center of the dance floor.

I pull her into me, welcoming the curves of her body pressed to mine. She tucks her head into my neck, and my knees go weak. I fight to stay upright and move to the music.

My eyes close and I sing the lyrics softly into her ear. *"Wherever you go . . ."* *I'll be with you.* This damn song is like a window into my soul, letting me sing all the truths buried inside. She was the first woman I ever fell in love with, and more than anything, I want her to be the last—the last woman I ever make love to. Like the song says, whatever she wants, I'd give it to her. A million times over.

I inhale her sweet perfume and shelter her body with mine, not wanting to ever let her go. I get to the final chorus, and she squeezes me back . . . hard. I lean back and tip up her chin. The pull of her lips taunts me.

The music fades along with the room, and the only thing that matters is Kat. My Kat, standing flush against me the way we stood on a different dance floor twenty-five years ago.

My lungs seize as I stare into her eyes, afraid to make the wrong move and lose her all over again. "God, you look so beautiful tonight . . . ," I say in a voice rough and raw with longing. My lips hover over hers and I swallow.

"Shaw?" Her voice is barely a whisper.

"Kat?" I stare into the face of the woman who has haunted my dreams for most of my life and try to remember how to breathe. I fail and clutch her tighter against my thumping heart.

"Kiss me," she says on a shallow exhale.

Time stands still, and it takes every sliver of control I have not to sweep my arms under her legs and carry her out of here.

My eyes close and I bridge the gap between us, inhaling our shared breath and her cherry-scented promise. My lips connect with hers and muscle memory takes over. I match the insistence of her tongue stroke for stroke as everything inside me disintegrates into raw burning need. A chill shoots down my spine and awakens my groin with one swift kick.

Her hands travel down my back, pulling me closer and raising the hairs on my arms. Our kiss is a familiar tango that's been relegated to my fantasies.

I cradle her neck in my palm and rest my lips next to her forehead as we sway to another song. "You're killing me, Kat."

Her fingers graze my cheek and she sucks my gaze to hers. I almost whimper from the desire burning in her eyes. She rests her other hand in my waistband under my suit jacket. "Shaw . . . Come home with me tonight."

I gulp. "You sure?"

She nods. "Yes . . ."

I laugh softly and dip in for another kiss, disbelieving my ears. "Can we leave now?" Before she changes her mind.

She bites her lip. "Yeah."

As far as I'm concerned, we can't get out of there fast enough. We say our goodnights, and I follow her with my police radio turned off from the hotel back to her new house on Pine Grove. I'm floating like a helium balloon. The world can melt in a nuclear disaster tonight for all I care.

I pull into the driveway behind her and shut off the engine when it hits me like a bucket of ice water.

One night won't be enough. To have a future, we need to unload all the secrets of the past between us.

I rest my head on the steering wheel then slam it twice. To knock some sense *out* of it this time. *Fuck it.* If once is all I get, I'll take it and worry about the rest tomorrow. I slam it once more for good measure.

Mission accomplished.

Chapter 32

Kitty

Reunion Night, My House

I PULL THE keys from the ignition and glance at John's car in my rearview mirror then have a momentary flash of panic.

What the hell was I thinking, inviting him back here? I'm fortunate he didn't think to check my blood alcohol level before we left to drive the two miles home. John, in combination with alcohol, is a lethal combination for both my heart and my libido.

I'm still cursing Jillian for this damn thong and the fresh memory of my ten-year-reunion night of passion that left me walking bowlegged for two days afterward.

Sitting next to John with a string and a little too much airflow teasing my vagina all night didn't help my decision-making. How do women wear these things?

But the dance is what pulled me over the edge. I'd been doing well enough until that Cheap Trick song came on, and I was in his arms on the dance floor with his sexy serenade in my ear. Lyrics he meant to be a personal message like his long-ago performance at the junior prom. Sealing the deal, my pounding heart matching his, beat for beat, alongside the unmistakable—and not unwelcome—feel of his arousal.

Now here I am in my driveway, lust-filled Kat without a plan.

Shit, shit, shit!

After drawing in a few deep breaths, I step out of the car to find him waiting a few feet away. The outside lights illuminate the brooding yet determined expression on his face. The corner of his mouth lifts into a half smile, and he reaches out a hand like he's testing the waters.

I hesitate a moment then lay my hand onto his outstretched palm and let him swallow it inside warm, clasping fingers.

He reels me in. "Kat, I—" There's a raw ache in his voice.

Nope. We can't go there. I press a finger to his lips and shake my head. "No talking. Not tonight," I whisper and remove my finger. His lips are too close to ignore. I'm living on borrowed time, so I improvise the best plan I can and kiss him, tasting the remnants of the Scotch he drank mixed with the heady scent of his cologne.

I savor every familiar touch of his tongue and almost groan with the soul-deep ache of how much I've missed him. Twenty-five years suddenly feels like yesterday. His free hand finds the small of my back and he presses me into him, his stiffening length growing between us. My body shifts to autopilot and I grind my hips into him. The string pulls taunt against my swollen center under the dress. *Oh, help me* . . . Whatever on God's green earth made me think I could resist this man?

I moan and he growls into my neck. "Is moaning allowed?" His voice is thick and ragged, but there's a twinkle in his stormy gaze.

"Most definitely," I say, and pull him toward the front door. My fingers tremble as the key seats into the lock and I let us in.

Draping my coat over the banister with only half a thought, I head straight up the stairs as he follows.

The room is dark other than a small reading lamp next to a chair across the room, which gives off a low ambient glow. Enough to see by but not enough to unveil flaws.

I'm halfway inside when John's hands gently grasp my shoulders from behind. He slides his arms around me and breathes into my hair. "Wait . . ."

"What?" I ask tentatively, melting back into him and hoping he's not having second thoughts.

He kisses my hair. "Do we need protection?"

The irony grips me and I stifle a laugh. Bob had a vasectomy, so I never had to worry. I'm still in perimenopause, so theoretically, yes, I could get pregnant though the chances are low. Still . . .

"Definitely." But the protection I need has more to do with my heart. "I have condoms, thanks to Jillian." Turns out I'll have to thank her . . . *after* I forgive her.

He huffs a laugh. "Should I ask?"

I snort and turn to see the amused gleam in his eyes. "Probably not."

"Would you hold it against me if I told you I came prepared?" His warm fingers wrap around my waist, and he presses me flush so my hips meet his.

I slip my hand between us and down the front of his pants to caress the erection underneath. "You always do," I whisper next to his ear then kiss his lower lip. "Now stop talking."

Letting out a low growl, he slides his hands up my arms and tugs me closer, claiming my mouth in a hot kiss.

Limbs tangle and clothing flies until I'm sitting on the edge of the bed with him standing in front of me wearing only his open dress shirt.

My hands clamp onto his hips and I swallow him whole. His fingers thread deep in my hair, and he groans. "Kat . . ."

I play his body, rediscovering all of his intimate hot spots.

He pushes my hair back and says in a rough whisper, "Babe, this feels too good. You gotta let me go." Then he shifts away and slides out of my mouth with a sharp moan and a mumbled curse.

He cups my face and tips it up, sealing his lips over mine and caressing my tongue before pulling away and dropping to his knees in front of me. Pushing me back on the bed, he slides my dress up my hips until he sees all that's standing in his way is a piece of string.

His eyes widen and he runs his fingers up my thighs over the bands of the thigh highs onto bare skin. "Holy fuck, Kat. If I'd known what was under this dress, we would've been here hours ago," he rasps, and then slips off the thong.

His face disappears between my legs and a second later his tongue hits my core. I close my eyes and sink into the sensation. The memories of us come back sharp and crisp, and he more than lives up to them.

It doesn't take long for my body to shatter under his touch. I clench the covers and exhale his name.

"That's it, baby," he whispers, and kisses my thigh, his fingers still stroking deep.

He rests for only a moment before dipping his head back for

another pass.

Oh my God.

After I've climaxed for a second time, he crawls up next to me and swipes a hand across his mouth. "Where are the condoms?"

"Bedside table," I pant, sending him on a quest for protection as I wrestle my way out of the dress and unhook my bra.

He stretches across the bed to reach into the drawer and find the box, and then he hands it to me and flips onto his back. He's always let me take control of this part. For some reason, I like it.

The corner of his mouth lifts. "Keep the stockings on." Fortuitous. It's the only thing I'm still wearing.

I rip the foil open and roll it over him. I'm happy to see he stands as tall and proud as he did that last time I had the pleasure of experiencing him. He slips his shirt off. His workout schedule with Raine has paid off. I get a full view of his chest tattoo and nearly flat stomach.

Seeing my name over his heart triggers a twinge of guilt that I promise myself I'll deal with tomorrow. Tonight, it's just us. No baggage, no reality. Just my love for him.

He pulls me down beside him and trades places so he's hovering over me. Then he kneels between my legs, hooking one around his waist. He dips down to glide his lips up my neck, sending a shiver over my skin as he positions himself at my entrance.

"I've missed you, babe," he whispers next to my ear and pushes inside with a slow thrust. A hiss escapes through his lips as I open for him and he sinks deep.

A shudder passes along his shoulders and his lips part. Then he moves in a steady, sensuous rhythm, massaging every inch of me with his length. Bracing on an elbow on one side and clutching my leg on the other, he adjusts his angle until he fills me fast and deep with raw, undulating motion that sweeps over my core.

I lose myself in his deliberate and skilled lovemaking. His body has always felt like it was made for mine. That hasn't changed. I'd almost forgotten how good sex could feel as the pressure builds in the most sensitive part of my body.

Time engulfs us, and I let go of every rational thought and drift toward my release.

He trails his tongue and lips along my neck through ragged breaths. A thin layer of moisture covers our skin where it touches—

his chest to mine. "Kat . . . you're close . . . come for me," he says in a gravel-filled whisper.

"Faster," I say and run my nails down his back over the scars and down the hollow. I arch my head back into the pillow, craving that moment of wild abandon.

His eyes slide shut and he releases a cross between a scream and a groan as he slams his way home and his entire body goes rigid. We find our release together in one unceasing wave. Letting it crest, we ride it home.

Exhaustion overtakes me and I turn to jelly beneath him with the ebbing retreat of our orgasms.

Our chests surge and I'm not sure who's sucking in breath faster before he shudders and collapses next to me.

He pulls me onto his slippery chest, his arm resting like a dead weight around my shoulders. We lie still for a few minutes, silent, with nothing but the sound of labored breathing and pounding hearts.

I run my fingertips through the damp hair on his pecs as they rise and fall and trace my name written over his heart. "I remember when you got this," I say softly.

He swallows over a panting breath. "That's easy. Do you still remember why?"

"Yes," I whisper. On the night of our tenth reunion, in the midst of our marathon lovemaking session, we poured out our hearts. Though I refused to answer his question on why I initially left, I had no problem expressing my hurt and anger over the fact that he left me, too. While my departure was meant to be temporary, he never came back. We lay in bed then like we are now.

"I may have been gone, but I never left you," he says, brushing my hair back and staring into my tear-filled eyes. Then he takes my hand and places my palm on his chest. "You've always been right here, Kat, in my heart. No one has ever taken your place. I'll prove it to you."

By the end of that day, he had my name tattooed over his heart. A mark that I'd staked a claim. A promise that I'd always be with him.

A promise I later forced him to break.

I continue to run my fingers through the short curly hairs over his tattoo, enjoying the soothing feel of them against my skin. "Did you ever regret it?"

He pulls me close, kisses my hair, and says, "Never. It's still true."

Tears prick the backs of my eyelids. My gaze snags on the circular, pink scar below his waist. Fighting back a wave of shame, I run my fingertips down to caress it. The thought of my secrets taking him away again guts me. I squeeze my eyes shut and fight back tears.

We lie quiet for a few more minutes before he excuses himself to use the bathroom and dispose of the condom. The toilet flushes, and when he comes out I feast my eyes on his glorious naked body. The washboard abs of his late twenties and early thirties are only a ghost of what they once were, but his appeal as a man in his fifties hasn't waned one bit. Neither has his lack of modesty, or the amused grin he gets as I ogle him.

He slips under the sheets with me, and I return to his embrace, inhaling the scent of our lovemaking clinging to his skin.

"Tired?" I ask.

He nibbles my neck and says low in his throat, "I'm not calling it a night until I have my way with you again. . . ." His arms tighten like steel bands around me, and we drift off for a minute anyway.

I flinch as a chiming cell phone in an unrecognizable tone shatters the silence.

"Shit," John mutters, and then rolls out of bed. He takes a few strides to his discarded suit jacket and fumbles in his pocket to retrieve it.

"Henshaw," he says through a low snarl into the phone.

My gaze drifts over the Grim Reaper and other assorted military tattoos that cover his back and artfully hide his scars, down to the birthmark over his left buttock. I admire the view. He still has one of the best tight ends I've ever seen.

He mutters another curse. "Give me twenty minutes." Then he tosses his cell onto the rug and comes over to sit on the edge of the bed. His brow furrows, and he runs a hand through his hair, looking less than happy. "Gotta go, babe. They called a raid tonight and need backup. Do me a favor?"

I sit up, draping myself in the sheet. "Sure . . ."

"Get my bag out of my trunk while I jump in the shower? I have to change."

I nod. He lays a kiss on my lips and lunges for his suit jacket again, then tosses me his keys. I let the sheet drop and catch them.

"Does your bag have another pair of underwear?" I ask, hustling out of bed.

His brow bunches and he cocks his head. "Yeah, why?"

"Good. Hope you don't mind if I borrow these." I grab his boxers and slip them on. "Jillian stole all my underwear and left me with that dental floss you took off me."

He breaks into a laugh and then heads to the bathroom, giving me another full view of his luscious backside. "Thank her for me."

"Ha! Not likely," I say, hastily pulling on clothes as the door closes.

I run down and retrieve a small black duffle bag marked FBI and place it on the bed. A chill passes through me, along with memories of why I left last time.

He comes out five minutes later, wearing a towel around his hips.

"FBI?" I ask.

"Joint task force with Tony," he says, unzipping the bag.

In less than two minutes, he's fully dressed in a black T-shirt, Kevlar vest, black cargos, and boots, his weapon holstered under a black jacket. He zips the bag and rounds the bed to where I'm reclined, watching him get ready.

He drops the bag, pulls me to my feet, and wraps me in an embrace. "I'll pick up my suit when I see you later. And Kat?" I meet his gaze. "I *will* see you later."

I nod and rest my head on his shoulder. I breathe in the fresh ocean scent of my body wash at the base of his neck. He strokes my hair and tucks me under his chin. "Tonight was amazing. I don't want to lose you this time, Kat. I want to be your last. . . . No more secrets."

His not-so-subtle hint that he's not going to do this without answers. My borrowed time is almost up. I squeeze him tight and tip my head back until I can see the stormy blue eyes I adore. "Be safe, Shaw." *I love you, and I've never stopped.*

"If this goes well, I'll be back before morning. Leave a key under the mat for me?" He gives me a sexy, crooked smile. "I'm not done with you yet."

"Deal," I whisper, and then we share another heady, passionate kiss before I see him out and his unmarked car is racing down Pine Grove.

Like all good things, this too shall end.

Chapter 33

Kitty

Later That Night . . .

THUNK! THUNK! THUNK!

"*Urgh*," I open my eyes from an exhausted sleep and squint in the darkness. Lifting my head off the pillow, I try to determine if I'm still dreaming or if the *thunk*ing is real.

The numerals illuminated on my alarm clock read 3:30 a.m. That was fast. John left only two hours ago. *John*. A sleepy smile slips onto my lips.

Thunk, thunk, thunk! The pounding takes on more insistence, and I wonder why he doesn't check under the mat.

"Hold your horses," I mutter, then silently berate myself for not just giving him a key as I switch on the lamp next to the bed. Wearing nothing but John's boxers, I throw on my robe.

I scurry downstairs. Flipping the lock, I swing the door open, "The key's under—" The words die on my lips, and an icy chill runs through my veins. "Jillian, what's wrong?"

"We tried to call. You didn't answer your cell." Jillian stifles her crying with the back of her hand and pushes inside. She looks like she dressed in haste, her coat thrown over a pair of yoga pants and hair barely brushed. Her SUV sits idling in the driveway.

She grabs me into a hug and whispers. "Get dressed, Kitty. We have to go." Her red-rimmed amber gaze meets mine, and she says softly, her lip trembling, "It's John. . . . He's been shot."

"But he was just . . ." *Here.* My knees almost collapse under me as the air rushes from my lungs. "Is he . . . ?"

"No, but it's bad." Jillian holds me up as I suck in breaths.

Oh dear God. The chill I felt earlier comes rushing back. "This can't be happening again," I murmur through my shock. *You better not die on me, Shaw!* My reflexes take over and I race up the stairs and grab a bra on the way to my closet. I strip off the robe and throw on a pair of jeans over John's boxers and top it off with the first shirt I can grab. Socks and running shoes are the best I can do.

I swipe at the salty trails streaming down my cheeks and unearth the seat of our secrets from my jewelry box. I stare at the letter postmarked last August, the day Vera died. Words she'd spoken before I left John the last time come rushing back to me. . . .

"Promise me something, Katherine." She doesn't wait for my response. *"That someday you'll tell him. That you won't take this to your grave . . . or let him go to his without knowing. Give him that. Return what you took from him. Regardless of the consequences."*

He can't die without knowing the truth. Why I left . . . and what I stole from him. Not when, for the first time in over three decades, I'm finally in a position to return it.

Any hesitation I may have had is gone. I stuff the letter into my handbag and race downstairs.

Rachel's asleep in her car seat when I join her in the back of the SUV.

"Hey," Raine says in stoic greeting. He looks just as much of a mess as Jillian, with his floppy hair in haphazard disarray.

It's not until we're on our way to Memorial Hospital that I'm coherent enough to speak. "Tell me what happened," I say in a steady whisper, fighting not to come undone.

Jillian sniffles. "His partner, Curt, called us. John listed me as his emergency contact and his health advocate as part of his living will." I'm not sure why that guts me, but it does. She continues, "I only know that he's in critical condition and on his way into surgery. Lucas is meeting us at the hospital. We'll find out more when we get there."

I press my eyes shut and say a prayer as the rest of me goes numb. He left wearing a bulletproof vest to protect his center mass . . . unlike the last time. I unconsciously touch the spot on my side where John carries the reminder of his last run-in with a bullet. "Did Curt mention where he was hit?" If she says his head, I'll lose it.

Jillian shakes her head. "No."

I rummage in my purse for my phone and understand why Jillian couldn't get me. My battery is dead. "May I borrow your phone?" I ask over the lump in my throat. "I want to call Jenny and Devon."

I hate bothering them in the middle of the night, especially tonight on such a special occasion, but she'll never forgive me if I don't tell her. Plus, I'm not above using Devon's hospital connections if necessary.

Jenny's groggy voice answers on the second ring. "Aunt Jill? Is everything all right?" I hold it together until I hear her, and then everything cracks inside of me and I choke out a sob. "It's Mom, sweetie."

She gasps. "Oh my God, what's wrong?"

Barely able to expel the words, my voice is a scant whisper. "It's John."

"What happened to him?" her voice rises an octave, flipping to minor hysteria. Like Jillian, Jenny has unnatural anxiety when it comes to death.

"He's been shot. He's in sur—surgery at Memorial Hospital. I'm—I'm driving over with Jillian and Raine now," I say through hiccupping breaths. Jillian reaches back and hands me a much-needed tissue.

I hear Devon whisper in the background, and she murmurs something I can't make out before she comes back on. "We'll be there as soon as we can."

"Thanks, sweetheart. My phone's dead. Text your aunt Jillian or Raine if you need us."

We say our goodbyes and I dab at my eyes to dry them.

Raine drops us at the entrance and takes my sleeping niece with him to park the car.

Dr. Lucas Wilson, a friend and our family's concierge doctor, meets us in reception. My age, with gray-peppered hair and glasses, he looks as sleep deprived as the rest of us despite the white coat. Watching our approach, he wears a grave expression, his hands tucked inside his pockets.

"Lucas," I say, getting there slightly ahead of Jillian. "Please . . . how is he?" I ask, ready to beg.

He nods toward a bank of seats. "He's still in surgery. Let's sit." Then he asks Jillian, "Is Raine here?"

Jillian nods and sniffles. "He's parking. He'll be here with Rachel in a moment."

"Good. Let's wait, so we only have to go through this once."

I do everything in my power not to lose my patience and bite his head off. Instead, I enunciate each word, "Just. Tell me. If. He's going. To live."

Lucas rubs his eyes. "We'll know more in the next couple of hours."

His noncommittal answer sends fear shooting straight to my soul and an involuntary shudder down my back. I resign to waiting for Lucas's full explanation, now not sure if I want to hear it.

The emergency room is on the quiet side. It takes only a few minutes for Raine to appear, with Rachel in a carrier and a diaper bag slung over his shoulder. He strides over to join us.

"Hey, Lucas," he says, giving a nod as he lowers himself into an empty seat.

Lucas leans on his knees, tents his hands, and lets out a breath. "Here's the deal. The Kevlar vest saved his life. Luckily we aren't dealing with armor-piercing bullets. The ones that hit his vest will leave some severe bruising, but one snuck through low and pierced his side above his hip. It didn't hit any vital organs or shatter bone. Again, that was fortunate."

I breathe a sigh of relief. "So far that doesn't sound life-threatening."

Lucas sighs. "The bullet wound isn't the worst of his issues. The impact of the shots knocked him off the roof of a two-story building. Thank God he fell into an open dumpster. Right now, we're dealing with internal bleeding from the bullet's ricochet and some swelling on the brain. He was unconscious when they brought him in. He's going to stay the night in ICU after he gets out of surgery." He glances at his watch. "They should be done by five or five-thirty, as long as the MRI doesn't show any blood clots on the brain that need to be retrieved."

I clasp a hand over my mouth. Raine cradles his head in his palms, while tears stream down Jillian's cheeks.

Jillian wipes her eyes and asks before I can, "Will he recover?"

Lucas scratches his neck, his mouth pressed in a grim line. "He was lucky. The contents of the dumpster cushioned his fall. The brain trauma appears to be only moderate. If the swelling stays down, he should make a full recovery. But the next two to four hours are crucial."

Lucas rises. "I'll take you to the surgical waiting area for family members. Jillian's his healthcare power of attorney. Once he's in recovery, you'll be allowed in two at a time." Lucas glances at me. "Raine will be allowed up because of the baby. I'll pull some strings and classify you as John's significant other to get you in. Is that okay?"

I nod. "Yes." Because, by all that's holy, I want that to be true. "Jenny and Devon are on their way. Will they have a problem?"

Lucas gives a wry smile. "Not unless Memorial wants to see their funding dry up." I had hoped he'd say that. Devon's family foundation runs the annual charity gala that funds a large chunk of their donations.

Jillian walks ahead and consults with Lucas about her responsibilities while Raine and I follow with Rachel. Our steps echo lightly along the tiled floors through the quiet and mildly antiseptic-smelling hallways on our way to the surgical wing.

Raine throws an arm over me, kisses my hair, and says in a low voice, "Hang in there, Kitty. John's tough. He'll be fine."

"Thanks." I accept his comfort and squeeze him back. At first, I may have balked at the age difference between him and Jillian, but I couldn't have been more wrong. He's warm, responsible, honorable to the core, and a stellar father. My sister is a lucky woman. I see a lot of him in Devon, which makes me happy for Jenny.

After we've checked into the empty waiting area, Lucas says, "I'll be back in a little while. Make yourselves comfortable, and have Devon text me when he gets here. I'll bring him up."

"Will do," I say, and settle into a seat next to Jillian. Mercifully, the televisions have been turned off for the night. Rachel stirs and her face screws into a tight frown before she releases a piercing wail.

"I spotted a microwave outside," Raine says, taking Rachel from her carrier in one arm and retrieving a bottle with his free hand from a cold pack in the diaper bag. "I'll text Devon with a heads-up while I'm out there."

Jillian brushes a hand over his forearm and gives him a look of gratitude. "Thanks, sweetheart."

Raine heads out to warm Rachel's bottle, bouncing her on his shoulder as she exercises her lungs.

"Have you called Rosita?" I ask, inquiring about John's mother.

Jillian nods. "She's looking into flights." A yawn slips out before she rests her head on my shoulder and whispers, "How did it go tonight . . . at the reunion?"

I rest my head on top of hers and fight the hollow feeling in my chest. "Fine . . . Your evil plan to steal my underwear worked," I admit, a wan smirk ghosting across my lips.

She shimmies out from under me with renewed energy. "What happened?"

I reach into my jeans and pull the shirred top of John's boxers out of my waistband.

Jillian's eyes widen. I wish I could laugh. Instead, I melt into tears that disintegrate into sobs as the gravity of John's situation grips me. Jillian wraps me in her arms. "Oh, Kitty . . . I'm *so* sorry."

I can't bear the thought of losing him like this. Even if I can't have him, I'm not sure I could exist in a world without him. Knowing he's alive and breathing has been enough for me, even in my darkest hours when I had no hope of us ever reuniting. The tears keep coming and I do nothing to stop them.

When I've wrung myself dry, devoid of enough moisture to make any more tears, Jillian asks, "How did you end up wearing John's underwear?"

I sweep my fingertips across my eyelids and come away with black streaks from whatever mascara was left on my lashes. "I invited him back to my place after the reunion. The call to join the task force raid didn't come until later. He said he'd come back when it was over."

Jillian's teary eyes shimmer. "It was good then?"

I nod. "The best."

"So you're not mad . . . about the underwear?"

My lips warp into a half smile and I cluck my tongue. "I'm livid. How can you call something underwear that has about as much coverage as a roll of dental floss?"

She wiggles her eyebrows and an amused grin slides into place. "What did John say?"

I roll my eyes and snort. "What do you think? He loved them, of course, and sends his thanks."

She dabs at her eyes and chuckles. "Told you."

"I'm so worried about him, Jillian," I whisper as a few more tears slip haphazardly down my cheeks.

Jillian runs her fingers down my hair. "He has a lot to live for."

I reign myself in. He does have a lot to live for, more than he realizes. I have so much to tell him. So much to be forgiven for.

"Kitty?"

"*Hmm?*"

"What did you mean back at house when you said, 'This can't be happening again'?"

I blow out a long breath and sniffle. Jillian digs into her purse and hands me another tissue, which I gratefully accept. I contemplate if I want to go there—to reveal more of our story.

John and I are both complicit in what happened next. He only agreed, because in a twisted way, we did it for Jillian. John being John, I know the reason he foisted her off on me for the retelling of our second breakup. He wanted me to be the one who made the choice to tell her, since the story can't be told without revealing what we hid. More accurately, what I asked him to hide. Not that our lie by omission matters much now, other than giving Jillian a reason to question her trust in me.

Once this is all over, there won't be anyone left who doesn't question their trust or hold some kind of judgment against me.

I no longer have a reason or the strength to fight her off. No more skirting around the truth. For better or worse, I crack open Pandora's Box. "You asked earlier tonight what happened—why John and I broke up the second time. . . ."

She nods.

Ready, set . . . I grab her hand, squeeze, and brace myself. "This isn't the first time John's been shot."

She frowns and sucks in a breath. "What do you mean? I don't remember him ever being shot."

I meet her probing, amber gaze. "That's because we didn't tell you."

"What?" she snaps, snatching her hand from mine. I shove down the sting of her retreat. "When?"

"September 1992. Right after you left for your sophomore year at

Villanova." The year after we buried Drew.

Hurt and a look of suspicion press her brows flatter. "What happened?"

I take a deep breath and stare down at my hands. "It was on a Friday. I'd just flown into Newark Airport from San Francisco for my monthly East Coast rotation," I smile softly, thinking back to those eagerly anticipated weekends after being away from John. "I was supposed to meet him at his apartment in the West Village for a date—dinner and late-night jazz at the Village Vanguard."

My smile fades and I meet Jillian's gaze. "But Vera intercepted me at baggage claim, and told me John had been shot and that she had a car waiting outside to take us to New York Presbyterian. He'd gotten caught in the crossfire during an undercover drug bust and was in surgery. They almost lost him on the table." I think of the circular pink scar on his abdomen, the feel of it under my fingers earlier, and I expose the crux of my fear. "It was the first time I understood how easily I could lose him forever and be left with nothing."

The hurt remains in her eyes. "But why didn't you tell me? I could've been there for you."

The same reason I kept all the darkness from her. I've done it to protect her, to try to ensure one of us had a life unencumbered by pain and loss. What I didn't count on was that loss would consume her anyway. Outside of my control. Yet where I could, I tried.

I absently twist the claddagh ring I now wear in place of my wedding band. "I didn't want to pass my fear on to you. Vera and I agreed. . . . You'd survived a year of hell after the accident with Drew, and you were just starting to smile again. I couldn't bear taking that away from you."

"John went along with this?"

I shrug. "At first, he wasn't conscious, so there was nothing to agree to. If he had died, we would've dealt with it then. When he didn't . . . we decided to wait. John loved you, and he didn't want to worry you any more than we did. When we knew he would recover, Vera and I discussed it with your therapist and decided it would be best not to mention it. Afraid it would trigger a relapse. Then it became easier never to mention at all . . . so we didn't."

She shakes her head vigorously. "That's not fair, Kitty! I would've wanted to be there . . . to know."

I press my eyes shut and sigh. "I'm sorry, sweetie. We did it with the best intentions." Like so many of the decisions I'd made with Vera throughout the years, they were made to shield, never to deceive.

Jillian cocks her head and blinks. "But didn't you return to California . . ." Then a look of shock and dismay crosses Jillian's face and she blurts, "Please tell me you didn't break up with John right after he was shot . . . and leave him like that . . . while he was *hurt*?"

I sigh and shrink away. "My timing wasn't great, but there were reasons."

Her mouth falls open. "Oh my God, you did! What kind of reasons would make that acceptable?" Her mistrust glares out at me.

Not for the first time, I recognize things in myself that remind me of my mother. And I hate it. Knowing I'm no better than the woman who gave birth to me unleashes the pain and loathing I've lived with since I left John that August day in 1981.

The day I destroyed the love of my life by making the best of the worst choices and sacrificing my heart to give him what I thought would be a better life. I've paid dearly ever since—losing Kat in the process and hiding behind a washed-out version of myself.

I let go of my rage and snap, targeting it less at Jillian and more at the woman I've become. "Don't judge me, Jillian! I've done enough of that myself. It's complicated! It's always been complicated with John. Nothing has ever been easy." My face heats in a twisted scowl. Needing space to explode, I push out of my chair. "When Drew died, you weren't the only one affected. It may not have been the same for me, but it was painful to lose him and to lose you in an entirely different way. Forgive me if I didn't want to end up in the same place!"

Her mouth snaps shut, and she stares at me like she's seeing me for the first time. "So it was my fault?"

Rubbing my temples, I grit my teeth. "No. That's not what I'm saying."

"Then what are you saying?"

"I'm saying that as much as you want it to be, sometimes love is not enough!" My voice escalates in direct proportion to my anger as I travel a back-and-forth path in front of the arranged seats. "Sometimes one choice cascades into a snowball of shit that takes away all of your other choices and sends you down a road you can never escape. Sometimes the decision is made for you, and all that's left is protecting the people you love!"

My whole body shakes when I'm done, and I realize that half of what I've said can't possibly make sense to her.

Her head snaps back. "I'm sorry. I . . . ," she sputters, and her shoulders slump. "I'm just tired and worried. I love you. I didn't mean to attack you." She pats the seat next to her. "Please, sit . . ."

I glance between the seat next to her and her pleading eyes. I shake my head, not calm enough to sit. Stalking to and fro feels good, cathartic, and I'll take all the catharsis I can get right now.

"Then just tell me what happened," she says in a gentler voice. "I promise. No judgments this time."

I release a breath and push my hair back behind my ears as I pace. "I didn't leave John because he was shot. I left him because I wanted something he didn't want to give me."

Her gaze tugs at me. "What did you want?"

Heaviness settles into my brow and I give her a pained smile. "A child."

Chapter 34

Kitty

October 1992 – Two Weeks After John's Shooting

"KAT, WE'VE TALKED about this!" John says, sitting propped up in bed with pillows stuffed behind his back. Vera generously offered him one of her many guest rooms to recuperate after the shooting. Her way of making sure, on behalf of his mother, Rosita, that the cranky patient took proper care of himself.

He looks like a vagabond with his hair grown out and a scraggly beard. Neither of which flatters him, but it's part of a disguise for the undercover case he's working on. Or should I say was working on, since he's on disability for the next few weeks and then at a desk job until he's ready to be put back into the field.

The only things keeping him from looking like a homeless person—one of the roles he plays—is that he's clean and wearing his NYPD sweats, which hide the bandages underneath.

I pace at the foot of the bed. "We haven't talked about it. You've only made your feelings known—*loudly*. On multiple occasions. I'm thirty years old, Shaw! I want a child. If you don't want kids, then I want to find someone who does!"

He locks his arms across his chest and squints through his scowl, his gaze carrying the gray-blue of a hurricane about to slam the coast. "Are you fucking *serious*? You're giving me an ultimatum? After all we've been through? We've only been back together for a year. I ask you to hold off for a couple more so I can get settled in the job, and you can't do that for me?"

"Admit it. You don't know if you really want kids." I snipe, planting my hands on my hips.

His jaw clenches and he stays silent.

I grind my teeth. Besides his issue with children, how do I explain that not knowing if he's going to come home every night scares the living daylights out of me? He almost *died*. Not to mention, although we've talked about marriage, he's yet to produce a ring.

Our last year has been passionate and heartbreaking all rolled into one. What I've discovered during that time is how much we've changed. My grown-up, ex-Marine Shaw is an adrenaline junkie—and I'm not. I want the white picket fence, the Volvo, the two-point-five children, maybe even a dog. But that's not who he is anymore, if he ever was that person. It doesn't help that my salary is twice as much as his, something that hasn't settled well with his fragile male ego.

I take a deep breath and stop pacing. "I've been offered a partnership role in our financial services practice." In San Francisco. At three times his salary.

His brows rise and his gaze fills with suspicion. "That's good, right?"

I release a breath and rub my eyes. "Only if you come with me."

His gaze hardens to ice and he gesticulates from where he sits on the bed. "So, I'm supposed to quit my job and go where, Cali-*fucking*-fornia? And do what, Kat, work as a waiter? Or maybe live off your salary?" His brow dips lower. "What's wrong with you working here? Living in New York? Isn't that enough for you? Or is it me? You ashamed of me? What I do for a living?" A combination of fury, accusation, and self-doubt churns behind his narrowed glare.

Rage surges up inside of me and I let loose, stamping my foot and making liberal use of the foul-mouthed language he's so fond of. "You're such an *asshole*! How can you even say that to me? I'm not ashamed of you. I love you, goddamn it! How about I'm scared to death that you're going to get yourself killed and I'm going to end up a basket case like Jillian? Do I have to have a fucking *dick* to get the privilege of making a decision in this relationship? How about what *I* want? *My* career? What about me, John?" I jab a finger at my chest. "I make all the compromises and you make none? Is that it?

Well, *fuck you!*"

His eyes widen and his head jerks backward. "Jesus, Kat! You want a kid that bad, or are you looking for another excuse to run away when shit gets tough?"

I freeze. That's the root of it all, isn't it? The source of his resentment.

I'd considered telling him over the last year why I'd left, but each time I rejected the idea, determining it would only cause him pain and leave him as powerless as me to change a past he had no choice in determining. Why should we *both* suffer? He has no idea what it's cost me.

My hands clench at my sides and my cheeks flame. "When shit gets *tough*? Really? Do you even know what it's like to give up everything because you love someone so much that you'd sacrifice your soul for them? Do you? Who was the one who ran, John? *Who?* It wasn't me. I came back six months later. You left for ten goddamn years!"

The storm behind his eyes erupts, twisting his face into squinting eyes and a twitching jaw. "You don't think what you did was run away? Are you fucking delusional? And you think *you're* the only one who gave up everything?"

John's face turns ruby red and there's murder in his eyes. "If I'm not enough for you, then go! Fucking go without me. Because my life, my job is here," he seethes. "You don't want to be part of it, I'm sure as shit not going to stop you. Go find some corporate guy to have kids with, drive your damn Mercedes, or whatever it is that I'll never be able to give you! Maybe your mother was right, maybe you should've married Marsh. Have a nice life, Kat. Don't let me get in your way!"

Tears prick the backs of my eyelids. I let out a scream of frustration, pick up the first object I can find—a hardcover book—and launch it at his head. "I won't!"

He ducks and the book hits the headboard.

All my dreams crumble in the second I turn and walk out the door.

Passion and love can only take me so far. The late nights, broken dates, weeks with no contact, and the near-death experiences have taken their toll on my resolve. Wanting a child is only a piece of it. I'm not cut out for the life John wants to lead. I'm not equipped to live like that without losing my mind and what's left of my soul.

Even though all of those things are factors, underneath it all, I'm terrified that—like Drew—he'll die, and that's a loss I'm not sure I'd survive. I love him too passionately, too deeply to stay in an uncompromising situation and end up losing him that way. I need distance, perspective, better choices than the ones I have.

I say goodbye to Vera on the way out and pick up my packed suitcase. My flight isn't until tomorrow, but I decide to take a red-eye back to San Francisco. I get on the plane despite the raw ache in my chest where my heart used to be.

My insides are numb for the entire six-and-a-half-hour flight. When I arrive early Sunday morning, there's a message from Bob. In a moment of desperation and utter loneliness, I return his call. The second I hear his voice, I sob uncontrollably into the phone.

Within an hour, he's at my door with breakfast.

An hour after that, we're in bed . . . and we don't get out until the next day.

Memorial Hospital Waiting Room

JILLIAN STARES AT me wide-eyed with her mouth agape. "Is that it? You went home and got back together with Bob?"

I run my hands down my face. "Not quite."

"Not *quite*? Did you talk to John after you left that night? He came after you, right?"

I wince and let out a breath. "Vera used to think our biggest problem was that we were both pigheaded." I give her a wan smile. "I didn't hear from him for a month . . . until flowers arrived at my apartment the day after Bob moved in."

Her eyes go wider. "That was fast . . . with Bob, I mean."

I shake my head. "I'd made up my mind, Jillian. For better or worse. Not only was I terrified of what John did for a living, but if he didn't want children then I needed to be with someone who did."

It wasn't until my own therapy sessions that I understood John's lack of desire had most likely been rooted in fear, related to growing up in an abusive household and the circumstances around his sister's death.

"So what happened when you got the flowers?"

"I ignored them." I shrug and take her hand, needing the contact. "You've got to understand, even though John and I got back together after our ten-year reunion, there was still a layer of pain and resentment on both sides. That kiss he gave me in the parking lot? That happened because I ran when I saw all the hurt and anger rise behind his eyes the moment his shock wore off. He loved me, but he never fully forgave me. He had to lose me before he could give me what I wanted."

She nods and the corner of her mouth rises in a half-hearted smile. "I can relate on the forgiveness piece. I had the same issue with Raine for a while. But we're past it now."

Her admission gives me a sliver of hope that maybe John and I can get past the hurdles ahead of us, too. We sit for a few quiet moments.

"So what happened? You said he had to lose you to give you want you wanted." Jillian asks.

I sigh. "Four months after our fight, he showed up on my doorstep in San Francisco."

February 1993 – San Francisco

Buzz. Buzz.

"Hold your horses," I mumble under my breath, fumbling with my earring as I head for the apartment door in stocking feet, only half ready for my dinner date with two of my closest single girlfriends. I have a big surprise for them and a ton of planning to do. It's my trial run before I share the news with my family. I hope my stomach settles enough for a meal.

Bob left with his team this morning for a two-week client audit in Europe after last night's celebratory dinner for two. I'm still walking on air even though the apartment feels empty without him.

I glance through the peephole, but whoever it is stands too close. All I see is a partial view of the hair on the back of someone's head. I swing open the door, expecting it to be my neighbor Sam looking for his spare key again.

My heart nearly stops as he turns.

John.

Clad in a black leather jacket, a black button-down shirt, and jeans, he's clean-shaven and has a fresh haircut. He's sexy and smoldering, and he epitomizes everything that ignites passion in my heart, and that's dangerous to my sanity.

I'd convinced myself I was ready to move on, leave him behind, but my galloping heart rate and shallow breathing say otherwise.

I have less than a second to read the pain and longing in his gaze before his hands and lips are on me.

My traitorous body responds to each and every touch. I ignore all the warning bells tripping inside of me and savor each hungry caress of his tongue, the hard press of his excitement between us, and the lingering touch of his large palms heating the base of my spine.

The protective layer I thought I'd built around my heart provides nothing more than a flimsy, inadequate defense. Until this moment, I'd been doing well enough focusing on a new life with Bob and letting that life wrap me in a cocoon of security that I so desperately thought I wanted.

One kiss is all it takes to realize how much I've lied to myself and the irreparable damage I've done.

He pulls away, sucking in heavy breaths. "Jesus, Kat... I'm so fucking sorry." He cups my face in his hands and runs a thumb softly over my cheek. "I can't live without you." He shakes his head, presses his forehead to mine, and says in an earnest, ragged whisper, "I'll move here. I looked into taking the exam. I'll leave undercover. I want kids with you, Kat, I do... if that's what you want. We'll do it. Together. I love you, babe. Please forgive me for letting you leave and not doing this sooner."

Every word is a hammer hit to my heart until it shatters into a million tiny pieces. The lump in my throat nearly chokes me as my body dissolves in uncontrollable shivers. I slide out of his grip. The first sob rips from my lungs a moment before I collapse onto the floor.

"Kat?" he croons, dropping to his knees next to me and trying to gather me into his arms. "Was that too much at once? I'm sorry to dump all that on you...."

I shake my head and push him away as irony and his bad timing coalesce to ruin my life within the space of a breath.

I'd underestimated the effect of the passion that has always existed between us, and to my own detriment, how deeply I still love him. Worst of all, I underestimated how much he still loves me.

He reaches out again. "Let me help you up."

"Goddamn you, Shaw!" I shove him away and run a wrist across my eyes. It comes away with streaks of the black mascara I put on just before he arrived. I stumble to my feet and make it into the bathroom in time to lift the toilet seat and throw up what little is in my stomach.

He hovers outside the door as I retch. Tears travel in warm paths down my cheeks. If he'd only come sooner, I would've made a different choice than the one I'm about to make.

I rinse my mouth and walk past him. His hulking frame steps in stride behind me back into the loft living room. I drop onto the sofa and cradle my face in my hands.

"What was *that*? Talk to me, Kat . . . ," he pleads in a low voice. "Please . . ."

I melt into tears again and raise my head from my hands to see him kneeling in front of me. He rests his warm palms on my knees. The naked vulnerability in his eyes slashes at my heart. I ache with how much John and I have lost, and once I share my news, how much I'll miss him. Why couldn't he have just stayed away?

The pressure behind my eyes rests heavy in my brow. I shake my head and run my fingertips down his cheek. "It's too late . . . *you're* too late," I whisper.

His eyelids drop to half-mast and his gaze darkens. "What do you mean?" he asks in a shaky voice. "Kat, what are you saying?"

I clutch my belly with one hand, my lips twisting into a sad smile. "I'm pregnant . . ."

He shoots to his feet and stumbles backward as if he can't get away from me fast enough. His gaze darts to my still mostly flat stomach. It doesn't take him long to do the math and realize it can't be his. "What the—? Whose is it?" he asks as a frown cuts fast and deep into his brow.

"Bob's . . . We're getting married this spring. I thought it was over between us."

His mouth drops open and his shoulders collapse as though I had just slugged him. And then something breaks behind the stormy blue eyes I've loved for half of my life, and his lip quivers. I've only seen John close to tears once before . . . the first time I left.

His hands clench at his sides and he fights to maintain control.

Seeing him like this craters my chest. He's been my strength, my pillar.

How did I think I could actually leave him behind? Stop loving him? I come to the realization that although I love Bob, I will always love John more. But love has never been our issue.

"Tell me you don't love me, Kat," he says in a hoarse whisper, "and I'll leave."

He digs into his jacket pocket and takes out a diamond ring. He shakes it at me as a tear escapes and slides down his cheek. His jaw tenses and his wrist jerks across his face to wipe it away. "Tell me you don't want this. I'll eat my fucking pride and marry you — even if that kid's not mine. Tell me you don't love me. Say the words."

My lips move, but no sound comes out. I can't speak. The lump blocking my throat is too thick. I can barely make him out through the wet warmth blurring my vision. It's my fault. All of it. I did this. Now I need to live with the consequences, which I will gladly do for my child. I may not be done making sacrifices, but I'm done making mistakes.

"Say it!" he screams, no longer trying to hold back the tears cascading down his face. "Say you don't love me! I may be a hardheaded asshole, but I made you a promise on my fucking skin." He rips open his shirt, sending the buttons flying and exposing the tattoo of my name over his heart. "I promised I'd always be there for you. I fucked up, but it didn't mean I stopped loving you. You couldn't give me one more chance to do right by you? After *everything*?" He shakes his head and stalks back and forth, brushing at his watery eyes. Then he asks more calmly, "When did you stop loving me, Kat?"

How can he think that's even possible?

My whole being goes numb. I ignore the hot tears spilling down my cheeks and whisper, "I've spent every minute since you first kissed me on Memorial Field loving you, Shaw. I'm not sure I'll ever stop. But that doesn't change a thing. . . ."

I rise from the sofa, leave him in the living room, and close the bedroom door behind me. I pick up the engagement ring Bob gave me last night from where I'd left it on my bureau after I took it off to put on some hand cream. I slip it back on.

When I come out, John's gone. All that's left behind are the buttons from his shirt, scattered on the rug like all of our broken dreams.

Memorial Hospital Waiting Room

I'M STILL CLUTCHING Jillian's hand, hard, when I finish. Even with the retelling, I take comfort knowing after all the decisions I've made, at least that one was the right one for Jenny's sake.

She leans her head on my shoulder, brushes at her eyes, and whispers, "Oh God, Kitty . . . I don't know what to say."

I rub her back in soothing circles and rest my head on top of hers, ignoring the new round of tears that have gathered in my eyes. I sniff them back, so done with crying. "Life is a series of hard choices and sacrifices for the ones you love. At least, that's been my experience."

It's not until I hear someone crying softly that I'm aware we're no longer alone. I twist in my seat. Jenny and Devon are seated in the bank of chairs behind us, wrapped in an embrace with their heads tucked together, while Raine brushes at his face as he stands rocking Rachel in his arms next to them.

"Sweetheart?" I say to Jenny. She and Devon, my sandy-haired future son-in-law, glance over with red-rimmed blue eyes.

It's a sweep. There's not a dry eye in the house. Warmth floods my chest and cheeks from a combination of embarrassment and the love I feel for my family.

"We didn't want to interrupt," Jenny whispers, brushing at her face. Devon releases her, and she propels herself across the room and into my arms. "I'm sorry, Mom. I had no idea," she says.

My miracle, my Jenny. "That's why this was always so hard to talk about," I say, hugging her close. "It was complicated, and I wouldn't change a thing if it meant not giving you the life you deserve, sweetheart."

Jenny bites her quivering lip and squeezes me in a tight hug. "I love you, Mom."

"I love you, too, sweetheart," I say through a teary smile.

She pulls away and Jillian swoops in with another tissue for each of us. Jenny dabs at her eyes and whispers, "If he lives, give him that chance now, promise? For me . . ."

"I promise," I say, nodding, and let the tears spill as I press her into a hug. "How did I get so lucky with you?"

Lucas clears his voice in the doorway. He's bleary-eyed but wearing a relaxed smile. "John's out of surgery and in recovery. It went well. He was very lucky."

I drop my arms from around Jenny, blow my nose with a proffered tissue, and release a huge breath of relief. "When can we see him?" I ask.

Lucas glances at his watch. "Thirty minutes, maybe? He won't be conscious for a while though."

As long as he wakes up, that's all I care about.

The irony of this situation isn't lost on me. Surrounding every major breakup in my relationship with John, he's endured a devastating physical injury followed by an emotional one, compliments of me. I can't promise the result won't be any different this time.

But what I can promise? This time, it won't be because I've left him.

Chapter 35

Kitty

Memorial Hospital, ICU

"I WANT TO set your expectations," Lucas says, barring the door to John's room in the ICU. "He's attached to a lot of machines. They decided to keep him in a medically induced coma for the next day to protect his brain from damage until the swelling from the fall recedes."

I nod and ready myself for a scenario similar to the last time he was shot.

"I'm heading home, but I'll stop by later," Lucas says, then steps aside. "Talk to him. They say it helps."

I squeeze his arm. "Thank you, Lucas, for being here."

Lucas and his father have been family friends for as long as I can remember. Lucas also happened to have close ties to Devon's father when he was alive. It's a small world sometimes.

He covers my hand with his and smiles. "Even if Jillian hadn't asked me to come, John's a good friend of mine, too. I'm happy to do it."

I'm not sure how long they've been friends, but I know they trade professional favors. John was the person Lucas called on when someone tried to kill Devon at the hospital gala this summer.

"See you later." I give Lucas a peck on the cheek, then push the door open and step into a symphony of whooshing, bleeping, and whirring. Lucas was right. Seeing John this way is jarring.

Still, I'm happy to be the first to visit. Jillian suggested I visit while she and Raine sit with the neurosurgeon to get a full debrief on John's condition. As much as I wanted to be there for the briefing, I wanted to see John more.

John lies in a hospital bed with the back elevated. He's hooked to monitors with tubes snaking in and out of him, nose, mouth, hand, almost everywhere.

A low fluorescent light behind the bed casts shadows over his still form. The breathing apparatus obscures his face, which carries only a glimmer of the strong, craggy-but-handsome middle-aged man I made love to a few hours ago. Other than some minor scratches on his face and arms, he doesn't look like he fell off a building.

I reach over and hold John's hand from where I sit in the chair next to the bed. It's cool to the touch. I take comfort from the steady beat of the heart monitor. It means he's alive and in there somewhere.

I say the first and most important thing that comes to mind, "I love you, Shaw . . . I never stopped. Come back to me. . . ." I lower my lips to his knuckles and kiss the nearest part of him not hooked up to something. "I'll be waiting."

I sit quietly for a few minutes like that, my hand covering his.

I stare at the man I've loved, at times secretly, since I was seventeen, searching for the boy he was in high school and then after that, with ten years of life behind us, and now . . . on the cusp of maybe a third and final chance after thirty-five years of me choosing the best of the worst choices.

He just has to live first.

A hot tear rolls from my eye onto his skin as I press my hand to his cheek. I can't believe this is where we are again. Life has taken me full circle.

Now, if he survives, I need to tell him the truth.

I need to tell him what I did in those months after I left for Stanford, and give back what I stole.

I need to tell him he's a father . . . and pray that he forgives me.

After

Chapter 36

Kitty

Memorial Hospital Waiting Room

WHEN I RETURN to the waiting room, Jenny and Devon are propped up against each other with their eyes closed. Heads tucked together, one dark, one light, supporting each other. They look so peaceful, so beautiful. It fills my heart with joy to see them like that after all they've been through this summer. I'm so very proud of them.

"Hey," I whisper, and lightly touch Jenny's shoulder. Her eyes flutter open and Devon wakes with her. They straighten up. Devon rubs his face while Jenny arches her back, stretches, and lets out a groan. My eyelids feel like they're sagging as much as theirs, but I have no intention of sleeping anytime soon.

"Why don't you both go and see John? I'll wait for Jillian and Raine, and then I'd like to go home for a quick shower and change."

"We'll drive you," Jenny says in a groggy voice and wraps me in a hug.

Devon runs a hand through his hair and stifles a yawn. "I put in a call to the hospital admin. John will get VIP treatment, and you'll have full access."

I hug him and he gives me a solid embrace in return. I like that for Jenny. "Thanks, sweetheart, I appreciate that. He's in room 353."

Devon twines his fingers with Jenny's, and they head toward John's room as I drop into a chair, exhausted. I close my eyes for a moment, not to sleep but to rest.

"Kitty . . ." A small but insistent hand shakes my shoulder.

My eyes snap open expecting Jenny; instead I find Devon's twin, Lettie. She's dressed as if she had never gone to bed after the induction ceremony. Under her fur coat, she's wearing a shimmery dress and heels, and her hair—cut short since I'd last seen her—is still fluffed, sprayed, and perfectly coiffed into a chic blonde cap.

"Hi, sweetheart," I say, straightening up in the chair. "Jenny and Devon went to see John. They'll be right back."

She drops into the chair next me and peers around with wild, pale blue eyes. "I know. I waited for them to leave. Tell me what happened." Her voice cracks as she sinks her fingers into my arm.

I snap fully awake. "What's going on, Lettie?"

Her fingers sink deeper. "Please . . . just tell me what happened tonight," she says in a desperate whisper.

I start with his injuries.

She cuts me off. "No. Before that."

My face heats and I skip the particulars. "Someone called his cell around one a.m. about a raid. He said he'd meet them in twenty minutes, and then he changed into FBI gear and left ten minutes later. Location must've been close by."

Lettie nods in a rapid bob then loosens her grip on my arm and slides back in the chair. "I missed his call. I should've called him back," she whispers, chewing her nail.

My heart rate accelerates. "What are you talking about?" As soon as the question passes through my lips, it dawns on me. "Are you helping the FBI?"

She turns her watery gaze on me and nods. "I'll make this right, Kitty. I promise." Then she leans in and kisses my cheek. "Not a word. Don't tell Dev I was here." Before I can open my mouth to speak, she's on her feet and walking toward the exit door.

I lunge from the chair and seize her fur-covered arm. "Lettie, wait!" I say in a hushed tone in case anyone wanders into earshot. "What's going on? What are you doing?"

She sniffles and her mouth pulls to the side. "Protecting the people I love." Then she depresses the release bar on the stairwell exit door and disappears behind it.

Her words freeze me in place, and, like an ice pick to the heart, they hit home. Part of me wants to run after her and convince her not to take the same perilous path I've followed, knowing how much it has cost me. Another part of me understands her, yet grieves for the piece of her soul she's sacrificing by keeping secrets. A third part of me hopes like hell she's not putting herself and my family in danger.

Sadly, of all the people Lettie chose to tell, I'm probably the safest. Though I hope it doesn't take her as long as it did me to recognize the consequences of her decisions.

I return to the lounge and take a seat. The rising sun peeks over the horizon and streams in through the windows, heralding a new day and filling the room with natural light. Other people have taken up residence with me in the waiting room, and a light buzz of activity has started on the hospital floor. A television suspended from the ceiling in the corner displays the news on mute with closed captioning.

I pick up my purse and touch the envelope inside. I have no control over Lettie's decisions, but I do have control over mine.

After I shower and change, but before I come back to spend the foreseeable future at John's bedside, I'm going to do something I should've done a long time ago. . . . I'm going to answer this letter.

Chapter 37

John

Memorial Hospital

"KAT?" I RASP, barely recognizing my own voice and assuming my sore throat is the cause. I squeeze the warm fingers clutching my hand. "Is that you?" My eyes are open, but I can't see anything but shadows.

"It's me," she says softly, lifting my hand and pressing it to her lips.

"What happened?" I ask, trying to make sense of all the mechanical sounds I hear. "Why can't I see?" My head jerks from side to side as I panic, my whole world feeling out of context.

"*Shh*," she says, and I hear her shuffle closer. One hand stays clasped around mine, while the other comes out of nowhere to cradle my head. She rests her cheek near mine, her breath warming my face. "Be calm for me, and I'll answer your questions, okay?"

I swallow past my parched throat. "Yeah, okay."

"You're in Memorial. You were hurt, but you'll be fine." Her voice is soft and soothing as she strokes my hair. It feels good. "A bullet passed through your side, but didn't hit anything vital. You fell and hurt your head. That injury is healing. The doctor will give you more details, but there's some temporary swelling that's affecting your vision. The doctors expect a full recovery. You're lucky. Nod if you understand."

I nod but it hurts to move.

"Good." Her lips brush my cheek before she retreats. Cool air replaces the void where she was a second ago, but she's still grasping my hand.

"Do you remember anything?"

Yes. No. What I remember is a jumbled mess.

I remember loving her and fearing I'd never see her again. Expecting her to be the person holding my hand ... but not knowing why. She's my lifeline. I know that, too.

I squeeze her hand. "I'm not sure."

"That's all right. You're healing. Things will get clearer. Do you remember our reunion the other night?"

A montage of images comes flooding back, how the press of Kat's body next to me in that dress made my blood heat and my heart soar. The song. Us. Together. "We danced, right?" I croak as the desire for it to be true nearly chokes me.

"Yes . . ."

More images. Kat's new house, her bed. Us naked. I pray this part is true, too. "We made love?"

"Yes . . ."

Somewhere between then and now, I remembered older images. Living? No dreaming, some of our early years. So afraid. So afraid none of the new stuff was real. That I was dreaming. Wishing so hard that I only thought it was true.

I gasp. Flashes in the dark. Gunshots. Pain. Agony. Losing Kat . . . again. Then nothing.

"*Shh,* it's all right," she whispers, never letting go of my hand. "I'm right here."

"Tired, don't remember," I say, feeling something wet leak from the corners of my eyes. "Don't leave me, Kat . . ."

"I won't leave, Shaw. Sleep . . ."

I release a long exhale and do what she says. Sleep sweeps me under.

Chapter 38

Kitty

Memorial Hospital, John's Room

"BLOOD," I SAY, reading off the word association list I've created, both as something to do with John and to test him while we wait to hear the results of the screening done by the neuropsychologist. I guess it's the tutor in me coming out. I'm finishing up on colors.

"Red." He looks peaceful resting on the pillow with his eyes closed. His skin color is better, and the early confusion during the first couple of days after the shooting is gone. Other than frustration over his limited eyesight, he's doing as well as Lucas and his doctors had hoped.

I've been here almost around the clock for a week. Thankfully, I've stockpiled enough vacation time to make it work. Devon called in favors to get John a private room post-ICU with a cot for me if the need arises. Other than the steady stream of doctors and nurses, having this level of privacy has been nice.

That being said, I'm far from the only visitor John has had. Marsh and Sue stayed a few extra days to see him before returning to California, and not without extracting promises from me that we would visit them—together or apart. John's work crew has stopped in several times, including his partner, Curt, and our friend Tony. Jenny and Devon. Lettie. Jillian and Raine. Rosita and José stayed for almost a week and just went back to Florida. Lucas promised to give José access to John's files with his permission as a professional courtesy. All in all, in addition to me, John's had a good amount of visitors since he left the ICU.

I move to the next pair on my list. "Sky."

"Blue."

"Sun."

"Yellow."

"Perfect! Next topic . . . Let's see if you can guess." I smile. It's a topic he loves—music. I start with my country favorite from back when we were in high school. "Dolly Parton."

He thinks a second then breaks into a wide grin. "Big tits."

I laugh despite myself. "Wrong topic."

He shifts his head in my direction and reaches out a hand. I discard my list and let him reel me toward the bed until I'm perched on the edge. His warm fingers slide up and down my arm. "Not when you're around, it's not," he whispers, his unfocused gaze rests on my face. "Thanks for being here. It means a lot."

I lean over and place a small kiss on his lips. "I'm not going anywhere this time, Shaw." Then I take his hand, cover my breast with it and chuckle. "But if you're looking for Dolly, you won't find her here."

His lips quirk up into a smile. "Don't need her. Everything I want's in the palm of my hand." He gently massages my breast to emphasize his point, and his smile turns wicked. This time, he's the one taking my hand. He brings my palm to his lips before pressing it into his lap. "Just in case you were wondering. No sustainable damage to the lower extremities," he says, low and husky.

I stroke his hardening length through the covers twice as payback. A groan rises from his throat, and I pull away. "You're unbelievable, Detective, you know that?"

He waggles his eyebrows, his wicked grin still firmly in place. "So I've been told." Then he gives me a mock frown. "Hey, tease, you started it."

I shift back to my seat and roll my eyes. "The answer was *country music*, ya big lug."

He waves a hand. "Yeah, yeah . . . what's the next question?"

"Stairway to Heaven."

Without realizing it, he mimics my eye roll. "Led Zeppelin, rock music, Robert Plant, Jimmy Page . . . take your pick. Too easy."

I smile. "Song you sang to me at the junior prom."

His lips quirk up again, instead of answering, he pulls out his best Robin Zander, closes his eyes, and sings the first few lines of "I Want You to Want Me" without missing a beat. "From *Cheap Trick at Budokan*," he adds to finish.

"Steven Tyler."

He clasps his hands behind his neck. "Aerosmith."

I glance at my list, fold it in half, and decide to go off script, broaching what could be a delicate subject. "I have a question for you, Shaw."

He smirks. "You have a lot of questions for me."

I weigh whether this is the time or place, or if I should even ask. Awkwardness aside, it feels like it's the right thing to do.

"It's not that kind of question," I say, twisting my claddagh ring between my fingers.

His brow crinkles and he flips his chin. "Ask me."

I draw in a deep breath and hold it. "Would you consider staying with me for the next couple of weeks while you recover?"

Other than his eyesight, the gunshot wound, and occasional dizziness, he's functional enough to take care of his own basic needs. I could tend to the dressing on his wound until his vision is back, cook, take him to doctor's appointments, do the little things that might help.

Guilt for what's to come only drives a small part of my offer. More so, the overwhelming need to be near him and the opportunity to build a solid bridge between us before I share the truth that might drive him away. That aside, there's no doubt I prefer him staying with me than sitting in a rehab facility, or in his fourth-floor walk-up apartment across town in Summit Gardens.

His expression darkens. "*Humph.*" He doesn't say anything for a few moments, like he's thinking about it. Then he asks, "You sure that's a good idea?"

I shake my head and tell him the truth. "Maybe, maybe not, but I'd feel better if you stayed. I can work from home. Between me and Jillian, we can help you get to appointments until you're ready to drive yourself." Then I add, "I'd enjoy the company."

He gnaws on his lip, and then the corner of his mouth lifts. "Does the offer include sponge baths?"

I laugh. "Will that sweeten the deal?"

"It might." He shrugs, rubs his eyes, and gets quiet. The dark, brooding look he gets when he's disturbed slips onto his face, and he releases a heavy breath. "Not seeing things is killing me, Kat. I'm losing my fucking mind over here. I'm not sure if I'll be great company. Might make sense for me to go to a rehab center. Not be a burden . . . We got our own shit to sort out, don't we?"

Yes, we do.

"It's up to you," I say softly and move over to the bed, lowering myself onto the edge and taking his hand. "But I wouldn't have offered if I didn't want you with me. Our *shit*, as you put it, can wait until you're better."

He squeezes my fingers and nods. "I want to be with you. Just not like this," he whispers, then pulls our clasped hands to his lips and kisses mine.

I rest my forehead next to his and whisper back. "I'll take you any way I can get you. Let me do this for you, please."

He presses his eyes shut and stays quiet again. Finally, he nods. " 'Kay. On one condition."

A tingle travels up my spine. "What's that?"

"Tell me why you lied about your mother having another child." His voice is soft, coaxing.

His question hits me like a blow, and my mouth falls open. I'm speechless. I rapidly assess all the possible answers as they run through my mind, knowing that a lie is out of the question. Also knowing that answering John's question will be like pulling a loose thread — one tug could unravel everything.

"Kat . . . you promised. No more secrets," he whispers and squeezes my hand. His breath hits my lips. "We've only got one more shot at this, babe. I gotta know you're all in this time."

I press my eyes shut, shove down the lump in my throat, and nod. "All right, I'll tell you . . . but everything else waits. There's something I have to show you when the time is right, but you need to see again first. Will you agree to wait . . . for the rest?"

He gives a small nod. "Yeah . . ." He swallows. "But if I never get my eyesight back, you gotta tell me anyway."

"Agreed," I whisper, kiss the tip of his nose, and shift away into the seat next to the bed. I need space to think clearly and figure out the best way to answer his question.

I organize my thoughts, then clear my throat. "Remember our first date in high school, the night you met my family? At your house afterward, we got into a fight over a snide comment you made about my family having money. Remember?"

He scrunches his face in distaste, his arms crossed over his chest. "I'll never forget that fucking dinner. Afterward? Yeah, vaguely."

"I mentioned that the house had been my grandfather's, and that my dad paid for institutional care for his sister with severe disabilities?"

John's brows pop up, then crease. I watch his mind whir behind his eyes as he makes the leap before I tell him. "She wasn't your aunt... was she?" he asks.

I wring my hands and prepare for impact. "No... she was my sister." I swallow and whisper, "But I didn't find that out until later." In case he has any doubt, I add, "Jillian doesn't know."

His mouth tightens into a grim line. "And they put her in an institution..."

"Yes." My mother's shame washes over me. "It was 1956. My parents were young... unmarried. Unequipped to deal with a child, much less one who was severely disabled." I stare at my hands as tears pool in my eyes. "She went into foster care until she was three. After that, she was placed in the closest state-run institution." I hesitate before saying the name out loud, anticipating John's reaction. As part of our generation growing up in New Jersey, he knows as much about the now-closed facility as anyone.

I cringe and whisper, "Willowbrook on Staten Island. She was there until she turned seven."

The horrified look on John's face pushes my tears to overflowing. "They dumped her in that fucking hellhole?" His tone borders on primal.

I had the same reaction when I found out. In middle school, they showed us the exposés on Willowbrook as part of our social studies curriculum. The graphic images of horrible care, overcrowding, and patients left to wallow in their own filth had made an indelible impression on my young mind.

I swipe at my face. "I hate that they did that. My grandparents were mortified that my mother had even gotten pregnant. The whole affair was shrouded in secrecy, and then when she had my sister..." I shake my head. "Neither set of grandparents was willing to step up. My parents weren't married yet and didn't have the means to support themselves, much less her. They chose the best of the worst choices." Placing severely handicapped children in institutions seemed to be far more commonplace in those days, especially when a family wanted the problem to disappear.

John's brow furrows. "Your parents weren't married, yet your father gave the baby his name . . ."

"She was his child," I whisper, my fathers' pain ripping through me as I utter the words. "This wasn't easy on my parents or without a cost. They loved her."

A look of understanding crosses John's face and he asks, "What happened when she turned seven?"

I sniff and stare at my hands. "My father had a good job by then, so they found a private institution in Connecticut, near Massachusetts. The costs grew to be astronomical over time, but the care and the facility were stellar."

He narrows his unfocused eyes. "She still alive?"

I shake my head. "No. She was born with a weak heart among other health issues. She died before I graduated college." A sad smile tugs at my lips. "I got to see her though, after my mom told me about her. The facility was beautiful."

He sighs and asks more quietly, "What was her name? The birth cert I found listed her as 'Baby McNally.' "

"Evelyn," I whisper. Sorrow for more than my sister overtakes me. Then, like a bucket of cold water, something strikes me. "Wait, why were you looking for my sister?"

John shakes his head and idly plays with the hem of the sheet folded over at his waist. "Something your mother said to me the day you left for Stanford."

My brow tightens. "What did she say?"

He waves a hand. "Something about how she had to give up her dream dancing with the New York City Ballet—because she'd gotten pregnant . . . all that time I thought the baby was you until I mentioned it to Jillian last month. She set me straight. I'd never stopped to do the math on your mother and Vera's ages."

A sense of dread hits my middle at the mention of Jillian.

"What about Jillian?" I flinch at the sound of Raine's voice as he strolls into the room carrying a wide-eyed Rachel, who's gurgling up a storm. I can't say the interruption is unwelcome as I shove down a sliver of panic, more than a little curious about John's conversations with both my mother and Jillian. But I'm not sure now's the time to tug those threads any harder.

"This a good time? Or am I interrupting?" Raine asks, stopping midway into the room.

John breaks into a wide grin and holds out his arms. "Bring me my goddaughter, would ya?"

Raine leans down to give me a peck on the cheek. Rachel uses the opportunity to seize two handfuls of his floppy hair and yank. "Ow! Jeez, Rachie, let go."

I chuckle and try to untangle her tiny fingers as Raine's eyes water. Rachel lets out a delighted high-pitched gurgling scream and tugs harder.

Raine swears under his breath.

"What's going on over there?" John grumbles.

I try to suppress a laugh. "She's doing her best to leave Raine with a bald spot."

"Not funny, Kitty," Raine gripes as he rubs the side of his head and takes Rachel over to John. "Careful, big guy, I don't want her getting grabby with any of that equipment you're hooked up to."

"It's okay. All the important stuff has been disconnected," John says, his arms open and waiting.

Raine positions Rachel in the crook of one them. Even though John can't see her clearly, he looks at her as if he does. His face lights up like the Fourth of July as he holds her. His finger finds her cheek. She grabs it and shoves it into her mouth. "Don't your parents feed you?" he asks.

Raine snorts and reaches into his pocket. "She should be twice her weight based on what she eats." He retrieves a pacifier and helps swap it for John's finger. Rachel happily accepts the trade. "Jillian told me to meet her here. She and the doctor should be by any minute."

"Maybe they'll let me out of this place," John says as he rocks Rachel. "My injuries didn't kill me, but if I stay here much longer, the food just might."

Raine cocks his head. "How's the eyesight?"

"Mostly MIA, but better every day. Fewer shadows, more contrast, things are starting to come back more in my right eye. The bruising in my head is healing, I guess. It's a waiting game."

"I'll hook you up with meals when you're out."

John's expression darkens. "Let's just say, if you were inclined to start early I wouldn't arrest you for smuggling."

Raine turns his gaze to me. "Kitty? What-up, girl? You couldn't do some smuggling for our guy?"

I roll my eyes and throw up my hands. "He's only been on solid foods for two days. It's unlikely he'll perish before I get him home."

"Home?" Raine's brow quirks up, along with his lips.

"Don't start," I whisper, and glare a clear warning.

"They're talking about me like I'm not in the room," John coos in a babyish voice as he rubs his finger over Rachel's chin. She breaks into a giggle and her pacifier slips from between her lips.

The door swings open and the neuropsychologist, Dr. Samuels, walks inside and gives a passing glance to the folder in her hand. "So, John, how are you feeling today?"

Jillian trails in behind her wearing a smile and gives me a wink.

"Just peachy," John says, bouncing Rachel until Jillian comes over to collect her.

"Hey." Jillian leans in and gives John a peck on the cheek. "I have her. Chat with the doctor, she's got good news. We'll see you in a bit."

Jillian clutches Rachel, who's rediscovered her pacifier, and then exchanges a look with Raine. They head for the door. I get up to follow.

"Kat, stay," John says, motioning with his hand for me to sit.

I retake my seat.

Dr. Samuels opens her folder and fixes her gaze on the contents. "I have the results of your tests, and it looks like everything is within normal range. Once you regain your full vision, we'll complete the rest of the testing." She closes the folder. "Your primary physician will be in shortly, but based on this there's no reason why you can't finish your work with me as an outpatient. That said, it's not uncommon to experience some residual headaches, sleep disruptions, fatigue, even dizziness and problems with balance. Since you live alone, we could arrange for a short-term stay at a rehab facility, at least until your vision stabilizes."

John glances in my general vicinity and the corner of his mouth lifts. "That won't be necessary, Doc. I have someplace to go."

I nod, give the doctor a smile, and pray this move is the right one.

Chapter 39

John

Two Weeks Later . . . November 2016

WAKING UP NEXT to Kat, I open my eyes. The sun streams into the bedroom windows underneath the half-shut blinds. I stare straight up at the ceiling fan and blink. My eyelids stretch wide.

Holy hell, I can see.

I blink again and sit up, ignoring the ache in my side. The doc said nothing strenuous for four weeks, much to the dismay of my libido. Too bad Kat's such a stickler for the rules. Then again, I've been a cranky bastard, not so much to her or Jillian, but pretty much to everyone who's had anything to do with my getting blown off the roof of a freaking building.

I'm alive, that's all that matters. At least that's what I've been telling myself when I open my eyes every day. It could've been worse. I get that. But the prospect of being permanently locked in a world of fuzzy shapes and shadows scares the shit out of me. Or it had until right now.

I'm giddy with the sheer joy of seeing the goddamn ceiling fan.

I look at Kat alongside me. She's sleeping with her back to me. Her hair is fanned out on the pillow she's hugging, and there's a peaceful look on the half of her face that's visible. She's the most beautiful thing I've ever seen, much better than the ceiling fan.

To keep things less tempting during my medical lockdown—or so she thinks—she's been sleeping in large T-shirts and yoga pants, and has stayed as far away from me and as close to the edge of the queen bed as she can get. The truth? The only way she'd be less tempting is if she slept in the next zip code.

In deference to Kat, I do my part in the temptation department by wearing boxers and a tee to bed. Under normal circumstances, I'd sleep naked.

When I first got here, she suggested separate sleeping arrangements, offering up her guest room. I convinced her it was safer for me to have her close in case I had a "balance issue" or trouble finding the john. Total bullshit, but it worked. I could see enough light and shadows not to fall down stairs or run into walls, and I've been more than okay finding the facilities even though I have to pee sitting down. A temporary blow to my manhood that I'll survive.

My hand hovers over her hair as I glance down at the stirring inside my boxers and fight back the urge to slide the yoga pants down her hips and slip inside her from behind for a celebratory wake-up call . . . but that might be overstepping.

My brain does a rinse and repeat as I glance at my hand, her hair, and the yoga pants. Screw overstepping, the bandages, and the waning ache in my side.

I stroke the soft strands above her ear. "Kat?" I whisper, and slide in behind her, spooning her close. In less than a millisecond, my morning wood makes a guest appearance. Lucky for me I don't have prostate issues forcing me to evacuate my bladder first thing. I move her hair aside, nuzzle her neck, and inhale the sweet scent of her skin.

"*Mmm*," she murmurs, and pushes back against me, more asleep than awake.

My hand slides down her arm onto her hip, sneaking under the hem of her T-shirt and slowly creeping underneath until my palm has a handful of warm, naked breast.

A smile slips onto my lips as I find her nipple and coax it to life between my fingers, still kissing her neck. I press my erection up against the swell of her delicious ass and softly grind into her.

Fuck. This feels good. I'm more than ready to celebrate.

She startles awake as if she realizes it's not a dream and swats at my hand.

"Shaw, what are you doing?" she says and jacks up away from me. "The doctor said—"

I'm smiling like an idiot. "God, you look beautiful in the morning."

A look of confusion passes over her crinkled brow a moment before her brown eyes light and her lips fall apart. She reaches a hand to touch my cheek. "You can see?" she asks in a mad rush.

I clasp the hand at my cheek and lean into it. "In Technicolor," I say, hooking my other arm around her and pulling her down on top of me.

"Shaw!" she half squeaks, half giggles.

I move my hips underneath her, positioning myself between her thighs despite all the fabric between us, and waggle my eyebrows. "Can I talk you into a proper good morning?"

She hovers over me and grins, her hair hanging down and curtaining our faces. "The doctor said—" she starts again in her schoolmarm voice.

I cup her ass in my palms and give her another slow grind. "Screw the doctor," I say in a low growl, letting my lust unfold. "We have some unfinished business from reunion night, and if my scrambled brain serves, plenty of condoms in that drawer over there." I glance at the nightstand.

She shakes her head and whispers through her smile, "You're unbelievable, Detective."

"Is that a yes?" I grin back, already sliding the hem of her T-shirt up her back.

She seizes my mouth and gyrates her hips in answer.

Holy mother.

My side stretches and I wince as I work the T-shirt over her head as fast as I can. Once her hands are free, she rolls off me and goes for the waistband of my boxers. I lift my hips, and she shimmies my underwear lower, springing me free on the way down my thighs. I kick them off the rest of the way.

She starts to crawl across the bed toward the top drawer of the nightstand. I grab the top of her yoga pants, and pull them—and everything underneath—down her legs.

"Wait a sec, babe," I croak before she gets too far. She stops, giving me a full rear view. *Fuck.* My balls tighten with the visual. I slide two fingers along the delicate skin between her legs. Hot and moist, like I'd hoped.

An "*mmm*" rumbles from my throat.

She moans and opens wider for me. I slip a finger inside her slick contours to test the waters, and deem her more than ready for me.

Desire chokes the ever-living shit out of me. I don't bother taking my tee off before I drag her back in my direction with the foil-wrapped packet in her hand. My rock-hard dick is lined up with her sweet spot from behind.

Bagging me has always been her job, but not this morning. I lay a kiss on her bare shoulder followed by a nip, and snatch the condom from between her fingers.

She doesn't protest. I rip the foil with my teeth and shift back to roll it on, wishing we didn't have to use these things.

I spoon behind her and nudge myself between her legs. She shifts position and guides me from the front until I find the sweet indentation I'm looking for. I sink in an inch or two, take a deep inhale, and thrust in up to the hilt.

The tight, hot feel of her, even through latex, rolls my eyes back and sends my lids down. *Fucking hell.* This feels better than good.

My instincts take over and I roll my hips in a steady pump, pressing her against my chest, while letting my free hand roam over her front. Caressing her breasts, I draw each nipple into a hard peak, pulling a moan from her throat. She arches into me, wrapping her arm around us and digging her nails into my ass as we rock in tandem.

I trail kisses along her shoulder as I slide my fingers across her belly and down farther until I'm teasing the heart of her core. Dipping into the "Kat file" in my brain, I unpack what I know gets her off. Small circles with the right pressure from my fingertips.

I could do this forever. Be inside her for the rest of my goddamn life, coaxing her to orgasm. She makes me feel alive like no one else ever has . . . like oxygen for my soul. Making love to her is the closest ride I've ever taken to Heaven.

I keep up my steady rhythm and start to sweat as the pressure builds in my groin.

A groan rips from my throat. I stroke faster and harder, picking up the pace on my pump, thrust, and roll. I slide into a steady, pounding rhythm that makes my toes curl.

Kat reaches between her legs, captures my balls in her hand and massages them like a pro. *Fuucckkkk* . . . I'm not the only one pulling shit out of my archives.

My heart slams against my chest as Kat stiffens in front of me and screams my name. Her body milks me with everything she's got. I let my fingers fall away from her core as she turns liquid in my arms.

I grasp her hips and ride her hard to finish with her hand still firmly attached to my nuts until my brain melts and my body dissolves into jerking, spasming euphoria.

The sound that breaks from my throat is one step from primal. I ride the wave of my release until it dumps me, empty and boneless, on the shore.

Every muscle I have quakes as I pull her flush against my damp shirt and drape my arm over her like a dead weight, leaving myself buried deep. We both draw ragged breaths as my heart notches down from a rolling thunder to a steady pound.

I kiss her hair. "God, that was good," I half pant, half whisper.

She takes my limp hand and brings it to her lips for a kiss. "It always is with us." Something about her tone sets off my warning bells and sends what feels like ice water rolling down my spine in a mad rush. I tuck her hair behind her ear and ask, "What's the matter, Kat?"

I don't want to pull out of her, but I do, because I need to see her face. I roll her onto her back and prop myself up on an elbow.

"Talk to me," I whisper, running a finger over her cheek to brush away a tear as she tries to smile.

"There's still so much . . . we have to talk about," she says.

"Yeah, I know." She's not the only one with disclosures to make. I pass a hand along the soft strands at the side of her head. "How about I cook us dinner tonight?"

Her eyebrows come up. "Can I help?"

I give her a crooked smile. "I'll think about it."

A loud buzz sounds from the alarm clock on Kat's nightstand. She lunges over to silence it then lets out a breath. "I have to go into the office this morning, but I'll be back in time to take you to your appointment this afternoon. You'll be okay?"

I cock a brow. "I'm a grown man, I'll be fine." Once I clean up the rubber raincoat mess and pee like a racehorse.

She crawls back over and leans in for a kiss. "I'm going to shower in the main bath. You can use this one."

I clasp her arm as she tries to leave and draw her gaze to mine.

"Have a little faith in me, Kat. There's not much you can tell me that could drive me away. I only want us to go into whatever's next with a clean slate. 'Kay?"

She hesitates for a moment before nodding.

Despite what I've said, she still looks like she's carrying the weight of the world on her shoulders when she disappears through the doorway.

Chapter 40

Kitty

The Shower

I LEAN INTO the pelting hot shower spray with a hand propped against the tile wall, wishing it could cleanse the pall clinging to my soul as much as the scent of sex lingering on my body.

Sex. God. I press my eyes shut and shake my head as if that could erase the last forty-five minutes. I had sex with John. Again.

That man has been my weakness since I was seventeen. Both the desire and the instinct to have sex with him are as natural as breathing. No one else, even my former husband of nearly twenty-five years, has ever awakened that kind of raw sexual energy and lust within me. And no one else has ever been able to snap my self-control faster.

For decades, I've hidden behind bad fashion and too much weight as my main weapons of choice to douse my desirability and to kill that heat in John's eyes. Funny, even then, a low burn always flickered in his gaze. A low burn that sparked into a bonfire after Bob left.

Inviting John to my bed, even for his own protection, was a dicey proposition—as this morning has just proven. So much for my intention to wait until after I'd shared the truth and given him the choice to be with me before enjoying the pleasure of his lovemaking again.

Not to say I'm not down-on-my-knees grateful that his vision has returned. I'll admit the thought of him near blind for the rest of his life gutted me. Though what I said in the hospital is true; I'd take him anyway that I could get him. Blind or not.

Caring for him these last several weeks has given me a deep satisfaction that I can't explain. A small way to make amends for what I've done.

During that time, we've been rediscovering one another. Sharing stories, filling in the gaps, trading new likes and dislikes. We've even agreed on a book, and I've been reading to him at night in lieu of watching television. It's been nice ... having him here. More than nice. Especially cooking for two instead of one. We've purposely held off on the heavy stuff, including talking about the night he was shot. That's been nice, too.

Having him in my bed has satisfied an even deeper part of my soul. I haven't slept this well in months. The only thing better would've been to sleep in his arms, which I shut down on the first night. A stipulation of sharing my bed. Being too close to him unwinds me, even with his injuries. He's like a drug that triggers an addiction.

I work a dollop of shampoo through my hair and press my eyes shut against the spray. My gratitude mixes with resignation. What we've had for the last two weeks could end tonight.

With the return of his eyesight, I'm obligated to keep my promise and share the secret I've protected for thirty-five years. No disrespect to John, but the thought of dinner later feels like a last meal before the electric chair.

After a quick rinse and some conditioner, I decide it's time for an emergency appointment with Dr. Graham. I'll tell her everything and fill in the gaps once he's been told, but in the meantime, I could use some advice.

I startle with the scrape of the shower curtain being pulled back; John's large tattooed frame fills the space behind me. "John," I squeak, covering my breasts with my hands. "What the —?"

I can't stop my gaze from trailing over his body, assessing him more closely. He's gotten thinner since the shooting, but he's still solid, and the change enhances his broad shoulders. The stitches have dissolved from the bullet wound on John's side, but it's still a nasty, angry red. It's only a few inches over from the thick pink scar he has from the first shooting. My gaze drops to the generous semi-hard length of him, the sight stealing my breath before I force my eyes back to his face.

There's a softness to his probing, stormy stare. "Hey..." He steps forward and wraps me in his arms. I respond in kind, my hands clasping in the hollow of his spine. "Drop me at my place on your way to work?" he asks in a low, silky-for-him voice as we stand flush in the warm spray.

Despite his sweet tone, the request hollows out my chest. I swallow and whisper, "Are you leaving?"

He adds a cockeyed smile to his penetrating stare as he whispers just as softly. "Only if you want me to. I just want to get my car. Pick up some things for dinner."

Relief washes the tension from my shoulders. I close my eyes against the cascading water and rest my head next to his chin. "Sure," I say, not ready to talk about a future, but not wanting him to leave, either.

He gives me a squeeze before letting go, and then tips up my chin and cups my face in his hands. He kisses me in a gentle dance of tongue, lips, and hands. Heat pours through my body from the inside out, and what was once semi-hard between us has turned to hot steel as it presses into my belly. If I ever thought age might have slowed him down, I discard that misguided notion for good.

"Stop," I gasp, and wiggle out of his embrace. As much as I'd like to christen every room in my new house with him, another round will only make things tougher later. "Rain check? I have to get ready."

"You're killing me, Kat...," he almost whimpers.

The recently revived sex kitten inside of me stretches. Despite my better judgment, I reach for him. My hand glides up and down his slick length a few times.

He grasps my shoulders to balance himself and his eyelids droop. "You're such a tease," he grits, followed by an "*mmm*" that ripples from his throat.

I can't help myself. My lips tip up in a half smile. "If I were really a tease, I would've done this...." I drop to my knees, take him in my mouth, and massage him with my tongue.

"You're evil," he mumbles, bracing himself against the wall.

Clasping his hips, I work his rigid length for another few seconds, ending with a tongue swirl around his head, and then retreat. "Gotta run, babe. Later," I say, mimicking his old Bayonne accent. Using him as leverage, I pull myself up to standing, and then wipe the water out of my eyes.

He huffs a laugh and sinks his fingers into my hips. "You think two can't play this game?" Then he's the one on his knees and it's his coaxing tongue between my parted thighs working its Shaw magic.

My nails dig into his wet shoulders as my lower half lights up. On my way to climax, I let out a moan. He pulls away and rises to his feet, wearing a grin. "Now you know how it feels."

I punch him lightly in the arm. "You suck."

He waggles his eyebrows. "I do, and I'm really good at it." He leans in for a quick kiss then winks. "I'll make it up to you later."

"Me too." I hope—with my whole heart. "Now hurry up, we've got to go if I'm dropping you at your apartment before my client meeting."

With that, I exit and leave John singing "I want you to want me" in the shower just to needle me as I scramble around like a lunatic, getting ready.

The pall, lightened for the moments with John inside the shower, returns. Only it's heavier than it was before.

Chapter 41

John

Later That Day, Charlie's Aunt

I'M STILL RIDING the high from the grand entrance of my eyesight and my morning with Kat as I stroll through the doorway of Charley's Aunt and into the lunch-crowd din. I take a barstool to wait for Tony and signal for a beer.

I'm still pissed about the cluster fuck the night of the raid. So much for the "all clear" on the roof. I'm not the only who got hurt that night. One of the newer guys got his kneecap blown off. That's two down because of a poor decision and a worse informant. Going through with the plan after a last-minute change in venue was a bad call, especially since it conflicted with Lettie's intel. We should've done an abort and regrouped.

Bottom line, I'm getting too old for this shit. I've ducked the Grim Reaper twice, and there but for the grace of God go I. Somehow, I don't think I'll get lucky a third time. I've officially resigned from the task force. It's not worth the risk. Not when I finally have a shot at some happiness. I once chose the job over Kat out of stubbornness, stupidity, and dick-based pride. It cost me big time—twenty-five years of my life. Not going to make that mistake again.

Time for something new and less dangerous to my health... which is why I'm here. Hopefully, Tony is about to do me a solid and make up for the near-death experience he's partially responsible for.

Jack, one of the bartenders, slides a beer in front of me, and I hand him my credit card as I raise the frosty glass to my lips and take a long pull.

The cool brew goes down so smooth I almost moan. It's the first drink I've had since reunion night. The pain meds are done, so I'm in the clear.

I'd cut way down on drinking as part of my training with Raine, and for the first time in twenty years, I have no desire to overdo it and ruin my svelte new waistline.

"Hey, Shaw." Tony claps me on the back and slides onto the stool next to me.

"Stella?" The question's almost rhetorical. Tony's a diehard Belgian fan. He's got me hooked, too.

He snorts. "Is there anything else?"

I flag down Jack and give him Tony's order.

"It's good to see you," Tony says. His sideways glance and the set of his jaw give away the pain and guilt he's still carrying over the call he made on the raid. I know that look well. I'm no angel. I've fucked up a time or two and have worn the same expression.

"Thanks. Good to be seen," I mutter, clutching my beer. "So what did your brother say?"

He takes a sip of Stella. "He said to drop by this afternoon, after three."

I nod. "Thanks. I appreciate it."

"We're trying to flip a new informant," Tony says, running his fingers down his glass.

My brow pops up. "Yeah, who is it?"

"You sure you're not coming back?" he asks, as if dangling a piece of intel is enough to get me to change my mind.

I dip my head and shake it. "I've got my twenty-five years. I'm done tempting fate. Two bullets are enough for one lifetime. Time for a new chapter."

He smirks. "An assistant coaching job on a high school football team is your idea of turning over a new leaf?"

I smirk back and shrug. "Always loved the game. Why not? Besides, it was your idea."

He chuckles. "Poor kids."

The corner of my mouth turns up as I sip my beer. "Maybe."

"How are things with Kat? Heard you've been staying with her."

"Good. Things are good." I purse my lips and nod, hoping it stays that way after tonight. I'm already anticipating how pissed she'll be when I tell her about my little encounter with Bob the night of the club raid on Route 22. Damn, I wish I could pull a rewind on that night.

When our beers are finished, we say our goodbyes and I head from Chatham Boro over to Jillian and Raine's house in the Township.

I'm dying to get back into Raine's gym, but I'm at least another four weeks away from getting medical clearance for something that strenuous. I thought I would pop a hernia just making love with Kat this morning, I'm not about to press my luck with weights. At this point, I'm happy enough to get back into his kitchen . . . literally. That kid can cook.

Lucky for me, Raine works from home on Fridays. We're having lunch, and then he's going to help me figure out what to make for dinner. He's taught me how to make a few healthy dishes, but I want something special for tonight.

God, I sound like a freaking girl. But Kat's worth it, and Raine's a master when it comes to food. He even writes a monthly recipe column for some romance publication because of Jillian's book. No one would ever question that guy's masculinity, so I guess I'm safe.

I park in the driveway behind Raine's garage then amble to the front door and ring the bell.

There's some shuffling inside before the lock clicks and Raine's grinning like an idiot in the doorway, all dimples and great teeth. His V-neck sweater stretches over his ripped physique. I eye him with envy after being out of commission for the last three weeks. If anything, compared to him I look underfed. No fault of Kat's. She's been shoving food on me like I might perish from starvation.

Raine pulls me into a man hug. "Good to see you, dude. Wait, scratch that. Better having you see me, if you catch my meaning."

I chuckle and give him a jab. "Thanks, kid. If I didn't know you better, I'd say you look like you've been hitting the 'roids."

He stumbles back in mock horror and clasps the center of his chest. "You wound me, dude. You know I'm all natural. I don't do that shit."

"Yeah, I know. I'm just jealous and pulling your chain."

He claps me on the back. "Don't worry, big boy. I'll get your ass back in shape once the doctor gives the okay."

"I'm counting on it," I mutter, and let the warm flush of our friendship fill me with comfort and ease.

Jillian's first husband, Robert, was a good guy, hardworking, ambitious; but Raine is a whole lot better for Jilly. Since she found him, I've never seen her as happy. And coming from me, who's known her since she was a kid, that's saying something. Kat says Raine reminds her of Drew. I never met Drew, so I wouldn't know, but I heard he had a pair of pipes on him. Not Raine. He can't carry a tune in a bucket. But he's an all-star husband and father, and that's what counts. I'm proud to have him as a friend.

I follow his hulking frame to the kitchen. "Where's Jilly and Rachel?"

"Pediatrician for Rachie's five-month check-up." He heads for the oven, grabs a potholder, and looks inside.

Whatever he's making smells incredible.

"What are we having?" I ask, pulling out a chair by the kitchen table.

"Baked salmon with dill-caper butter over a Caesar salad with a low-cal dressing," he says, and shuts the door on the Viking Professional before discarding the potholder. "Light, healthy, omega-3s, lots of protein." He runs a critical gaze over me. "Got to get you back with the program. You're looking a little runty."

I snort. "Gee, thanks. Have a little respect. I fell off a goddamn building. I'm lucky to be here."

Raine's brows draw together and he breathes deep. His teasing tone is gone. "No lie. You scared the shit out of us, John," he says, low and serious. He pins me with a stare and then shakes his head and rests his hands on his hips. "How about not doing that again, huh?"

I lay my hands on the table. "I don't plan on it. Thinking it's time to retire. Do something else."

He cocks an interested brow and grabs a bowl of greens from the fridge. "Yeah? What's your plan?"

I tell him about the potential opportunity for the assistant coaching job at Summit High School. Lucky break. The guy they had is moving to Ohio after Christmas for his wife's new job. Football in the fall, baseball in the spring. Between that and my pension, I should be fine financially. Though I can't decide whether or not police work might be less dangerous than dealing with a bunch of high school meatheads, as Kat so fondly used to call us.

Raine nods, takes out the fish, and rests the pan on the stovetop. "Sounds cool. Perfect, actually. What did Kitty say?"

I shake my head and tap my fingertips together. "Haven't told her yet. Figured we'd talk about it over dinner."

"For the record? You seem happy . . . in spite of your swan dive off the building."

"Yeah . . . but Kat and I got some stuff to work out. I'm hopeful we can spend some more time together."

Raine sniffs and throws me a crooked smile. "That all? Jillian and I have higher hopes for you two."

I shrug. "No point getting ahead of ourselves. Like I said, we've got some shit to sort out. Then let's see where the chips fall." As much as I downplay my situation with Kat, my hopes are probably as high as Jillian and Raine's, but I'd like to keep that to myself for now.

An unconvinced *um-hum* comes from Raine's throat as he plates the food. "You coming for Thanksgiving next week?"

I hadn't thought about it. "I guess. If Kat doesn't mind."

He gives me a sour look. "I'm inviting you. You're not obligated to come as Kitty's date. You comin'?"

I grin. "Yeah, I'll come, but hopefully as Kat's date."

"That part's up to you." He grabs my gaze. "You're family with or without Kitty, remember that."

"Yes, sir," I say, giving him a two-fingered salute.

He scoots a plate in front of me. I inhale the aroma. "Shit, man. Jillian's one lucky woman. I'd marry you myself if you fed me this well every day."

He chuckles and slides into a seat across from me with his salad. "Then I guess Kitty's chances are pretty high. She's a great cook."

Yes, she is.

I cut into my salmon. "Speaking of . . . what should I make that's not too complicated? My repertoire doesn't stray far from rice and red beans, and whatever else you taught me."

Raine tucks into his salad. "Doesn't need to be complicated to be good. I wrote up a shopping list and jotted down some notes for you with a simple dressing recipe. A salad, roasted potatoes, and those chicken thighs with rosemary and lemon you like. Easy . . . and impressive enough."

I nod, liking his suggestions. "Done."

We chat for a while longer as I help him clear the dishes. We decide dessert for tonight is best purchased, along with a nice bottle of wine. I'm in the mood for a Philly Fluff cake, so I make a mental note to stop by Natale's. I ponder whether to desecrate it with strawberries and whipped cream, and then add those to my shopping list.

I let Raine get back to work and cruise over to the north side of Summit to close out my last piece of unofficial FBI business.

Lettie answers two seconds after I ring the bell. No jeans today. She's in full makeup, a tailored business suit, and heels.

"John." She throws her arms around my waist. I do my best not to flinch at the twinge in my side. "God, I'm so sorry."

I run a soothing hand along her tiny back. "*Shh*, let's go inside." She pulls the door shut and leads me to the kitchen where she's set up a makeshift office on the granite-topped island.

She grabs the teakettle on the stove and fills it with water. "You're lucky you caught me. I was supposed to be in the city this afternoon." She sets the kettle to boil and sits on the stool next me, her blond brows pulled painfully tight. "You have no idea how relieved I was to get your text."

I take her hand and give it a squeeze. "What do you know about that night?" I ask, taking the first opportunity we've had to speak alone since the shooting.

"I don't know who the other informant was or where he got his information. All I can tell you is the shipment arrived when and where I said it would, and the FBI wasn't there to intercept it."

I huff and shake my head. "I'm out, Lettie. I want you out, too. Hear me?"

She nods with a dipped head and stares at her manicure; when she looks up tears pool in her eyes. "I might be in too deep."

Fuck. I swipe a hand down my face and shove back the fear that slides across my middle. I expel a breath and grab her hand again. "Doll, listen to me. You're not. You've done enough. Walk while you still can. If anything happens to you, I'll never forgive myself. Understand me?"

She nods. "After . . ."

I tug on her delicate fingers. "After what?"

"After I turn Howard."

The informant Tony mentioned. Damn it.

"Lettie. . . ." I sigh and mumble a curse. I hate this. A lot.

"After that, I promise."

My mouth drops into a grim line and I shake my head.

A tear trickles down her cheek and she wraps me in a hug. "Really, John. I promise." I circle her baby-bird frame in my arms, and even though she's a capable twenty-five-year-old woman, all I can think is: "What if she were my daughter? What would I do?"

"Unlock your phone and give it to me," I whisper.

She pulls away. "Why?"

I pin her with a glare, hold out my hand, and stay silent.

Wiping her eyes with one hand, she hands me her cell with the other. "7458."

I extract my phone and program both cells so that we can find each other using GPS, and then hand it back to her. "This is just until I get you a device you can put in your bra. You call me if you get in trouble. Understand?"

She brushes at her eyes a second time and gives me a wicked smile. "Trying to get close to the girls?"

I snort. "Got my own set at home, smartass." Home. Let's hope.

Her smile dampens. "Hey, Detective, thought you were out," she whispers, waving her phone and looking fourteen again.

"Not for you." I slide off my stool, pull her back into arms, and kiss the top of her head. "Never for you, sweetheart. You're family."

She pushes away and wipes her eyes again. "Damn. I wish my father would've been more like you."

"*Humph.*" My cheeks heat at the compliment.

The kettle whistles and a stream of wispy steam shoots out the nozzle. "Rain check on the tea?" I ask. There's still one more stop I need to make before tackling my errands and the appointment at my alma mater.

Five minutes later, I'm heading across town to my apartment. I haven't been here since the night of the reunion. When I walk in, the place has the stale smell of being shut tight and not lived in. I can't say I've missed being here.

I've never been much of a decorator. The apartment is utilitarian and crying out for a woman's touch. Same as it's been for twenty years. The opposite of Kat's place. Even though she's only been there a month, the atmosphere is warm and inviting. Someplace I'd enjoy living.

I head to my bedroom and reload on clean clothes. Whatever I have at Kat's, I'm getting sick of. I gave her my key to pick up some stuff once I agreed to come home with her, but she hasn't been back since.

But that's not why I'm here. What I came for is in my safe. I shove my clothes aside in the closet, spin the lock, and open the small metal door. Next to my firearms, I have some paperwork, emergency cash, Ben's tags, and an old envelope with Kat's handwriting. I take it out and give it a little shake. The contents slide between the paper. Satisfied, I stuff it into the pocket of my jeans.

If tonight goes well, I plan to return what's inside.

It represents a promise I hope she'll let me keep.

Chapter 42

Kitty

Pine Grove House, The Last Supper

MY HAND SHAKES as I open the door from the garage into the kitchen. "I'm home," I say in the most upbeat tone I can manage. With Dr. Graham's help, I've prepared as much as possible for what will likely be a painful discussion that holds the potential to explode into a mushroom cloud and touch everyone I hold dear.

There's a nice smell coming from the oven. John's in a pair of jeans and an untucked button-down rolled to the elbows, revealing his dive watch on one wrist and a simple silver link bracelet he's worn on his other for twenty-five years. A present from me during the year we dated after the tenth reunion.

He smiles, a dish towel casually resting on his shoulder as he works the corkscrew into the neck of a wine bottle. He comes over, bottle and all, and drops a soft kiss on my lips.

"How was your day?" he asks, and gives me a lazy grin. The table is set with the lights dimmed. Soft jazz music, which I recognize as Dave Koz, plays in the background.

"Busy but good," I reply, placing my handbag and keys on the counter. "How did your appointment with the doctor go?" He had volunteered to drive himself when I dropped him at his apartment. A relief, since I needed the time to juggle my day.

He takes the towel from his shoulder, places it on the counter, and pours Cabernet into two glasses. "I took the rest of the tests. Results seemed to be good. No headaches or dizziness, so the doc thinks I'm in the clear." He hands me one of the glasses and catches my gaze. "Toast?"

I smile despite myself and nod. "Sure." Steadying my hand, I touch my glass to his.

"To new beginnings and putting the past behind us?" He says with a subtle note of challenge in his tone, his stormy gaze tugging at mine.

If only . . . I nod again. "Hear, hear," I whisper, and take a long sip, hoping it settles my nerves. I understand he wants to get past this, but more than anything, I understand this is a test of trust. And I owe him that. I'm long past due paying my debt.

Something Dr. Graham pointed out made me feel better. Despite not knowing all the details, she noted the complexity of the situation and that my decision to share my secret doesn't affect only John. Many people have been living under the protective umbrella I've created. Some of them now dead, but plenty still alive. Ironically, the timing is finally right to minimize the fallout. It's now or never, and I won't live with never.

John nods toward the table. "Sit. We have a few minutes until the chicken is done."

I take a seat, unable to get fully comfortable.

He lets out a breath. "Raine invited me to Thanksgiving dinner. You okay with that?"

"Of course." I drop my gaze, clutch my glass, and lose any ability to make small talk. Now that I'm ready to confront this, the weight of my task bears down on me.

"Kat?"

My gaze darts up to see a pained expression on his face. He reaches across the table with his palm up.

I stare for a moment, tension knotting the center of my back, and then lay my hand in his. He enfolds it in warmth and pulls it to his lips. "Relax. Let's start small . . . all right?"

I nod, staring at the glimmering silver on his wrist, and reach for a question I've always wondered about. "What made you marry Carmela?"

He half snorts, half chuckles, but there's an amused gleam in his eye. "That's your idea of starting small?"

I shrug and give him what I hope looks like a smile rather than a grimace.

He squeezes my hand before letting it go, then leans back in his chair and rubs his chin. He gets a faraway look in his eye, shakes his head, and blows out a long breath before he meets my gaze with an unwavering stare. "I don't like admitting this, but since I want the God's honest truth from you, I'll give you the same. I'm not going to pretty this up. I'm gonna lay it out plain and ugly. You okay with that?"

I nod slowly.

He nods back, looking satisfied, and continues. "After you shot me down in San Francisco, I had a couple of bad years. Way too much drinking, bad attitude, and I'll be honest . . . I fucked my way through more women than I could count. One-night stands. All of them. No romance involved, just release. Worst time of my life."

His admission sends a knife through my heart, especially since I can still count the number of men I've been with on one hand. Not to say he and Bob were the only two — they weren't, but still . . .

He leans on the table, resting on his elbows. "I'm not proud of that time in my life. I was pretty empty and disgusted with myself when I ran into Carm one night at a club in New York. She was divorced, no kids. I took her home. We understood each other . . . and I was so damn lonely." He pauses and shakes his head, regret shining in his eyes. "She could never hold a candle to you, Kat. But she was the closest I could come to finding some happiness. So I took it. We hopped a plane to Vegas a few months later. I don't know when she started using, but the minute she hit crack, I threw her ass in rehab. She cleaned up. We made it another year and a half before I found her in bed with some loser, and that was it. . . ."

"I'm sorry," I whisper, and shake my head. "I . . . I never knew the whole story."

His lips hint at a half smile. "That's because I never told anyone before."

"Thank you for telling me." I sip my wine, warmed by his honesty despite the grittiness of his story. I'm sorrier than he knows for the part I played in his unhappiness.

He folds his arms over his chest, lifts a brow, and asks gently, "My turn?"

Giving the only acceptable response, I nod.

"Why didn't you invite me to Vera's memorial service last summer?"

I press my eyes shut and shake my head. "Something happened . . . the day she died. It sent me into a tailspin. Seeing you . . ." Heading into dangerous territory, I swallow and shift approaches. "I already suspected something was off with Bob, but I was in denial. I was vulnerable . . . brittle. Sharing my grief with you over Vera would've unwound me. God, I'm sorry. It was selfish and inexcusable."

His gaze is intent and assessing, but his tone is soft and a mere whisper. "What happened?"

I reach for his hand. "I'll get to that in a while. But please know I didn't do it to slight or hurt you," I say in earnest.

He closes his fingers around mine, enrobing me in warmth. "How so?"

"I was one step from shattering. I would've been tempted to lean on you . . . get you involved in something you shouldn't have been. It wouldn't have been fair." I squeeze his hand and beg, "Forgive me?"

He nods, and then his brow tightens to the point that he almost looks like he's in pain. He blows out a long breath. "There's something I need to tell you" — The timer rings on the stove. — "Let me take out the food first." He drops my hand and pushes his chair back. Grabbing potholders on his way to the oven, he pulls out pans with chicken and potatoes that smell heavenly, and sets them on the stove. "Before I possibly ruin your appetite with what I'm going to tell you, how about we have dinner first?" he asks with a pleading look in his eyes. I can't imagine what he has to say will be any worse than what I plan to tell him.

"That would be fine." After all his effort, I don't have the heart to admit I'm not that hungry. I join him at the counter with our plates from the table.

He scoots around me to the refrigerator and pulls out a large bowl of greens for a salad and my glass Pyrex measuring cup with homemade dressing.

"Sit, babe. I got this," he says, giving me a more relaxed smile.

Rather than argue, I return to my seat. The kitchen is warm and cozy from the oven. With the mood lighting and music, it would qualify as romantic if there wasn't such an undercurrent of dread.

"This looks wonderful," I say when John places the meal in front of me. "Thank you for doing this."

He lifts his fork. "It's the least I could do after all the cooking you've done for me these last couple of weeks."

I smile. "It's no bother. Cooking for two is easier than for one." I cut into the chicken and have a bite. It's surprisingly good. Not that I didn't have confidence in John, but during our shared history his prowess in the bedroom didn't extend to the kitchen. I swallow and dab at my lips with a napkin. "It's very good," I say.

A satisfied smile settles on his lips. "Thanks."

"How was your day?" I ask, starting simple.

"I met with Tony's brother Frank over at Summit High school this afternoon," he says, cutting a piece of chicken.

"Really? About what?" I ask, and stab some salad greens.

A smile warms his face. "Retiring from the Force and applying for an assistant coaching job."

An unexpected sense of relief floods through me, knowing that he's taking measures to stay out of harm's way. His news brightens my mood like sun peeking through storm clouds. "That's fantastic!"

He pokes at his plate. "I haven't gotten it yet."

"You will, and you'll be amazing. I'm so proud of you," I say, confident that he's perfect for the job.

A blush creeps onto his clean-shaven cheeks. "Thanks, babe."

We manage to get through the rest of dinner without discomfort. Trading tidbits about the people we know, the conversation flows to the relaxing sounds of smooth jazz. We do an admirable job of avoiding the other white elephant in the room—his ongoing living arrangements—but by the end of tonight, that might be a moot point.

By the time we finish the meal, my wineglass is empty and so is the bottle. Two glasses of white have barely taken the edge off. I'm still stone-cold sober.

I rise to clear my plate, but John motions me to sit. "Let me get this." He pushes out his chair and chuckles as he takes my plate. "You have a hard time letting people do things for you, you know that?"

My mouth opens for a rebuttal, then snaps shut. He's right. I'm the giver. But that role wasn't my choice. Not at first. The iron grip of control was forced upon me, and once it took hold, it became a mantle that consumed every aspect of my life, especially within my own family. The giving shifted the focus away from me, allowing me to hide.

"You're right," I say finally, and glance down at my work clothes. "How about we meet in the living room in a few minutes? I want to change."

He shoots me a glance as he flips on the faucet. "Sure. There's not much to do here."

I escape up to the bedroom and stand in front of my open closet. As I reach for yoga pants, I stop. *No hiding,* I remind myself.

Instead, I take out a flattering pair of new jeans and an attractive top that Jenny insisted I buy. One that clings to my slimmer curves and does its part to make me look younger and more hip. Something Kat would wear.

I dress quickly then run to the bathroom to brush my teeth and hair, doing my best to freshen up. Satisfied, I take a deep breath and return to the closet.

My heart beats with a strong thump as I retrieve the envelope that contains the tipping point for the rest of my life.

It's time.

I take to the stairs with an iron resolve.

John's sitting on the couch with his legs crossed at the knees, drinking a glass of water. There's a second glass on the coffee table waiting for me.

I slip onto the sofa, leaving some space between us, and tuck a leg under me. Something I hadn't been able to do easily for over two decades when I'd been carrying an extra forty pounds.

He points to the glass. "To hydrate. Strict instructions from Raine."

"Thanks," I say, slipping the letter next to me on the far side of John before I pick up the glass.

As I'm swallowing, John says, "Kat, I . . . knew about Bob."

I almost choke on the water. Coughing hard, I put down the glass and swipe a hand across my mouth. My face heats from a combination of water going down the wrong pipe and my blood pressure escalating. "What are you talking about?"

He blows out a breath, rubs his eyes, and then turns his regretful gaze on me. "Not too long before you asked for Ray's info, I did a raid down on 22 at the Wayfarer's Club. As we cleared the front rooms. . . ." He shakes his head and then says. "I found him with Carl."

His words ring in my ears as I stare at my hands, my insides slipping off their axis. I chew my lip, resisting my first impulse to take this as a betrayal. After a silent prayer for patience and fortitude, I ask in a quiet, measured tone, "Why didn't you tell me?"

He gives a half-hearted shrug, accompanied by a look somewhere between sorrow and pity. "I planned to tell you if he didn't come clean before the reunion."

"But you'd found out months ago," I snap.

He presses his eyes shut for a second and lets out a breath. "But then you asked for a PI. If you had told me it was for you, I would've told you." His brow drops into a frown and his tone gets less apologetic. "But you lied. You said you were asking for a friend. So I thought you wouldn't appreciate the fact that I already knew." He clenches his jaw and shakes his head. "You didn't trust me, Kat. And that hurt."

I sway back like I've taken a blow. "It wasn't a matter of trusting you, John. It's the same reason I didn't tell you about Vera's memorial service. I didn't trust *me*," I whisper, feeling tears well in my eyes. "You've always been my Kryptonite, Shaw. My weakness. Leaning on you is like breathing for me. I couldn't use you like that after everything . . ." After everything I've done. I fight back tears, needing to stay strong.

His shoulders fall forward and he passes a hand over his pained face, and then he motions for me to come to him.

I shake my head and stay where I am. If he was hurt because of that, I can't imagine how this can end well. I pull the letter out from next to my leg. It quivers in my hand.

"Not yet," I whisper, and brush away an escaping tear.

He tips his chin at my hand. "What's that?"

"It's everything I stole from us," I say.

His gaze turns wary as he stares at the letter. "What do you mean?" he asks, his voice crushed gravel.

"Promise me something first?"

"What?"

"You'll hear me out once you see this. You'll listen and let me explain," I say, no longer able to stop the tears as I anticipate the impact this will have on him. Wishing I could lessen the blow.

His spine straightens and his body coils like he's preparing for what I'm about to deliver. He hesitates, his eyes fixated on what's inside my hand. Then he gives a slow nod.

I open the envelope and remove the contents. Still folded, I slide the sheets of paper across the cushion to his waiting fingers.

Chapter 43

John

The Reckoning

MY HEART POUNDS and I swallow hard as my fingers connect with the papers Kat passes me. Every instinct I have screams a warning. Once I read what's inside, I can never go back and "un-see" it. I know Kat well enough that whatever this is . . . it's significant.

I take a deep breath, hold it, and unfold the sheets of paper.

I blink.

I blink again and I try to process why Kat's handed me a photocopy of a birth certificate from Santa Clara County, California. At first, I think it's for her sister, the one who died.

A second later, the air seizes in my lungs when I see the name. My sister's name—but not. Mine and Kat's. All three of them. Together. As one.

Denise Henshaw McNally.

My jaw drops and my whole body turns numb as the synapses in my brain fire and I suddenly understand.

Born January 15, 1982. Mother: Katherine Ann McNally. Father: John Doe.

The center of my chest caves in and I don't breathe. I forget how.

"Say something," she whispers, hugging herself as tears stream down her cheeks.

I stare at her, uncomprehending how she could keep something like this from me . . . for all these years. "What the fuck?" I whisper on a shallow exhale, one step from imploding.

Shock doesn't even begin to cover it. I rise to my feet.
I need out. A place to breathe. Now.

"I gotta go," I mumble with barely half a thought, and head to the door.

"Shaw . . ." Kat sobs softly behind me. "I'm sorry."

My car keys end up in my free hand, and before I even remember getting into my car I'm driving the half mile down Pine Grove to Memorial Field. Shit. I should've just walked.

My whole body shakes, rocked from the impact of Kat's revelation. I'm tempted to grab a bottle of something and drink myself into oblivion, but if I do that I'll never come back. Alcohol won't solve this problem.

Every emotion I have does battle inside of me. I don't know which to tackle first: the pain of betrayal, the anguish and rage of lost possibilities, the fucking regret, the guilt . . . The guilt that this was somehow my fault.

Of all the things Kat could tell me, I never expected this. I. Never. Expected. This. Or for her to make this kind of decision without me thirty-five fucking years ago. For someone who prides himself on his powers of observation, how the fuck did I miss this? How didn't I see it? Know it? Feel it?

I pull into a spot, kill the ignition, and slam the steering wheel with the palms of my hands. Then I roar in frustration at the top of my lungs into the darkness until I'm desperate for air.

Fucking hell.

My eyelids slip shut. I draw in deep breaths and lean back on the headrest. All I see blazing behind my lids, accompanied by an ache in my chest, is the name on the birth certificate: Denise Henshaw McNally.

I snap on the overhead light and pick up the crumpled sheets of paper I'd thrown onto the passenger seat. Unfolding them, I stare at the birth certificate again as the paper rattles in my hand.

A lump grows in my throat. There's significance packed into what Kat chose. Kat didn't list my name as the father, yet there it is. Pressure builds behind my eyes and my lip quivers as I remember a conversation we had not long after we met.

"What's this?" Kat asks as she stares at a framed certificate written in Latin on my bedroom wall during a study break.

I drape my arms around her from behind and rest my chin on her shoulder. Bittersweet feelings tug at me as I look at it. Denise had died the week after. "I got it when I made my Confirmation at St. Andrew's."

She points at my name. "But . . . this says, Juan Henshaw Rivera. I thought Henshaw was your last name?"

I chuckle and kiss her neck where it meets her shoulder. "It is. I don't have a middle name. It's tradition in Hispanic cultures. Parents give their kids two last names. The father's name is first. The mother's is second. So if it's a girl, she keeps her father's name when she gets married."

She named the baby . . .

Denise *Henshaw* McNally.

My eyelids flutter and my vision blurs as I start to crack. What's written on the certificate is all for me. A tribute to my sister. My place claimed in my child's name. Kat's love and respect for me clear as day.

I pass a hand across my eyes to catch a few hot tears as they spill over, and then turn the page to see what's behind it.

It's a letter dated August of last year. My heart picks up rhythm when I read the first line. A second later, my heartbeat's pounding in my ears.

Chapter 44

John

The Letter

THE PAGES JITTER between my fingers. I clutch them tightly, making the movement stop so I can read on.

Dear Katherine,

It feels odd calling you by your first name, but even stranger calling you "Mom," though I'm sure neither of those things compare to how odd or strange getting this must be for you. I desperately hope this letter isn't wholly unwelcome or painful to receive.

I've wanted to reach out and find you for many years now, but out of respect for my adoptive parents, I waited until my mother passed away. My father has already been gone for several years, so now seemed like the right time.

All I know about my birth is that you had me as an unwed teenage mother, and you weren't in a position to keep me. I confess that it wasn't until I had children of my own that I truly understood why you gave me up, not because you didn't want me, but because you wanted to give me a better life than the one you could provide. I understand. I really do.

315

My parents never changed my name or hid that I was adopted. I'd always wondered why you chose not to seal the records of the adoption. In my heart, I'd hoped that you'd done it so that I could find you someday if that's what I wanted.

The people who adopted me were wonderful and loving parents who couldn't have children of their own after years of failed fertility treatments. My father was a surgeon, and my mother a college professor. My childhood was happy, and I wanted for nothing.

In high school, I played varsity soccer and graduated as the class valedictorian. I was accepted to Stanford and received a scholarship named the Liam McNally Grant for Scientific Study in Molecular Biology. It was that ironic twist of fate that led me to you. I found it odd that a prerequisite for applying was having McNally as a surname.

On a whim, and what my mom used to call an investigative binge, I dug deeper and found the scholarship was originally an endowment meant for Liam's granddaughter, Katherine, who dreamed of becoming a molecular biologist. Although she attended Stanford, she turned down the endowment to pursue a major in accounting.

The timing triggered my curiosity, and after some additional research I exercised my legal right to request a copy of my original birth certificate, which I found in Santa Clara County, CA. My mother's name was listed as Katherine Ann McNally. The same Katherine listed as the intended recipient of the endowment.

I had chills for a week.

After that, I continued my search and found a record that listed you living in Summit, New Jersey, with your husband, Robert Lynch. Since my father was listed as John Doe, I had no idea if Robert was my biological father. After further investigation, I ruled him out due to timing, and decided there was a high probability that you meant to protect my birth father's identity, and I had to respect that.

From that moment on, I knew I would try to find you someday.

I haven't searched for my father. The choice to share this letter with him will be yours. My intent is not to cause pain, or to harm either of your current or potential relationships. I just wanted you to know that I am alive, I am well, and I am eternally grateful that you decided to have me rather than the alternative. What you did took grit, determination, and courage.

The last thing I will share is that you are a grandmother two times over—gosh, I'm so sorry to make that sound as if you are old! My husband, James, and I are the proud parents of twins, Samuel and Sarah, who just celebrated their tenth birthdays. They are wonderful children—smart, athletic, and kind.

Well, I guess that is it for me. I'll leave this in your capable hands. If you have the desire, I would be honored to meet you and thank you in person for the chance you gave me. I'd also like to give you the option of being a part of our lives if that's something you wish to do. On the off chance you are in touch with my father, and you feel he is someone I should meet, please extend the same offer to him. We still live in Santa Clara County. . . . Surprise, surprise, I became a molecular biologist and teach at Stanford University.

We've never met, but I've dreamed of you for years . . . and, as impossible as it sounds . . . I love you.

Yours truly,
Denise (Henshaw McNally) Crawford

The letter drops onto my lap. I cover my face with my hands and come undone.

All this time. . . . My life and my choices speed past me like time-lapse photography while unbridled sadness takes my heart into a death grip.

As much as I want to blame Kat, I can't. I know what I did to drive her to this. . . . I know how this happened. I'm not blameless. Not one bit.

That doesn't mean I'm not angry — nuclear angry — that she stole choices I should've been allowed to make. Angry she let me believe that she left me . . . and yeah, I believed she lied about her promise to stay together after high school. Sadly, I just thought she didn't love me enough.

My fucking pride took a hit and got in the way of my pursuing the truth.

My whole goddamn life I thought it was me. And it was, but not in the way I thought, and not because she didn't love me.

I drop my head to the steering wheel, and force myself to breathe.

In. Out. In. Out.

Anger aside, I admire the sheer courage it took for Kat to do what she did without me. The sacrifice she thought she was making for me, knowing that I didn't want kids young like my mom . . . the sacrifice she made for our daughter.

What she did was wrong, but it was right, too. Therein lies the rub.

For the first time, I understand her parting words from the summer of '81, *"I'm doing this for you."* She did do it for me . . . because she loved me enough to gamble what we had so that I could live a life she thought I wanted. But she missed the point. The life I wanted always included her.

My shoulders shake and I sob, loud and ugly, for the first time since Vera delivered the news that she hired Sven before she left that same summer as Kat.

Kat's decision changed the course of my life for the next thirty-five years. I've spent every moment since I was nineteen living in the shadow of my past, hoping against hope to someday be with the only woman I ever truly loved.

Kat told me after I gave her the locket the night of the junior prom that forever seemed like an impossible word. That no one could guarantee it. But I never stopped believing. I promised I'd always be there. It's why her name is inked into my skin. It's her, or it's no one.

Fuck it. I promised I'd listen. If I can't do that, I don't deserve her anyway. And wasn't I the schmuck who told her this was our last chance to get it right?

I may not be happy with the news, but she did right by me this time. She can't erase a decision she made thirty-five years ago.

I pass a wrist across my eyes then reach for the napkins I keep in the glove compartment to blow my nose.

Picking up the letter again, I stare at it. She has a chance to make this right, too. We both do. *Together.*

Far be it from me to fuck up again.

I toss the letter back onto the passenger seat. A few deep breaths later, I start the car, ready to begin life on the other side.

Chapter 45

Kitty

Aftershocks

I CRUMPLE NUMB and broken when John leaves. The shock and devastation on his face sliced my heart open and left me hemorrhaging. As much as I tried to anticipate and manage the pain, somehow it didn't lessen the blow for either of us.

I'm not sure how long I stay curled in a ball on the couch, trying to draw breath. It could have been minutes, or hours. I've lost track of time.

When my limbs are too cramped to stay like that, I get up and walk to the kitchen on autopilot, carrying the empty water glasses. All the dishes from dinner have been loaded into the dishwasher, thanks to John. There's nothing left to do. The kitchen's clean.

The life and energy I've felt inside the house since I moved in fled with John's departure.

Bracing myself on the sink, I drop my head, feeling wrung out like a dried husk. My emotional well is empty. There are no tears left to cry. Our fate is in John's hands now.

Tomorrow, I'll deal with the fallout. My daughter needs to know she has a half sister. My sister needs to know she's an aunt. And my ex-husband needs to know his ex-wife has a child with another man . . . because I plan to take Denise up on her offer.

I plan to get to know my daughter, my child with John. I plan to be a part of her life and my grandchildren's.

Her response to my letter came last week, and we've already

spoken once on Skype. She knew what I was about to do, and that there's a possibility she may meet her father.

Carrying this burden for so long has cost me dearly. It's forced me to hide my grief from everyone but Vera, and it's twisted me into someone else. Beyond that, nothing can ever make up for holding my baby and then signing her away, especially when I loved her and her father with every fiber of my being.

Despite all of that, I can't lose sight of the life I did choose. Not for one second do I regret Jenny, or my years with Bob.

In the end, I made the best of the worst choices for all of us. I've carried this burden out of love. No matter how it turns out for me and John, in my heart I'm finally at peace, knowing I made the best choices for both of my children.

I've scrubbed off my makeup and I'm pulling out a pair of pajamas when the front door opens and shuts. My heart rate spikes as I hear John's heavy footfalls on the stairs.

I suck in a breath as he dips his head and rests a hand on the jamb like it's holding him up. He runs his free hand through his hair before he looks up. His eyes are bloodshot and his face slightly mottled. He can't quite meet my gaze. For a moment I think he's been drinking, and then I realize, no . . . he's been crying and he's fighting for control.

Silence lies heavy and pregnant between us.

I have nothing to say until he asks. I want to explain but only if he wants to listen.

A few more moments pass and then he lets out a long breath. "Kat . . . I . . ." When he looks at me, I see the sorrow and regret in his stormy blue gaze. He swallows and starts again. "I'm sorry," he whispers, and passes a hand over his face. His eyes water and he bites down on his quivering lip. He swears under his breath and glances away.

A spark of hope ignites inside of me. I stand statue still, afraid to move.

"Let's do this. Together. All of it," he whispers, and holds out his hand, lessening the distance between us.

A moment passes before I nod, speechless, and tears spring to my eyes. He nods again, a tear spilling over and cutting a path down his cheek.

For a heartbeat, I look at him and see the boy with the cast I left that summer day in August. The day I left the most essential piece of my soul behind, and I propel myself straight into his waiting arms.

He closes them around me and I melt into sobs that rise from a depth I didn't even know existed. I lean into the warmth of his chest and his stomach, letting his body enfold me. His heat seeps into my pores. I clutch his shirt tight in my hands. I never want to let him go.

"I promised forever, Kat, and I meant it," he whispers, his lips resting on my hair. "I love you, babe. I always have, and I always will."

I sob harder . . . Happy sobs. Joyful sobs.

I left that day in 1981, and now I've finally come home.

He squeezes me tighter. "I'm ready to listen. . . ."

Chapter 46

Kitty

Revisiting the Past

I WRAP MY hand around a fresh mug of coffee, letting the warmth heat my palms. As tempting as it was to loosen up with a glass of wine, I rejected the idea in favor of a clear head.

John patiently sits on the couch next to me. At my request, he's left half a cushion of space between us. To recount this story, I need to stay free of distraction and stand on my own.

I open my mouth to speak but nothing comes out. I feel like I'm teetering on the edge of an abyss that's waiting to swallow me up.

He sets down his half-drained mug and gives my hand a gentle squeeze of encouragement. "Go on," he coaxes softly, "I'm not going anywhere this time."

Giving him a wan smile, I strengthen my resolve. "Neither am I."

With a deep, sustaining breath I revisit the three days that changed my life.

Clearing my throat, I clutch my coffee and start. "After our fight that day, when you wouldn't come to the movie, I threw up halfway home on the side of the road. My periods were so irregular, I never suspected . . ." I pass my finger around the ceramic rim. "We'd been safe every single time. But I guess I was proof that protection doesn't always work." I stutter, "Wh-when I did the math, I figured I could be three to four months pregnant. So I bought two pregnancy tests and took them to Vera's."

August 1981 – What Happened After I Left John That Day

MY AUNT, EVER my protector, throws her slender body between myself and my mother. "Viv! Come with me," Vera says, controlled fury in her voice that's barely constrained within her clenched fists. To say my mother didn't take the news of my pregnancy well is the understatement of the century. She might have strangled me on sight if Vera hadn't kept her away from me.

My mother's beet-red face looks like it might explode straight off her shoulders. "Get out of my way, Vera! She's my daughter. You have no right—"

Vera pushes into her space, her voice an icy blade. "I have every right. . . . It's you who needs to back off. I will *not* let you punish this child for your mistakes. Unless you want to have this conversation in front of her, I suggest you turn around and head toward the door." She speaks her last word with a low growl. "*Now.*"

My knees give way and I drop down, quaking, onto one of a pair of tufted leather sofas in the library. Too devastated to defend myself, I gratefully allow Vera to act as my shield.

My mother's expression twists into pure ugliness as she jabs a finger at her mirror image. "Vee, you don't own me," she grinds out. "And you sure as hell don't own my daughter."

Vera glares at my mother with a cold ferocity that sends a shiver down my spine. "No, but I own all your dirty secrets. Now, let's head to that door before Kitty gets an earful."

My mother stamps her foot and bares her teeth in a feral grin. "Don't you dare blackmail me!"

"Then grow the hell up and let's deal with this like adults," Vera snaps.

My mother's golden eyes hold frigid disgust when she glances around Vera and scowls. "I hope you're happy, Katherine. I told you to stay away from that boy. Instead, you've ruined your life because of him."

Her words hit me like a blow to the midsection, and I crumple into the corner of the sofa.

"Don't you *dare* shame that girl after what you've done. She loves him, and you better respect that. They acted responsibly. The odds just worked against them." Vera grabs my mom's forearm. "Let's go," she says, and hauls my mother toward the library door. Mom jerks her arm free and storms through it without looking back.

"Stay here," Vera says, paired with a stern, no-nonsense stare.

The shouts begin the moment the heavy wooden door closes. I may be a mess, but even through my panic and devastation some of what Vera has said piques my interest.

Despite my aunt's warning, I can't just sit here. Chess taught me the importance of studying an opponent's weaknesses in order to gain leverage. Life is the most important chessboard I'll ever play, and I'm desperate for a move. I won't let my mother or even my aunt determine my fate, or John's, without having a vote . . . or leverage.

My instincts take over. I shove down the sick feeling in the pit of my stomach, kick off my sandals, and creep across the library in my bare feet. The voices grow hushed by the time I press my ear to the wood-paneled door.

"Unless you want to be overheard, I suggest we take this to the kitchen," Vera says as their shoes tap along the polished mahogany floors.

"Fine," my mother snipes.

Their footfalls recede. Only when the kitchen door closes down the hall do I twist the doorknob to the library and let myself out.

My heart pounds as I sneak soundlessly along the corridor past the museum-quality oil paintings and flatten myself against the wall next to the closed door. The kitchen's Spanish-style, clay-tiled floor inside does an excellent job of amplifying their voices.

"How could she do this to me?" my mother asks to the sound of pacing.

"This isn't something she did to you," Vera says brusquely. "This happened to her and we need to help her decide what is best . . . for her. Not you."

"What's best for her? I think she should get rid of it," my mother spits, "and then stop this silliness with NYU and go to Stanford like she's always planned. Use the endowment her father and I traded our souls for. Consider a relationship after she graduates. If John really loves her, he'll wait."

"No abortion," Vera snaps. "She doesn't want one. It's her baby. Her choice."

"Oh! And look how well that decision worked out for me!"

I flinch, thinking my mother's talking about me as her words slice a swathe across my heart.

"She's not you, Viv! She's not hiding her mistake in a high-priced group home for the mentally disabled! And at least her mistake is with the man she *loves*! Not with some male dancer she screwed in a drunken stupor. A child you passed off as your husband's own flesh and blood!"

My whole world tilts on its axis, knocking the breath out of me. I swallow a shocked gasp. *Not me. She's not talking about me.* Blood surges through my veins and I fight back dizziness as my knees buckle and I slide down the wall with my fist jammed into my mouth.

Holy God. My father's sister who lives in an institution? She's not his sister at all . . . *She's mine.*

I take some calming breaths to quell my pounding heart.

If leverage is what I wanted, I just got it in spades. An ill-gotten gain paid with my mother's pain.

Numbness seeps into my bones. Part of me wishes I'd stayed in the library and that I could erase this secret from my memory. Whatever I had hoped to learn, this wasn't it.

"You bitch!" my mother screams. Sounds of scuffling and shattered crockery echo from inside the kitchen. I scramble to my feet and agonize whether to barge in and keep them from hurting each other, but I don't want them to know that I'm here.

A crack of skin on skin—a slap. "Enough!" Vera says, breathing heavy. "Let's focus on Kitty. She deserves a chance at her best life, and I for one am going to make sure she damn well gets it. Unlike what *you* did to me." Vera's tone is low and hostile. Her vehemence startles me and I wonder what my mother did. "So, whatever she wants, I'll support . . . financially and emotionally. She may be your child, but you won't use her as a pawn in your personal melodrama. Not this time. And so help me God, Viv, if you do anything to make her feel ashamed, I'll tell her everything."

"You wouldn't dare," my mother grits, her voice cracking.

"I swear on her life, I *will*."

My skin prickles uncomfortably as I absorb the shameful family secrets my mother so desperately wants to keep hidden. My heart hurts for my father most of all, for the deception my mother perpetrated on him, and for the secret my aunt has been forced to keep amidst the echo of her own secret layered in between. . . .

Vera lets out a sigh and her voice softens. "Viv, don't make me break my promise. Give her and John the chance they deserve at happiness. Help me . . ."

The sound of sniffling and nose blowing. "Fine," my mother says thickly, then adds quietly, "I never meant to hurt you, Vee . . . I thought I was helping."

"I know you did . . ." Vera says. "We can't change history, but we can be there now for the ones we love and try to do right by them. Let's do that for Kitty, together."

I hear my mother's heavy sigh through the door. "I don't want her to live in my hell. Is that so wrong?"

Tears gather in my eyes. I keep my mouth covered as the warm drops spill down my cheeks.

"There are no perfect choices here, Viv."

"This will break William after everything that's happened."

I drop my head in my hands and rehash every option as they talk quietly inside. I come up with the only plan I can live with. One that affects the least amount of people. I can't hurt my father, and I can't hurt John.

Right or wrong, I love John more than myself, and I won't enslave us in the situation he fears most. I won't force him to become his parents.

My plan will cost us less than a year, and for once, I agree with my mother. If John loves me enough, he'll wait . . . and he'll forgive me for leaving. In my gut, this feels like the best choice for our child and for us. What I'm doing is unfair. I know that, but I'd trade my soul and my last dying breath to protect my unborn child and the man I love—and give them both the lives they deserve.

Satisfied, I dry my tears and open the door to the kitchen.

My mother and Vera freeze. Their mirror-image stares turn assessing. But it's Vera whose gaze hardens and who speaks softly. "How much did you hear?"

I throw my shoulders back and say evenly, "Enough to know that we'll be doing this my way."

Kitty

I STOP THERE. Somewhere midway through my story, John has sealed the gap between us on the sofa and pulled me into his arms, my chest pressed to his. I take comfort in his warmth, the only warmth that has ever brought me to equilibrium.

"I wish you'd told me," he whispers, pressing his lips to my hair.

I tip back my head to meet his gaze. The storminess has been replaced with deep ocean tranquility. "And what would you have done?"

The corner of his mouth lifts and he brushes my hair behind my ear. "What do you think? I would've asked you to marry me."

That's what I was afraid of . . . I sigh and avert my eyes. He tips up my chin. "Hey. I'm not an idiot. You would've been right to say no. We were too young. Whatever you decided, I would've supported you, Kat. I would've been there for you, no matter what."

I close the space between our lips and press a kiss to his, relaxing into the familiar soft feel of them. "I'm sorry."

He cups my face with a rough but gentle hand and rests his forehead on mine. "I hate that this kept us apart, but I get why you did it."

The remaining tension leaches from my shoulders. I twist in his arms and melt into him. He shifts back and pulls me closer, cradling my back with his chest. "Tell me the rest. Your plan. What happened next?"

I shrug. "You know some of it."

"I want to know all of it," he coaxes softly, stroking my hair. "Don't leave anything out."

He deserves every detail. Sharing them has been more healing than I expected. The more I share, the more I feel the fabric of our lives knitting back together.

"Fair enough . . ."

Between Vera calling in personal favors and what felt like a half day of frantic phone calls, together in an unholy alliance, the three of us set my plan in motion.

August 1981

"I'LL HAVE MONEY deposited into your account at the end of every week," Vera says into the phone from the desk in the library. Her voice softens. "I love him like my own, Sven. Make him as good as new."

After a couple of nods and a tight smile later, she hangs up and glances at me and my mother, who has the good sense to stay quiet. She's as white as a sheet, the last eighteen hours having taken a toll on her. I'm relieved that John will be taken care of after Aunt Vera and I leave for California.

My aunt releases a heavy sigh. "Well, that's the last of it. Our rental is secure; the plane tickets are booked for Saturday; Katherine is enrolled for classes at Stanford; I've secured her an obstetrician's appointment for Monday in California." Vera consults her fingers and continues to tick off each item. "The one-year deferral to NYU has been processed; John's physical therapy is taken care of . . ." She pops up a seventh finger and glances at my mother. "After you get Katherine's things to the shipper, we should be set."

Even though my father thinks I've lost my mind with this sudden change in plans, he's none the wiser, thanks to my mother's embellishments. I'm amazed we've accomplished so much in such a short time. But *set*? Not exactly.

"I want to see my sister before I go." I say, and brace myself for a fight even though my mother is in no position to argue. Not that I feel good about backing her into a corner.

The fight doesn't come. Instead, I'm awash in my mother's guilt.

"Kitty . . . ," she says, a look of anguish in her eyes. Her shoulders cave in around her. "Why?"

"Because . . . she's my sister." My sister who has caused so much strife by her very existence. "And I want to see her," I say, leveling my mother with an unsympathetic stare. Maybe it will help me find peace with my decision. Maybe because I want my sister to know someone cares.

She lets out a defeated breath and nods. "Fine. We'll drive to Connecticut tomorrow morning."

Satisfied, I give her a tight smile that's far from triumphant.

Vera rises and grabs her purse. "While you both tackle packing and the shipper, I'm going to see Johnny and share the news about Sven."

Hearing John's name sends an agonizing blow to my middle. I need to muster the courage to see him before I leave. Leaving him will be the hardest thing I've ever done, though I don't plan to be gone long. If I can take enough classes during and after the pregnancy, I should be able to transfer my credits and start as a second-year student at NYU. I plan to stick to my pursuit of accounting. As long as John doesn't change his course of action in my absence, he should start Rutgers in the spring.

I haven't figured out how I'll win him back when I return, but I'll do whatever it takes to pick up where we left off.

I want to marry John someday, but not today and not like this. For better or worse, I'm not a martyr, and I won't make him one, either. And I'm definitely not someone who can end a life, so this is the only option I'm willing to live with. I'm doing this for him. For our baby. For my parents. Least of all, for me.

If he truly loves me, he'll forgive me for leaving. At least that's what I have to believe. Otherwise, I might go insane.

I clasp my head between my hands. "Tell me again what you're going to say to him?"

She gives me a look of wide-eyed innocence. "I plan to tell him to the truth—that a former client asked me to take on a project near and dear to her heart."

I squint at her. "How's that the truth?" I hate the deception already.

She shrugs. "Your mother was one of my first clients and you happen to be near and dear to both of our hearts. And, as of now, you're my new project until this baby comes." Then she frowns and taps her lips with a finger. "*Hmm.* I reserve the right to fib about the location and when I'm leaving to eliminate suspicion."

What scares me? I'm all right with the last part of what she just said. John is perceptive, and to make this work over the long-term, there can't be any careless clues. My mom and Vera both agreed that no one outside of the three of us would know the truth. The burden would be ours alone. The fact that carrying this secret makes me a liar and no better than my mother rips at my psyche.

I feel as if I've given up a slice of my soul.

Because I have.

Chapter 47

Kitty

August 1981

THE TWO-HOUR drive to Connecticut the next day borders on agonizing. We drive with the radio on, and no more than a few sentences pass between us during the journey.

"Try not to judge me," my mother whispers as she parks the car in the small pea-gravel lot next to a lush rose garden.

I ignore her, unbuckle my seatbelt, and reach for the door handle.

"Wait." My mother clasps my shoulder. "There's something you should know."

I turn back and give her an impatient stare. "What's that?"

Her lip trembles as her hand drops away. "Our silence was the price for the endowment."

The words cut through me like a knife through butter, and I do nothing to hide my distain. "So it's my fault that Evelyn's here? Thanks a lot, Mom." I sneer and jerk the car door open. "I hope it was worth it."

She trails a few paces behind me to the entrance.

True to her word, the facility is incredible. Located on a wooded property a mile from the road and overlooking a lake, the English Tudor mansion looks more like a private estate than a high-end group home and hospital. According to my mother, with a limit of thirty-five residents the care is highly personalized and costs as much as a year at an Ivy League college. A cost my parents have shouldered for the last seventeen years. Suddenly, all those weekends my parents went on "romantic getaways" and dumped us at Vera's house take on a new light.

I follow my mother inside to a small office on the first floor.

A jovial-looking woman around my mother's age rises to greet us. She's well put together in a blue suit and pearls. "Viv, luv, how wonderful to see you," she says in a crisp English accent and rounds the desk from where she's seated to embrace my mother. "Evelyn will be so pleased you're here."

My mother touches my shoulder. "Sophie, this is my middle daughter, Kitty." I push down the shock of hearing myself referred to as a middle child.

Sophie's smile lights up her cherubic face, and she takes my hand in a warm shake. "Welcome to Sunrise Manor, Kitty."

I mumble my thanks.

"How is she today?" my mother asks with some trepidation.

Sophie's joviality falters and she motions to the guest chairs. "Please. Sit a moment." She returns to her seat behind the desk and glances between me and my mother. "May I speak freely?"

My mother's eyes tear and she nods. "Yes."

"We have her on an oxygen tether full-time now. Her heart is deteriorating at a faster rate than we expected, so she gets tired very easily." Sophie brightens with a gentle smile. "On the positive side, she adores the colored pencil set you brought the last time. They give her so much joy. On good days, she spends her time drawing. Today is a good day."

I swallow, not sure what I expected. Part of me believed my mother cast Evelyn aside, unwanted, not believing her claims that this was a better place for my sister than living with us. Now, I'm not sure.

"Does she have friends?" I blurt, fidgeting with my rings and holding out hope that she's not lonely and that this is truly where she should be.

Sophie's smile blooms. "Of course. She's created many meaningful bonds with the staff and residents and seeks their company when the mood strikes her."

My brow knits. That doesn't fit my definition of friendship.

As if sensing my dissatisfaction with her answer, Sophie leans over her clasped hands, her expression softening. "Evie has an interesting mix of talents and handicaps."

"Like what?" I ask, more comfortable posing the question to Sophie than my own mother.

"She's a rare bird, your sister Evie," she cocks her head. "How much do you know about autism?"

I shake my head. "Nothing, really."

She leans farther forward and speaks more softly. "She's what we call an artistically gifted savant. She has extreme developmental disabilities that mimic autism but don't fit cleanly into the spectrum. For instance, she has trouble with eye contact and physical touch, which is common among our autistic patients, while her emotions are easily reflected in her facial expressions, something more uncommon with extreme autism. She doesn't speak, at least not using language like you and I do, though she's an uncanny mimic when it comes to replicating sound. She's exceedingly observant and expresses herself mostly through her artistic talent." A soft smile touches Sophie's lips. "In some ways, Evie's like an angel. She has such a gentle heart, and a wonderful—at times, almost unnatural—calming effect on the other residents. She loves animals and has a soft spot for Patches, our resident Persian cat."

"She sounds special." Wringing my hands, I ask the question that's been weighing heavily on my mind. "Does she have to be here?"

Sophie nods with a knowing look that's both sympathetic and absolving as if she expected my question. I'm sure it's not a new one. "Although Evie's keenly intelligent in some ways, she still needs assistance with more mundane tasks like personal grooming, feeding, and taking her required medication. Beyond that, her health has always been fragile. Our onsite medical staff has been a godsend for her. She's happy here and loved. This is her home."

Sophie's impassioned honey tone soothes my angst but not my guilt, which has less to do with Evie and more to do with me.

Avoiding Sophie's kind, dark eyes, I glance around her office and take in all the framed photographs. I spot several of Sophie with a girl ranging in age from childhood into adulthood—a girl with Down syndrome. The rose garden and lakefront at Sunset Manor provide the background for most of them. I point to one. "Is that one of the residents?"

She follows my gaze to the photo and a sad smile slips onto her lips. "She used to be. We lost Maggie two years ago. . . . She was my daughter."

The hairs rise on my arms along with the lump in my throat. "I'm so sorry. I didn't mean to pry." Next to me, my mother wipes her eyes.

"Don't be sorry, dear. Maggie gave us joy for the time she was with us. Just like Evie does."

"Thank you," I whisper, the guilt lingering. "May we see Evelyn now?"

Sophie returns to good humor as she rises. "Of course, sweetheart. She's looking forward to meeting you."

I wonder how true that is as I trail behind her and my mother up the central staircase and into the resident's quarters on the second floor. The only indications that this isn't a private residence are the red exit signs hanging from the ceiling and the wall-mounted fire extinguishers dotting the carved wood paneling along the plush, carpeted hallway, otherwise lined with artwork and small furniture. Classical music floats in through unseen speakers and provides a tranquil backdrop.

Sophie stops with my mother in front of a door midway down the hall and knocks.

I intend to follow but my mother holds up a hand. "Wait here, Kitty. Let me see her first." She goes inside with Sophie and leaves me to sit on a decorative bench in the hall.

Cut roses, same as the ones that line the parking lot, sit on a nearby table in a perfumed bouquet. Breathing in the fragrance, I rub slow circles over my abdomen and the life growing inside of me. I wait, half terrified that I won't know what to do once I get inside.

The door cracks open ten minutes later. Mom's wearing a wan smile when she emerges with Sophie. "Go on in, Kitty. Meet me downstairs in Sophie's office when you're finished. You remember how to get back?"

Nodding, I take a deep breath to calm my pounding heart and walk inside.

My mouth drops open the moment I cross the threshold. Evelyn sits at a table near a large bay window, working intently on a sketch. The room looks closer to a small studio apartment. Besides the table next to the window, there's a small kitchenette, a double bed with a pretty pink coverlet, a seating area, and a bathroom. Artwork in every medium covers the walls. I'm stunned silent by their beauty.

Compositions of people, animals, sunsets, landscapes, dreamscapes; realistic and impressionistic, her range of subjects and styles is beyond impressive.

Once I regain my senses, I clear my throat. "Hi, Evelyn... I'm Kitty."

Evelyn looks up from her drawing. A clip feeds oxygen into her nose from the portable tank next to her. Her straight, dark brown hair falls to her shoulders, the sides held back by tiny flower barrettes. Her small, golden eyes flicker to a point past my shoulder. My first thought is that she looks so much younger than twenty-four, probably because she's so petite. Her face is full, making her eyes look a little too small for her face, but there's no mistaking she's my sister. Besides having my mother's odd eye color, she resembles her.

Evelyn's mouth stretches into a smile and she purrs deep in her throat. Like a real cat. Sophie was right; her mimicry is uncanny. I smile back.

She returns her attention to the drawing. I shift awkwardly on my feet before tentatively approaching where she sits. Slowly, I slide out a chair and join her. The view from the window overlooks the lake. The midday sun reflects off the surface, shimmering like tiny diamonds.

I catch that faint sense of peace Sophie mentioned downstairs regarding Evelyn's presence. Words don't seem like the right way to communicate. Instead, I tap her blank pad of drawing paper. "May I have a piece?"

She drops her colorful masterpiece to the floor. Without looking up, she removes two clean sheets and pushes one in my direction. She taps it with a finger. "*Meow.*"

I take the proffered sketch paper and smile. Art was never my best subject, but I'm better than average when it comes to drawing. I select a few pencils and start my life map. We did them our senior year as part of my sociology elective.

As we draw, Evelyn breaks into the most beautiful birdsong. I stop and stare, moved by the sweet chirping sound coming from my sister.

"That's beautiful," I whisper.

The sound stops abruptly and her cheeks redden as her pencil glides over the page.

I return to my drawing. A soft purr comes from across the table over the low hiss of the oxygen tank. Then the birdsong resumes with an even lovelier melody.

Forty minutes later, I'm almost done with my life map when Evelyn tugs on my sleeve. She won't meet my eyes, but a broad smile sits on her face. She slaps her palm on the paper in front of her containing a colorful mural.

"May I see it?" I ask, motioning at her picture.

She bites her lip and pushes it toward me. I spin it around, and my heart misses a beat. The drawing has the delicate touch of a gifted artist and requires no explanation. My mother stands in the middle with my father. My parents are bookended by their daughters—one short with dark hair and golden eyes holds my mother's other hand; the other, tall with dark hair and a cat sitting at her feet, holds my father's. Sophie stands on the other side of Evie with her arm wrapped around her and Maggie pressed to her opposite side. The likenesses are uncanny, down to what Evie and I are wearing. Songbirds hold an elaborate garland of hearts and flowers over our heads with a plaque in the center containing one word: "Family."

Tears gather in my eyes and I smile at her. "May I keep this?" I ask, a realization dawning inside me that family doesn't have to be biological, and that, yes, this is exactly where Evelyn is supposed to be. Her life here is better than any my parents could've given her.

She nods and *meows*.

"Thank you. It's beautiful, just like you," I whisper, brushing away the wetness spilling onto my cheeks. I consider myself blessed to be here and for having this opportunity to meet my sister. To me, she's beauty personified. For a moment, I forgive my mother and understand her better. I have no doubt she loves Evelyn, or that Evelyn loves her. Like me, my mother is a victim of having to make the best of the worst choices for the people she loves.

It's not the stunning beauty or clarity of Evelyn's drawing that's stolen my breath . . . it's the baby she drew in my arms.

Chapter 48

Kitty

One Last Tale

JOHN'S ARMS TIGHTEN around me as I finish. "Sweet Jesus, Kat," he says in a thick whisper, his breath warming my ear from where his chin rests on my shoulder. "Did you see her again? After that?"

I shake my head and wipe my nose with the crumpled napkin in my hand. "No. Mom promised to take me back after the baby came, but Evie died of pneumonia right before Denise was born. All we had was that one amazing day." My voice cracks as tears cut a searing path down my cheeks. Visiting my sister gave me as much joy as it did sadness over dreams lost and found. "Meeting Evelyn even once was a gift. I hate that my parents kept her a secret."

"I'm so sorry, babe . . . that you didn't have more time with her."

I sigh. "I gave her my life map in exchange for her beautiful sketch. I still have it . . . someplace safe." Turning, I snuggle against John's chest, taking comfort in his warmth and the steady rhythm of his heart against my ear. "You were on my life map, you know."

He makes a chuffing sound into my hair. I feel him smile and puff out his chest. "I'd be insulted if I wasn't."

His cocky, teasing tone gets him a gentle pinch to his waist, eliciting a chuckle and sending a protective elbow to cover his side. "Hey! What was that for?"

"Always so sure of yourself, Shaw," I say, teasing him back.

He cups my cheek and lifts my face to meet his gaze. His jaw tightens and he shakes his head. "Not by a longshot, babe," he says, rough-graveled emotion replacing the playfulness in his tone. "Not when it comes to you." He rubs a thumb over my cheekbone. "My pride got in the way with us, more than once. That wasn't confidence, that was stupidity, and it cost us. Big time. Make no mistake, what happened is as much on me. What you did took strength. Strength I'm not sure I would've had."

His admission brings new tears to my eyes. That he assumes part of the responsibility means the world to me and makes me fall in love with him even more. "Thank you," I say softly.

He clears his throat and says in a raw whisper, "Don't thank me. Just let me make it up to you."

I nod. "All right."

He cradles me in his arms, my head resting under his chin. "Now tell me the rest, so we can leave this behind us and never look back."

With a lighter soul, I return to that fateful day — one last time — to complete the circle and close the door on my past.

August 1981 – The Day I Left

WIPING MY EYES, I crack open John's front door at eleven-thirty Saturday morning and brace myself. I can't imagine he's pleased that I left him twisting in the breeze for the past three days without so much as a phone call. Wednesday feels like a decade ago.

When I walk in, he's on the couch, where I left him, glued to MTV. Butterflies flit around in a psychotic dance inside my stomach over the agony I'm about to inflict.

His head jerks over and he freezes the moment he lays eyes on me. A mix of anger and concern blazes in his gaze. Then he releases an exhale and the tension drains from his shoulders.

A golf ball–size lump rises in my throat. My body screams out to touch his. I want to anchor myself in his warmth, but an invisible barrier lies between us. A barrier he doesn't even know is there.

He holds out an arm. "Babe, what's the matter? Where've you been? I almost went out of my mind. . . ."

Unable to speak, I let my feet carry me over. I crawl into his lap. He wraps me inside his warm embrace and I memorize the spice and pine scent of him, the feel of his arms heavy around me, his breath on my hair.

He presses his cheek to my crown. "Talk to me, Kat." The ache in his voice tears at my heart.

"I'm sorry," I whisper, letting my hair fall around my face, hiding behind its dark curtain.

He squeezes me tighter. "I'm the one who's sorry. For being an ass. I've been trying to call you for days. Where have you been?" he whispers back.

I don't answer. This is harder than I expect. My insides feel like they're being ripped to shreds. I don't want to leave him. I don't want to be pregnant with our child. I don't want the shitty hand I've been dealt.

I love him so much. His muscles tense around me, his worry pulsing off him in waves. "Kiss me, Shaw," I murmur.

He brushes back my hair and tips up my chin. I can't look at those stormy blue windows into his soul. I'll lose any sense of control I have left.

He takes my mouth with tentative licks and caresses, running his hands down my back and pressing me close. We're midway through the kiss when I pour my soul into his—one last time. I have to feel him under my fingers in a desperate attempt to remember how this feels in case I lose him for good. My hungry touch travels over his terrain: back, arms, chest . . .

He captures my wrists as I run them over his torso.

"Stop," he breathes into my hair. "What's going on?"

I freeze in his arms and rest my head on his shoulder. Panic rises up and grabs me. *Oh God. What am I doing?* My resolve wavers for a second, I'm about to hurt him . . . to shatter a piece of our trust that I might never earn back. So I have to start with the truth while he can still listen. "I love you, Shaw. . . . I'll always love you."

He grasps my shoulders and holds me at arm's distance. "Kat, what the hell?" His voice shakes, and I see the fear in his eyes and look away. Pain assaults the center of my chest in an unceasing wave.

Tears blur my vision, and I try to meet his gaze. "I'm . . ." I swipe my fingertips at the corner of my eye, hating every word I'm about to say. My lip moves in an uncontrollable quiver. "I'm leaving."

He digs his fingers into my arms. "*What?*"

I force out the words, choosing the most honest ones I can find. "Stanford . . . I'm going to Stanford," I whisper, and catch my lip between my teeth.

He pushes me away and my heart cracks in half. His frown is deep and immediate, but there's no mistaking the look of devastation written on a face I know as well as my own. "What? What are you talking about?" he croaks. "You're going to NYU."

His body folds in on itself, and layered inside his hurt is a look of disbelief and betrayal.

Something breaks inside me with his next words. His voice has a flat and hollow ring. "We're going to make this work. That's what you said."

I can barely breathe. He may never forgive me, I realize. This hurt may go too deep. I barely manage a whisper. "I can't . . . not now."

He blinks and blinks again, like he's in shock.

"What did I do?" he asks. His voice cracks, and he presses his eyes shut. This is the closest John has ever come to crying in front of me.

My self-loathing has never been greater than it is in this moment. I'll never forgive myself for hurting him like this. I don't care that this is for the greater good. In this moment, all that matters is that I'm ripping out the heart of the person I love most in the world. The man who promised me forever — a forever that I still want.

I brush my tears away. "Nothing. You didn't do anything wrong."

"I don't understand," he says, his eyes glistening and his ruggedly handsome face twisted in so much pain.

Oh God. Before everything inside me shatters into a million tiny pieces, I kiss my fingers and press them to his lips. Then I give him the last truth that I can manage and pray to God for forgiveness. "I'm doing this for you."

Before he can say another word, I run for the front door and leave the better part of my soul behind, knowing I may never recapture it.

I can barely see the road as I drive home to meet my mother. She's my ride to the airport. I curse my naïveté for thinking I could do this without sacrificing the thing I hold most dear. We can never go back to the way things were before.

I've just realized it too late.

John

I'M QUIET FOR a moment when she finishes telling her side of one of the worst days of my life. But I meant what I said—I'm ready to put it behind us and move on. Time and heartache have taught me hard lessons, and pride is a sonofabitch that's no longer welcome on my personal turf. What time I have left is precious, and spending any more of it living in the past will do nothing to give us a future. And a future is all I want. With Kat. For the rest of the time I've been given.

"You left from there for California, lived with Vera, and had the baby," I say, confirming my understanding.

She nods. "I only decided to stay there after I'd found out you left."

"I know," I whisper, letting it all go.

She pulls away to sit up and stretch, then stifles a yawn with her hand.

I glance at my watch. It's four in the morning. We've been at this for hours, but I'm not going to bed until this is done. Because once my head hits the pillow, I want this chapter closed. There's only one question left that I'm curious about, "Did you ever find out what Vera had on Viv?"

Kat rubs her temples and nods. "She told me when we lived together in California. It also explains why she aided and abetted the actions of two lovesick teenagers behind my mother's back." She gives me a wry smile.

I'd be lying if I said it hadn't crossed my mind more than once during high school why Vera put herself out on a limb for me and Kat. It didn't take a brain surgeon to figure out we were having sex and indulging in libations before we were legal. These days that could get an adult thrown in jail. But back then, phones still had cords and parents didn't GPS their kids. They trusted that if another adult was present, things were cool. A lot of trust existed then that doesn't exist now.

"So what happened?" I ask.

Kat takes a deep breath and sighs. "Get ready for more tragedy."

I nod, pressing my lips together, and brace myself. "Let 'er rip."

Kat pulls her legs under her and her gaze drifts off. "When Vera was seventeen, she fell in love with a nineteen-year-old boy named

Avi. An Irish Catholic girl and an Orthodox Jewish boy isn't an easy match today, much less in the '50s, so they dated in secret."

My stomach falls as I listen. Wasn't easy in the late '70s as a poor half Cuban in a rich WASP town, either. I raise my eyebrows. "Yeesh. This didn't end well, did it?"

Kat frowns and shakes her head. "No," she says quietly. "It didn't."

I take a deep breath and pinch the bridge of my nose, my vision getting fuzzy from exhaustion. "Shit. What happened?"

"Avi hatched a plan for them to run away together and live in New York City. He was a tradesman and had saved a little money that he'd hidden from his father. They were supposed to leave the night after Vera's high school graduation, but Viv found out and told her parents."

I scowl. "Why am I not surprised?"

Kat shrugs. "That wasn't nearly as bad as what happened when my grandparents told Avi's parents. Not only did his father shame him, but he found Avi's escape fund and took it. Then he forced Avi into an arranged marriage with a girl from a nice Jewish family." Kat swallows and her lip quivers. "Avi shot himself in the head on his wedding night."

Her words hit my gut and I press my eyes shut. "Fucking hell."

"Vera never forgave my mother." Kat wipes her eyes. "Vera saw in us what she had with Avi. That's why she helped us." She reaches for my hand and squeezes. "That, and she loved us like her own."

I shiver as if I had just walked over Vera's grave, and then my detective's brain officially shuts down for the night. I'm wrung out and ready to collapse.

"Come here." I hold out a hand and Kat crawls into my arms. "What do you say we go bed and kiss this night goodbye?"

"Shaw?"

"Yeah?"

"Stay with me?"

"I plan on it." I'll be lucky to drag myself off the couch.

"Not just for tonight . . ."

Chapter 49

Kitty

Six Days Later – Thanksgiving Morning

"MORNING," JOHN PURRS, whispering a breath over the back of my neck. "Happy Thanksgiving. . . ."

A smile touches my lips as he pulls me close enough that his naked body is flush behind me under the sheets, warm, inviting, and more than a little aroused.

"*Mmm,*" I purr back. "Happy Thanksgiving." His lips travel across my shoulders while his hand glides down my side and over my hip.

He nips my earlobe. "I plan to show you just how thankful I am, but first . . ." Sliding back, he rolls me over. "I have something for you." I catch a mischievous glint in his eye before the covers fall away from his tattooed torso as he stretches to retrieve something from the top drawer of the nightstand.

He rolls back and hovers over me, propped on an elbow. "Remember this?" The corner of his mouth lifts. A heart-shaped locket on a silver chain dangles from his finger.

It's the necklace he gave me the night of the junior prom. The night I gave him my virginity and he promised me forever. I sent it back to him a few years after we broke up the first time in a fit of anger and defeat.

My breath catches and I clutch my heart. "You kept it. . . ."

"You bet I did. Here . . ." He releases the locket into my waiting hand and says in a half snort, half chuckle, "You really know how to hit a guy where it hurts. Came in the mail when I was in Germany on my first tour. When I saw your handwriting, I'd hoped like hell it was a letter. Cruel move, Kat." He scowls and drops back onto his pillow.

Tangling my legs with his under the covers, I pout and look regretful. "How come you didn't give it back after the tenth reunion?"

His expression softens. He pushes a lock of hair behind my ear and then helps me secure the clasp at the back of my neck. "Never got the chance. Found it in a moving box at my mom's in Florida after you left," he says, resting a palm on my cheek.

I cover his hand with mine and lean into its calloused warmth. "I love you, Shaw. Forever, this time."

He kisses my nose and moves my hand to the KAT tattooed over his heart. "It's always been that for me, babe." His half-lidded gaze, like the deepest ocean, draws me in, and when he takes my lips with his, he doesn't let go until we're panting and breathless. My heart races with an unbridled freedom it hasn't known since I was eighteen, and I inhale the warm, familiar scent of my soulmate.

I say a silent prayer of thanks to Vera for all she did for me and John, and for recognizing the love we shared from the beginning.

He rests his forehead on mine. "Does that mean you'll wear my ring and be my wife?" he asks in a rough whisper.

A smile blooms on my lips. I can't imagine living the rest of my life without him. I never could. "Yes. One hundred percent, yes." I run my fingertips over the soft salt and pepper whiskers on his cheek and seal my answer with a kiss.

But before we can bask in our engagement bliss, there's one more hurdle to clear. We decided to wait until today and share our news at a family meeting before Thanksgiving dinner. Empty and lighter with the shackles of the past behind me, I'm ready to face anything as long as John's by my side. "You ready for later?" I ask with some trepidation.

Jillian and Raine were more than a little surprised when I told them I'd invited Bob and Carl to our family meeting.

Now that John and I are together and we've cleared the air, his animosity toward Bob seems to have dulled. If anything, he's grateful we have another chance, and so am I. In a weird way, we owe it to Bob.

I've made peace in my heart with my ex-husband, and I hope to renew the warm friendship that's always been at the foundation of our relationship. Despite my choices, I've spent my life putting my family above all else, and there are no bounds to how many people that should include.

"Hey." John strokes my hair and meets my eyes with a penetrating stare. "It'll be fine. You're not your mother, Kat. Give yourself a break. You've been punished enough trying to protect us all. Let go of the fear and forgive yourself. I have; they will, too."

My lips curl into a smile. "Maybe I should be paying you instead of Dr. Graham."

He pulls me closer so we're sharing the same pillow. "All I'm saying is have faith in your family and their love. Sometimes you gotta surrender your heart and go all in. That's what I'm doing. With us. One life, Kat. That's all we've got. They'll understand, I promise."

I run my fingers through his dark, salty hair. "You're going to be an inspiring football coach, you know that?"

He chuckles. "Thanks, babe. Let's hope they think so."

The call came yesterday with an offer to take the assistant coaching job, starting in January when John comes off disability and officially retires from the police force.

His eyes light up. "Hey, that reminds me. I need a new car after I turn in the cruiser." The side of his mouth quirks up. "Thinking about getting a Camaro."

I chuckle. "Really? A '74?" He'd sold the Black Beast after Ben died.

"Hell, no! That thing was a death trap. New. Like us." The look in his eye turns to sizzling hunger. He drags a hand down my side and we're back to where we started with his body pressed into mine. He plants his palms firmly on my naked backside and gives it a squeeze. "But we can talk about that later. We have a little business to attend to first."

I giggle as he buries his nose into my neck and nibbles. I slip my hand between us, circle his growing length with my fingers, and stroke him. "Nothing little about it."

His eyes slide shut and he groans. "You're killing me, Kat. . . ."

"There are many things I plan to do to you, Detective, but homicide isn't on my list," I whisper before seizing his earlobe between my lips.

"Tease," he says in a low voice, digging his fingers into my hips and baring his throat to me.

Still stroking velvet skin over hard steel, I caress his lobe lightly with my tongue before moving my lips over the light stubble on his neck and inhaling my favorite pine and spice. "Oh, I plan to deliver. . . ."

"PLEASE TELL ME this isn't a bad idea," I mutter as I ring Jillian and Raine's doorbell three hours later. Devon's Aston Martin and Bob's vintage Mustang are already parked in the driveway.

"It'll be fine," John reassures me, a Natale's bag containing a Philly Fluff in one hand and his fingers threaded through mine with his other. "Trust them. We made it through. They will, too."

The door swings open a few seconds later and Raine's muscled frame fills the doorway. He's dressed in slacks and a button-down under his apron, and his once-spiky blond hair is tamed with gel. Jillian likes it long, but I think the shorter cut suits him and camouflages the gap in their ages.

An easy smile slips onto his lips, lighting up his vibrant blue eyes and Viking good looks. "Hey, you two. Happy Thanksgiving." He motions for us to come inside. "Everyone's perched in the Roost."

Jillian renamed her kitchen "Raine's Roost" in April when Raine moved back in and assumed exclusive rights as their in-house chef. I love my sister, but her cooking is toxic. At least now I can sleep at night, knowing she's properly fed and not existing on a diet of boxed macaroni and cheese, coffee, and yogurt.

John follows me into the foyer's cozy warmth. Conversation and laughter float up the hall from the kitchen.

"Hi, sweetheart," I say, trading a hug and kiss with my much younger brother-in-law and catching a whiff of pumpkin pie mixed with something more distinctly masculine. I chastise myself for thinking he feels like Devon and that I'm old enough to be his mother. Ah, well. Some things are harder to let go of than others. Doesn't change the fact that I love him dearly.

"Hey, man. Happy Thanksgiving. Glad you're here," Raine says, grasping John in a man hug. The affection in Raine's voice sends warmth through my chest. I love that they're close.

Raine pokes a teasing finger in John's gut. "You coming back to the gym next week? Treadmill's better than nothing."

John thrusts the Natale's bag at him. "Only if you go easy on me. I'm still on the mend. Treadmill's fine. No weights."

"Deal," Raine says, giving him a lopsided smile and taking the bag. "But no falling into bad habits." He shakes a finger at me. "No aiding and abetting Big Boy over here, Kitty. As of now, no comfort food after today's dinner. No bacon, butter, baked goods or any other crap for this guy, or you're going to make my job harder. Agreed?"

I nod and do an awful job of suppressing a snicker when John groans and gives Raine an unhappy stare as he hangs our coats in the closet. "Anybody ever tell you that you're a pain in the ass?"

Raine smiles wide. "You, all the damn time, but you'll thank me later like you always do."

John mutters something under his breath and laughs. He threads his fingers through mine and squeezes as we follow Raine to the party inside the kitchen.

I brace myself as we step over the threshold. Heads turn and the room falls into a hush. Jenny, Devon, Bob, and Carl stand in a cluster next to the island across the kitchen with drinks in hand, while Lettie and Jillian resume their conversation in low voices at the nearby table. Rachel, wearing a party dress and bib, sits nestled in a highchair next to them and contentedly gums her teething ring.

"It's okay, babe," John whispers, and squeezes my fingers.

"Excuse us, Dad," I overhear Jenny say across the room. She sets her drink on the island and approaches with Devon in tow, her face splitting into a delighted smile.

"Hey, guys." Jenny wraps me in a hug first and then John. "Happy Thanksgiving."

Devon takes her place when she steps back, hugging me then John. His smile is easy and lights up his eyes. "Can't wait to hear your news."

"Uh . . . great," I stutter, momentarily dumbfounded, realizing the whole room is expecting us to announce our engagement. Oh my. I glance over to where Bob and Carl are sipping drinks and looking uncomfortable.

"Let me go talk to your father," I say to Jenny and unthread my fingers from John's.

"Do you want me to come with you?" John asks, rubbing a hand down my arm.

I brush a kiss across his lips. "I need to do this alone."

He presses his lips shut and nods with understanding. "I'll be here."

I take a deep breath and cross the kitchen. Without much thought, I trade a hug with Bob. "Thank you for coming." Then Carl. "Good to see, Carl. Happy Thanksgiving."

"You too, Kitty," Carl says, his embrace welcoming and friendly.

"You look good, Kitty," Bob says, wearing a genuine smile as his gaze travels over me. He casts a glance at John. "I'm happy for you." His words warm me this time, unlike when he said them last.

Placing a hand on Bob's arm, I ask Carl, "Mind if I borrow him for a minute?"

Carl winks at him and says with good humor, "As long as you promise to return him."

I nod and whisk him into the living room.

"What's up?" Bob asks as we duck inside.

"I just wanted to say that I was sorry—"

"No, Kitty." Bob tugs on my arm and shakes his head, an earnest look filling his bespectacled eyes. "I'm the one who needs to apologize. For everything that's happened over the last few months. I'm sorry. . . . I never wanted to hurt you."

I take a breath and press my eyes shut for a second. "But you were right about so many things. I want you to know that I never regretted what we had. You're a wonderful father and you were a good husband." I swallow as my eyes fill. "I loved you. . . . I still love you. I don't want to lose my friend."

Bob's lip quivers and he takes off his glasses to wipe his eyes. Then he pulls me into a hug. "I love you, too, Kitty. You'll always have me as a friend. I promise to do better."

"Thank you," I whisper, and give him another squeeze before letting him go. I pat under my eyes. "We should get back inside."

I check my watch as we return to join the others. It's one o'clock. John's at the table holding Rachel with the rest of the crew, except Raine, who's stirring something in a pot on the stove. The kitchen smells divine as it always does with Raine at the helm.

"How much time left on the turkey, sweetheart?" I ask Raine.

"Ninety minutes." He frowns. "That enough time for the

meeting?"

Let's hope so. I smile and nod.

Raine whistles between his teeth. "Hey, everyone, family meeting in the living room. Scram. I'll join you in a minute." Then he winks at me and flashes a crooked smile. "That good?"

Five minutes later, John and I are snuggled in a love seat while everyone else is draped over the remaining couches and chairs.

Rachel's drifting off to sleep in Raine's arms with her pacifier in her mouth when he calls everyone to order. "*Shh*, quiet down." The room falls into a hush like before. "It's all yours," Raine says to me and John.

I clutch John's thigh and we trade a glance. He nods with an upward twist of his lips. "I'm right here. Every step of the way."

I clear my throat and look at Jillian, locking my gaze to hers. "For years, you've asked about . . ." My brow furrows. "Things I couldn't tell you. Things about me . . . things about John." I glance at Jenny and then Bob. "So much has been hidden. To protect the ones I love." I wring my hands, stare at my lap, and swallow. "But not all the secrets were mine." Then I look into John's eyes and take his hand. "But keeping them cost me something dear. Cost us something dear." I shift my gaze back to my family. "Cost *all of us* something."

I stop to gather myself before moving on.

"Kitty," Jillian whispers, a look of worry and panic brewing in her eyes. "What is it?"

John gives me a gentle squeeze of encouragement. "Go on," he says softly.

All eyes lock on me, and one last time, I revisit the three days that changed my life. "In the summer of 1981 . . ."

Sharing all the relevant points, I unpack each and every secret that has touched our family, ending with the letter. When I'm done, my family sits in stunned silence.

Jillian wipes her eyes and comes over. She pulls me and John into a hug. "You have a child and two grandchildren. That's so wonderful." Then she turns to me, "I'm so sorry you had to go through that all alone."

Jenny arrives next and throws herself on top of the pile. "I love you guys, and I can't wait to meet my big sister."

"I'm sorry," I whisper to no one in particular and everyone in general.

We crumble into a tangle of arms as I laugh and cry together with my daughter, my baby sister, and John. "I love you all," I whisper.

The timer rings in front of Raine. "Turkey's ready." He gets up and hands a now wide-awake, gurgling Rachel to Bob. "Jeez, Kitty. Here I thought you were going to tell us you guys were getting engaged."

I glance at John, who's beaming at me. "That, too, kid. That, too."

Jenny and Jillian jump up and squeal with delight, giving each other high-fives while John takes the opportunity to lean in for a kiss in the newfound space. I feel his sizzling touch all the way to my toes.

"You'll always be my Kryptonite, John Henshaw, in a good way."

He gives me one of his classic smiles that lights his eyes, turning them from stormy to tranquil. "And you'll always be mine, Kitten. Forever."

The room explodes into hoots and hollers, and the rest of the family rushes us as I breathe in the sweet smell of home.

Epilogue

Kitty

Three Months Later, February 2017

"HEY, MRS. HENSHAW-RIVERA," John whispers the last part with a proper Cuban accent, then kisses our clasped fingers. "Wake up. We're landing."

"*Mmm*," I purr, opening my eyes to look at my husband of less than twenty-four hours. "Hey, Mr. Henshaw-Rivera. I'm excited. Are you excited?"

"Absolutely." He waggles his brows, lounging back in the first-class seat next to me. "I've never been to Disneyland. But I've always had a fantasy involving those tea cups."

I chuckle. "What kind of fantasy?"

His eyes dance with wicked merriment. "The naked kind."

"*Hmm*. Dr. Graham may be able to help you with that." I laugh and reach for one of his ticklish spots. "Save your naked fantasies for when we're alone in Hawaii." I packed a few thongs and a pair of thigh highs for the occasion.

Clamping a protective elbow to his side, he licks his lips and snickers. "*Mmm*, Kitten. I can't wait to feed you fresh pineapple and get *lei'd*."

I roll my eyes. "You're such a big kid."

He snatches my hand back. "Blame it on my tragic teenage years. Got a lot of time to make up for to get us to forever," he counters, and rubs the diamond eternity band he gave me as a combination engagement ring/wedding band.

351

"Please don't make me regret my decision," I say, suppressing a grin.

"Which one's that?"

"The vow I made to laugh at your jokes for the rest of my life."

He frowns and looks crestfallen. "Oh, come on, that was funny."

I shake my head, tightlipped. "Nope. I definitely think the vow about listening to you sing to me in the shower was a much better deal."

He *tsks*. "You're a hard woman to please, Kat McNally Henshaw-Rivera."

My lips tip up in a smile. "John Henshaw-Rivera, you of all people should know I've never been easy."

"I'll say." He shakes his head. "Who would've thought it would take thirty-five freaking years for you to marry me? That's got to be some kind of record."

I laugh softly.

His expression turns contemplative. "It's a mouthful, you know. You can clip off the Rivera if it's easier. I won't be offended."

I shake my head vigorously. "Nope. I'm proud of you and your heritage. I always have been. It's your name and I love it."

His lips tip up and his eyes turn a little misty. "I love you, babe."

My gaze drifts to his mouth and I let the gravitational pull of his lips reel me in for a kiss.

The plane rolls to the gate and stops. When the seat belt lights ding, we're up and taking our carry-on bags out of the overhead. We're the first passengers to make it off the plane.

John clasps my hand and draws me to a halt at the end of the jetway. "You ready?"

I smile and brush a kiss across his lips. "You bet."

We step into the terminal and the next phase of our new life together.

But we've already come a long way. I'm thrilled that John no longer carries a gun for a living. He started his coaching job in January and absolutely loves it. Seeing his passion reignite for football has been a joy to watch. He's as excited now about the game as he was when he played in high school. Right before Christmas, we took Jillian and Raine to the last Giants home game of the season. Had it not been for a gallon of hot chocolate, we would've all frozen to death. But the Giants won, and despite the cold, we all had a wonderful time.

John's workouts with Raine have resumed, while I've stuck with Bar Method. What hasn't killed me has made me stronger. The classes have done wonders to reshape my body, and John's blood sugar has never been better. Together, we've agreed to maintain our commitment to health and wellness. I'm happy leaving my frumpy clothes and extra weight behind. There's nothing wrong, I've decided, with sexy grandparents.

We've found that we enjoy cooking as a couple. A lot. So much that I've booked two weeks at a cooking school in Tuscany after the school year ends for John. Jillian's agent and dearest friend, Brigitte, recommended it. Raine tried to talk Jillian into making it a family vacation, but she said as much as she loved us all, she'd rather stick hot pokers in her eyes than cook. Ah, well. Among the three of us, at least she won't starve.

In a surprising shift, our relationship with Bob and Carl has taken a pleasant turn. So much so that they have recently become a fixture at our Sunday family dinners. Raine has allowed me to take one week a month, although it kills him not to help in the kitchen. Most surprising of all, Bob and John's relationship has warmed, and for the first time there's a glimmer of mutual respect. Jenny is walking on air having two fathers to claim as her own.

I say a prayer of thanks every night for this chance with John to make everything right. I've searched my heart and believe I've found forgiveness. For myself and for my mother.

I pray that the dead are at peace and that the living find joy.

Me? For the first time in thirty-five years, I finally have both.

So here we are. . . . It's winter break for John and the grandkids. What better way to spend the first part of our honeymoon trip than with our family at Disneyland? A family we've been given this precious chance to know.

John and I make our journey through Los Angeles Airport and exit security. His fingers tighten around mine, and he draws me to a halt. The air squeezes from my lungs as I spot the dark-haired woman who has my cheekbones. She's standing with a tall, nice-looking man and two children, a boy and a girl. A teary smile comes to her lips when she sees us. Like the limo drivers clustered around waiting for their charges, she's holding a sign that says, "Mr. & Mrs. Henshaw-Rivera."

As we get closer, I catch the color of my daughter's eyes before tears blur my vision and my heart swells to overflowing.

They're a familiar stormy blue.

John

MY FINGERS PRESS Kat's hand tight against my sweaty palm the moment I lay eyes on my baby girl. A lump rises fast and furious in my throat when I see shades of my sister, Denise, in our daughter. But it's not until I look at the kids that I feel an iron fist clench my heart.

Our grandson, Sam, is the spitting image of Ben. He has the same chocolate brown eyes, pointy chin and dimples that had the girls falling at Ben's feet in high school. Sarah's gorgeous too, like both her mother and my wife.

A year ago, I could've never imagined I'd be here. Though I kept the faith that, by some miracle, Kat would come back to me someday. The day my prayers were answered, I made another vow to myself—I'd live every moment like it was my last and savor every day I had left. I may have come from nothing, been banged around a bit, but I did good in the end.

I locked up people like my father for over twenty-five years, and for all my fear, I've never come close to being anything like him. Still, like Kat, I punished myself for my shitty decisions. For years. But I've paid my dues. For Denise's death. For letting Kat go. When Kat left her past behind, I left mine with it. What lies ahead now stands in front us—this beautiful family we helped make with our love and Kat's strength. That's something to be proud of.

I'm one of the luckiest SOBs alive. For the first time, I have a family of my own. The feeling splits my chest open with happiness. Happiness I never thought I'd experience.

Kat and I had a small Valentine's Day–themed wedding ceremony last night at the Grasshopper in Morristown where Raine used to work. Our buddy Declan, the owner, gave us the top floor, and his brother, Father Pete, performed the ceremony. Since Kat and I are both divorced, we couldn't do the church thing, but my theory is God is everywhere, even in Declan's Irish bar.

Kat wore red velvet for the occasion—Jenny and Jillian's idea—

and only admitted afterward that she'd been afraid of getting struck by lightning for her choice. Raine stood up as my best man, with Devon and Tony as my groomsmen. Jillian did the honors for Kat, along with Jenny and Lettie.

My mom and José came up from Florida and we filled the room with some of our closest friends and family. Best part? I sang our wedding song, "The Flame," to Kat. She cried. It was beautiful.

Never thought I'd see the day, but Bob gave Kat away. As a surprise wedding present, he helped me find a black '74 Camaro and restore it. Okay, so I threw in a red herring early on about it being a death trap so she wouldn't suspect what I planned to give her as a gift if she agreed to be my wife. Bob and I have been working on it together in Carl's garage for the last two months. Brings back memories of me and Ben customizing the original Black Beast. I plan to give Kat the keys when we get back from our honeymoon.

Only two bones of contention came up during the wedding. The first involved my private powwow with Tony and Lettie. Lettie managed to flip Howard as an informant and claims to be out. I'm not sure I believe her. Tony gave me a look of wide-eyed innocence. I promised to snip off his 'nads with garden shears if anything happened to her from here on out. She just kissed me on the cheek and told me all was well and not to worry. That would've been fine until she slipped in a comment that "the girls were well protected." I checked my phone. The device I gave her to carry in her bra still shows up on my GPS.

The second bone came by way of Jillian. Now that my story with Kat ends in a "happy ever after," Jillian begged to write it . . . as a sequel to *Caught Up in Raine*. I'm not sure who barked "No!" faster, me or Kat. Either way, Jillian slunk off, disappointed.

Oh, and I added a little embellishment to my tat before the wedding to show my renewed commitment. Now it says, FOREVER MY KAT. Yeah. I'm one lucky SOB.

"Dad?" asks the lovely woman in front of me as she releases Kat from a hug. My heart nearly freaking stops, and for the first time this all feels real.

I'm a father.

I embrace my daughter, hold her tight to my chest, and momentarily lose the ability to speak. I catch a hint of her mother's honeysuckle and moonlight and choke up. "Hey, beautiful . . . I'm glad to finally meet you," I whisper, and savor the feeling of holding my child for the first time. "Sorry we're late . . . it won't ever happen again."

Dear Readers,

Thank you so much for reading *SURRENDER MY HEART!* I hope you enjoyed Kitty & John's story. Want to get caught up in love again? Turn the page to find out how. If you haven't read it yet, the *CAUGHT UP IN RAINE* Collection is Jillian and Raine's complete story. Also consider Jenny & Devon's story (and a heavy dose of his twin sister, Lettie) in *SHELTER MY HEART.* Both are emotional journeys you won't want to miss!

In *SURRENDER MY HEART*, you probably noticed that I left an open thread with Lettie's story. Knowing Lettie the way I do, it's going to be a wild ride and what happens in Vegas might not stay in Vegas! Her love interest might surprise you...because it's not Howard. Go to the DOWLOADS page on my website, **lgoconnor.com to get a preview chapter**!

Before you go, please consider leaving a review on Amazon, Goodreads, or sharing on Instagram or TikTok (#BookTok). Please and thank you! Truly, word of mouth is what helps authors sell books. Request these books from your local library, or read it with your Book Club (questions to follow)! Did you know that you can request this series from your local library? Stay in touch!

Warmest Regards,

LG O'Connor

Book Club Discussion Questions

1. Popular music provides a gateway between the past and present for Kitty and John's story. Did any of the songs from their playlist stir up memories for you? Were they related to a past love?

2. Kitty shoulders the burden of her family's secrets for thirty-five years to protect the people she loves. Was she justified in her resentment toward her mother? What could her mother have done differently?

3. Vera's death cut off Kitty's one avenue for relief from bearing her secrets alone. If you were Kitty, what would you have done? Would you have told Jillian everything on the beach?

4. Kitty learns in therapy that the weight she carries, her preference for outdated clothing, and her choice of lipwear unconsciously tie back to her past. What did this tell us about Kitty?

5. Kitty's aunt Vera has a relationship with Kitty's mother (Vera's identical twin) that contains an underlying tension. Vera freely encourages and protects Kitty's relationship with John. She loves them both as if they were her own. At critical times during the story, she clearly condones and becomes a conduit for teenage behavior that Vivian would clearly not approve of. Was Vera justified in her support of Kitty and John given the secret between her and her twin sister, Vivian? Or do you think part of her motivation was payback?

6. It's clear from John's first meeting in 1979 with Kitty's mother that Vivian treated him with thinly veiled prejudice. John attributed her judgment to his socioeconomic position and his Hispanic roots. Do you agree? Or do you think she told him the truth after Kitty left: that her prejudice was grounded in the threat he posed to Kitty's future?

7. Kitty maintains that she made "the best of the worst choices." Do you agree that she did given John's fears and issues?
8. Was Kitty justified in keeping her secret again when she reunited with John at the ten-year reunion knowing there was nothing either of them could do? Do you think they would've lasted had she told him the truth either time, or do you think her early sacrifice led to a better life for all involved and enabling her and John to achieve a well-deserved "happy ever after" thirty-five years later?
9. Many themes are presented in this novel: loss, secrets, family politics, love, resilience, forgiveness, and acceptance. Which of these themes resonated most with you?
10. Given everything you've learned, how much would you sacrifice for the ones you love? Under what circumstances would you do those things?
11. Vivian and Bill made a moral choice to keep a secret in exchange for a free college education for Kitty. Were Kitty's parents justified in the end?
12. Tattoos are a symbolic device used in the Caught Up in Love series to represent commitment and wearing what matters most to us forever on our skin. What did you think in regards to John and his commitment to Kitty? Is this something you would ever do to symbolize what you hold most dear?

Order a 5- or 8-pack of author signed print copies with FREE eBook companions at a 40% discount off the retail price + shipping

Interested in me joining your Book Club meeting?

For either, use the contact page on my website, www.lgoconnor.com.

L.G. O'Connor

Want more?

Get Caught Up again and again…in the *Caught Up in Love* series. Missed the full story? Get caught up in Jillian and Raine's story from the beginning…

CAUGHT UP IN RAINE (Novel)
Two hearts. One soul-shattering decision. Plagued by loss, bestselling romance author, Jillian Grant, enlists a young landscaper with an uncanny resemblance to the boyfriend she lost at eighteen—and the male lead in her next novel—as her cover model. When Raine ends up in the hospital with no place to go, Jillian offers him a place to stay until sparks ignite, giving Jillian more than she bargained for and forcing her to confront the past that she has tried to forget.

REDISCOVERING RAINE (A Caught Up in Raine Novelette)
Two Hearts. One Magical Night. Pick up where we left off in CAUGHT UP IN RAINE from Raine's point-of-view and experience his magical night with Jillian. But putting a ring on Jillian's finger doesn't mean all is easily forgiven.

CAUGHT UP IN RACHEL (A Caught Up In Raine Novelette)
Two Hearts. One Small Miracle. Giving birth at an "advanced maternal age" isn't without peril, as Jillian discovers when she develops a condition that threatens mother and child.

SHELTER MY HEART (Novel)
Two Weeks. One Life-Changing Proposal. Devon, an ailing young CEO persuades Jenny, an engaged, young woman to accept a two-week proposal: spend her vacation with him and attend his family's society gala so they can convince the Board of Directors that he's healthy and going to marry to fulfil the

terms of his inheritance and save his family. No strings. No future. Until the stakes rise, forcing Jenny to choose between her heart and saving Devon's life.

SURRENDER MY HEART (Novel)

Two old flames. One new destiny. Kitty McNally knows sometimes you need to make the best of the worst choices for the ones you love. Ever since their high school breakup, Kitty McNally has secretly loved Detective John Henshaw. The hardest thing she'd ever done was leave him behind—not once, but twice. Decades later, a hint of what they had still shines in his eyes. But only the dead know the secrets she still keeps. At their 35th High School reunion, Kitty has one last chance to confront the past and rekindle their love—if John can forgive her once he learns the truth.

Acknowledgments

I want to say thank you to my tremendous team for all your love and support. Thank you to my critique partner, Joan Sorensen, for sticking by me through my writing journey and giving critical feedback; the "cross-stitch" beta reading crew (Marilyn, Pat, and Lesley); authors Carla Susan Smith and Kilby Blades for all their support and friendship; beta reader and editor, Rachel MacAulay; my editor, Ray Rhamey, for his guidance and for making me laugh with his editing comments; Tom C. for answering my questions about law enforcement and FBI task forces; and to everyone else who has supported me along the way.

Thank you, my wonderful support team; without you this book wouldn't have reached its full potential.

About the Author

L.G. O'Connor writes romantic women's fiction, paranormal, and suspense that touches the heart with themes of family, redemption, forgiveness, and most of all, hope. She's the author of the multi-award-winning romantic women's fiction trilogy: *Caught Up in Raine, Shelter My Heart,* and *Surrender My Heart,* which follows a family of three New Jersey women who must confront the past to find redemption and second chances. She is also the author of the epic angel & demon fantasy, *The Angelorum Chronicles.* Besides writing, L.G. is a Mayo Clinic & Board-Certified Wellness Coach. She's passionate about connecting with readers and loves food, antiques, and excellent coffee. Find her books or stay in touch:

| Website | Amazon | Bookbub |

| Goodreads | Instagram | Substack |

Photo credit: Oak & Ivy Photography

Looking for something different?

Try The Angelorum Twelve Books

From L.G. O'Connor, award-winning author of **Caught Up in Raine**, *comes a 4-book epic angel & demon fantasy series with forbidden and fated love, enemies-to-lovers, found family, and sizzling romance that will leave you wanting more.*

Science and spirit meet in The Angelorum Twelve, an epic angel & demon fantasy. For 2,000 years, the Angelorum—the next generation of angelic Watchers—has maintained the balance of good and evil between humanity and Lucifer's Dark Ones. Both sides have played by the rules…until now. Lucifer has a score to settle and a celestial loophole to seize to restore his rightful place in the final battle of good and evil. Twelve souls will stretch the limits of Heaven and Earth to stop him…

TRINITY STONES, Book One.

There are no coincidences, only destinies to be fulfilled.

Cara Collins is questioning her choices. Between a back-stabbing boss, a non-existent social life, and lingering feelings for Dr. Kai Solomon, a man she can never have, things need to change. After discovering she has the power to restore the gift of youth the same day she receives an unexpected $50 million windfall, it seems Fate agrees.

Learning she is part of a Trinity, Cara is shaken to discover she can become the angelic weapon needed to defeat Lucifer and his Dark Ones in their quest to conquer Heaven and enslave humanity. Torn between her duty to save the world and the promise of a new love, the timing couldn't be worse.

Cara's unseen Nephilim Guardian, Chamuel, knows he has a problem the moment he sees his new charge. His heart stirs for the first time in over a century for the one female on earth forbidden to him under Angelorum Law. After a chance encounter under his human identity, he's powerless to resist her—regardless of the devastating price he will pay if anyone, including Cara, discovers the truth.

When dark forces kidnap Kai and his daughter, forbidden love, betrayal, and destiny collide, forcing Cara to make an impossible choice to save the people she loves without sacrificing the future of humanity, and playing right into Lucifer's hands.

WANDERER'S CHILDREN, Book Two.

Los Angeles. San Francisco. Chicago. New York. The Wanderer's mission three decades ago: secretly sire children to hide his bloodline, and protect them until their destinies unite to fight the final battle between good and evil.

Duty will call soon to gather the rest of the Angelorum Twelve and prepare them for battle. Before that happens, Cara Collins wants one peaceful weekend with her bridesmaids before her wedding to her former Trinity Guardian. But we don't always get what we want …

Life has changed. Cara's newly acquired Nephilim DNA is wreaking havoc on her body, with an overabundance of pheromones triggering a mortifying outbreak of "insta-love" among her friends that would make Cupid proud. If only she could point her arrow at her Trinity Messenger, Michael Swift, who has been running from his attraction to Cara's brazen best friend, Sienna, the only woman ever to skirt his defenses. Even if he wants a future with her, first, he must confront his tormented past, or risk threatening the future of the Angelorum.

After a chance encounter, runaway rock star Brett King is harboring a crush on Cara, but, infatuation aside, Brett is more than he appears. One of the Wanderer's children he and his siblings are the key to gathering the rest of the Twelve souls destined to fight in the final battle of good and evil. With the growing threat of Lucifer's fallen angels, Cara has more to worry about than petty jealousy, drunken debauchery, and a bridal shower. An enemy within the Angelorum is determined to see them fail, if a traitor in Cara's inner circle doesn't destroy them all.

HOPE'S PRELUDE, Prequel Novella, Book 2.5.

Save the *One* who will save them all.

Enter the world of the Angelorum for a glimpse into its origins as destinies entwine to deliver us one step closer to battle …

Stolen as an infant by Achanelech, the Archdemon of Fire, Samuel has lived in his kidnapper's dungeons for over a century. Unaware of his angelic origins, he is persuaded to help capture his Nephilim brethren in exchange for a longer leash and a chance to plot his own escape.

While dealing with visions of her death, Dr. Sandra Wilson races against the clock with research partner, Dr. Tom Peyton and her Nephilim mate, Isa, to develop a vaccine that will save the One.

With Isa ensnared in Achanelech's trap, and the Archdemon closing in on Sandra, it is Samuel who must risk his freedom to ensure the future of the Angelorum … and the mother he has never met.